Marian
WITH
THE FLAXEN HAIR

Marian
WITH
THE FLAXEN HAIR

DONALD SINCLAIR

authorHOUSE®

AuthorHouse™
1663 Liberty Drive
Bloomington, IN 47403
www.authorhouse.com
Phone: 1-800-839-8640

Published by AuthorHouse   02/29/2012

ISBN: 978-1-4685-0753-9 (sc)
ISBN: 978-1-4685-0752-2 (e)

Library of Congress Control Number: 2011961394

Any people depicted in stock imagery provided by Thinkstock are models, and such images are being used for illustrative purposes only.
Certain stock imagery © Thinkstock.

This book is printed on acid-free paper.

Because of the dynamic nature of the Internet, any web addresses or links contained in this book may have changed since publication and may no longer be valid. The views expressed in this work are solely those of the author and do not necessarily reflect the views of the publisher, and the publisher hereby disclaims any responsibility for them.

Chapter 1

The first date Howard Keck had with Marian Harbaugh, they went to the Fox Theatre in downtown Detroit to see *Spartacus*. Marian was way overdressed in a tan sheath and had her hair up in a swirl at the back of her head that made her look like a fashion model.

Howard had to turn away from watching her walk; she had the lines of a racing hull that moved under the sheath and it made him very excited.

After the movie, they drove back to Marian's sprawling house, and walking into the front room, Howard saw the antique furniture and oriental rugs that made the place look like a musty museum. He had the thought that it looked like her family had moved Dusseldorf to Grosse Pointe.

When Howard was following her across the room to the French doors that opened onto a porch where the television set showed, he asked, "Where's the family?"

"Up at the farm," Marian said, snapping on the television. "We call it the summer house because it has two small lakes—and we go up there when it gets hot down here."

"Where's it at?" Howard asked before he slid his arm around her waist, he could not resist touching her.

"Near Lapeer," she said turning to face him. "It's a small town up near Flint," she said slowly before he kissed her.

Howard could feel she wanted him as much as he wanted her.

Only the flickering light from the television set lighted the room as they sat down on the long couch. Her dress slid up her legs, and when Howard pushed it higher she did not resist.

When they were making love, the only thing she said was, "Don't . . . don't . . . come," her eyes closed, her face wet, her hair falling down.

Later, when they were laying, breathing heavy, their faces touching, spent, she whispered, "I love you, Howard. From the first day we met—I felt it. I knew."

He raised his face, his jaw falling open, "I felt that way too—amazing. I can't put it in words, the exact words," he said slowly, "but that has never happened before. It's a new—a total—feeling."

She moved to straighten her clothing, and he raised up on his left elbow.

"Every—thing," she said, "that came before in my whole life is gone now."

"Yes," he said raising himself higher as she pulled down her dress, "the only thing that matters is that we be together. From now on out."

"That will make me very happy," she said before he kissed her, then sat up.

Howard was looking over the back of the couch, and through the glass in the French door, glanced out to the living room. At the far end of the room, in the window, he saw something round, the light from the street behind.

When it moved, he realized it was a head; then it was gone.

"Someone was looking in the window," Howard said quietly. "Someone was watching us."

"Where?/" she asked sitting up.

"That window out there next to the bookcase," he said, but did not point. "I saw it just for an instant."

"Well," she said, "maybe you just imagined it."

"Yeah," he said. "Could be I'm hallucinating or something like that." He grinned. "You have that effect."

But when he stood up, a sinking feeling filled him where his stomach was, as if he had something to dread.

"Come out to the kitchen," Marian said, "We'll make coffee and . . . sober up." Smiling, she stood up.

~ ~ ~

That summer, Howard was taking classes to speed up getting his degree in Journalism at Wayne State University. One of his classes was a physical science course that included viewing the star groups. The astronomy study required the student to actually view, first hand, The Big Dipper, The North Star, and the Sirius Dog group, and it suggested to go outside the city, away from the glow of the lights, and lay down and view the stars.

When Howard told Marian about the star-study, she invited him to come up to the summer house but he said he would not stay until dark if he came up for a visit.

Howard felt nervous about spending time that close to Marian's family, they being Grosse Pointers at their *second* and him a student, struggling to get a degree at a city college. The father made Howard uneasy with his bluntness.

There was that first incident with the father on the Fourth of July that upset Howard. He had come to pick-up Marian for a Bar-B-Q up in affluent Birmingham given by a Journalism professor. Howard wore white-duck pants and a blazer to fit in at the upscale suburb.

At Marian's house, they stood in the foyer after he kissed her, their foreheads together, whispering, "You look so cute," she said taking him by the hand. "Come and show my mother your sporty outfit."

Out in the kitchen, the mother and sister were popping popcorn and greeted him, all smiles.

Then Marian led him to the patio outside the kitchen door, and Howard greeted the father who was stretched out on a lounge chair, reading legal papers.

"Look at his white ducks, Daddy," Marian said with pride, smiling. "Just like in the movies."

Howard noticed all the women in the family called the father "Daddy," even the mother.

"Probably from an army surplus store," the father said without looking up.

"Oh, Dadd-dy," Marian said smiling at Howard. "He looks so nice."

The father was right, Howard had bought the ducks at an army surplus store; and trying not to show emotion, he said, "We have to get going—Jennifer and Tom said dinner was at six sharp."

"Have a good time," the father said without looking up.

Howard caught the message the father was throwing; you are from a lower economical class, and you will soon find it out, that you are in over your head.

"'Night, Mister Harbaugh," Howard said as he and Marian turned away.

Marian whispered, "His business is being sued by a disgruntled lady who's taking him to court."

"Maybe," Howard whispered, "he's trying to be funny and . . . clever."

"He's been crabby all week," Marian said and pulled open the screen door to the kitchen.

~ ~ ~

The Sunday before final exams for classes, Marian wrote Howard to come up to the summer house.

Howard smiled reading the note, sensing Marian's concern about him in the heat and humidity of Detroit. She did not know there was no air conditioning at his apartment house—that the nights were like trying to sleep in an oven—but, he though it better not to give her too much detail, dwell on the shabbiness he lived sometimes.

Driving up the road to the house, he beeped the horn looking through the trees, he saw Marian come out the door onto the porch.

He liked the feeling that she had been looking for him.

"Wow," Howard shouted, his head out the car window, "You look like something out of a magazine."

She was wearing a pink shirt and tobacco-color Bermuda shorts.

She stood smiling, watching him get out of the old Ford, the door making a *ka-runk* sound when it opened, and again when he closed it.

"I've missed you Howard," she said quietly.

When he kissed her, he suddenly felt warm all over. Holding her against his chest he could not move.

"We have to go inside," she said, and as she turned, took hold of his hand, leading him. "We're finishing lunch in the kitchen," she said in a normal voice going up the steps, then whispered before opening the screen door, "We can be alone later."

There was an awkward silence after Howard said hello to everyone seated around the kitchen table. The mother, and Marian's sister, Ardis, were all smiles, again, but the father sat at the head of the table, moodily.

Marian, walking around the table, to break the silence said, "Are you ready for the final exams for your classes?"

"I'll ace the Geography course," Howard said taking the seat across from Marian, "but, I'll be lucky to get a B in that Physical Science course."

"That's ready good, Howard," Marian said grinning.

"Well," the father said, "I hear the work whistle bowing." He pushed back his Captain's chair from the head of the table. "Back to the grind," he said walking past Howard to the door.

"They are cutting up a tree that fell during a storm last week," the mother said, pointing out the window to the smaller lake.

Howard looked out and saw the tree, uprooted, the top out in the water. Two men were standing next to an old Jeep watching Mister Harbaugh walking down the hill.

"They're trying to get the part in the water out," Ardis said smiling, "but they're not doing too good."

"Have you had lunch?" the mother asked Howard.

"I had a late breakfast," he said.

"We had tuna fish salad," the mother said, "and there's cream of tomato soup left."

"I'll get it mother," Marian said getting up and shaking her head, passing her sister looking out the window down at the lake, smiling widely.

"'Wonder if they know what they're doing," Ardis said.

"Sit up here Howard," Marian said, "in Daddy's chair—by the stove."

Howard moved up to sit in the heavy chair at the head of the table.

"Those guys are going back into the water," Ardis said watching intently. "They don't look enthusiastic."

"Don't be so quick to criticize." the mother said. "They're just doing what they're being *asked* to do."

Howard took a quick look and saw the father sitting on a camp stool down at the edge of the water. He was leaning forward on a stick, intent, like a general.

"Well," Ardis said, "They're been at it all morning. And not much has changed."

"Dear," the mother said, "it's a very large tree, and it will take some doing to remove it. Daddy will see to that; he will devise a plan to remove it."

"How tall is the tree?" Howard asked as Marian set a bowl with tuna fish salad in front of him, smiling.

"Daddy says the ground near the water is soft," Marian said, "and the high winds pushed the tree over, pulling up the roots."

Howard took a slice of bread and was spooning tuna out of the bowl.

"Daddy says the tree is nearly sixty feet tall," Ardis said slowly, still looking out the window. "It's a monster—that's for sure."

"Want some soup?" Marian asked looking down at Howard. "it's still warm."

"Don't bother," Howard said and smiled up at her, "I'm warm enough already."

"Well," Marian said, grinning, "We have Ice-tea. I'll get you a glass . . . to cool you off."

"Don't bother," Howard said picking a potato chip piece from the bottom of a bowl off to the side of the table.

It was then Howard noticed the mother and Ardis watching him and Marian, they could see the magnetism between them, the attraction working on each of them. They could sense they were crazy for one another.

"You sure you want to skip the tea?" Marian asked, then put her hand on Howard's shoulder and squeezed.

"I want to go down there by the tree," he said pushing back the Captain's chair and standing up. "Maybe I can help out, somehow."

Over Marian's shoulder, Howard saw Ardis smile and look quickly to the mother, who turned to look back out the window.

"Be careful," Marian said stepping back.

"You bet," Howard said. "Thanks for the lunch."

Down by the water, the father gave Howard the job of driving the Jeep, for pulling the rope the two locals from town had tied around the section of tree cut away from the trunk.

As Howard drove forward, the rope shredded, then snapped.

"There's a length of chain up in the garage," the father said leaning on his stick. "We'll try that."

The two locals went up to the garage while Howard backed the Jeep back down to the edge of the water as close as he dared.

"Here Daddy," Howard heard Missus Harbaugh say; she had come down the hill with a glass of ice tea.

The old man took the glass, then, pointing with his stick, shouted to Howard, "Now, don't get the Jeep stuck."

Howard nodded, then smiling, turned forward, and there was Marian, wearing a bathing suit.

"Who-a," he said to her, "you looking for a ride, Miss?"

"Keep your mind on the job," she said, grinning.

"I am, babe. I am."

"You-u."

Harbaugh's wife took off her straw hat and set it on her husband's head. The afternoon sun was growing hotter by the minute.

"Now he looks like a photograph," Howard whispered to Marian, "like some French painter spending the day at the seashore—leaning on that stick and that wide-brim hat . . ."

As he was speaking, Howard tried not looking at the crotch of Marian's bathing suit, where it was tight.

"We can go for a swim," Marian said, "when you get done here.": She sat up on the right front fender of the Jeep. "The water is *always* cold."

"How come?" Howard asked looking out to the raft in the center of the lake.

"It's a spring-fed lake," she said. "Water bubbles up right out of the ground all the time—just the other side of the raft. I'll show you . . ."

"Marian," her father shouted, "move away from the Jeep. The chain might slip—you might get hurt if it does.

"Okay, Daddy," she said in a loud voice, then made a long face as she looked at Howard, as if to say she had to go and had no choice, then slid off the fender.

"You might get hurt," Howard said, grinning.

"It's getting hot," she said, "so I'm going up and wait in the house—in the air conditioning. Come get me as soon as you get done here."

"You bet, babe," Howard said, feeling the bite of what old man Harbaugh said; a warning to her about getting hurt, and not from a chain.

In the rearview mirror of the Jeep, Howard saw Marian and her mother walking up the hill to the house. He liked her long legs taking measured steps up the grade; he felt lucky to have met her.

"Okay," Harbaugh shouted. "Pull ahead. Slow."

Howard drove, the section of the tree began to follow, then, when the entire length was dragged up on the shore, someone shouted, "Who-a-a. Good."

When Howard was backing the Jeep so they could unhitch the chain, he wondered if the women had come down to the lake to see how the old man reacted to working with him; if they got along, something like that.

Later, swimming with Marian near the raft, he kissed her.

"They can see us," she said, pushing him playfully, "and you sort of got to act accordingly."

Howard glanced up to the house and shook his head.

"I really missed you, babe," he said swimming behind her to where the ladder from the raft hung down in the water.

They climbed up and stretched out on the hot boards in the sun.

She was silent for a moment, then said, "I'm glad Daddy sent those two guys home," with her eyes closed to the glare of the sun. "There's a little more privacy."

"Yeah," Howard said, taking a sweeping look at the length of her. When he laid back, closing his eyes, he added, you look like a million, babe. I'm going crazy just being near you."

"I want you, too," she whispered without opening her eyes. "I'll ride back to the city with you—I have a dentist appointment tomorrow morning."

"Terrific," Howard said fighting the impulse to sit-up and kiss her; instead he continued laying flat with his eyes closed. "That's the best news I've had today, babe."

"I know," she said, "and for what it's worth—I think you made a good impression on Daddy by driving the Jeep. Despite the fact you're not having a very good time today, you scored some points with Daddy."

Howard with his eyes closed still, grinned, and said, "'For what it's worth', babe, you're the only one I want to 'score'—anything—with."

"Oh-h," she groaned, "I know, I know, but they are my *family.'* She swiped at a fly on her shoulder without opening her eyes. "You have to expect them to react with suspicion toward you. They don't know you—like I do," she said smiling.

"Okay, okay," Howard said. "I get the message, babe."

Howard did not grin; he sensed a deeper 'reaction' going on in old man Harbaugh and it was not just suspicion.

He felt it this past spring too, the night he and Marian walked down to the Detroit River behind her Grosse Pointe house, crossing the yard of a half-built house to the water's edge. Seagulls were out in the dark screeching and flapping out where the breaking ice made *crunching* noises. Howard could not see out on the river in the dark, only hear the sounds.

When they walked past the unfinished house again, Marian had mentioned it was owned by a Negro doctor, who the neighborhood association did not want to move in. All the members of the association, including Daddy, donated a thousand dollars each to buy off the builder.

It was that kind of action "Daddy" was capable of that bothered Howard now. The old man was the kind who wanted his own way and was not squeamish about how he got it.

At first Howard though the problem with the old man was the economic gap; the old man had money and he, Howard, did not. That had to be part of the problem, that as obvious, Howard thought, but there was more—and he did not want to lose Marian because of it.

Howard felt accused of something and was—already—found guilty. He felt confused about it, what it could be.

"Mari—an! Oh, Mari—an!" came a shout from the direction of the house.

Both Marian and Howard rose up on their elbows and could see Ardis up on the house porch, waving her arms.

"Wha-a-at?" Marian shouted, looking up.

"Dinner—in an hour!"

"Oh—kay,—we'll be up!" Marian shouted.

9

Shading his eyes from the sun with his hand, Howard said, "After dinner, babe, I should get going—back to the city—if that's okay with you."

"Don't—be—so serious," Marian said while brushing the back of her legs that had been against the hot raft boards. "Stay away from black—dark—thinking. Relax."

"Right," Howard said, grinning. "I've got to lighten up. But I don't know what it is lately. *Everything* is getting serious all of a sudden, *and* I didn't know it showed."

"It's on your face," she said. "It shows—you're wrestling with some kind of problem." She moved her legs and folded them to sit Indian-style, her elbows resting on her knees, holding her face. "Well, I've got some news about the New York trip . . ."

"Oh, yeah," he said brushing his elbow that had been against the boards. "I've been busy—these final exams . . ."

"I told Daddy . . ."

"Ah-h, no wonder he's been looking daggers at me."

"He says it's okay," she said calmly, "as long as we fly, and we don't drive in that—ancient—car of yours."

Howard grinned.

"Naw," he said waving a hand, "he thinks we'll stop in a small town in Pennsylvania and get hitched or something stupid like that. Right, babe?"

She put her hand on his arm.

"It's nothing like that, honey. He just thinks it's safer to fly—and avoid all that high-speed driving—he thinks is too risky.

Howard was surprised she could go, and pleased at the same time. He had a friend in New York, Bob Foskett, an architect with an office in the city and a house out on Long Island at Sag Harbor for his wife and kids.

Foskett wrote Howard a letter with a picture of his new sail boat, and invited him to come to New York for a jaunt on the new sloop.

The boat, Foskett wrote in letter, was built special for the 1956 Olympics. It was thirty-six feet long and made of molded plywood, the letter said, and with the hull painted with epoxy, the surface "was as hard as a cue ball, and just as slick."

Foskett's father was a local building contractor, who got involved with the new building material called pre-stressed concrete, and after World War II, made a fortune and moved to

Grosse Pointe. Foskett's father was a Canadian who came from a sailing family, and he always kept a sailboat down "at the foot of Alter Road," the border between Detroit and Grosse Pointe and frequently sailed for recreation.

Bob Foskett married a girl he met at the University of Michigan, and they lived for a while in Grosse Pointe, while he became a master in designing buildings from pre-stressed concrete. But his wife missed her family in New York, and she had an uncle in a large architectural firm, and soon they moved to New York and Bob worked at the firm.

Howard did not mention the letter he wrote Foskett telling about the interviews for work with a news service that was scheduled for September. He did not want to mention the four positions open, work in Paris, Washington, Uganda and the far East. It would mean going away, and he did not want to upset Marian.

He did not tell her either about when he was in the Army taking a training course in journalism at the Fort Slocum Information School. That was the summer before he went to Germany for a year and a half. That summer he went to Sag Harbor and sailed frequently because it was just a short jaunt from Fort Slocum at New Rochelle over to Sag Harbor.

It was Howard's letter about the interviews for the news service to Foskett, that prompted Foskett to fire the letter off about his new boat.

Now, looking at Marian getting up on the raft, stepping to the edge, he said, "I thought your father wouldn't allow you to go because—of the *sleeping* arrangements."

She was grinning, watching him get to his feet.

"Daddy trusts me," she said, then dove into the water.

Howard followed her.

Chapter 2

Howard as sitting at the dining room table when Marian came back from changing her bathing suit. She was wearing an Oxford-cloth, light blue, button-down shirt.

"You look Preppy," Howard whispered across the table after she sat down.

"I am 'Preppy,'" she whispered back. "After all, I went to school at Dobbs Ferry, New York."

"It shows, babe," Howard said quietly, then clenching his teeth, added, "and I'm very impressed."

Ardis came in carrying a latter platter of chicken and a yellow bowl the size of a wash basin filled with salad.

"I hope you guys are hungry," she said setting the platter in the center of the table, and the yellow bowl up at the end where her father sat.

When the mother came through the door with a large bowl of mashed potatoes and a platter of corn on the cob, she said, "We're all here now, so we can start the dinner."

Following her was old man Harbaugh carrying a tall pitcher of lemonade with ice cubes.

"Can I help with something?" Howard said, pushing back his chair.

"You did your share, today," the father said sitting down at the head of the table, the mother on his right, next to Howard. "We appreciate that."

"Glad I could help," Howard said, pulling his chair forward.

"We always feed our help, don't we mother?" the father said reaching for the chicken.

"Say Grace, Daddy," Marian said, looking at Howard and shrugging, "so we can start."

The father said the prayer quickly, and Howard only caught the words, "'for these thy use . . .'"

"I forgot the gravy," Ardis said and stood up and darted out to the kitchen.

"We always feed our workers,'" Marian whispered, grinning.

Howard moved his eyebrows up and down, then made a smirk in appreciation of Marian's parody of her father.

When Ardis came back, she set the gravy boat in front of her father. Then took her seat on his left.

"If you want lemonade," she said, "pass me your glass."

The mother leaned over to Howard and said, "We're very informal at meals. Please begin while everything is warm."

She passed him the bowl of mashed potatoes.

Marian reached across the table with the gravy ladle, and after pressing the potatoes on Howard's plate, made a puddle of gravy by tilting the ladle—the same as a parent would do for a child.

When he raised his eyebrows, she moved her leg against his under the table.

Marian smiled and he smiled back, then tilted his head to one side and began to eat.

Glancing around the table, Howard saw Ardis watching him and Marian. She did not miss what the two were doing.

To break the silence, Howard asked the father, "Are the chain saw guys coming tomorrow—to buzz-up the rest of that tree?"

"No," the father said stabbing his fork into the salad bowl by his plate. "They have a landscaping business . . . they won't be back until next Sunday."

"There is a lot of wood in that tree," Howard said to the father. "You'll have a lot of logs."

"We have a big fireplace in the living room," the mother said, and with tongs, put a chicken breast with the leg attached on Howard's plate. "When the weather gets cool, we burn wood all day—to heat the house."

Marian's leg brushed Howard's just when he poked the fork into the chicken to cut a slice with a knife, the entire piece, breast and leg, slid off the plate.

Glancing around the table, Howard saw that no one but Ardis had caught his fumble, and she was smiling, when he quickly slid the piece of chicken back on his plate.

Howard liked Ardis, maybe because she was always smiling. He liked the mother too, she was very considerate.

"It's not very good wood for burning," the father said, holding his fork with salad on the end in front of his face, "that tree is maybe Ash—or some kind of Elm."

Howard began eating evenly now, cutting pieces off the breast that was cut open, easy to remove morsels.

When Marian's leg moved against his under the table, again, he did not look up, but he did smile.

"That tree," Howard said, "is pretty good size. There'll be a lot of wood—it'll keep you warm for a long time."

He bumped Marian's leg to make her smile.

"Would you like more corn?" the mother asked Howard.

"No, no," he said. "Thanks, I'm good." He glanced at Marian, then at the mother and said, "I'm . . . going to have to get going right . . . after dinner," he said looking at the mother next to him. "I have to get back to the city and finish writing a term paper—that's about a third of my grade for the class."

"Oh," the mother said nodding, "I understand. Your classes are important. Marian told us you were studying for final exams."

Howard knew it was a clumsy exit, but it was the only excuse he could come up with that would seem valid. He had come up to be with Marian today, but it turned into a session where the family was sizing him up—as a possible husband for Marian. Even though the father's hostility was offset by the mother's kindness, he felt an urge to run away; flight. He was tired of being judged, looked over like a used car.

"I hope," Howard said to the mother, "that you don't think me the 'eat-and-run' type, but this week is going to be hectic."

"No, no," the mother said looking at the old man, who was wiping his chin with a napkin, not showing any emotion. "Your final exams are important."

Marian, smiling across the table, said, "We have ice cream for dessert."

"Great," Howard said.

Ardis was smiling like a Cheshire cat; she was two years younger than Marian, but knew what was going on, that her sister and Howard were aching for one another.

"Not for me, mother," the old man said. "I'm going to skip dessert today," he said folding his napkin. "I'm full up."

When the women carried the dishes out to the kitchen, Howard found himself sitting alone with the old man.

"That tree," Howard said slowly, "was really a monster—it's lucky it didn't fall on anything."

"Yes," the old man said leaning back in his Captain's Chair, "that old stag shaded the pond—but everything has it's time—and now, it's gone. Tipped over by the wind . . ."

Marian came through the kitchen door carrying two bowls heaped with strawberry ice cream.

"Daddy," she said, "are you sure you don't want any dessert?" as she set one of the bowls on the table in front of Howard.

"No, no, daughter," he said smiling. "I'm sweet enough." Then getting to his feet said, "I'm going to watch some television—for dessert—that chicken filled me up."

Just then the mother came in followed by Ardis. They both carried bowls heaped with ice cream.

"We made coffee," the mother said to the old man.

"I think it's too hot for coffee," he said to her before going through the kitchen door.

While they were all eating, Ardis leaned forward against the table toward Howard and said, "Daddy watches wrestling on television. I think it's the *only* thing he watches."

Howard noticed she spoke like her mouth had something hot inside. The mother was the same. The only difference was Ardis, spoke faster than the mother, and the words she spoke sort of piled-up—bumped into one another—and you had to listen closely as she spoke.

"Ardis, dear," the mother said. "I would like a cup of coffee with my ice cream. Would you get me a cup."

"Sure," Ardis said and went out to the kitchen.

Marian caught Howard's glance and smiled at him.

15

"Do you have time for coffee?" she asked.

"Sure," he said grinning at her; then biting his lip.

Later, when he was getting ready to leave for Detroit, Howard went into the small bathroom off the kitchen to get his wet bathing suit, which he rolled in his damp towel.

Coming back out, he could see into the living room where the old man was watching wrestling on television.

He almost burst into laughter. There was the old man, who acted so practical in making life judgments every day, sitting and watching the phony, staged, action of a wrestling match, totally enthralled. The crowd at the match was shouting, the noise blaring on the television, as the wrestler's slammed one another to the canvas in the ring with grunts and groans.

Howard, grinning, just shook his head.

When he walked into the kitchen, Marian was talking with her mother while putting up her hair in the mirror on the back of a closet door. She was making her hair into the twist at the back of her head.

On the counter next to the sink, where Marian's mother was rinsing a coffee pot, lay a pile of envelopes; someone had gone down to the road and brought up the mail. One of the envelopes had been opened, the letter on the counter.

Howard liked when Marian wore her hair like that; the swirl made her look sophisticated. It showed her face more too.

He remembered once, when he and Marian were at the horse races, he heard one guy say to another, "'there's a Miss Blue Gem,'" nodding at her over his racing form. The other guy nodded, looking at Marian who was rated on a par with an outstanding filly that ran often at the track.

Howard remember smiling, feeling proud of her good looks being appreciated.

When the mother turned away from the sink, Howard said, "Thank you for lunch and dinner, and I really enjoyed this afternoon—away from the city—it took my mind off final exams."

"We are glad you could come," the mother said, and Howard sensed she was concerned about something; her voice was flat, not the usual musical tone: she and Marian had been talking.

When the mother said to Marian, "We may stay until next week," Howard stood silent, listening, leaning against the counter. The mother began sorting through the mail pile. "We would like it if you came back up after you go to the dentist. It's too hot to be in the city."

"I don't think so, mother," Marian said looking at Howard in the mirror, her chin low. "Sandra McDonald is having a birthday party. In that letter on the counter she asks me to help her—in the—preparations. She says she invited twenty people . . ."

Marian stood for a moment, then looking in the mirror, patted her hair slowly.

"My-y goodness," the mother said, still looking at the pile of mail, sorting through slowly, setting some aside, "Sandra sounds awfully—ambitious."

"It's her twenty-first birthday, mother," Marian said turning around. "The party is set for Friday night."

"That doesn't give her much time," the mother said looking at Marian. "She'll need your help—and then some."

"I know," Marian said, nodding. "Her parents are still—over in Italy—buying *more* art works."

"Yes," the mother said picking up the letters, "I've heard that too." Then holding up the stack of letters, she said, "I'll take these in to your father."

Howard, tired of waiting, walked to the kitchen door, then said, holding it open, "Marian, I'm going down to my car and wait." He hesitated a moment, then added, speaking to the mother, "Thanks for dinner, again. I really enjoyed that baked chicken."

"Hope," the mother said smiling over the compliment, "you come again soon and see us."

"Where's Ardis, mother?" Marian asked walking to the door.

"Down in lake Veronica, swimming," the mother said pointing in that direction.

Howard stood holding the door open for Marian; she shouted back to the living room, "Daddy, Good-bye."

"What?" the old man shouted over the loud television.

"Marian's going," the mother shouted, "back to the city."

"With *him*?" the father shouted back.

"Yes, Daddy," Marian shouted. Then she put her hand on Howard's arm and whispered, "Let's go."

Driving down the hill to the main road, Howard saw Ardis out on the lake through the trees. She was standing on the raft, a teddy-bear shape like her mother, waving. Where the road came near the lake, there was an opening in the trees and Howard sounded the horn.

17

"Your mother called the lake 'Veronica,'" he said. "Why is it named 'Veronica?'"

"Daddy," Marian said grinning, "named it after his favorite movie actress—Veronica Lake."

"'You kidding me?'"

"No, honest," Marian said putting her hand to her eye, "the blond with the long hair that hangs over one eye. She always starred in movies with Alan Ladd."

"Huh," Howard said turning onto the paved county road, "you'd think he'd name the lake Marlene—for Dietrich."

~~~

They arrived back in the Grosse Pointe house as it was getting dark, Howard following Marian into the kitchen that was still hot from the heat of the day.

She threw her keys on the counter in the kitchen and turned without speaking.

Howard kissed her, but when she lifted her up and set her on the counter, pressing himself between her legs, she reached for his hands.

"We can go upstairs to my bedroom," she said.

"You're driving me crazy," he said as she slid off the counter, pressing against him, then, after kissing him quickly, pulled his hand, leading him to the stairs.

Howard pulled her hand at the bottom of the steps, and when she turned, kissed her, and laying her down on the carpeted edges, pulled open her shirt.

"You-u," she said smiling. "You-u."

"Hurry," Howard said pulling off his clothes, kneeling between her legs, helping her take down the Bermuda shorts.

When they were without clothes, Howard, to lay on top, raised his weight on his elbow on the step near her head as she moved her legs up.

They both began perspiring, the warmth in the house from the heat of the day making the air heavy, close.

"Ohh-h," Marian whispered. "Oh-h, man. More, Howard. More. Oh-h, more—oh-h."

He was between her legs, thrusting, sliding against her wetness, unable to stop the frenzy, having it all now.

Marian's hair came unraveled, some of the strands clinging to the wet on the side of her face.

Then, spent from the frenzy of the love making, they lay side by side, resting, Marian, her eyes closed, said, "We'll go up on my bed—put on the air conditioner."

Upstairs, Howard lay against her on the bed, and said, "I want—you—so much. I can't stop myself."

"Do it," she said softly. "I *need*—you to do it."

Howard made love to her two more times.

"When I'm with you," he whispered, when they were laying side by side again in the dark, "I just can't stop."

Marian lay resting next to him, her eyes closed.

They both lay silently for a moment.

"We—are one person," she said softly, "in two bodies."

~ ~ ~

Later, driving back to his campus apartment, Howard had to urinate so bad, he stopped the car and bolted into the dark alley behind a hardware store. It took a long time for his bladder to empty. The stream of urine on the ground, flowed, running on the sloping ground back to where the light began at the edge of the alley.

"That's odd," Howard said looking at the stream while walking back to his car, "seems everything connected to my peeper is working overtime tonight. That's strange."

Chapter 3

Hal Parsons was a friend of Howard's from Journalism class. They had taken three classes together. Parsons was married, had a young daughter, and worked in Wyandotte, the city downriver from Detroit, as a general assignment reporter for the Sentinel, a weekly newspaper.

Whenever Howard met Parsons in the hallways at the university, he always stopped to talk. But, they were not close friends, just acquaintances, who had an interest in journalism careers.

Now, this summer, Parsons was taking summer classes, the same as Howard, wanting to get his degree as soon as he could.

"Where you going?" Parsons asked Howard in the stair well of Prentis Hall. Harold had just come from the final lecture for his Geology class.

"To the library," Howard said, still tired from yesterday's drive to Marian's summer house. "I have to try and absorb more for my Physical Science final exam. Most of it just doesn't sink in," he said slowly, leaning a shoulder against the wall.

"Got time for a beer?"

Howard hesitated, looking at the old acne scars on Hal's cheeks. He knew Parsons had no time for beer drinking between working, attending classes, and being with his family. Something besides their common goals in journalism was bothering Parsons.

"I'm flat broke," Howard said in an attempt to get out of the situation. "My G.I. Bill check doesn't until next week."

"I can loan you a couple of bucks," Parsons said, then stepped backward down one step. "C'mon. We won't be more than a half-hour."

They went to the Dean's List bar on Woodward Avenue and sat at a table near the window that looked across the wide street to the Detroit Art Museum.

The bar was more a meeting place for faculty than students, but still offered a large glass of draft beer for a quarter.

Howard kept waiting for Parsons to spill what he had on his mind, and sat patiently waiting, sipping beer.

When they ordered a second draft, Parsons was telling Howard how hard it was to cover school board meetings that ran to late night hours. Parsons went on about how tired he was in class the next morning, when suddenly he said, "You should find a nice girl and settle down, Howard. A nice middle-class girl. A girl from your own class."

Howard looked at Parsons pock-marked face, the scars showing more prominent in the bright light from the window, but did not react, only slowly slid his empty beer glass away on the table and lifted the full one.

"Not right now," Howard said, holding the glass up in front of his face. "I want to get my degree first—and foremost. Marriage is—a ways down the road, Hal."

"Don't wait too long," Parsons said still sipping beer from the first glass in his hand that was half full.

It was Parsons' words "'own class'" that had jolted Howard. This guy was an acquaintance, a classmate, not a confidant; he was way out of line. Howard felt like telling him to mind his own business.

Glancing out the window at the flow of cars on busy Woodward Avenue, Howard suddenly realized that he had never talked about Marian to Parsons. How this guy knew about her, he found out on his own.

Then a though hit Howard like a thunderbolt: someone *sent* Parsons to talk this way to him.

Howard turned to look at Parsons, and was determined not to show any emotion.

"I should have my degree in about a year," he said calmly, "or—maybe a little longer—I'm working on it—steadily," he said and smile.

"You're not getting any younger," Parsons said. "you shouldn't wait too long to settle down—with some working girl."

"Yeah, you're right, Hal," Howard said smiling. "You've given me a lot to think about today."

Parsons slid his full glass of beer over in front of Howard.

"Here," he said, "drink this. I've got to get going—drive down to Wyandotte—get to work at the newspaper. One beer is my limit."

"Sure," Howard said smiling; he was keeping up a front so Parsons would not have any hint he was now considered as an enemy.

Instinctively, Howard sensed Hal was involved in something against what he, Howard, was doing with Marian. Hal was in the enemy camp, Howard could *feel* it.

~~~

Two weeks later, Howard was sitting in a student chair in his Advanced German Language class, when Melanie Marsack came in and sat down next to him. The instructor was late, the class sat waiting.

"You find a writing job yet?" Melanie asked, crossing her thick legs under her pleated skirt.

Howard and Melanie were in the same Journalism classes over three terms, all taught by Doctor White. The eleven students all knew one another from progressing through Research Journalism, Editing, Feature Writing, and the Law and The Free Press, all with Doctor White, the instructor.

"No," Howard said to her, "I'm still out making the rounds at the weekly newspaper around town."

"I might of landed a public relations job," Melanie said. "I'll find out today or tomorrow . . . for sure."

"Good luck," Howard said, then changing the subject said, "This German class takes a lot of my time," he said. "All these daily vocabulary assignments, the translation pages, and going to the lab listening to the spoken word—man, it burns up the hours."

"Yeah," Melanie said, "but it's a Liberal Arts requirement. What can you do?"

"Yeah," Howard said. "Well, I'm not doing very good. I was in the Army in Germany for two years, I thought I had a head start in the German Language requirement—but these kids in this class are—way—ahead of me."

"Don't you know what's going on?" Melanie asked grinning.

"No," he said. "I've heard them answer the instructor in the Past Perfect tense German. I think I'm in way over my head in this class."

"You *really* don't know, do you?"

Howard looked at her soft face for a moment.

"I guess not," he said quietly.

"These people take this class two—or three times," Melanie said evenly. "They drop the class, take an incomplete, then take it again. When they are sure they can get at least a B mark—they take the final exam. They want to be sure to keep their overall grade average up."

"Wow," Howard said. "Who can *afford* to repeat classes like that—in money—and, time?"

"Well . . . that's what's going on," she said showing her teeth. "Now you know why they know all the answers." Then she added, "Your girlfriend *could* afford it . . ."

"What about her?"

"She's from Grosse Pointe. She can afford *anything* she wants."

"Yeah," Howard said slowly looking for a sign of jealousy on Melanie's face, "I guess you could say that."

"She's going to break your heart, Howard. You should be aware of that."

Howard, grinning, watched as Melanie began flipping the pages of her own textbook.

"Yeah," Howard said, "it seems lately—everybody—is aware of that."

The German instructor, a short woman in a gray suit carrying an arm full of thick manila folders, came into the classroom. She close the door, quietly

"You don't have a chance, Howard. She's wealthy."

"We'll see," Howard said watching the German instructor walked to her desk

Twenty minutes later, Howard's stomach began to make a *growling* sound. It started as a low sound, but grew louder. His stomach was empty, the last time he ate was two days ago at noon.

"Go drink some water," Melanie said in a loud whisper.

"That'll work," Howard said, and as he passed some of the men students on his way to the door, they began snickering.

But at the last chair near the door, a girl in a mauve sweater said, "have a Lifesaver. It's peppermint."

Nodding a thanks to her, Howard moved silently out the door, into the hallway and headed for the drinking fountain. He slipped the candy onto his tongue.

He wished he had a tuna sandwich instead of a Lifesaver, but he did not have a quarter; he tried filling up with the cool water arcing out from steel fountain. He thought of asking Melanie for some money, but shook his head, and changed his mind. He tried to be content with the Lifesaver on his tongue, and rattled it from side to side against his teeth.

Tuna fish sandwiches were sold over in the Student Center Cafeteria. The Negro ladies who made them, piled on this tuna salad, almost a can on each sandwich, and wrapped them in waxed paper. The tuna sandwiches were the cheapest food on the cafeteria menu; the Negro ladies knew hungry students with little money were grabbing them up. The white bread sandwiches went first, and the students who came later, were left the ones made with whole wheat bread, and the wheat tasted different; not as sweet as the white. But they did not complain about the wheat bread, concentrating more on how to get to the cafeteria earlier.

Standing in the hall, Howard thought for a moment and decided not to go back to his German class. He had disrupted it enough, he felt, standing, still rattling the Lifesaver from side to side against his teeth.

He knew Melanie would bring his German textbook to the Friday journalism class; he smiled thinking she probably knew he was embarrassed and would not be returning the class.

Where the stairs began at the end of the hallway, Howard stopped; he felt a growling noise that stopped, and stood grinning for a moment, before starting down. He was thinking of the student Raskolnikov in the Russian novel he read in a literature class. In that book, *Crime and Punishment,* the student is tired of being broke all the time, then murders an old woman money-lender for her rubles.

Grinning, he started down the steps, and said to himself, "there are a lot of poor, broke, students in universities, all over the world—I'm not alone, that's for sure."

Walking down Cass Avenue toward his apartment, he stopped and went in the Campus Club Bar, hoping to borrow some money. The walls inside the bar were covered with photos of sports teams from past years, and college pennants with TARTAR'S the name for all the school athletic teams. The older photos showed the Gas House Gang, the name used by the football team when the college first opened. The bar had been a campus fixture since the 1930s.

Tim Etherly was sitting on a barstool, talking with Mona, wife of the bar owner. She tended bar during the morning when students were in class and business slow.

"What's new Howard?" Tim said watching as Howard climbed onto the barstool next to him. They knew one another; Tim attended the music school across the street, and Howard lived just a block away, both frequent customers in the bar.

"Same old stuff, Tim," Howard said looking at Mona just across the bar from him.

"Beer?" She asked.

"Can you put it on the tic?" Howard said quietly. "My G.I. check don't come until next week."

"You're . . . in kind of deep already," she said, holding both hands on the beer tap as if Howard was going to try and remove it.

"I can loan you a deuce," Tim said smiling. He had been on a Coast Guard icebreaker in Alaska for his military service. He played saxophone and was going to teach when he earned a degree. But he failed English twice, a composition course, and had to take a remedial class for no credit. He asked Howard to take the test for him once, offering $20, but Howard had to refuse because he had a class at the time of the test.

"Thanks," Howard said watching Tim take two dollars from the money he had folded in his shirt pocket. "I'll have a draft beer," Howard said as Tim slid the money to him on the bar. "And . . . two hard boiled eggs."

The bar door swung open and a man in a uniform, pushing a cart with beer cases labeled Budweiser, came in backwards at first.

"In the back cooler," Mona shouted to the deliveryman, as she filled a glass from the tap and said it in front of Howard. Then she took two eggs from the rack on the back bar and quickly set them on a napkin in front of Howard and rang up the sale on the cash register.

When she set Howard's change in the bar, she shouted to the deliveryman, "the empties are outside the back door. I'll show you."

Howard watched her go to the back room almost running behind the bar.

"She's almost as wide as she is tall," he said peeling an egg, grinning.

"She'd fit right in," Tim said, pointing to the pictures on the wall, "to any one of these teams," then watching Howard peeling the egg, added, "what are you having? Breakfast or lunch?"

"Both," Howard said before he bit the egg in half, stuffing the other half in quickly. "And I think supper as well, lad," he said peeling the second egg.

"That bad, huh?" Tim said and took a drink of beer. "I was going to ask," he said setting his glass on the bar, "if you're still going with that Grosse Pointe girl. But, maybe, I won't."

"What about her?" Howard asked before putting the second egg in his mouth.

"Does she like Opera?"

"I never asked her," Howard said wadding up the napkin around the showpieces, then sliding across to the edge of the bar. "Why?"

"Well my girlfriend's father passed away—bad kidneys," Tim said turning his glass in a circle on the bar. "We were going to see the New York Metropolitan Opera on Saturday night—but of course she can't go."

"That's a tough break," Howard was looking at Tim over the beer glass he held up to drink just in front of his face. "Things like that happen."

"Forty bucks worth of tickets," Tim said shaking his head. "Simone Boccanegra is playing. It's opening night here at Masonic Temple downtown. Big blow-out, all the city bigwigs will be there. And all the socialites."

There was loud noise from the back room; cases of empty beer bottles being stacked.

"I was sort of hoping you'd show here today," Tim said. "I had you and your lady in mind—I mean you would really impress her, if you took her to the opera."

"Tim—I don't have forty cents—so the $40," Howard said and drained the last of the beer from this glass, "well—just—I can't help you, no matter how much I'd like to take her . . . That's all."

"Tell you what Howard, give me $20," Tim said and finished the beer in his glass. "It'll help me—I mean I won't have a *total* loss."

They both watched Mona come back and held up their glasses for more beer.

Howard turned to watch the deliveryman going to the front door pass behind his stool. Then looking at him, said "I can't. Sorry."

When Mona slid the two beer glasses she refilled in front of Howard and Tim, Howard asked for another hard-boiled egg.

"Okay," Tim said "give me $10 for the tickets, Howard," and flipped open a notebook on top of his textbooks sitting on the bar. He picked up an envelope with two orange tickets sticking out; he held it toward Howard after sliding the tickets back inside the envelope.

"What if she says no?" Howard said peeling the shell off the egg.

"She won't, Howard."

Chapter 4

On the night of the opera, Howard put on his only suit, charcoal gray, three button, that made him look like an Ivy Leaguer. He bought the suit when he came out of the Army to wear on job interviews. And he put on the vest he bought in Munich, pool table green with the roll of small silver dome buttons down the front, because he thought it made him look like some kind of *foreign* celebrity.

At Marian's house, when he went to pick her up, and she opened the front door, his mouth dropped open when he saw her.

"Wow," he said looking at her, "I can't breathe—you take my breath away, babe." She wore a champagne color sheath dress and her mother's mink jacket. Looking at her hair swept up in French twist she always wore he said, softly, "you . . . look like royalty."

"And look at you, Howard," she said smiling, closing the door. "Honey, you could pass for Franz Liszt . . . or something. You look so trim and beautiful."

When he slid his arms around her waist, she pulled back.

"No, no," she said, running her hands down her thighs to smooth her dress, "I don't want to go with my dress . . . rumpled."

Howard, exaggerating, put his hands behind his back, then leaning forward, kissed her gently.

It was then he smelled her perfume.

"Or, babe," he said backing away, "that perfume . . . and the look of you . . . my knees are buckling."

"Howard, honey," she said putting her hand on his face, "I know how you feel . . . but after the theater we'll have more time . . ."

"I'm going to . . . explode," he said raising his arms toward her.

"Sweetie," she said, "we have to get going if we want to get there on time," and moved her shoulders under the mink coat, then with her hands, pulled the fur against her face.

"I guess . . . you're right, babe," he said quietly, and looked up at the ceiling of the foyer for relief.

"We can take Daddy's car," she said picking up a small purse from the side table in the foyer. When she picked up a set of keys, she jingled them, and handed them Howard.

"How did your folks get up to the summer house?" He asked reaching for the keys. "I mean the family car is here . . ."

"Oh Daddy bought a new AMC station wagon," she said pulling open the front door. "They all drove up in it . . . trying it out. It's white . . . something new for a car color."

"I can't stop looking at you," Howard said. "From every angle . . . you are . . . perfect."

"Oh, Howard, please try to calm down, honey," she said shifted her shoulders under the mink "we *have* to get moving . . ."

After stepping out on the front porch, and down the one step to the grass, he turned, "why did he by AMC station wagon?"

She smiled, and said, "he's been buying a lot of their stocks lately—I guess he wants to boost the price or something."

"That figures," Howard said. "I hope you like the white color . . ."

"Howard, I'm going to the kitchen and push the automatic door button for the garage door . . . and the lights go on. I'll lockup the house and I'll be out in a minute."

"Yes, your Majesty," he said jingling the keys.

In the parking lot across the street from the brightly lit Masonic Temple, Howard gave the attendant two dollars and that left him with only sixty-three cents in his pocket. He had not figured he had to pay a fee for parking the car when he came out tonight.

He had to smile while walking around the car to open the door for Marian, thinking he had a champagne taste but a beer budget.

"Oh," she said, "isn't this exciting, Howard?" When they walked into the street, crossing into the bright lights.

"You bet, babe," he said feeling her hand holding tight on his arm.

Flashbulbs were going off when celebrities climbed out of the limousines that took turns driving up to where the red carpet came down the steps and ended at the curb. Press photographers were moving around in front of the crowd, that stood watching.

Just as Howard and Marian reached the curb and stepped up onto the sidewalk, a Lincoln limousine pulled up and the crowd gave out a sigh.

Marian pulled Howard to a stop.

"That's the Henry Ford daughter," she whispered in Howard's air. "The oldest one."

"Don't do that, babe," he said. "When you whisper like that—it drives shivers down my spine."

A young woman wearing a long black dress and a fur cape stepped out of the limousine, the chauffeur standing at attention as he held the door open.

Her hair was piled high on her head like a beehive.

Flashbulbs seem to go off all at once, and some of the crowd were taking flash pictures with their own cameras. There was a hush, the crowd silent.

A second woman stepped out of the limousine. She was young and thin, dressed in light blue and the dark fur jacket.

Suddenly, a full-faced man appeared out of the limousine, pulled his suit coat down straight, then with one of the women on each side holding his arm, started up the red carpet.

Flashbulbs lit up everywhere at once.

Someone in the crowd said, "that's Henry Ford II—just look at him—with his daughters—isn't that something?—isn't that charming?"

Marian leaned against Howard and said, "aren't you impressed?"

"Yeah," Howard quipped, "must be a good opera."

"Oh-o you," she said pulling Howard's arm. "That's not funny, you-u."

"Okay, okay," he said grinning, "I'm impressed. Now, can we go up the steps?" Taking Marian's arm, he added, "maybe we'll get our picture in tomorrow's society page too."

"Oh," Marian said "it's all just part of the excitement—enjoy it Howard. I am."

"Yeah, yeah," Howard said grinning, aware that the photographers were shooting pictures of them, unsure if they were celebrities are not. Then, as they neared the top of the stairs, he added, "I think you're the best looking celebrity here tonight, babe."

She squeezed his arm as they walked through the doorway into the lobby, following the red carpet.

"You're prejudiced," Marian said smiling, looking at him as he presented the two orange tickets to the usher at the door who led them to their seats. "You know that?"

"I know a good thing when I see it," he said helping her take off the fur jacket.

"Have you ever seen an opera before?" she asked, taking two programs the usher held out to her, then sitting down.

"Well," he said dropping into the seat next to her, "I saw the movie *"Three Penny Opera"* in Munich once. It was in German. Does that count?"

"Could you follow the story?" Marian asked slowly.

"Yeah, there were English subtitles." And when he saw her holding the bulk of the fur coat, Howard added, "can I hold the coat for you?"

"No, sweetie," she said. "It's no bother."

"I think," Howard said leaning in his seat to speak quietly toward her ear, "you're worried about that fur coat—that it might get damaged or something."

"No, no," she said smiling, looking at the photos in the glossy program after handing Howard his copy. He sat holding the program, watching the people being seated in front of him. "It says here," she said quietly, "this opera is rarely performed because the costumes and the scenery are so elaborate—it's *very* costly."

"I'm sure you will like it then, babe," he said grinning.

When intermission came, they waited, seated, until the crowd thinned out.

Then, walking through the doors into the lobby, Marian said, "you like the opera, so far?"

"Yeah," he said. "And, you are right about the background scenery—it's really something. It looks like the real thing. The buildings, especially. But the singing is mostly back and forth, like talking."

"You're right Howard about that; I'd rather hear *La Boheme*," she said smiling. "That's why I've seen it for five times. I like the emotion . . ." then turning to face him, she said the Howard, "now you can hold fur cape—while I go to the ladies powder room."

He took the fur and stood holding it, watching her walk across the lobby, her bottom moving. He pursed his lips, but was silent, watching her go the rest room door.

To his left was a long table against the wall with a large mirror behind it. Howard looked at the stacks of pamphlets, all on the subject of Opera, all laid out in neat rows, and grinned widely when he saw the sign: BROCHURES $5 DONATION.

He walked along the wall where the group of people stood smoking, some sipping from small paper cups. Over near the door he saw the stand with the girl behind the counter with the sign: ORANGE JUICE $1.50. He shook his head, then shrugged, he only had sixty-three cents.

When he was walking back along the table, shifting the fur jacket to his other arm, he saw a paper cup sitting on the edge where someone left it. It was almost full, so we picked it up.

"Okay," he heard Marian say from behind, "it's your turn—if you want to go the boys room."

"Oh-h," he said, turning to her, then sliding the fur to her arm, "you startled me there for a moment, babe."

"How nice," she said, "you bought juice," and took the cup his hand.

"No," he said watching her drinking from the cup, "I found it on the table here I'm too broke to buy anything right now . . ."

"Oh, Howard, do you always have to keep trying—to be funny," Marian said wiping her lip with a finger. "Hurry—go—so we can get back to our seats."

Howard shrugged, then turned walking toward the door marked: GENTLEMEN.

Later, when the opera was over, and they were outside walking across the street the parking lot, Marian said, "I'm just bowled over seeing that Opera, honey. I really enjoyed it." She squeezed his arm. "It was so rich—and elaborate—some of the scenes could've been a painting in a museum—from the 18th century—or something."

That she had enjoyed it so much brought a wave of satisfaction over Howard. He liked doing things for her, and when his efforts made her happy, like today, it made him feel good too.

"Yeah," he said looking at her for an instant as he was unlocking the car door, "the opera production guys sure got it right, babe. It must cost a fortune to ship all those stage props—and costumes . . ."

"Yes," she said, "it is very expensive." Then when he opened the car door, she asked, could you follow the story—the words?"

"I followed the words in the program," he said as she sat down on the car seat and he caught a flash of her legs when her dress pulled up.

"The *libretto*," she said.

"Yes," he said teasing, "the liber-retto," wishing he could make love to her right now. She was so perfect from any angle that he felt that way more when he looked at her.

Smiling to himself, walking around the back of a car, he suddenly felt as if something cold touch the back of his neck. Turning, he saw people the parking lot getting in their cars, but none of them were looking toward him. But he could not help feeling someone, somehow, wanted him to know he was being watched.

When he climbed into the car, he said to Marian, "thank you for looking so terrific tonight, babe." He leaned over to kiss her, and felt the fur against his face.

"Howard," she said putting her hand on his face, "everything went terrific tonight. I enjoyed *everything,* the opera, the hoopla out front with the flashbulbs. It was a night I won't forget . . . what we . . ."

"Babe, he said sliding a hand on her leg, "I know one way you can thank . . ."

"Stop, honey," she said pushing his hand away. "You have an audience out there . . ."

He looked out the windshield at people walking between the cars, and sat up, then turned the key to start the car.

"I hope these people realize," he said driving out of the lot, "what an imposition they are to Yours Truly."

"I'm sure they don't sweetie," Marian said smiling. "Sometimes—you have to use—constraint. You just can't have it your way *all*—the time. Life doesn't work that way."

"You're right, babe," Howard said stopping the car at a red light. "If there was no—constraint—well, people would be making love in the streets."

"Oh, Howard, there you go again . . ." she said as the car started away from the traffic light, "trying to make everything funny."

"Babe, I *am* funny," he said. "And you're too serious."

"Howard, you should be—serious. Really."

"I'm working on it," he said looking at her for an instant, "but being serious—*is* serious."

They both smiled.

Driving on Jefferson Avenue, they passed the last of the tall, brightly lighted buildings that make up downtown Detroit, when Marian made a moaning sound.

"Hey, babe. what's the matter?"

"I feel—terrible."

"Are you in pain? Where do you hurt?"

"It's my—stomach. A cramp," she said putting her hand on Howard's arm. "We might have to make an—emergency stop."

"Can you hold it?" he said taking his eyes off the road for a moment to look at her. "Grosse Pointe is just ten minutes up ahead . . ."

"Stop *now*, ple-ase. Anywhere there is a little girl's room. Oh, Howard, please."

"Okay, babe." The only lights ahead on the street were coming from a Toddle House restaurant, a small cottage size building set back from the roadway. Howard stopped the car and said, "There isn't many places open; it's sort of late."

Marian opened the car door, "This will do," and stepped out, slamming the car door hard.

Howard followed behind at a short distance as Marian pulled open the door. He caught the open door and followed her inside.

The restaurant was empty, a chubby lady behind the counter was smoking a cigarette near the cash register. When Marian asked for the rest room, the woman pointed to a narrow hall at the end of the counter.

After Marian handed Howard the fur jacket, and he was standing behind the row of swivel stools when she disappeared around the corner, the woman asked him, "Can I get something for you?"

"Ah-h, yeah," he said, feeling he owed her something. But he only had sixty-three cents.

Looking up at the overhead menu searching for the cheapest item, he saw that hot chocolate was twenty-five cents.

"Two hot chocolates, please," he said and sat down on a stool slowly, resting the fur on his knee.

"Anything more?"

"Hot chocolate will be all," he said, looking at the woman, realizing what she thought of the two well-dressed customers with a mink jacket.

"Two hot chocolates coming up," she said and set two dark brown ceramic mugs on the counter in front of Howard. Then she ripped the tops off two packs of chocolate powder, and after emptying one into each mug, filled each cup with hot water from the giant coffee urn side spigot.

Howard sat smiling, watching her drop an extra-long spoon into each cup, then begin writing the check. When she slid the bill on the counter in front of him, he saw the fifty cent cost, and smiled wider with relief.

Stirring the chocolate, Howard was beginning to have second thoughts about leaving the waitress the thirteen cents he had left for a tip.

Some of the things he did forced people to look at him, disbelieving. The word was *incredulous.* It would not be hard to imagine the waitress giving him that look after a thirteen cent tip.

He got that look last fall from the old lady in the Lost and Found department, downstairs in the Detroit Art Museum. When Howard told the old lady he lost a raincoat, she looked at him through her thick eyeglasses the same way the waitress did. The incredulous look.

But, Howard remembered, he did get the Burberry raincoat with the wool lining to wear in the coming cold last winter. And he remembered filching the wool scarf from the pocket of another coat the old woman had set on the counter. He remembered thinking about asking to search the box of gloves he saw on the floor behind the counter, but he decided to skip it, the old lady was getting too suspicious. She might call a Museum guard. She had that incredulous look.

It was not easy being broke all the time, Howard thought. That Raskolnikov in *Crime and Punishment* wound up in big trouble because of it. Being broke is some kind of stigma that people can sense, Howard thought, or maybe they can spot it because they are just naturally suspicious.

"Oh, hot chocolate," Marian said from behind Howard.

He turned to watch her sit down, looking at her face, closely, for any sign of distress, then said, "Hope you're feeling better, babe. Here, you can have your fur back."

"As good as can be expected," she said stirring the hot chocolate, taking the fur onto her lap with the other hand.

Seeing the emergency was over, Howard said, "You know what guys usually ask when you come out of the bippy?" he said, stirring his chocolate, "they say, hey, did everything come out all right?"

"Oh-h, Howard," Marian said grinning, "there you go again—trying to be a *comedian*." She took the spoon out of the mug and set it on the counter, looking at him. "Take a break, honey—and give me a break, too. No jokes."

When she took a drink of cocoa, he did the same.

The front door of the restaurant opened and an elderly man in a raincoat and Tartan driving cap came in slowly, limping.

"Ah, Myrna," he said to the waitress, "you look ravishing."

She stood folding paper napkins and stuffing them into empty chrome containers at the far end of the counter.

"Oh, Robert, quit," she said smiling, watching him lower himself onto a stool, gripping the counter. "how come you're all dressed up?"

"I went over to my daughter's house," he said.

"You want coffee, Robert?"

"Got anything stronger?"

"I'll be there in a second."

Marian had finished the hot chocolate, and was lifting the fur around her shoulders, when Howard reached over to help her. As she stood up, he slid thirteen cents on the counter, then followed her to the door.

"'Night," Marian said from the door, Howard holding it open.

The waitress came walking down the counter, and when she saw the thirteen cents, her mouth dropped open.

Howard followed Marian out the door.

Walking to the car, Marian said, "Did you see the look on her face? Didn't you give her a tip?"

"Yeah," he said. "I put two quarters on the paper receipt, and some change at the side of the cup. Why?"

"She looked like she was hit by a bolt of lightning," Marian said getting in the car, Howard holding the door.

"Maybe it wasn't enough," Howard said. "I mean two well-dressed people stop in and only have cocoa . . ."

"It must be something like that," Marian said before Howard closed the door, making a face; showing his teeth the way people do when shirking away.

In the driveway at Marian's house, she stepped out of the big sky-blue Oldsmobile to push the button on the garage wall that opened the automatic door.

For a moment, Howard turned to look at his 1953 Ford parked off the side of the driveway. For some reason the old car had turned obscene, he thought. It was out of place in these surroundings at Marian's house.

When the automatic door of the garage opened, he saw watching her long legs in the car headlights while she walked into the dark garage to pull the light chain on.

When the lights came on, he sat for a moment looking at her round bottom.

"She's perfect," he said out loud to himself. Then driving the car forward, added, "She's like a dream. Like a dream—too good to be true."

Marian had left the kitchen door open; and had turned on all the lights leading to the hallway.

Dropping the car keys on the kitchen counter, Howard walked out to the hall. Marian had the fur jacket on a hanger from the closet and was dropping a plastic covering over it.

"The garage" . . . she began, talking to his reflection in the mirror on the closet door.

"Door down," he said, "and all the lights out."

"That old guy in the Toddle House," she said reaching to hang the jacket in the closet, "I thought I knew him." I just remembered—he goes to our church," she said turning and closing the closet door.

Howard stood for a moment, thinking, about the whole congregation, and Marian's father, hearing about the thirteen cent tip.

"The guy in the Tartan cap?" Howard said, "Are—you—sure?"

"Yes," she said putting her arms around his neck. I thought I recognized him—but I had to remember from—where."

"He's not a cop," Howard said slow, his nose against Marian's, "or something like that?"

"I don't know," Marian said. "Why?"

"It just struck me," Howard said. "I had the feeling when he came in the restaurant—he was a snoop of some kind."

"Oh, Howard, you sound like someone with a guilty conscience—on the run, or something."

"Yeah," he said rubbing his nose against hers, "it does ring a little paranoid, doesn't it."

He kissed her once, and the second time, he began pulling up her dress from behind.

"No, no," she said quietly, moving her face back from his. I can't do anything now. It's my time of the month—that's why I had the cramps."

"Are you kidding?" he said tilting his head. "I'm internal combusting here."

"You'll have to wait a few days," she said softly, shaking her head. "That's all, honey."

"I can't wait," he said and bent forward and looking down at his crotch. Taking a step back, he said, "Damn. My good suit. Damn."

"Wha—at, Howard?"

He took off his suit coat, then pulled at the front of his pants where he was wet.

"What a mess," he said holding his pants out.

"Howard, I'm sorry, but I can't help it—I'm wet, too."

"I'll go in the bathroom," he said, "and use some toilet paper. Clean up some."

He went into the bathroom and snapped on the light while holding out his pants.

"This would be funny," he said to Marian, "if it happened to someone else."

She turned away, smiling, and said, "I'll make coffee. Take your time, Howard. You poor dear."

"Whatever," he said, moving the door for privacy but not closing it. "Hell of a night, hey, babe?"

"It was a terrific evening, honey," Marian said loudly in the direction toward Howard. "I'll never forget—what we had at the opera house. It was unbelievable—I think the word is *sublime*, well, anyhow," she said, counting scoops of coffee into the percolator, "what happened tonight, doesn't happen too often in a lifetime."

After she snapped the lid on the coffee pot and plugged it in, she pulled open the freezer. There were two turkey pies frozen in boxes. She took them out of the boxes and set them in the stove oven, and turned the heat setting to four hundred.

Howard walked into the kitchen, the blotch on his pants bigger from where he washed the stain. It had taken him much longer than he had wished.

"You look real domestic," he said and put his arms around Marian. She put her arms around his waist. "What are you making?"

"Turkey pies in the oven," she said just before he kissed her.

They stood holding one another, neither one wanting to move.

"What a night at the opera," he said slowly. Then, when he smelled burning, he said, "That can't be us."

"Oh," Marian pulled away. "I forgot to set the timer for the turkey pies." When she pulled open the oven door, the pies were smoking, the tops black; smoke rose up to the ceiling.

"I'm not that hungry, anyway," Howard said watching her use a hot pad to set the pies in the sink.

"Are you sure, honey," she said dropping the hot pad on the sink. "I can make something; eggs, maybe?"

"Naw," he said watching as she came over and put her arms around his neck. "It's getting late—it's almost one—and I have a ton of stuff to read for class at the library tomorrow."

"I guess we should call it a night," she said leaning against him. "We'll make up for lost time," she said before kissing him. "And we got the trip to New York when you're out for the summer—to look forward to."

"I can't hardly wait," he said and kissed her.

"That goes for me, too," she said watching him put on his suit coat.

Outside, in the car headlights, he looked at the large house as he backed down the driveway, and shook his head.

"Every time I come here," he said out loud driving down the street, "something is out of sync. It's uncanny; something *always* goes wrong."

Chapter 5

In New York City, standing with their luggage on the curb, watching the taxi go off down the street, Howard said to Marian, "Well, that's "Wolfie's Deli"; the loft is just up there, babe."

It was seven in the morning, the June sun growing warmer.

"He lives here?" Marian asked looking where Howard pointed.

"No, no," he said, "he lives out on Long Island—the family has a house in Sag Harbor. that's where they keep the boat." Picking up his duffle bag, then Marian's large suitcase, he said, "Bob keeps this loft as a combination office and pad—for business—in the city here."

"How do we get out to Sag Harbor," she asked, looking across the street at Wolfie's in an absent-minded tone, standing in her wrinkled skirt, holding a small suitcase, looking like a refugee.

"You okay, babe?" Howard asked looking closely at her eyes. "I mean, you've been acting—distant—since we got on the plane this morning."

"I'm just tired," she said, smiling and returning his stare, "if that's what you're asking. No, it's been awhile since I was here in the city—a lot of memories—it's—overpowering—being back; that's all."

"Want something to eat?" Howard asked quietly. "Corned beef hash, or coffee or something? We can pop into Wolfie's."

"No," she said smiling. "Let's go to the loft, Howard—and stop being so sweet, honey."

"Sometimes, babe," Howard said quietly, "you rattle the hell out of me—I don't know what to say."

"I know," she said following him as they walked, looking up at the buildings, "I can be like that sometimes—distant."

"Bingo," he said looking up, then at the stairs in front of him. "Up we go. This is the loft building."

Up on the second floor, Howard found the key hidden on top the window sill he knew about. He bent down close to the lock in the dim light to find the key hole.

"The lettering says," Marian read slowly, "R. M. Foskett *and* T. M. McMillan, Associates."

"McMillan was, ah," Howard said, Bob's wife's father's partner," as he swung open the door glancing at the lettering before turning on the lights. "He's dead, so is Bob's father, but Bob kept the name."

All the office walls were navy blue, and off to the left near the windows, as a large desk stacked with folders of pencil sketches.

On both sides of the desk were four drafting tables with lights hanging from the high ceiling. Large potted plants with wide leaves made a passageway to the bookshelves on the left wall.

"The windows," Marian said, "all you can see is a brick wall on the other side of that air shaft."

"That's New York, babe, no office with a view," Howard said walking to the back of the loft pointing. "The bedroom is back this way."

When he swung open the door and snapped on the light, she said, "Wow, your friend certainly likes basic colors," standing and looking at the orange walls, running her hand on the stainless steel sink.

Howard swung open another door, "This is the bedroom where we can drop these suitcases and unload."

"All dark blue walls again," Marian said and set her small suitcase on the large bed. Then looking into the bathroom, she said, "Unbelievable—even the tiles in the shower are blue."

"Maybe he likes everything blue because it reminds him of sailing," Howard said and grinned when he opened his duffle bag and pulled out a dark-blue, wrinkled, t-shirt. He stood taking off his white dress shirt.

"That could be," Marian said while stepping in front of the two sliding doors of a large closet.

Howard looked at her and said, "Don't get too nosey," but she already pulled opened the doors.

"Look—at—this," she said. "It looks like a magazine store. Look at this collection . . ."

"We're just guests," Howard said and dropped his dress shirt over the back of a chair before stepping up behind Marian. Looking into the closet, he said grinning, "Oh-h, yeah; that goes all the way back to his college days in Ann Arbor."

"This whole stack is all *Playboy*," she said putting her hand on the magazines up nearly to her hip. Those are *Penthouse*," she said pointing to a smaller stack. That bunch there is *Hustler*."

Howard shrugged and walked over to the bed and sat down, and took off his shoes, then the pants he wore on the flight from Detroit.

"He told me he started saving the copies of *Playboy* in nineteen fifty-two," Howard said, "when it first came out." He folded his pants and set them on the chair next to the bed. "Those first issues were in black and white."

"Howard, this guy isn't some kind of sex-weirdo?" she said, moving over to the end of the bed, then opening her small suitcase.

"Naw," Howard said pulling the blue t-shirt over his head, "he's just—enthusiastic. He told me about *Playboy* when he came home for Easter vacation one year. That the guys would line up to buy the magazine at a place called the "Blue Front" bookstore—and that it sold out in minutes."

"Are they all like that in Ann Arbor?" Marian said as she slipped off her seersucker jacket. "I mean, I'm afraid to even hang my clothes in there—with all that—pornography."

Grinning, Howard said, "*Playboy* was a bombshell back in those days, babe. The girls were nude—completely. The store had to keep the magazine under the counter—so guys couldn't sneak a peek."

She began taking off her white shirt, and Howard saw the wetness stains on the seams under her arms.

"I'm going to jump in the shower," she said.

"You're wearing a bra," Howard said sitting down on the bed. "You never—wear a bra."

"Yes I do—always—when I travel."

"Man, oh man," Howard said sitting down on the bed. "It makes you look even more—sex—ier."

"Sometimes Howard," she said grinning, "you say some—unusual—things, honey."

He reached for her arm and gently pulled her on top of himself where he lay on the bed.

"The bra just makes—you—more feminine, babe."

"I wear it to be—respectable out in public," she said when he slipped off the remainder of her clothing, not resisting him.

"Respectable," he said to her face just **about his,** "and more—fetching."

"You're pretty fetch—," she said when he entered her. "Oh-h, Howard," she added, and put a hand on each side of his face, holding it.

He thrust up, holding her bottom, wanting to make love for her total enjoyment. He wanted to give back all the pleasure she gave me—and for being with him.

Without speaking out, or moaning like some girls, she gave back in a pushing motion, until they perspired so much they were becoming slippery. It was then she began a jerking motion, suddenly, coming against his stomach.

Howard felt the inside of her dropping down, around him, where he was inside her, as he climaxed, letting go, after holding back the release because she was enjoying the moment.

Resting, laying side by side, Marian whispered, "We should get married," in an even voice, and he knew she enjoyed everything.

When she was in the shower, Howard dug out a pair of canvas deck shoes out of the duffle bag. He smiled, feeling good because she was with him, today. He did not want to think about the future—the economics of it. He had to grin thinking about her attitude toward Bob; then he shouted as he was tying his shoe, "you'll see how normal Foskett is when we get to Sag Harbor; I mean kids, and a wife—and a dog even."

She came out of the shower in a towel wrapped around her body beginning under the arms.

"How come he's so far—advanced—in life?" she said sitting down on the bed, dressing while covered still by the towel. "I mean, you and him are about the same age."

"I know what you mean, babe."

He watched her pulling on Bermuda shorts, and turned away. He heard the money in her voice, her wealth speaking.

"He didn't have to go in the Army for two years, like everybody else," Howard said and swallowed hard to clear the tightness in his throat. The question upset him. It was not a simple question; Marian was digging, and Howard felt she was looking for money.

"How come he didn't have to go into the Army?" Marian asked while slipping her travel shirt wet under the arms on a hanger, then carrying it into the bathroom.

"He had a medical deferment," he said tying the laces of his second shoe. "He's got a 'lazy eye' or something—it prevents him from seeing correctly."

"No wonder," she said coming out of the bathroom and standing in front of him as he sat on the bed, "after reading those smut magazines—he can see at all."

Howard laughed and leaned forward getting up.

"Wow," he said, "you look so—fresh—crisp in those shorts." She had put on a light blue oxford shirt over her bra and was now opening a vile of perfume, dabbing behind her ears. "And you smell good . . ."

"Howard," she said grinning, "control yourself—at least try . . ."

"I just can't help it, babe. I can't stop looking at you," he said, putting his arms around her.

"Howard, honey," she said pushing him slow, "go take a shower. You need it." Grinning she added, "And you better make it a cold one . . . so we can get going out to Sag Harbor."

He sat down on the bed and began untying his shoe.

'Okay, okay," he said, "I get the hint."

~ ~ ~

Howard was driving the Volvo station wagon on the Long Island Parkway when Marian asked, "How does Bob get out to Sag Harbor? . . . I mean, we have his car."

"He flies out," Howard said looking at her for an instant. "They have some kind of light plane shuttle service, that buzzes people out and back to the city."

She was wearing sunglasses because of the afternoon brightness, and she lowered them for an instant. "Ahh," she said to Howard, looking over the top of her glasses, "that sounds typical New York," she said and pushed them back up.

"Those sun shades," he said smiling, "make you look . . . mysterious . . . and at the same time, babe, sort of New Yorkish . . . at the same time."

"You've been out here before," she said. "Last summer? When?"

"Two summers ago," he said, turning to her. "I came for a job interview at Reuters . . . and stayed a week . . . but I was here, too, when I was in the Army, just after they bought the place."

"Howard, keep your eyes on the road. Ple-ase," she said shaking her head. "You're making me nervous."

"I can't help it," he said looking at her. "those Bermuda shorts show you off," he said and put his hand on her leg, where it was bare, below the line of the Bermuda shorts. "With you sitting here—I just get—excited."

"Don't do that," she said, pushing his hand away.

"You're cruel sometimes," he said shaking his hand. "You know that, babe?"

"Keep your mind on driving, Howard. Or we might not get to Sag Harbor."

"Aye, aye, Captain."

"Are you sure—Howard—where—we are going? How to get there, I mean?"

"The Parkway to Riverhead, then left and we're in Sag Harbor. Bingo," he said and waved his hand. "You can't go further than Riverhead, because out here the island is shaped like a claw, and Riverhead is at the inside of the claw. The top left of the claw is Sag Harbor."

"Howard—sometimes you're too much," Marian said grinning, "and—it makes—you charming."

"Kiss me," he said, "or I'll have you keel-hauled."

She kissed his face, next to his ear, slowly.

When Howard saw the name Foskett on the mailbox, he turned, heading the Volvo up the Foskett road through the trees.

"It looks like an old farmhouse," Marian said leaning forward, then pulling off her sunglasses, to look through the windshield.

"Yeah," Howard said grinning, "and it's all furnished with Bean catalog stuff."

After Howard sounded the car horn, Bob Foskett came out on the porch barefooted, wearing a t-shirt that showed his muscular swimmer shoulders. He stood grinning, watching the station wagon come, leaning against the post that supported the overhanging roof.

"You came just in time, Howie," Bob shouter. "We're just having a snack." He watched Howard getting out of the station wagon, then added, "Then you *always* show up where there's food, right slick."

"You still wear Levi's, man," Howard shouted. "Some things never change, right, Bob-o?"

"It's my mid-western upbringing," Foskett shouted back. Then when he saw Marian, he stood up straight, and watched her close the car door. "Howard you sure are lucky, but I didn't realize how lucky—until now."

"Marian," Howard said walking toward the porch next to her, "meet Bob Foskett—don't believe anything he says."

"Hello, Bob, she said. "I've heard alot about you."

Bob came down the porch steps, holding out his hand toward Marian.

"I didn't know we were going to be visited by royalty today," he said gently shaking her hand. "You're fantastic, Marian. You deserve much better than this slug you came with."

"Don't be so generous," Howard said. "And drop the pick-up line you always spiel at parties, you rotter."

Bob pulled up the collar of his golf shirt as if to make his appearance more presentable.

"Howard," he said grinning, "it's mind-boggling to see how fortunate you are to be in the company of this lady."

Marian stood smiling and listening.

"Clean living," Howard said putting his hand on his heart, "always merits a reward. But you wouldn't know what I'm talking about."

"He's getting hostile," Bob said to Marian. "We'll avoid him." He pointed up the steps saying, "Come into the house and meet my family, come."

"Great," Marian said, and getting into the light-hearted banter while going up the steps, added, "Tell the porter to bring the bags into the house."

"Howard," Bob said grinning, turning around at the top of the steps, "you heard the lady."

"I'll expect a tip," Howard said, turning, walking back toward the Volvo. "A very generous one."

Bob, at the top of the steps, holding the door open for Marian, shouted, "You'll get the tip of my boot, swab, if you don't make it snappy."

"Aye—Captain," Howard shouted as he pulled the suitcases from the back of the station wagon. Then slamming the heavy car door and walking to the house, muttered, "Don't worry dude, I'm watching you—especially when you're near Marian."

When Howard pulled the porch door, that opened into the kitchen, he held it with his knee, as he passed the two suitcases inside, and he heard Bob saying, "Deborah has a cousin in Traverse City—she runs a cherry orchard farm up there."

Marian was next to Deborah, nodding, "Ah, we have friends of our family with a cottage at Glen Lake—we go up there to Traverse City alot—it's such beautiful country up in that area—I never miss a chance to go up there."

"Oh, hello Howard," Deborah said smiling. "Bob give our guest a hand . . ."

"He's not a guest," Bob said grinning, taking a smaller suitcase from Howard. "He's more like a relative."

"Well, show him where to put the luggage in the guest room," Deborah said evenly, at the same time looking at the baby in the high-chair next to the kitchen table.

"Thanks, Debbie for keeping Captain Bly in line," Howard said, then looking down at the baby, added, "Caroline is really growing—she's what? Almost three?"

"She'll be three in two months," Deborah said and put her hand on the top of the child's head.

"Hey, Howard," Bob said, "put your suitcase out here in the hall for now. And quit soft-soaping my wife—I'm up to your game."

Passing to drop the suitcase out in the hallway, Howard plunged his elbow into Bob's midsection. the women did not see the move; the only sound, a grunt coming from Bob.

"I can offer you some clam chowder," Deborah said to Marian. "I made bread this morning and there's tea . . ."

"Sounds wonderful," Marian said sitting down at the table.

"When you're done," Bob said while squeezing the baby's cheek to make her smile, "we'll go down to the harbor and see the STRAY CAT—my thirty-six foot—*other* baby."

"Right, Bob-o," Howard said watching Deborah set a bowl of chowder on the table in front of him, "we've come a long way to see this new yacht, man."

"How—ard," Marian said, "maybe you should tone down the aggression a bit." Then she turned to Bob, "I want to change clothes before we go sailing on your boat."

"Sure, no problem," Bob said. "We have time—do you what you have to do."

Howard, holding a spoonful of chowder, made a long face as if to say to Bob to quit the soft-soap.

After lunch, Marian changed into khaki shorts and a dark blue t-shirt, and when she came outside, Howard and Bob were standing next to the Volvo.

"Hold it a minute," Bob said, "I just had a flash . . . we need extra life preservers."

Marian climbed into the front seat of the Volvo and Howard followed, pulling the door closed. They both saw the bronze Mercedes sedan in the garage when Bob lifted the garage door.

"Cripe," Howard whispered, looking at the luxury car through the windshield, shading his eyes from the sun, "he's certainly doing all right."

"But," Marian whispered back, "look how he lives."

After Bob flung two orange vests in the back seat, and climbed behind the steering wheel, Marian asked, "Where did you meet Deborah?"

She was standing on the porch holding Caroline.

"In Ann Arbor—when we were both students," he said waving to her before turning the Volvo down the gravel driveway. "We met in French class in the old Romance Languages building."

"Seems like the right building to start a romance," Howard said.

"Do you *always* have to say the obvious, Howard?" Marian said, smiling.

"Don't be too hard on him," Bob said to Marian. "He's a journalist—they're *all* like that."

"I take that as a compliment," Howard said.

"You would," Marian said.

"Well, we all can't be architects," Howard said.

"Thank heaven," Bob said grinning.

~ ~ ~

When they were walking on the dock at Sag Harbor, Bob pointed to a black hulled sailboat.

"There she is—my new baby—purpose-built for racing in the Olympics. She's made with pressed wood and painted with epoxy that makes her hull slick as a green onion."

"But, Bob," Marian said, "then stopped when she dropped her life preserver, and stooped to pick it up," there's no top. Where's the cabin part?"

Howard took hold of her arm, grinning widely at her.

47

"No cabin," Bob said, then stepped on the deck and a hand on the mast, "because this is strictly a racing machine—not a floating kitchen—for cruising weekends."

"Who we going to race today, Captain Bob?" Howard said helping Marian step on the boat, holding her arm.

"No race today, lad," Bob said stepping down into the cockpit opening. "Not today. Just a leisurely jaunt to familiarize the guests with the working hardware."

Marian sat down on the bench seat in the cockpit opposite Bob and Howard, and pulling on her life vest, said to Bob, "I like all this varnish and chrome and the white ropes—but, where is the little girl's room?"

Bob reached under the bench seat up forward and pulled out a brass spittoon.

"This will have to do," he said in a matter-of-fact manner, "when the situation arises."

Howard looked at her in disbelief. "Hope you didn't drink too much tea at lunch," he said grinning.

"That's not funny, Howard," she said watching Bob put the container back under the seat.

"We promise not to look," Howard said. "How's that?"

"I'm not," Marian said in a flat voice, "going to use that thing."

"Okay," Bob said, "we'll just have to face the problem when it comes around," as he began untying the lines. "Howie, go forward—pull up the jib—so we can get underway."

"Don't you have an outboard?" Howard asked going forward. "Don't you pull out of slip with the motor—the auxiliary?"

"No. No auxiliary," Bob said pushing the boat away from the dock. "Real sailors," he said sitting down and taking the tiller, "leave the slip on the jib—they don't need a motor."

"A purist," Howard said when the jib was up and he was coiling the line. "Hey, Bob, what's this track thing running next to the cockpit?"

"For a Genoa—a Genoa jib sail," he said steering the boat out in the channel. "It's for racing—it runs parallel to the main. It gives you more zip."

"You two know about sailing," Marian said. "You can talk about it—both of you."

"Yeah," Howard said dropping down on the bench seat opposite her, "we took classes at North Shore, the club out near Lake St. Clair."

"We only capsized two lightning's," Bob said laughing.

"I hope we don't do any—capsizing—today," Marian said looking back at the dock.

"No, no," Howard said, "when they turn turtle—it's to teach you to right the boat again—from the water. It's part of the class."

Bob made a long face; he knew Howard was just reassuring Marian. He did not say anything as he turned to check all directions as they moved out into Long Island Sound.

"Up with the main," he said. "Marian, hold the tiller while we crank it up."

"Does Deborah like sailing—on your boat?" Marian asked watching them raise the main sail, holding the rudder exactly where Bob left it.

"No," Bob said, when he took the tiller back, standing, one hand on the boom overhead, steering with his knee, "she doesn't like sailing—she thinks it's too dangerous." Then he caught Howard's grimace, and he added, "Ah, for the baby—and she won't bring Caroline out here."

"And I bet Deborah won't leave," Marian said smiling, "the baby home. She's a good mother."

When the wind caught the main sail, the boat suddenly heaved to the left and began moving fast.

"Wow," Howard said dropping down on the bench seat opposite Marian, "this is terrific—she really moves, Bob-o."

"I didn't know it would move like this," Marian said, brushing her hair away that was blowing over her face. "It moves so fast—it seems almost—alive."

They were passing another sailboat coming out of Sag Harbor, and just as the guy with a full beard nodded to them, a wave broke over the bow, spraying everybody in the cockpit.

"Salty," Howard shouted to Marian. "It tastes salty," he said wiping the water from his face.

"Sure," Marian shouted back, "we're out here ripping along in the Atlantic Ocean—it ought to be salty."

"No," Bob said grinning, "it's really just the Long Island Sound, Marian—not quite the Atlantic."

"That's just a techni—cality," Howard shouted at bob. "It's still *part* of the At-lantic."

"Okay, okay," Bob shouted back. "Don't start a mutiny over it."

Just before another spray broke over the front of the boat, Marian shouted, "We're leaving that other boat from the harbor way back," then, when the water hit her, she turned her face to the side.

"Howie," Bob shouted, 'get ready to jib the spinnaker pole.

"Aye, aye, captain," Howard said moving forward in the cockpit.

"Coming about," Bob shouted.

Howard stood up on the bow, pulling the wide jib over to the other side of the mast.

"Marian," Bob shouted, "watch out for the boom—when it swing back over—"

She rose up on her right knee when the boat tipped sharply to the right.

"What do I do now?" she shouted.

"Mar-rian," Bob shouted, "the boom—behind you—watch out," and tried to reach her, to push her down, while still holding the tiller.

The boom swung, hitting her back and she fell over, face forward, into the water.

"No-o," Howard yelled before he let go of the sail and jumped into the water after Marian.

She came to the surface in front of him, her mouth open, the life vest holding her head up.

"Wha—at happened?" she shouted at Howard. "What did that?—Ooh, it's cold—the water."

"You're okay, babe," Howard said taking hold of the collar of her life vest. "Don't be afraid—you'll be all right."

Bob shouted across the water, "I'm turning around," and when Howard looked, he saw the main sail dropping.

Then, the sailboat that had come out of the harbor behind them, veered toward Howard and Marian. The man with the beard, held out a hand as his boat drew near, then when it was over the swimmers, he shouted to Marian, "Your hand. Reach me your hand."

When Marian held up her arm, the bearded man pulled her out o the water in a sweeping motion. Howard grabbed at the gunnels of the passing hull and swung a left leg up. Then the bearded man pulled him into the cockpit by his life vest, as the boat continued moving.

"Thanks alot, man," Howard said, breathing hard.

"Oh, yes," Marian said. "thank you for helping us," she said, shivering, her clothes dripping water. "We might have gone under—if you didn't come over."

"I could see you needed help," the bearded man said, turning the tiller, "And I was nearby—to help."

"Where's Bob's boat?" Howard said in a loud voice, turning to look behind.

"There over port," the bearded man said. "He's just furling his main sale—we'll head over there."

Jeez, Marian," Howard said turning to her, putting his hand on her face, "my heart stopped when I saw you tumble into the water. Man."

"I think mine stopped, too," she said smoothing her wet hair back. "It happened so fast—I didn't have time to think."

"Are they all right?" Bob shouted from his boat running on the jib, drawing closer. "Are there any injuries?"

"Both are okay," the bearded man shouted. Then when the two boats were closer, he said, "coming alongside." Then to Bob, "Grab the bow before it strikes."

"Right," Bob shouted. He could not hold the weight of the two boats for long, and the bearded man took hold to help, as Howard and Marian stepped back onto Bob's boat.

"Damn," Bob said, "I was really scared, Howie—for a minute there . . ."

"That makes two of us," Howard said and put a hand on Marian's shoulder. "Luck was with us today."

"Here," Bob said, pulling two yellow slickers out of the box he slid out from under the seat. He went back to holding the tiller, watching the other sailboat skidding along his hull. "Oh, man," he said, "we're taking a pounding . . ." But, when the two boats separated, he shouted, "Thanks again," and waved.

Howard saw the word *Portsmouth* under the name *GIGI* on the stern of the other sailboat as it moved away.

"Portsmouth, Maine?" Howard shouted, helping Marian pull on the yellow slicker.

"New Hampshire," the bearded man shouted back, still within earshot.

"Who do I send the Christmas card to?" Howard shouted as a wave broke over the bow.

"The Barlows'" came the shout back over the growing distance between them.

~~~

After dinner at the Foskett house, Howard and Bob sat out on the front porch steps, away from the clatter of dishes the women made back in the kitchen.

Howard sat looking at the setting sun, thinking about what Marian had said when he helped her off the sailboat: "What are we doing here?"

Later, she said she did not want to stay the night with the Foskett's, so Howard told Bob before dinner they would not be staying.

"I hate to put the bite on you, man," Howard said, "but I'm really short of cash."

Bob had not spoken since they came out on the porch, and now he used a tone as if he just woke up: "How much you need, Howie?"

Howard had an inkling Bob was rolling over in his mind about Marian going overboard. There could have been a tragedy, and he was feeling responsible.

Howard had pushed the event out of his own thinking. He let Bob alone, not mentioning it, to let him draw his own conclusions.

"Fifty bucks," Howard said, then shook his head. "Man, I hate to have to tap you for money. I feel like a—piker."

Bob set his snifter down on the porch next to his leg, slowly, then pulled out his wallet.

He handed Howard three new twenty dollar bills.

After Bob put away his wallet, he said, "You're going to need a *lot* of money." Then picking up his snifter, added, "Girls like Marian—are expensive."

"I'll send you money when I get home," Howard said folding the bills and sliding them into his shirt pocket.

"Yeah," Bob said nodding, "you better."

"She's never known—money problems," Howard said swirling the cognac in his snifter. "You think—I'm in over my head—going with her?"

"Who knows," Bob said and took a sip of brandy. "Hey, Howie, don't lay a question like that on me, man," he said, holding the glass under his nose, then adding slowly, sniffing, "it's *too* personal. Okay?"

"I can tell," Howard said, "by you dodging the question, that you think I'm in trouble with her—because of money." He looked up at the dark sky above full of stars. "Practically everybody I know has been telling me I'm going to lose her."

"Howie, there are alot of jealous people in this world—believe me, man."

"Marian and I dig each other so much—I just can't believe—we would ever—be apart. I mean—I couldn't take being away from her. I'd crack-up, or something."

"Howie, after a woman has a child, her attention is *all* on the new baby," Bob said sniffing his cognac again and swirling it. "The guy is only necessary for the income—to pay the bills. He becomes second fiddle. I guess, what I'm saying is *everybody* sort of loses his girl—as things change. That's the way life is, kid."

"Naw, Bob-o, that ain't the same. I mean, she ain't gone forever—like with some other guy, or something. It ain't—drastic, man. Okay, her time—just for awhile—is tied up with the child—she's occupied—but she'll come back after awhile."

"You know, Howie, some guys go looking for—bimbo's," Bob said quietly, swirling his cognac glass. "Maybe because they miss the attention—they had from the girl they married."

"Or maybe," Howard said, looking at the cognac in his snifter, "they just got—bored. Well, not bored exactly—but sort of tired of the same thing with the same woman: guys go looking for—variety."

"Could be," Bob said and finished cognac, tilting the glass up high. "Could be all that stuff," he added and set the glass down on the step in front of him.

Howard stretched his back muscles by sitting up straight, then raising up his arms over his head. "Who knows for sure," he said. "Everybody is different, man."

The screen door screeched open behind them and Marian came out on the porch.

"Howard," she said, "maybe we can head back to the city. You haven't had too much cognac?"

"No, no, babe," he said turning to look at her, seeing she was wearing Bermuda shorts again, her long legs above him. "I'm okay to drive," he said feeling he should be accommodating because of what she had been through today out on the boat. "Whenever you're ready—we'll roll."

"Where's Deborah?" Bob asked looking up at her.

"Putting the baby to bed," she said. "Hey, you sure you guys didn't down too much brandy?"

"I'm okay," Howard said looking up at her, "I had a big dinner, babe."

"We have to drive back in the dark, Howard."

"I know, I know," he said. "We'll be okay."

Pulling open the screen door, Marian said quietly, "I've had enough excitement for today." When the door screeched and closed, she said from inside back through the screen, "I'll get my wet clothes—and say goodbye to Deborah."

When he was sure she was gone, Howard said to Bob, "I guess I'm going to listen to the 'Man Overboard' stuff for awhile."

"What you expect, man?" Bob said, standing up.

Chapter 6

The building in the shape of a large white duck near the town of Riverhead appeared in the headlights as Howard turned the Volvo station wagon onto the Parkway.

Marian moved her legs forward to stretch, and said in an even tone, "I'd like to visit a friend I went to college with—she's working for an airline."

"Sure," Howard said without turning to look at her in the dark. "As long as we take it easy on the cash."

"You mean, Howard, we have no money?"

"Nothing like that, babe," he said feeling his face go flush-warm. "We just have to—not be extravagant—that's all."

He took a quick look at her in the dark; she was sitting looking forward.

By her not saying anything, Howard felt the distance between their lives come out into the open. He felt inferior for the first time; it was a shock. They had never talked about money before, their time together as boy-girl looking at one another, learning about each other's habits.

"Your friend, Bob," she said still facing forward, "had a stroke of good fortune—everything he's got now, he got by good luck. Deborah told me while we were washing dishes—she told me all about it."

"Right," Howard said, nodding, "I know some of it." He did not look at her, he knew what she was feeling, what she was leading up to. She was wishing that he could conjure up some good fortune like Bob and make enough money to live a comfortable, secure life. A life with no money worries.

"It seems you friend Foskett and McCullough—the firm's partner—"

"Not McCullough," Howard said, "McMillan, babe. Yeah, I know they were in the same architecture class in Ann Arbor."

Deborah doesn't like McMillan," Marian said. "For some reason, she told me she has never been to the firm office."

"McMillan is kind of—fruity," Howard said grinning.

"Fruity?" Marian said looking at Howard in the dark, only the lights from the oncoming cars lighting his face on occasion.

"Effeminate," Howard said quietly.

"Well, okay," Marian said, "anyhow, McMillan's father had the firm here in New York with a partner, who had bad kidneys. The father had the son working for him, until the doctors told him to retire. So daddy told the son to get a partner because the workload was growing—they were designing buildings all over the country, and even down in South America."

"And," Howard said, "Brian McMillan asked Bob to join the firm—and the rest is history."

"Deborah told me, Howard," Marian said shifting her weight on the car seat to get comfortable, "that Bob was one of the few people on campus—who even bothered—to talk to McMillan."

"Now," Howard said grinning, feeling Marian had snapped out of the somber mood cause by her 'overboard mishap', "you're going to tell me the moral here is that an act of kindness can lead—to a good job."

"There you go again," she said looking at him," trying to be funny. This is serious, Howard. I'm just trying to say you should look for opportunities . . ."

"I know what you mean, babe. And you're right—being without money is no joke."

"I wish," she said continuing looking at him, "that something like that happened to Bob—a lucky turn—would happen to you, honey." She wetted her lips with her tongue, "Even my family—Daddy in particular—would breathe easier—if something like that happened."

"I know, babe. Those with money—only have to worry about keeping it—and entertain themselves in the meantime." Howard did not want to go into the tirade against rich people and upset Marian. "The people without money," he began, "are stuck. I mean, they have to earn a living—while, at the same time, *trying* to figure out how to make a fortune."

"I just wish," Marian said looking forward again, "you could have a stroke of good luck—like Bob did, that's all."

"I know, babe, but—unfortunately—I'm in the newspaper business. And this business has a building, a bunch of editors working there, and some writing employees, reporters at the bottom of the totem pole. I go to them for a job and a salary."

"Howard, I meant . . ."

"I know what you mean—the luck part," he said, the headlights of the cars lighting his face now as traffic grew heavier near the city, "and I'm trying to explain that the news business is different from an architectural design office. And here it is—those design firm people can charge a pile of money for their work. A newspaper man—gets a salary. And—that's the difference, babe."

"Well," she said quietly, "I just wish you could get some kind of lucky opportunity like Bob did in his job—it would really be great."

Howard turned to look at her again in the headlights of the oncoming cars. For some reason, her face looked surprisingly like her father's in the glare. It startled him for an instant.

"Babe," he said, searching for something to say to make her feel better, "you never know when something unexpected will pop into your life."

"Yes," she said turning to look out the car side window, "I had a sample of the 'unexpected' today—when I fell out of that boat. Talk about the 'unexpected' . . ."

"We were lucky, babe," he said without looking at her. "I mean, I was right there when you went over the side."

"I know, I know, honey," she said putting her hand on his arm. "But how am I going to tell my parents? You know they don't understand us—they're going to go crazy."

"Well," Howard said sensing what was bothering her now, "it's pretty obvious—if you don't want them to know, then don't tell them."

"Oh-h, How—ard," she said turning to face him, "I've *always* told them—things that happen to me. I'm not good at keeping secrets." She put her hand to the side of her face. "Things are getting—so—complicated."

"Well, babe, you would be doing them a favor—mom and dad—by *not* telling them—look at it that way."

"Yes," she said "that would work—but it seems too—sneaky." She looked out the passenger side window and said quietly, almost inaudible, "I've always been—open—with them."

Howard trying to soothe her feelings, said, "Think about it for awhile, babe. You'll do the right thing for *everybody* involved, I'm sure of it. Just step back and take some time—and think about it. The answer will come to you, you'll see."

"Yes," she said, putting her hand on his arm again, "that's what I'll do, honey; maybe I'll feel different about all of this later. Thanks. I suppose it's all right."

"Now," Howard said, "we should enjoy being in New York City, babe. I mean, we have all day tomorrow to bum around before we fly back Sunday. We can go to the Guggenheim and . . ."

"No, no," Marian said sitting up straight, "I want to see my classmate—Nancy Rousseau. Okay?"

"Yeah, babe."

~ ~ ~

Howard's second drink of White Horse scotch on the rocks, as he sat at the White Horse Bar, made him light headed. He had skipped lunch to save money, after he and Marian visited the art museum, then walked Fifth Avenue window shopping, and she said she was not hungry, when he asked her about having a sandwich.

"Nancy lives right over there," Marian said pointing, then looking at her vermouth on the rocks glass in front of her. "She lives with a couple of other girls who work for the airline, so you'll have to listen to girl-talk—but, I want to see her. She'll know about a lot of the other girls—who were in our class—and I'm curious how they're doing now—and all that."

"Sure," Howard said, "why not?" feeling dizzy now.

Outside the bar, crossing the street, Howard put his hand on Marian's rump. She was wearing the tan suit again that she had worn on the plane, and her long, round legs made him excited.

Last night she would not make love, saying that the incident of falling off the boat, made her feel guilty about her life and she did not want to make it worse.

When he tried to use his tongue on her, to give her some pleasure, she refused.

"Your trip to the White Horse Bar is showing," she said pushing his hand away. "You should go to the other White Horse—up there in Canada—or the Yukon—and cool off."

"Babe," Howard said taking her arm, "sometimes you can be—cold. You know that?"

"It's just the way I feel—right now," she said stepping up on the first step in front of a brownstone apartment.

"It's new to me, babe," he said following her up the steps. I've never seen this side of you. It's new territory."

At the door, Howard expected to see a slender, graceful Nancy Rousseau, who glided gracefully through the aisles of airplanes, serving drinks and peanuts.

But the Nancy who opened the door of the apartment, was a short girl with wide hips and a stack of black hair.

When Howard was introduced and he shook her hand, he felt a firm hand.

"It's pure luck I'm home this week," Nancy said taking hold of Marian's hand. "I'm on standby for the Paris flights."

"You haven't changed," Marian said, pulling Howard to the couch with a pattern of large flowers. "Nancy, you're the same when you were at school," Marian said, and gently forced Howard to sit, without looking at him.

"And you're attractive as ever," Nancy said, standing now with her hands on her hips. "You're a lucky guy, Howard. This lady is beautiful inside as well as outside."

"I know," he said nodding, fighting sleep, the scotch making him groggy.

"Well," Nancy said, "I want to offer you folks something—refreshments." Moving to the kitchen door, she said, "I can make coffee, or if you want—I have vodka—Smirnoff—in little bottles that I snitch from the airline supply."

"Vodka," Howard said, "sounds good—for me."

Nancy ducked into the kitchen and there was the sound of the refrigerator door opening and closing. Nancy came out carrying a bowl of small bottles of vodka and a carton of orange juice.

"Glasses are there in the cabinet next to you Howard," she said, and dropped into the large chair with a floral pattern opposite where Marian was sitting.

"How do you feel these days?" Marian asked Nancy, who was pouring orange juice into glasses. "Any kind—of medical problems?"

Howard winced at the question to Nancy, thinking it an odd question, but he did not say anything.

"No, Nancy said as she twisted the top off a bottle of vodka, then pouring it into a glass. "I've been lucky, I guess, in that way—so far—anyhow."

Marian pored a small part of the vodka from her bottle into her glass, then handed the bottle to Howard. he emptied the full bottle into his glass, then added Marian's leftover portion.

"I think about that time we had at school, often," Marian said. "I don't know if I can ever forget. It may last—a whole lifetime. It doesn't seem to *want* to go away for me."

"Me neither," Nancy said and drank from her glass.

59

"Okay," Howard said, "Here's to the memory of your school days—rah-rah."

He took a long drink from his glass, but neither of the two women looked at him.

Then Marian asked, "Have you seen—any—of the other girls we knew at school?"

"Bippy," Howard said in a falsetto voice and slowly stood up. "Bippy time."

"Second door down the hall," Nancy said pointing with the glass she held in her hand.

When Howard came back into the living room, Marian and Nancy were sitting, leaning forward, their knees almost touching, as they were talking.

Stumbling over the corner of the couch, he dropped heavily onto the cushions. The women had seen his fall, but said nothing. He sat a few moments, then rolled his head back against the top of the seat and closed his eyes.

Later, he woke up, Marian shaking his shoulder.

"Are you all right, Howard?"

"Yeah," he said, rubbing his eyes. "I just dozed . . ."

"Are you ready to go?"

"When you are, babe."

Nancy held one of the small bottles of vodka.

"Howard," she said, "take one of these home. You'll probably need it—later."

He took the bottle.

"I'll drink it on the plane home," he said and dropped the bottle in his shirt pocket.

At the door, the two women were crying, so Howard went out and stood in the hallway.

Then, downstairs, going out into the street, Howard said, squinting in the sunlight, "You two were close—really—to say the least."

"I didn't tell you before, honey," Marian said. "I should have told you—Nancy had an abortion at school. I went with her to the doctor. I even loaned her—a hundred and fifty dollars—for the—operation."

Howard stopped walking, looking at Marian.

"Wow, babe," he said slowly.

"She wants to get married now, and she has to tell a priest about it."

"I see, I see," Howard said, nodding.

"Since we landed . . . here in New York, it's been pressing down on me, like a big load on my shoulders. It all came back—all of a sudden."

"I see," Howard said, putting his arm around her shoulders, "that's why you were—distracted—at the time we were out front of Wolfie's when we climbed out of the cab."

"You don't miss a thing, do you?" she said looking up at him.

"Not when it comes to you," he said and squeezed her, and kissed her forehead.

"Howard, don't ever go away. I need you—to stay with me. No matter what happens—we should not be apart. I couldn't stand to be away from you and go on living. I need you with me."

"That goes for me, too," he said and kissed the side of her face.

When they were walking again, Marian said quietly, "Nancy said she wonders what the child would have looked like today. And she said she wonders if she did the right thing—about destroying it."

They stopped at the corner, waiting for traffic.

"I don't like it you—being—involved," Howard said looking at her. "Technically—abortion is murder—that makes you—an accessory—to murder. If not legally, morally."

"There you go again, Howard," Marian said. "Ridiculous again. You're not funny, Howard, not at all."

"I guess, you're right, babe," he said when they stepped off the curb. "I'm no one who should talk about morality."

"You know what Nancy said about you?" she said looking up at him, grinning, as they crossed the street.

"No," he said, "I can't imagine."

"She said you're drinking is going to be a problem—that I should let you go—and find someone else."

"Jeez, she said *that*?"

"Yep, she did, honey."

"Well, babe," he said as they stepped up on the curb, "her being up there on the moral high-ground—gives her the advantage to take shots—at us low-life."

"How—ard," Marian said shaking her head, "try to be nice. She's a friend—you should be nice."

"I'm trying. I'm trying, babe," he said looking at her as they were walking. He paused before asking her, "Who was the guy involved with Nancy? Her lover boy?"

"I think he was a Greek or Italian guy," she said at the top of the stairs to the subway. "He sold gelato from a pushcart—on a street near campus. He was a young guy with black hair. I saw him a couple of times—out there."

She turned to go down the steps.

"One more question, babe," Howard said following her down the steps. He leaned forward next to her ear and asked, "Did you get back the hundred and fifty bucks?"

"Oh, Howard," she said, "You're so crazy. That's not funny," she said as they stepped into the subway car. "You're always trying to be funny. But to answer your question, yes."

"Couldn't you say," he said watching the automatic doors close, "that I'm just too—curious. After all, I am a news man."

"All right, all right," she said holding onto the pole for balance as the subway car began to move, "now I have a question—for you."

"Shoot, babe," Howard said dizzy with vodka and the motion.

"Well," she said looking up, holding the pole, "I have another classmate—friend—I'd like to visit. She paints. She has a loft downtown, a studio, down on Pearl Street. I would like to go see her."

"Okay," Howard said, exhaling, then inhaling deeply.

"Are you okay, honey?" Marian asked putting her hand on his face. "You look—pale."

"Your painter friend isn't violent—or anything?

"No. She paints pictures that look like a ball of yarn."

"Okay," Howard said, nodding.

"She says the viewer—has to see through the labyrinth—of her paintings."

"Labyrinth," Howard said, and made a long face.

"You're still loopy from drinking, aren't you?" she looked up at him. "Daddy says that news reporters—all drink a lot."

Howard was going to ask her how Daddy knew that, but, grinning, holding the pole to steady himself, swaying with the subway car movement, he said, "reporting and news writing is all—mental—and reporters use drinking as a form of relaxing.

~ ~ ~

The note on the door loft read : AM TAKING CLASSES IN ITALY. BACK IN MID-SEPTEMBER. JULIE BRAMPTON.

"Well," Howard said, "that settles that, babe."

"Yeah," Marian said, turning. "Hey, are you hungry by any chance?"

"What you got in mind? Pizza?"

"No, not today, honey. But the Fulton fish market is just over a few blocks. You like fish? Julie took me to a great restaurant—a fish place that makes bouillabaisse soup.

"I don't know, babe," Howard said, sliding his hand in the pocket with the money he had left. "Well, okay."

"Great, honey," she said taking his arm. "You'll really enjoy it, they use seven or eight kinds of fish. In fact, it's more like a stew than a soup."

"I know what bouillabaisse is," he said, knowing that it was like any other seafood. "But, I've never had it."

"It's a real treat," she said. "You can't get it everywhere."

Howard was looking up the street when they turned the corner, and saw water, then boats at the dock.

They were walking past stalls stacked with boxes of fish packed with ice, when Marian pulled Howard's arm, "That's the restaurant, there."

They sat at a table near a window.

"Man, that fish smell," Howard said, looking out the window, "that's a *real* smell of the sea. And those boats out there at the dock, are *real* ocean-going jobs. And it's all here—a stone's throw from Times Square. Fantastic."

"Julie says she likes the atmosphere down here at the fish market, "Marian said leaning forward across the table, "because it's authentic—she says."

A bald waiter came to the table, and Marian ordered the bouillabaisse, and Howard sat watching him write the order on the pad, hoping it was not too expensive.

Looking around at the walls for a price list or menu, Howard did not find either, but he noticed the elderly couple come through the door. The woman hand a nose that was sharp, so much so, it made her look like a bird.

"I'm getting hungry," Howard said across to Marian as she was unfolding a large linen napkin. "I must have been excited—or something. I wasn't hungry before."

"I know why you weren't hungry, Howard," she said spreading the napkin on her lap. "You were trying to save on money."

Howard turned from looking at her, and saw the old man, sitting at a table near the center of the room, both he and his bird-wife, looking straight at him.

"Je-ez, Marian, can't you give me a break? I mean, I only got twenty, maybe twenty one—two, bucks."

He looked up at the pattern in the metal ceiling, thinking for an instant, it dates back to the turn of the century.

"I'll help," Marian said, "when you run out of cash. But, not to change the subject, honey, I want to tell you I've made a decision about telling them at home—about my falling out of the boat."

"Oh," Howard said unfolding his napkin as the waiter arrived with two large bowls stacked with cooked pieces of fish, a lobster claw at the top." "What'd you decide?"

"I'm not going to say anything about it."

Howard looked across at her; she was looking intently at the lobster claw.

~~~

Back at Foskett's loft, as Howard came out of the shower, he saw Marian sitting on the edge of the large bed in her panties.

"Don't ask me to make love, honey," she said to him when he sat down next to her. "I'm scared—too much as happened to me today. I guess the falling out of the sailboat has sunk in. I don't know—how to think about it now. I'm sorry."

"I was right there to help," Howard said and put his arm around her shoulders. "You were never in any danger. I mean of drowning. You had a life vest on. Look at it as a quick dunk in the water to cool off—on a hot afternoon—like jumping off the raft in the lake up at your summer house."

"I feel—somehow—it was a—warning," she said looking him in the face. "I can't shake the feeling off. I can't find the words, exactly, but it's guilt sort of mixed with something bad—terrible—is coming."

Howard kissed the side of her face, but when he reached to touch her breast, she took hold of hand, stopping him.

Then she laid back on the bed.

"I'm crazy for you babe, all the time. I can't help it. I'm sorry you feel bad," he said standing up as she pulled the sheet. "It's all I can do—to keep my hands to myself—when I'm around you."

He walked around the end of the bed, and dropping the wet towel on a chair, climbed under the sheet and lay next to her.

"I want you, Howard. I always want you," she said slowly, "and nobody else. You know that." She turned her face on the pillow to look at him, "But since I fell out of that boat—I can't shake this feeling—a deep, dark, feeling, something is going to happen. No matter how much I try to make it go—it always creeps back. All day it's been bothering me."

"I admit, Marian, falling overboard can be a frightening experience," Howard said reaching to turn out the bed lamp. "But, you shouldn't let it influence . . ."

"Going overboard . . . is just part of it," now that I'm thinking about it. It's been a few weeks now, that the feeling has been around. I don't know why."

Howard put his face next to hers.

"if you're worried about getting pregnant," Howard said in the darkness, lowering his voice, "I brought some—protection. I've got two of them in my pants pocket over there."

"Howard, not now—tonight."

"You can be cruel, babe," he whispered, "and slid his hand down her thigh. "Don't be like that—we're on a trip enjoying one another."

"I can't help it," she said pushing his hand away. Then she asked, "Am I really an 'accessory'—to Nancy's abortion?" in a tone Howard never heard before.

"What's the matter, babe?" Howard asked her back. "All this stuff is guilt—thinking—it's like a confession of some kind." He raised his arms and turned to put his hands behind his head, laying looking up at the darkness. "You're being too hard on yourself. Think of something else for awhile, babe. Give your—conscience—a rest."

"I made a promise—about sex," she said, almost whispering.

"What kind of 'promise'?"

"Daddy. I promised I wouldn't have sex on this trip to New York. I gave my word."

"So *that's* it," Howard said, rolling onto his side to look at her. "Daddy's long arm reaches—all the way to New York, huh, babe?"

"Just for now," she said. "just for this—trip."

"That's doesn't make sense," he said. "I was surprised they let you come with me to New York at all—your parents. Now, I understand."

"I *knew* you'd understand, honey."

Chapter 7

When the summer term ended at the university, Howard moved back home with his family. He was tired of being without money all the time, and decided to get a job, not pay rent, and save to make a bank account.

His mother and father were tolerant at having him home again, but his sister did not conceal dislike about it.

He planned to take night classes at the university, continue his studies, while working.

Two Saturday nights later, Howard parked his old Ford out front of the house at the curb, and a beer bottle was smashed on the windshield making a crack. A witness saw the man do it and left a note under the windshield wiper:

I was coming home from work last night about 1 a.m. and

I saw a guy get out of his car and break a bottle on your windshield.

His car license is EW 6419.

Jack Gascoyne, a neighbor.

Howard's father was mad about it, and called a police friend of his, who traced the address for the license number. The address registered to a young man who lived with his parents in Grosse Pointe Park, three streets west of Marian's house.

Howard's father was mad after he found the name and address in the telephone book.

"Let me call this kid's father," he said to Howard, who was grinning, when he nodded. Howard had been studying in the kitchen and took a break.

"What the hell was your son doing over here in our neighborhood—at that late hour—in the first place?" his father said in a loud voice into the telephone.

Howard sat at the kitchen table, grinning, holding is face with both hands, listening.

"Give him hell, Dad."

There was a pause, then Howard's father said in a low tone, "Yeah, you better have a talk with him."

After the two men talked on the phone for over ten minutes, Howard went back to reading his history textbook.

When he heard his father say, "All right, we'll have the windshield replaced at this Ford dealer you want us to go to—and you'll take care of the bill. Okay, and goodbye." Howard looked up, smiling.

"Hey, Dad, the car is ten years old."

"So what?" his father said hanging up the phone on the wall. "You can't let it go—a thing like that—besides, they live in Grosse Pointe. They can afford it."

Howard, smiling, watched his father go out the kitchen door to the living room where the television was blaring.

Howard had the windshield replaced, but more than that realized he was being watched *all* the time. He first thought it was only when he was with Marian, but now he was certain he was under surveillance around the clock, day and night.

There were accidental things happening also, that he began to look back on, as happening by design, and not accidental at all. A light bulb flashing and burning out when he turned on a light, the radio suddenly changing stations, electric appliances quitting when he tried to use them, all were things happening to him now. He could only think, someone was deliberately causing these mishaps. Why, someone would do that, he kept asking himself.

A week later, Howard had car trouble again. The mechanic said it was just a low battery and re-charged it. But it would not stay charged. Then two days later, the mechanic said it might be the generator, now called the alternator. But a test showed it to be working. Then, checking the wiring, the mechanic found the flat copper ground wire to the battery—severed. When he replaced the copper wire that grounds the battery to the metal of the car body, the battery system began charging again.

Howard looked close at the ground wire when the mechanic handed it to him, after collecting fifty-four dollars for his repair work. The mechanic said nothing.

The braided copper ground wire, Howard could see, had been severed with a clean, sharp edge, the way a chisel cuts, and had been smudged over with grease and dirt.

Howard did not say anything to the mechanic.

~ ~ ~

In September, with Labor Day coming, Howard wanted to head to Saugatuck, the party town over in the sand dunes on Michigan's west coast. The town had a Cape Cod look, and in the off-season, was headquarters for a ritzy art colony.

There were all-night beer parties on the beach that brought students from campuses all over Michigan.

Plush yachts from Chicago came across Lake Michigan and tied up outside the jam-packed bars in the town called Douglas, on the waterfront, near Saugatuck.

The biggest Party times were Memorial Day at the beginning of the summer, and Labor Day at the end of summer. Howard had been going to festivities every year, since he learned about the resort back when he was in high school.

Marian said she would like to go to Saugatuck when Howard asked her on the telephone. Then Howard added, "Besides, I want to look up Jerry English, a journalism classmate. He graduated and got married, and landed a job on a newspaper over in Kalamazoo."

"You seem to know people, honey," she said, "every town we travel to."

"I know, babe. They rent a place—maybe we can sleep overnight on the floor—take a shower, that kind of thing. It helps my wallet." He paused, exhaled, then said, "When I get a job, things will be different, you know?"

"When classes start," Marian said slowly, "I'm going to try to find a job, too."

"You must really like to ski, babe. I mean, you like it enough to—go to work—make money just to go skiing."

"Yeah," she said, "In the two years since I began to learn, it's gotten in my blood. I'm sort of crazy about it. I want to get on the slopes as much as I can."

"Good for you," Howard said. "You need something like that—something you like doing." He shrugged, not having any more to say, and added, "Okay, then, I'll pick you up Friday after six. We'll drive at night—and be there the day before the partying begins on the beach."

"I'll be ready," she said quietly. "Howard—I miss you. These past few days—have been lonely, honey."

"Me, too, babe. In a double-dose."

On Friday, when Howard rang the front doorbell, Marian answered, dressed in a peach color long sleeve shirt and tan Bermuda shorts.

"Yikes," he said, "you are a feast—for all my senses. Babe, you glow. I'm stunned and getting weak. I'm—overcome. You—look—delicious."

"Howard, don't come in the house," she said, smiling, and reached for a small suitcase next to the door. "If you come in—we'll *never* get going to Ka-zoo."

"I need emergency medical attention," he said putting his hand over his heart.

When she moved next to him, the fragrance from her caught him, just as she was at eye-level and he studied her blond streaked hair pulled back into a swirl at the back of her head.

He leaned against the wall as if wounded.

"Honey, control yourself, ple-ease. The neighbors can all see us out here," she said pulling the door closed with her free hand.

"Okay, okay," he said, standing up straight, taking the small suitcase from her. "The family up at the summer house?"

"Yep," she said bending to lock the door.

When she turned and stepped off the low porch, leading the way to the old Ford across the grass in the driveway, he followed, smiling, watching her walk.

"I can't stop looking at you, babe," he said putting her suitcase on the back seat. "We got time—I mean, I've got an *erection*. I'm horny as hell," he said, closing the car door, looking at the bulge in his pants.

"You're not funny, Howard," she said when he slid behind the steering wheel of the car. "you're just being—ridiculous—and it's not funny."

"You knock me out, babe," he said and started the car.

"I just might do that," she said smiling.

"All right, babe. I get the message."

They were silent until Howard turned onto the Expressway.

"How long has your friend English and his wife been out in Kalamazoo?" Marian asked as they drove in the rush-hour traffic.

"Almost a year," Howard said. "I had heard about an opening out there on the newspaper staff and I told him about it. He wanted to get married, and he needed to find a job. Fast."

"Did he marry a girl from the university?"

"Yeah. Denise Dixon, a theatre major."

"I *know* her," Marian said smiling. "So do half the guys in my age group—around Grosse Pointe."

"What does that mean, babe?"

"She would date one guy to meet other guys—looking for 'targets—of—opportunity', that sort of thing. She was trying to hook up with some G-P ninny with money," Marian said taking a quick look at Howard.

"You mean a gold-digger, babe?"

"Not that strong, honey. She just wants to marry money and be comfortable—like everyone else—with money," Marian said grinning. "I'm not sure."

"Well," Howard said grinning, looking at Marian for an instant, "she married Jerry English. He's not G-P. And he's certainly not flush with money."

"They must be in love," Marian said quietly.

"I guess so," Howard said and switched on the car headlights as the orange streak ahead from the setting sun faded.

"Ah," Marian said, "Maybe Denise just ran out of G-P guys to date. The Pointes are—close-knit communities. Word gets around fast."

"Ah, yeah, babe. Life is better in Grosse Pointe," Howard said and stuck out his tongue.

"Quit being so smug, Howard."

"You're the smug one," he said.

"I'll let that pass, Howard. And I have a question."

"I know, babe, should Red China be admitted to the United Nations Assembly?"

"No, Howard the comedian' who makes these beach parties?" She was grinning looking over at him driving. "I mean, who builds the fire—goes and buys the beer—and all that?"

"Well, it could be anybody," he said, "but a lot of the time it's Red McNiven, the beach maintenance guy. He's got an office on the road right on the beach. He sleeps in the back room."

Marian laughed and said, "I bet a lot of girls flock to that beach house."

"Yeah," Howard said lifting a hand off the steering wheel to wave, "the house has hot and cold running girls."

"Ah," Marian said smiling, "then Red is a local celebrity?"

"If he's still there."

"You mean he might have moved away?"

"No babe, I meant to say, if he's still *alive.*"

They both laughed.

~~~

It was just after nine o'clock when they drove into Kalamazoo. Howard did not want to intrude on the young couple too early on a Saturday morning, so he filled the gas tank and afterwards, drove around the town.

"Howard, what's growing in all these swampy farms?"

"Celery, babe. Kazoo is the celery capitol of the world."

"Oh, over there," Marian said pointing, "the sign says onions for sale. Wholesale and retail?"

"How should I know, babe? Maybe it's both."

"Yeah," Marian said smiling, "'maybe'". then, putting her hand on his arm, she asked, "Honey, where do you learn all this kind of stuff?"

"Just the same as you," he said. "I asked the same question." He turned and looked at her while driving, "you know, babe, you look terrific this morning—even after being up all night. You're incredible, babe."

"Well," she said looking out her side window, grinning, "you look like you could use a coffee. You don't look 'incredible' by any stretch of the imagination, Howard."

"You want breakfast, babe?"

"Maybe a coffee," she said looking at him. "I could watch you eat—if you're hungry."

"I'd like a cold Budweiser."

"You look like you've had too many Budweiser's," she said.

"Yeah," he said looking in the car mirror, "I guess I have been hoisting quite a few Buds—lately."

"It shows.," she said. "Those dark circles under your eyes—make it look like your nose is riding a bicycle."

He rolled his eyes, and shook his head, grinning.

"I'm just a little tired, babe, don't try to make a federal case out of it." Then turning an ear to the engine, he said slowly, "I think I better check my car oil. could be my rods are clacking. Damn, I should have checked it when I bought gas."

"Cut it out Howard, that's not funny."

"This clunker burns a lot of oil," he said stopping the car at the curb next to a grass field with a backstop for baseball games. "We ran this old bus all night on the highway."

"Howard, you're so practical, it's amazing sometimes."

"Yeah, 'practical' about getting back to Detroit," he said getting out of the car. "I carry a spare can of oil in the trunk. I'll be back in a flash."

"See," Marian said grinning, "I was right about you being practical, honey. It's very—charming—to see you act so competently. Really."

Grinning, Howard looked at her, hesitating, "You keep that kind of talk going, babe, and you're going to get me all excited."

"There you go again, honey, trying to be funny. Stop it, Howard."

"Okay, boss," he said before going to open the car hood.

When he finished pouring oil into the engine, throwing the empty can into the trash barrel near the baseball backstop, Howard, looking in the car window while wiping his hands, said, "I think it's time to visit the English's, babe."

"Okay, master," she said grinning. "You're so cute, when you're being master-ful."

"I'm not sure, babe," he said sliding back behind the steering wheel, "but, I'll take what you're saying as a compliment." Leaning toward her, he added, "Give me a kiss."

"Uh-h," she said drawing back after kissing, "you smell like oil."

Starting the car, he shook his head.

~~~

"They live in the apartment with the orange painted door," Howard said. He had parked at the curb, and held up the notepaper Jerry had sent him. "Each door is painted a different color. that's the address he gave me."

"It looks like a motel," Marian said, turning, looking at the low building that stretched up the street.

"That's the college over on the left. These rooms must be the no-nonsense living accommodations for the students. Jerry tapped into that, I guess. His newspaper salary probably isn't anything to brag about."

"Oh, I see," Marian said. Then stepping out of the car and looking up at the sun, she added, "Ah, it's beginning to heat up; today's going to be a scorcher—and it's sticky out here."

"The humidity," Howard said closing the car door, walking around the front of the car, "is bad here because we're close to Lake Michigan."

"They have air conditioning, at least," Maria said, as she and Howard walked across the grass, she pointed at the unit in the window. "You need a conditioner when the temps get nasty hot."

Howard rang the door bell, saying, "Here we go."

The orange door whipped open, and Jerry English stood in the opening, dressed only in a pair of green Tartan shorts.

"Ah-h," he said, "you made it—finally. We've been up since about eight, waiting for you."

Howard, shaking Jerry's hard hand said, "this is Marian Harbaugh. Don't crush her hand, okay?"

"Wow, Howie," Jerry began, shaking Marian's hand lightly, "you don't deserve such a fine lady; nice to meet you, Marian."

She smiled at the blatant compliment and said, "Howard says you're a fellow newspaper . . ."

"How you been, Sluggo?" Howard said interrupting the reference to news work.

"Hello," came a voice from the kitchen. "I just made coffee," said Denise as she came out. She wore a denim work shirt over a pair of white shorts, and was wiping her hands. "Marian, you can fresh up there, the second door in the hall."

"You first, babe," Howard said.

"Yes, yes," Marian said.

Denise took her by the arm and said, "Jerry tells me you're from Grosse Pointe."

Jerry rolled his eyes up, looking at Howard, at his wife's "Grosse Pointe" comment.

To Howard, she had used the words as if Grosse Pointe were a distant planet.

Howard smiled at Jerry, watching the two women move away, and noting the contrast between the two: Marian, thin and blond, while Denise was heavy with black, curly hair. He noted, too, Denise's blunt manner of speaking, and the effect it had on Jerry.

"How you getting along on the newspaper?" Howard said to Jerry in the kitchen, watching him fill two coffee cups.

"There's not all that much hard news," he said, "so I wind up writing a lot of feature stories about farming stuff—and things like that."

"Well," Howard said slowly, "you're out in the sticks here, Jerry. But, don't feel bad, man, we *all* begin on small papers."

"I know, I know," he said, and pointing back at the living room, said, "Let's go out there."

Following, Howard watched as Jerry moved quickly to the bookcase and slid a thick book out. Opening the book cover, Jerry lifted out a pint of Jim Beam bourbon, hidden where the pages were cut so the bottle fit down in the hole.

Grinning, Howard turned the book over to read the title while Jerry was pouring bourbon into the coffee cups.

"Ah," Howard said, "*The Collected Works of Shakespeare*."

"Hey, Howie," Jerry said, after quickly returning the book to the shelf, then holding his finger over his lips.

Howard nodded, "Don't worry," he said smiling, watching Jerry as he sat down on the couch opposite him.

"The newspaper work I'm doing here in Ka-zoo," Jerry said in a loud voice for the women to hear, "is good training. Kind of the apprentice work I'll need—for when I get to work on a big city newspaper."

"You're right," Howard said, and sipped the coffee with whiskey. "I'm making the rounds of all the weekly papers in the Detroit suburbs, now, and living home. I want to save up—get some money ahead. But I still want to get the degree, so I only want to work part-time and take night classes."

"Maybe," Jerry said lighting a cigarette with a lighter that was a giant eight-ball that sat on a table next to the couch, "you could land an intern job at one of the dailies in Detroit?"

"Yeah," Howard said shaking his head, "that works out to a Saturday night stint at the Sports desk. Answering the phone to settle bar arguments and bets, and sometimes typing up the info on a hole-in-one. You get fifteen bucks for the one night. Phooey. I need more than that."

Marian came out of the hallway followed by Denise carrying a towel.

"We're going to town to do a little shopping," Denise said folding the towel. "Can you guys get along without us for a little while?"

Marian stood grinning at Howard.

"She wants to show me the school—where she works," Marian said grinning.

"Bring a six-pack," Jerry said to Denise, and she nodded while digging in her purse for car keys.

"About an hour," Marian said to Howard before following Denise out the door, smiling.

After the door closed, Jerry said to Howard, "Man, that's some fine chick you latched onto, pal. She's a winner."

"Yeah, I know, Jerry," Howard said. He leaned back in the stuffed chair, swirling the coffee and whiskey in his cup. "Everybody says that."

"Hey," Jerry said standing up, "you want another Jim Beam?"

"I haven't had breakfast yet."

"Aw-w, don't give me that," Jerry said taking out the Shakespeare book again. "You never let that stop you before—that I can remember. Man, those parties on campus—that went on all weekend," he said pouring more bourbon into Howard's cup.

"How can I forget?" Howard said grinning.

"Those chicks from the nursing school that lived upstairs from my pad—they were something else."

"That was a party for the books, all right," Howard said, looking up to watch Jerry take a drink from the bottle.

"Yeah," Jerry said putting the bottle back, then setting the book on the shelf. "It's all different now," he said dropping on the couch again, looking across at Howard and shaking his head. "You know—sometimes I phone Denise from work and say I have to work overtime. I do it so I can be alone for awhile. Denise is all over me when I'm here at home. I mean, man, I don't have *any* time here—when—she's not clinging to me like wallpaper."

"When you have a baby," Howard said, "things will be different, man. You'll see."

He took a drink from the cup, that was mostly bourbon now.

"No, no," Jerry said, "I can't afford a kid right now. Not on what I make—even with Denise teaching part-time. If she quits her substitute job at the school—and stays home—even now, we'd go under. We're living on short money as it is now."

Howard wanted to change the subject, get away from listening to Jerry's problems. He did not come to listen to money problems, he had his own.

"It will all work itself out," Howard said and took a sip from his cup. "Everybody goes through the short money problem when they're just getting started in life."

"Maybe so," Jerry said getting up, reaching for the Shakespeare book. Then, after drinking from the bottle, said, "working on a big metro newspaper would solve a lot of problems."

He offered the pint bottle to Howard.

"No thanks," Howard said. "I've had my limit."

"Last call for me, too," Jerry said. "Just a short one," he said and lifted the bottle.

"Hey," Howard said, "Denise is going to know you have been nipping—if you get swacked."

"Yeah," Jerry said putting the bottle away, "I'll eat some pretzels. Come out to the kitchen."

When Howard was following him, Jerry said, "I go to the bar sometimes, when I tell Denise I'm working overtime. I just sit there—drinking beer."

"You're not alone, man," Howard said. "Everybody does that at one time or another."

They were eating "Cheez-Its" because there were no pretzels in the cabinet, and after filling their coffee cups, were sitting at opposite ends of the kitchen table.

Howard was feeling lightheaded from the bourbon; he sat, holding one side of his face, resting his elbow on the table.

"You couldn't loan me twenty-bucks, could you" he said to Jerry slowly, his voice flat. "This trip is steep—I mean, it's costing more—than I estimated."

"I don't have twenty to spare, honest. Denise keeps the money and she keeps me on an allowance." Jerry sat silent for a moment. "I mean, she'd know if I came up twenty-bucks short."

"Okay, man," Howard said, nodding, his face flush from the refusal. "I understand."

Jerry looked at him, squinting for a few moments. "Ah, hell," he said quietly taking out his wallet, "I know you're up against it with that money chick, man. You don't want to look like a bust out."

"You don't know the half of it, man," Howard said, sitting back in the chair, both hands on the table.

"O-ops," Jerry said, "I only got ten. I bought gas and cigarettes on the way home last night. Will a ten spot help?"

"Sure," Howard said, and reached across and took the worn bill that Jerry put out on the table. "I'll pay you back as soon as I can, man."

"Right," Jerry said, stretching up to put his wallet back in his hip pocket. "That lady you got, Sluggo, *looks* expensive. I mean, you better make a lot of loot; you don't want to lose her. She's never had to live without money, like us. So, you got your work cut out for you: make a bundle of money."

"I know," Howard said. "I know what you're saying. Everybody I know says the same thing," he added, feeling the bourbon working on him, and Jerry too, was talking freely now; Howard knew it was the bourbon.

"I'm not trying to bust your hump, man," Jerry said leaning forward, elbows on the table, "but, I got my own big, big problem."

"Yeah," Howard said, "you got a big money hurdle . . ."

"I got a problem with Denise," Jerry said nearly hoarse, whispering. "She don't want kids, man."

"She'll come around, Jer."

"Man, you don't understand."

"She'll change," Howard said, thinking the bourbon was making Jerry maudlin, causing him to exaggerate.

"She says she's afraid," Jerry said leaning back away from the table. "She never had German measles when she was a kid. She says if she has a child, the baby, if it catches the disease—well, it can cause blindness in the baby."

"Damn, man," Howard said. "I got woman problems, too," he said leaning back in the kitchen chair. "I mean, Marian doesn't want to screw sometimes—and me, I want to screw *all* the time. She drives me crazy. I don't know if it's my fault, or what, that she doesn't want to do it. We only screw, when *she* wants to—it seems."

""It really changes things," Jerry said, leaning back, looking up at the ceiling, as if he had not heard Howard's lament at all, "I mean, I got a lot to think about—about the future with Denise, man."

Howard felt regret suddenly for his outburst of emotion, about his feelings for Marina, talking about their personal relationship. He felt embarrassed for Jerry, too, his spilling his problem with Denise.

A light blue Volkswagen came up the driveway next to the house and passed under the kitchen window.

"Well," Howard said standing up. "The girls are back—and it's time to hit the beach."

"Hey, Sluggo," Jerry said pushing back his chair and standing up, "what's the hurry?" He took both cups and began washing them out at the sink. "Stay for lunch, man. Denise will like that—we don't get much company."

There was an open pack of cigarettes on the sink, and Howard took one and was lighting it, when he said, "We just came by to say hello, Jer. We don't want to impose . . ."

"It's not no "imposition'—you and your lady are more than welcome, man. You can see it in Denise that she's enjoying being with your lady—that don't happen too often out here—company for her. You know?"

Marian came in the back kitchen door, followed by Denise carrying a shopping bag and a six-pack.

"You guys don't have the conditioner on," Denise said, "and it's like the Sahara out there. How come?"

Jerry went out to the living room and Howard heard the air conditioner come on.

79

"Did you enjoy shopping in downtown Ka-zoo?" Howard asked Marian. When she rolled her eyes up, grinning, he knew it was time to go.

"I'll thaw some hamburger for lunch," Denise said, taking a head of lettuce out of the shopping bag on the table, then turning to put it in the refrigerator.

"No, no," Howard said to her, "you don't have to bother. We're sort of in a hurry to get down to the beach. Honest—we don't have much time before we have to head back to Detroit," he said putting an arm around Marian's shoulders.

"We thought we'd walk the beach," Marian said, "you know, the end of summer thing."

"It's no bother," Denise said, hesitating after she took a frozen chicken out of the shopping bag.

"Let them go to the beach, honey," Jerry said to her from the doorway. "I'd like to go, too," he added, "but I'm on the night shift this weekend," he said to Howard. "That puts the kibosh on the Labor Day festivities."

"My fall classes begin next week," Howard said moving Marian toward the door.

"We have a lot we want to see," Marian said putting a hand on the door jamb, "so—I hope you don't think we're being selfish."

"No, no," Denise said taking a large can of tomato juice out of the bag. "I understand—you came all this way to enjoy the beach and the sun—you're pressed for time."

Jerry stood light a cigarette at the sink.

"Maybe," he said, "if the weather turns bad, Denise, they'll come back for a while."

"That's a promise," Howard said, and when Marian waved and nodded, he followed her out the door.

The English's stood in the front door, Denise waving, when Howard climbed in the car next to Marian.

"Man, this sun's getting hot," Howard said. "The heat shimmers are rising off the car hood."

As they drove away from the curb, they both waved back to the English's.

Putting on her sunglasses, Marian said, "Howard, you smell like whiskey."

"Yeah, I needed it, babe. Jerry gave me an awful earful of his family troubles."

"Denise kept introducing me to her friends at school and at the market," Marian said in a flat voice, "as her 'house guest from Grosse Pointe'. Can you imagine that?"

"Well, we're away now, babe."

"We weren't very graceful in our exit, were we, honey?"

"We did what we had to do, babe. Think of it that way."

"Well, at least we stopped to say hello, right, honey?"

"Yeah, babe. I—sort of wish—that we skipped it."

"How—ward."

"I'm just being candid, babe."

"Or, it's the whiskey talking," she said. "I can tell."

He smiled at her.

"At least it makes me feel better, babe."

Chapter 8

On the road to the sand dunes "oval" turnaround, Howard saw the new sign: "NO PARKING AFTER 11 P.M. WHEN BEACH CLOSED." And, as he drove down the hill to the beach, he saw there were posts where chains could be stretched across the road.

"Jeez," Howard said, "I guess progress has come to Saugatuck. In the old days, we could park here for the weekend. Now they lock it up at night."

"Howard, things change," Marian said looking up the beach that stretched to the horizon.

"And not for the better, babe," he said and thumped the top of the steering wheel with the palm of his hand.

"Honey, this place is beautiful," she said lowering her sunglasses down her nose. "The white sand goes all the way up to where it curves. Miles. And the sky is so blue."

"Cripe," he said parking the car, "there's a house over there—up the beach. *That* wasn't there before."

"I've seen the Sleeping Bear Dunes up near Traverse City," Marian said as she climbed out of the car. "They're higher than these—but, these are just as beautiful, the way they roll. It's kind of a paradise here; I'm glad I came, Howard."

Walking on the white sand, they passed the beach custodian's office, a wood building the size of a garage, and there was a sign on the front wall: NO GROUND FIRES.

"What else are they going to eliminate?" Howard said and shook his head as they were walking. "They're probably working on that right now."

"How—ward," Marian said putting her hand on his shoulder, "can't you see they're trying to preserve what they have here?" Then she pointed out to the lake, "Look how calm the water is today—and that mist is burning off."

"That means today is going to be a scorcher, babe." Then he pointed to the west, "Chicago is just over there—about ninety miles. Want to swim over?"

"I would like to swim," she said looking at the few bathers standing in the water, "but Chicago? That's out."

"Okay, we'll go swimming," he said, "but not just now. I'm getting hungry. I'd like to get a burger." Then he said, when she looked up as if under strain, "maybe if you went wading—that would hold you until we come back, huh?"

"I feel—gritty," she said, "and the water looks inviting."

"I know, I know," he said. "We'll only be gone an hour. You can do what you want then—swim all you want."

Marian kicked off her sandals and walked down and into the shallow water. Howard stood watching her a moment, then he sat down on the sand to take off his sneakers and socks.

As he stood up, two girls in bathing suits ran past him down to the water, then the mother came past with towels draped over her arm. The mother kept looking at Marian, Howard noticed, and it made him uneasy.

Marian turned as Howard waded in behind her, "Oh-h, the water *feels* so cool. This place is terrific."

He grinned, "And you look 'terrific', too," he said quietly. "I mean—I can barely keep my hands to myself, babe," he said putting his hand on her shoulder, then rubbing her back.

"Don't rub any lower, honey," she said scooping a handful of water, splashing it forward, "there are people around—with their families."

Speaking to the side of her face, he said, "I'm going to explode . . ."

"Come on," Marian said smiling, "we'll cool you off—with cold water."

They waded out, almost to their knees, walking on the sandy bottom in the clear water.

"They can keep the Bahamas," Howard said. "I've got paradise right here—I mean with you, babe, and the sun and this water—it makes you want to stay here forever." He looked up at the sun and closed his eyes, and then said, slowly, "I might just stay here."

"Ah," Marian said, squeezing his hand, "dream on, honey. You know things aren't like that—you have to be more—realistic."

"Babe," he said lowering his head to look at her, "I've been—'realistic'—most of my life. Huh—what has it done for me? You get rid of one realism, and bingo, behind it is another realism waiting."

"O-oh," Marian said looking up at the sun, "I'm getting thirsty. Maybe we should get going, it's time for lunch."

They turned and were wading toward the beach, when Howard said, "Babe, I'm going to show you a place that has the coldest root beer you ever had."

The beach sand was hot from the high sun, and they had to run for the parking lot, Howard picking up his socks and sneakers, and Marian's sandals.

"Put these on," he said, but she was half-way to the car, when he held up the sandals.

"I don't want to stop," she shouted, moving quickly with each step painful; Howard bolted up next to her.

"Cold root beer," Marian said slipping into her sandals in the gravel parking lot, watching Howard put on his sneakers without the socks, "sounds good right now."

"Everybody's left the beach," Howard said making a ball of his black socks.

"I don't blame them," Marian said as they crossed to the car.

"This root beer comes in a thick glass mug." Howard said as he opened the car door for Marian, then tossed the ball of socks in the back seat. "They freeze the mugs and it makes the root beer so cold—it hurts your teeth."

"I can hardly wait, honey," Marian said, as Howard closed the door and walked around the car, looking up at the sun.

Then, he saw the mother with two daughters, sitting in the parked car behind his, the mother in the front seat, looking at him. When she did not look away, Howard did, then shrugged.

"Yeah," he said to Marian as he slid into the car, "we had bad hangovers from the beer we had all night at the beach party. We'd stop for a frosted mug of the root beer for breakfast. It did the trick—a great cure for the common hangover."

"How long ago was that, honey?"

"About—two summers ago," Howard said starting the car. "Why?" He said looking at Marian, his mouth open. "You know, Howard, she said, "things can change in two years. I don't want you to be let down . . ."

"Things like that don't change," Howard said, looking in the rearview mirror as he turned the car, seeing them mother talking to the girls in the back of their car. "You'll see."

"You never know, Howard."

Driving back up the steep roadway through the trees from the beach, Howard said, "Let's take a quick tour of town—just a drive-through. You'll get a kick out of it."

"Everybody must be in town," Marian said looking at Howard, lowering her sunglasses she just put on. "The beach seems deserted."

"The heat of the day, babe."

The traffic on the main street was barely moving, one car behind the other, creeping so slow, people were walking between the moving cars. Some of the young people carried cans of beer.

Groups of people stood on the sidewalk, some were in bathing suits, most wearing shorts. The biggest groups were outside the bars, where people stood talking and laughing, and loud music blaring from the bar rooms.

"Yikes," Marian said, "it looks like the northern version of the Mardi Gras."

A convertible moved next to their car, crowded with young students, all shirtless, one sitting on the trunk waving.

"Looks like a good time, babe, for one and all?" Howard said smiling, trying not to miss anything as he drove slowly. "The revelry—goes on into the night—and spills out on the beach. They build a bonfire, and they drink all night."

"I believe it," Marian said. "They look like they're having a ball—before starting classes—going back to the study grind." Then she added, "I see college names on T-shirts from all over."

"Yeah," Howard said, "it's a popular place all right."

After 20 min. to drive through town, they came to the railroad tracks, and Howard turned onto a gravel road that ran along the track.

"That root beer stand is right down here, babe. It's a big wood barrel—maybe 40 feet high—varnished wood, a real barrel they serve you through a little side window. I remember the barbecue beef sandwiches—were super."

"I don't see any barrel, honey," Marian said leaning forward, looking in all directions through the windshield, "varnished—or otherwise."

"It's got to be here," Howard said looking. "I'm sure—it was right here."

"Howard, maybe you can ask over at that building there. They might know."

"I'm sure it was right here, babe."

A man wearing a work shirt splattered with paint, and carrying a wide window screen, was walking on the opposite side of the roadway.

"I'll ask this guy," Howard said, "he looks like a local yokel."

"He would know," Marian said, grinning.

Howard stopped the car opposite the man, and shouted, "Wasn't there a root beer stand around here—a big barrel thing?"

"There was," the man said resting the screen on his foot while talking, "but they moved up closer to town—up near the post office. It's a Dairy Freeze stand now."

"Oo-h," Howard said, quietly, "I see. Thanks."

"Well, Howard," Marian said grinning, "so much for the varnished barrel—and those thick glass frosted mugs."

"Don't rub it in, babe," Howard said grinning at her, then added, "Would you like a Dairy Freeze?"

"Why not," she said slowly. "Poor Howard."

"Yeah, things can change fast," he said to her, turning the car around. "And not always for the better."

"Poor Howard," she said smiling at him.

~~~

Later, after they changed into bathing suits at the bathhouse and were wading into the water, Howard said, "since they put chains up over the road at 11 and close down the beach—we got two choices."

"Whatever you want to do, Howard," Marian said. "You make the choice."

"Well, I don't want to park up in town—and walked back here," he said as he waded now in water up to his waist. "That means were stuck here until they take the chains down at seven in the morning."

"All right," Marian said in pushed off into deeper water using her arms.

Howard turned to look back the people on the beach, before he pushed off with the backstroke, and caught a glimpse of the two girls, sitting on the sand at the edge of the water. Their mother was standing behind them, and Howard caught her looking at him again.

"That's it," he said to himself. "I'm being watched, all right."

He heard a loud *ka—wonk* sound from the parking lot; one car hitting another.

He smiled after the noise, thinking someone will need to have their car fixed Monday, and swam backwards to catch Marian.

He came up next to her, where she was standing in chest high water.

"Oh, look," she said, "there's a crowd up by the parking lot." She smoothed her hair back using both hands, "something must've happened."

"Yeah," Howard said standing up in the water, quote I heard a crunch—like two cars hitting," he added, wiping his face with both hands, his mouth open, eyes closed. "Must be a traffic jam in the parking oval."

"You think you're car is okay, Howard?"

"Yeah," he said looking at her.

"Maybe we should go check."

"I just got out here," he said sliding both hands around her waist under the water, feeling her firmness.

"There's people standing near your car, honey," she said, looking over her shoulder. "I think it's your car. We better go check."

He turned to looked, then said "all right, babe. We need my old Ford to get back to Detroit, so will check."

"It'll only take a minute," she said. "Then we can come back out here."

They came out of the water near the lady with the two girls, who were now making a pile of wet sand.

"It's my car all right," Howard said to Marian.

The sand was hot in the afternoon Sun, but they both ran hard to lessen the pain is much as they could, Marian scooping up her towel, as she followed Howard.

Howard saw a red Jeep stopped at an odd angle behind his old Ford.

A young man wearing a T-shirt with COLGATE printed on the front, came toward Howard as he walked into the parking lot.

"You own the Ford?" Young man asked.

"Yeah," Howard said, reaching down to run his hand on the sharp crease in the rear fender, that ran the length of the wheel opening.

"I sort of misjudged," he said pointing at the damage, "when I was trying to park in the space here—and my bumper creased your car. I didn't mean . . ."

"Yeah," Howard said backing up a bit to look at the dent.

"If you want to make a police report," the young man said, scratching his stomach under the T-shirt, "—for the insurance . . ."

"Well," Howard said, catching the young man looking at Marian as she tied the towel around her waist, "it's a pretty old car, man. The dent won't mess up the driving . . ."

Turning, he saw the young man's friends looking at Marian to, as he leaned against the side of the Jeep.

". . . Ah, let's just—let the whole thing go away," Howard said, glad Marian covered herself with towel, particularly the tight spot between her legs. He smiled, thinking she was striking, and wet bathing suit, whatever she wore, and people sensed her attraction. Howard felt lucky.

"Oh okay," young man said. "Tha—anks."

His two friends stood up straight, looking at one another.

"Thanks for sticking around," Howard said looking at the Jeep that had no top, and he saw the six-pack behind the front seat on the floor. "You did the right thing."

"There were a lot of witnesses," the young man said grinning.

Howard turned to Marian, "Let's get back in the water—this Sun is frying my skin."

"Let's go," she said looking him in the eye, and pulling at the not on the towel to untie it, "this parking lot is like the Sahara."

They ran back across the hot sand, Marian dropping her towel again.

Before he reached the water, Howard made a quick search of the beach for the woman with the two girls, the woman who always seem to be looking at him. She was gone. When he was waiting in the water, he glanced at the other parts of the beach for her, and did not see her.

"Ah," he said wading back in the cool water just over his knees, "this is more like it, babe."

"Are you looking for someone?" Marian asked as she swam on her back, moving her arms.

"No. Why?" He said swimming facing her, moving his arms, his mouth above the water.

"You, seem to be looking—studying—the beach, Howard. "You, still thinking about the dent in the fender?"

"Cripe," he said, "no, nothing like that, babe. I was just looking to see if there was anyone—I know. That's all."

"That was funny," she said, floating for moment, eyes closed to the Sun, "when you—complimented—that jerk about staying at the accident . . ."

"Why?" Howard said and rolled over on its back to swim next to her.

"Well, the whole beach saw the accident, silly," she said, "or—they heard the crash—he couldn't very well take off."

"Yeah, you're right, babe."

"It was a nice—gesture—though, honey," she said smiling. "You made everybody feel good—after you said it."

"Yeah," he said smiling, eyes closed, "I'm a charmer."

"You—are," she said glancing for a second at his splashing, "and you don't know it. That's why I—like you. It's your—nature."

"Speaking of nature," Howard said taking a breath, "you look so sharp in that bathing suit—everybody was staring. Long legs—that tight butt—you look like a young colt."

"How—ard," she said looking at him, trying to hit him, but only making a splash.

"I'm just being my charming self again, babe."

"That's—not charming—that's being, horny."

"It's my—nature," he said looking up, eyes closed.

"Now you're being facetious, Howard."

"The conversation is getting too deep for me, babe," he said and rolled onto his stomach to swim forward.

"Don't try acting dumb," she said. "It doesn't work."

"I wouldn't think of it, babe," he said taking a mouthful of water and spurting it out in front of him, then grinning.

Later, back on the beach, Marian changing in the bathhouse, taking longer than Howard, he had time to look for the woman who'd been watching him.

It reminded him of last year when he saw an elderly woman watching him in a gas station in Detroit. When he drove out after buying gas, he saw the woman's car come out of the station behind him. He watched her car in the rearview mirror, he recalled. It was a busy road to the shopping center, and he thought her following him was a coincidence, that possibly she was going shopping also.

We drove in the parking lot at Sears, and saw her car follow, he thought she was just going shopping at the same time he was. That was the reason she was behind him.

Downstairs at the service desk to pick up the pants he ordered from the catalog, Howard remembered standing while waiting for his turn, when the elderly woman walked up and stood behind him. He did not say anything to her, but look at her pink framed eyeglasses, that swept up at the edges, making the glasses look like a butterfly.

Driving home, he remembered looking in the rearview mirror, and he did not see her car.

He remembered he shrugged at first, thinking it was a super coincidence, but the more he thought it once in a lifetime occurrence, he finally realized he was being watched; and the watching was now being used as harassment. But he could never figure out who was doing the watching, and why.

Howard grew impatient waiting for Marian now, standing in the hot sun. He started walking to the oval on a hot sand, then ran when it was torture on his feet, and came up breathless to his Ford. The windows were down, he left it that way because the burning sun would make the inside an oven. He pulled open the rear door and hung his wet bathing suit on the clothing hook behind the driver seat.

That was when he spotted the money, folded, sticking up from the horn ring on the steering wheel.

"Wha-at?" He said grinning, unfolding the build. "Man, it's a twenty."

Dropping down to sit on the hot seat, he pulled the door closed, looking around the parking lot. The red Jeep was gone; it must have been him, Howard thought. He gave the twenty for car damage.

"What a windfall," he said. "Twenty is real nice."

He saw Marian come out of bathhouse, carrying her rolled bathing suit and towel, and waved out the window, then beeped the horn.

He saw her look up at the car, then run across the sand, not grimacing; she had her sandals on.

"I won't tell her about my windfall," he said, grinning, sliding the bill into his pants pocket, watching her run, looking at her long legs.

"What's the hurry?" She asked to the open window. "You got a hot date?"

"You bet," he said reaching across the seat open the door for her. "I'm just getting hungry around the edges," he said, and pushed open the car door. "Swimming does that—I must burn a lot of energy—swimming."

"I'm a little hungry to—now that you mention it," she said. Then she added as she unrolled the towel, "should I hang my suit—like yours?"

"Naw," he said, "we don't want to look like gypsies. The girls suit—does that—somehow—when it's hanging."

"Okay, Howard, if you say so—but I'm not—so sure."

"Babe, lay the stuff out on the backseat," he said pointing. "The suit and the towel."

"They're wet, honey."

"The seat's plastic. It won't hurt."

When she climbed in the car front seat, after spreading her swim things out flat, Howard said, "There used to be a great restaurant in town, Martha's Garden, we used to go to. It is set right in a real garden. The food is terrific."

"Maybe it's not there," she said, smiling. "Remember the root beer barrel?"

"Yeah, yeah," he said looking at her for a second. "Well, there's only one way to find out, babe."

Driving back up the hill, he could smell the pine trees, as they pass under the long branches hanging over the road.

"This place is so beautiful," Marian said quietly. "Thank you for showing me Saugatuck, honey. I'm so glad to see all this . . ."

"You're repeating yourself," he said and added, "it smells good, too."

"Oh, Howard, there you go again—the comedian bit."

"I know," he said. "I know."

At the restaurant, they walked through the dining room, out to where there was a screened-in porch filled with potted plants. They sat at a table in where the screen touched the bushes outside in the yard.

"Howard," Marian pointed, "just look at the size of those yellow roses . . . Their magnificent. Look there . . ."

He turned and looked at the potted roses, then said, grinning, you're right . . . In fact they look good enough . . . to eat."

"Ah, you," she said slowly, "always the funny man."

A waitress in a yellow dress with a large white lace handkerchief in her chest pocket, came up to the table.

"Hello," she said. "Can I help you folks?"

"Can we see the dinner menu?" Howard said.

"Our dinner menu is only available after five the clock," she said softly. "But I can offer our luncheon menu, were still serving from that . . ."

Howard looked at the clock above the entrance door; it was just five min. after four.

"Okay," he said, nodding, the luncheon menu is fine."

"Can I bring you something from the bar?"

"No, no," Marian said, "we're too hungry right now."

The waitress, trying to look impassive from the refusal, handed them the menus, and said "I'll be back in a few moments to take your order."

"Don't look at the prices, babe," Howard whispered. "Just order what you want."

"We're not eating the gas money—for the drive home, are we, honey?"

"No, babe," Howard said grinning, "I have that money locked up. That's nothing to fool around with—give me more credit than that, huh?"

"I didn't mean to step on your toes," Marian said. Then looking down the menu it, asked, "what looks good?"

"Beef au jus," Howard said running his finger on the menu. "Sounds good to me."

"Oh, yes, yes," Marian said. "You just saying it makes me hungry. I didn't realize I was hungry—famished is more like it."

When the waitress returned, Howard ordered the beef for the both of them.

Writing in her order pad, the waitress said slowly, "it comes on French bread like a sandwich—you dip it in the bowl of beef juice . . ."

"And I'd like a salad," Marian said handing the menu to the waitress, who nodded.

"Will you have a beverage?"

"Yes, "Howard said handing her the menu, "ice tea." Looking over at Marian, "you too, babe?"

"Yes," she said, "with lemon."

"Thank you," the waitress said and stepped away.

"Babe," Howard said quietly, "later, you might want to go to the partying in town tonight—join the festivities?"

"No, not really, honey," she said studying his face.

"Okay," he said and shrugged.

"Is something bothering you, honey? I noticed when I climbed in the car at the beach. You're sort of—preoccupied—distant—or something. Has something happened?"

She was looking at him steadily, and he said, "you're pretty perceptive."

"Did I say something that upset you?"

"No, babe, it's not you—it's that—accident in the oval."

"It wasn't *that* bad, honey. I mean—your car still runs. It's still—usable . . ."

"I wonder," he said turning the water glass on the table with his fingers, slowly, "if it really was an accident."

"You mean—it might have been done—on purpose?"

"Yeah," he said and took a drink from the glass.

"But why—would someone—just dent a fender?"

"Well," he said, turning the glass on the table again, "a lot of odd-ball situations have been going on lately—in my everyday life. Somebody is trying to mess me up—make my life miserable, it seems. Something like that."

"That's practically the definition of paranoia, Howard."

"Okay, my problem is with the accident—that I benefited. I mean—I wasn't damaged by it happening, and it don't fit with all the negative stuff that's gone on."

"Benefitted, honey; what—how benefitted?"

"Twenty bucks stuck on the steering wheel."

"And you think the guy in the COLGATE t-shirt . . . ?"

Howard nodded, then took another sip from the water glass.

She smiled and said, "That's why—you're splurging on dinner, now? You got the—bonus money?"

Howard nodded, looking across at her.

"Howard, honey," she said reaching to touch his hand on the table, "I thought I might have said something—that ticked you off at me. You could give me a heart attack, or something, if you—distance yourself like that. You don't want to be the cause of me dying—don't act like that. Okay?"

"Well, now you know, babe," he said looking at her and wishing he had *not* told her.

The waitress came with two tall glasses of tea, the ice tinkling, lemon wedges on the rim.

Squeezing the lemon into the tea, Howard thought Marian seemed to have a sixth-sense when it came to finding out about his money. He looked at her, thinking, maybe they have a course at Grosse Pointe High where they teach how to ferret out money.

"Here's to your car, honey," she said holding up her glass. "It's dents for dinner—isn't that a stroke of luck?"

"Yeah," he said, clinking his glass against hers, "as long as the fenders hold out—we're okay."

"Howard," she said laughing, covering her mouth. "Stop. You're too funny, now. Really funny."

"I was going to ask," Howard said after he drank near half the glass of tea, "that guy from the Jeep—if the COLGATE was for the toothpaste or the college . . . ."

Marian, caught with a mouthful of tea, hit the table with a flat hand, then covered her mouth with a napkin.

"I love it," she said when she took the napkin away.

It made him feel warm to see her elated, enjoying herself.

As he said, "no telling what's next," the waitress came and set a thick sandwich on the table in front of each of them, then a bowl of hot beef au jus, and Marian's chef salad.

"Bon appetite," she said smiling, and went away.

Howard looked across at Marian's salad, wishing he had ordered one for himself, when he saw slices of hard-boiled egg, Swiss cheese shards, and bits of salami in the greens.

"Time to enjoy our ill-gotten gains," he said.

"Look at it as good fortune," Marian said. "The fender bender came at the right time, honey. I think it's just—delightful—and we should enjoy—all of it."

"Right, babe," he said picking up his sandwich. "Look at the size of this," he said before dipping the end into the au jus.

"You'll have to help me with mine, I can't eat this whole sandwich," she said, pouring oil from the cruet on the salad.

Howard, chewing his mouthful, nodded, watching as she set the cruet in the rack at the side of the table, then pick up the one with vinegar.

He waited for her to say she would share the salad, too, but she did not, and he felt a pang of resentment.

~~~

After dinner, they drove through town that seemed to be packed more than before with weekend party goers.

"Let's go back to the beach," Marian said. "I don't want to get into this craziness."

"Man," Howard said, looking from his side of the car at the people crowding the sidewalk, "the place is overflowing."

"We'll walk on the beach," Marian said slowly as she studied the crowd. "We can see the sunset and walk off our gigantic dinner—burn up some calories."

"I don't like that stuff with the chains," Howard said driving ahead slow, behind the car in front. "But, I can see why they pull the plug on all this partying at eleven."

"There's plenty of time, honey. You'll see."

The sun was lower now at the beach, the sand warm, not blazing hot, and when they walked down to the edge of the water, Marian took off her sandals.

"Look at that," Marian said, waving the hand holding the sandals at the giant orange sun that sat just above the water out on the horizon. "It's like we're in a movie."

"You mean, *'The Wizard of Oz'*, babe?"

"Can't you ever stop—the comedy stuff?" she said without looking up at him.

He took hold of her free hand, and said, "I'll try."

She bumped her hip against his, hard.

Howard was going to make a wisecrack, when he saw the man and woman walking along the water's edge, coming toward he and Marian. When they came closer, Howard squeezed Marian's hand, and she squeezed back, as if to say she saw it, too, that the man was shorter than the woman, nearly a head shorter.

As the couple passed, Marian stepping into the water, kicking, splashing the water out in front of her, until the couple moved off down the beach. No one spoke.

Then Howard whispered in Marian's ear, "They look like Mutt and Jeff."

Smiling, Marian whispered back, "That's—not nice." She looked in the direction of the couple, and said, "It's funny—but it's not nice."

They walked watching the sun going down, and when they came to a long tree washed up on the sand, its root system intact, they sat down on the end near the roots.

"Labor Day is sort of the official end of summer," Howard said, leaning back on the slope of the roots, as if it were a lounge chair. "Summer went by fast," he said sitting up, then putting his arm around Marian's shoulders.

"There goes the sun," she said as the last of the orange ball sunk into the Lake Michigan horizon, leaving only a thin streak of light.

Howard kissed the back of her neck; then when she turned to him, putting her arms around his neck, he kissed her again and they moved down onto the sand next to the log.

After her shirt was off, Howard took away her Bermuda shorts, countering her moves from side to side.

"Don't move so much," he whispered feeling his heart pumping hard as he quickly undressed himself.

She pushed at his shoulders, saying quietly, "This sand—I can't help it—it's so gritty." She pulled her legs together, and said, "Let's stop. Not now. Okay?"

Howard sat up slowly and repeated, "'Not now,'" as if speaking to himself. Then, leaning back against the log, his elbow resting on it, looked at her, "Maybe—we can go—for a swim. I can cool off—before—I explode."

"Okay, honey," she said taking his hand to pull herself up. "I can wash off this sand. I hate the feeling of it on my skin."

There was no moon as they waded into the cool water that was dark now, Marian splashing herself to wash away the sand.

Howard felt himself grow an erection, seeing her small pointed breasts and the curves of her hips showing white in the water. He moved her against his body, feeling her firmness as they stood in the water, waist deep, and she slid one leg up, then brought the other up to hold him, when he was inside her.

Later, she was standing in the water, pushing her hair back in the swirl at the back of her head, when she said to Howard, "There's a fire—down the beach there."

He was laying on the water, floating, arms and legs out, looking up, and he stopped and stood up. "Yeah," he said wiping his face, "somebody is having a party. Let's get our duds on—got take a look—join the festivities."

"Sounds like fun," she said, bringing her arms down when Howard slid his arms around her, and kissed her quickly.

"I've already been to one—party—tonight," he said putting the side of his face against hers.

"Are you bragging?" she said, her face in front of his, "Or—are you complaining?"

"No," he said, "it's more an—endorsement. An endorsement of—satisfaction. How's that?"

"See," she said taking his hand, "I told you—about being a charmer."

Wading back to the beach, Howard said, "I hope I didn't start a family, babe. I mean I should use—protection. I couldn't get to a condom."

She turned to him as they waded in shallower water and said, "I don't like doing it with a condom—it's not—natural."

He looked at her, shaking his head, not able to take his eyes off her trim form.

He felt contentment for being with her, and he felt lucky for having found her. But having a beauty for a girlfriend had a dark side, mainly, other guys, like bird-dogs, will *always* go after good-looking chicks. A guy with a super chick has to be alert, always. A party, for instance—when she goes into the kitchen, some guy will try to corner her behind the refrigerator where she went for the ice cubes.

On the beach, getting dressed, Howard tried not to watch her, but he told himself he just wanted to know everything about her. He could not help himself.

Mixed with this contentment Howard felt, was a burden that seemed to press down on him. The burden of getting a degree, finding a job, and making a pile of money. That was the cost of having a super-chick. You had to be a success.

"You all right, honey?" she asked, as they were walking toward the fire up the beach. "I can almost hear the gears turning in your head. What are you—thinking about?"

"Ah-h," he said squeezing her hand, "I guess you could call it—nostalgia."

"What about it? Why is it absorbing you so—strongly?" she took hold of his arm. "I don't like to see you—so distracted—off in some distant place. It upsets me, honey."

"Ah-h," he said kissing the side of her face, "It just dawn on me—I probably won't be coming back to the beach here—maybe for a long time—with a job—and all that."

"How-ard," she said, stopping to stand and look at him, "you make it sound like you're being—condemned—to work in the coal mines, or something."

"Yeah, I guess I made it sound like that, babe."

"You know," she said, "everybody in the university faces the same—problem—or hurdle—after they get their degree. When they go out—into the working world—they have to begin—at the beginning. Things are all changed—life takes a different path."

"I didn't think of it that way," Howard said, then put his hands on her shoulders. "I guess—I enjoy drinking beer on the beach too much. I was thinking about it going out the window—that's all."

"Well you know, honey, you can't go to 'drinking beer on the beach' the rest of your life, can you?"

Howard felt sheepish about saying what he did. It was all he could come up with to cover how he felt about her, and more importantly, *keeping* her.

"Yeah," he said and kissed her. "Nothing stays the same," he said taking her hand. "Everything changes."

"Remember the root beer barrel, Howard?" she said as they started walking again.

"Yep," he said, "that was a shock—but I think I'll get over it. Maybe you'll forget to mention it—later."

"I get the message, honey," she said. "Now let's crash the beach party—and 'drink beer on the beach,' okay."

Howard counted nine cars beside his on the oval parking lot, as he walked closer to the bonfire with Marian. the fire was in the first deep sand dune away from the lot.

A young man without a shirt, came out of the dark and waded into the water and picked up a case of beer cans that had been cooling in the lake.

"The sign says," Howard said to him, "they put the chain up at eleven." He and Marian had stopped walking when the young man came down to the water's edge. "Does that go for the party, too?"

"Naw," the young man said, balancing the case on his shoulder, "the cops just hook it—they don't lock it. C'mon, have a brew—it's a holiday.

"Well, just for a few minutes," Marian said. "We might have to drive back to Detroit—tonight."

Howard looked at her, surprised by what she said; so tactful.

"I won't tell," the young man said. "C'mon up."

"This is Howard," Marian said to the back of the young man walking ahead up to the bonfire, "and I'm Marian."

When they were in the firelight, the young man said, "Everybody—this is Marian and Howard from Detroit."

A man with a heavy mustache, held up a can of beer and saluted. He was seated next to a girl wearing an army fatigue shirt, who sat cross-legged on the edge of a blanket. "Wel-come," she said and let out a 'whoop' sound.

Red McNiven, who some people called "Pinky" because of his red hair, sat next to the fire, strumming a guitar. He was the red trunks that were his badge of authority as beach maintenance boss. Recognizing Howard, Red raised his chin at him and smile. Next to him, a blond girl in a bright chartreuse t-shirt, sat drinking from a large plastic cup.

Howard and Marian sat down next to a girl wearing a t-shirt with KENTUCKY on the front. She sat holding her legs.

"Welcome to our leper colony," she said, after making room for Marian to sit on the edge of her blanket.

"Why a 'leper colony?'" Marian asked moving to sit on the blanket.

"Everybody who can walk," she said smiling, "is going to see The Kingston Trio perform at the Seagull Bar tonight. A sell-out crowd. We decided—the beach was better."

Howard rose up on his knees, reaching to take a can of beer from a young man in a WESTERN MICHIGAN sweat shirt, who held it out. The girl next to him, in a sweatshirt with the same college name, said, "Buffy St. Marie was here last summer. They had an overflow crowd—for that show, too."

"The beach is better," her boyfriend said. "The crowds are ruining everything in town."

"'In China they never eat chili." McNiven sang as he strummed the guitar. "'Now here's the next verse; it's worse than the first, so waltz me around, again, Willie.'"

Howard sat down cross-legged, opposite Marian, who was talking to the girl in the KENTUCKY shirt next to her.

When she caught Howard looking, she smiled at him. He smiled back, thinking here was the Wonder Woman of my life. He remembered the saying he heard once, on a Canadian television program from across the Detroit River, that said, "'If the women are happy, then everybody's happy.'"

Leaning back, he drank most of the beer from the can. Looking back at Marian, her holding her beer, not drinking but talking, he reached out and took it, and put his can in her hand.

She smiled.

"'There was an old hermit name Dave,'" McNiven was singing, "'Who kept a dead whore in a cave,'" making the people laugh and make noises.

"' . . . And they call me . . . depraved,'" the song went, "'but look at the money . . . I save,'" and everyone was cheering and joined the chorus, "Hi, yhi, yhi-yhi, In china they never eat chili . . . '"

The girl in the KENTUCKY shirt stood up slowly, and looked like a giraffe; she was over six feet tall, and Howard's jaw dropped. She touched the guy from the beach, who took the beer from the lake, on the shoulder, and said, "I'm going to the little girl's room."

"You want me to come . . . ?"

"No, no," she said, and walked toward the bath house.

Marian nudged Howard's knee, "That's your Mutt and Jeff, honey," she whispered, grinning, and sipping beer.

Howard nodded, watching the young guy with no shirt, sit down.

"Are you from Kentucky, too?" he asked the young man.

"Uh-huh," he said, sitting up straight and scratching his bare back, "we're from Lexington. Carrie's folks have—own a home here—she comes every summer."

"'Now here's the next verse, it's worse than the first, '"the crowd sung in unison with the guitar.

"Are you her—boyfriend?" Marian asked him.

"Don't I wish," he said and popped open a beer, the foam running down the can. "I'm just an—escort—for her."

"You a cop? Something like that?" Howard asked, reaching for an unopened can the young man held out to him.

"Sort of," he said, offering a can of beer to Marian, who was listening, and held up her hand, refusing the offer. "Carrie is from," he said looking off in the direction she went, "a very . . . important . . . family."

When she came back into the light of the bonfire, he seemed to relax.

"I'd like to stay a while—longer," she said kneeling down on her blanket, then dropping into a sitting position.

The young man nodded, and lifted his beer to drink.

"It's supposed to rain tonight," the girl in the army shirt said. She had walked over from the other side of the bonfire. She was holding up two fingers, meaning a beer for her boyfriend with the mustache. "I heard it on the radio," she said, taking the two cans, "but it's held off so far," she said, to the young shirtless man. "Everybody wants to stay until dawn."

Howard turned and saw Carrie talking to Marian again; he heard Carrie say she knew people from Grosse Pointe.

"We don't need rain," the shirtless man said.

"Do you carry a gun?" Howard asked him.

"Naw. I was a Marine—embassy security," he said taking a short drink. "There's a lot of things I can do—without a weapon."

Howard, his newspaper instincts at work, asked, "Is Carrie a relation of the governor of Kentucky? Or Maybe she's the daughter of a senator—something on that line?"

"Nothing like that," the young man said. "her family owns a thoroughbred horse stable. There's a lot that goes on—in horse racing, and they want her protected from any trouble-makers."

"Wow," Howard said and took a swallow of beer. "That's some job you got, man."

He nodded, then reached into his back pocket and brought out a flask, took a sip, and put it back, leaning forward, not offering Howard a drink.

"'Now here's the next verse, it's worse than the first,'" came louder, everyone singing at the top of their voice.

"Your lady—" the shirtless guy said, leaning forward, looking at Howard, "has the look of—money, besides her movie-star looks. I figured you—for some kind of Sheppard like me."

"Is that," Howard said slowly, "why you told me you were 'security' for Carrie? You thought I was 'security' for Marian?"

Nodding, he said, "*Somebody* is watching her. You can count on it."

The girl in the fatigue shirt came back, singing loud with the rest of the chorus behind her, and took two more cans of beer.

Howard held up a finger, and said, "Help."

"Refill?" she said. "Coming up," and handed him a fresh can, as she rocked from side to side with the music.

'*Gracias,*" Howard said, glancing to see Carrie waving her arms, talking to Marian, both of them smiling, obviously telling a story.

The shirtless guy took out the flask again, and held it out toe Howard, "Tequila?"

After Howard shook his head, he sat and watched the shirtless man take a drink, then lean forward and say, "It was either security, or a clerking job at Piggly-Wiggly."

"What's 'Piggly-Wiggly'?" Howard asked grinning; popping open his beer can.

"They have stores all over Florida," the shirtless guy said, waving the flask. "They sell beer, pop and cigarettes—to people in a hurry."

"Ah, a convenience store."

"Yeah."

Something wet hit Howard's left arm, and surprised him; then something hit his ear on the same side, and when he looked up, heavy rain drops hit his face.

The girl in the army shirt let out a *whoop*, then said, "here it comes. Run for the cars," as she pulled up her blanket. Some of the girls covered their heads with blankets, the guys following, carrying the leftover beer cans.

Howard took Marian's arm, the rain coming down like it was poured from a bucket, "Let's run, babe. Head for the car."

"I didn't know it could rain this hard," she shouted, running in the sand that slowed everyone.

A cardboard beer carton lay at the top of the dune where they came up; Howard picked it up, flattened it, and set it on Marian's head. She held it in place while running to the oval.

McNiven ran past them with his guitar, his orange shirt stretched out over it.

"It would have to rain—tonight," he shouted.

Howard jumped in his car at the oval, and began rolling up the windows on his side. Marian doing the same on her side, said, "Oh-h, the seats are wet."

Well," he said, grinning, "at least we're out of the downpour."

They sat for a moment listening to the rain hitting the roof.

"I'm just drenched," Marian said pulling out her wet shirt, the points on her small breasts showing through.

"Makes you sexy," Howard said, grinning, sliding his arm over her shoulders.

There came a tapping on Marian's side window.

Howard reached over and rolled down the glass a few inches to see Carrie's bodyguard standing outside.

"Carrie sent this note for you," he said to Marian, his hair plastered down, water running down his face.

"Get out of the rain," she said taking the folded piece of cardboard through the opening.

Before Howard cranked up the window, the bodyguard was gone.

Marian turned on the car dome light to read the note.

"It's Carrie's address in Kentucky," Marian said. "She invited me to come for a visit."

Howard started the car to run the heater for Marian.

"Look," she said, "the bonfire is going out."

"Yeah," he said, looking at the front of her shirt, again, "there goes the weekend, too, babe. Sort of washed out."

"Could you get my suitcase in the trunk?" she said. "I want to get a dry shirt."

"Okay," he said, shaking his head, looking at the rain running down the windshield.

""It's either that or the Piggly-Wiggly," he said quietly.

"What did you say, honey?"

"Just a—joke—I heard," he said, opening the car door. "It's nothing."

Chapter 9

Howard found a job working part-time, reporting for a weekly newspaper chain. He knew it was nothing more than a glorified shopping news, made up mostly of local advertisements. The front page different for each of the cities the paper circulated in, offering a few local stories, but the insides were all the same advertisements in all the editions. He took it because the job paid money.

His job was to comb the five Grosse Pointe cities, the nearby Harper Woods community, and St. Clair Shores over on the lake in Macomb County, for local feature stories, report on council meetings and any interesting police blotter happenings.

Council meetings were in the evening, and he had to juggle his times for night classes at the university around the schedule of meetings.

On registration day at the university for fall term, he was seventeen dollars short for the tuition payment due to a new rate hike. He did not want to ask his parents at home, and it would be a week for his first newspaper paycheck to come. He would have to look for somebody to tap for the money.

Sitting in the Campus Bar with a twenty-five cent beer, he sat up straight when Tim Etherly came in, carrying a small portable television set. Etherly, Howard still owed for the price of the opera tickets, so asking him for money was out.

"I'm going to pawn it," Etherly said setting the TV on the bar before sitting down on the stool next to Howard.

"Yeah," Howard said, "we're all having money problems. I came up short at registration. I was thinking—the crap game. It still going? Over that bakery shop?"

"Far as I know," Etherly said, and ordered a beer for Howard, too. "You going to use your tuition money at the game?"

Howard shrugged and said, "Might as well. Look at Columbus, he took a chance—and look at what he found." Howard drank his beer glass empty, and setting it on the bar, picked up the fresh on Etherly order. "Hey, man, maybe you want to come, too?"

"Yeah, okay," Etherly said slowly. "Maybe I'll get lucky—I need enough to get my car fixed. I was going to see what I could do at the pawn shop."

"They only give—peanuts—for the pawned stuff," Howard said and took a drink from his glass.

"I've got to leave around dinner time," Etherly said, watching Howard drink. "I'm driving my girlfriend's car—and I got to pick her up at work."

"I'll follow you over to the game," Howard said, nodding.

When Etherly pulled over to the curb on the side street next to the bakery on Grand River Avenue, Howard was behind him. Getting out of his car, Howard walked with Etherly through the street littered with newspapers, cardboard boxes, and broken glass.

They stepped in front of a steel door and Etherly knocked.

A short man in a tan suit and Panama hat, stood in the open door, and recognizing Etherly, swung the door out further. No one spoke.

At the top of the dusty stairs, the room opened out into a long room, a crap table at the far end under bright lights overhead.

An Oriental man in prescription sunglasses, sat on a high stool at the end of the table, holding a large bundle of money, watching the dice intently. He ran the game.

"Nine is the number," the white-haired stick man said, standing at the half-way distance of the table, reaching out over the numbers on the table for bet positions with a thin stick with a curved end. "Place your bets."

He scooped the dice, after a shooter threw them and they were read, and gave them back.

As Howard was digging out his money from his pocket, he counted nineteen players at the table.

He watched as Etherly bet five dollars against the guy with the nine point, and win, grin at Howard for a second, and pick up his winnings.

Howard started betting the odd-even line with two dollars; not numbers themselves, but rather if they were odd or even numbers on the dice coming on the throw. He began to win, and the Oriental guy he was standing next to, paid him promptly.

A guy in a yellow sport shirt came over to the Oriental guy, "Lou, give me a vigarish."

"You only come with five," the Oriental said.

"Six, Lou. I had six bucks. I come all the time, and I need the two bucks vigarish to get home."

"Not this time," Lou said continuing to watch the dice on the table.

Howard played until he had thirty-one dollars, then turned to Etherly, "I'm ready to go."

Etherly looked at him and said, "I'm up near seventy—I'm going to stay. I've got a little time before I have to go . . ."

"Okay," Howard said, "see you around—and good luck."

As he turned, the Oriental said, "You won—today."

"Yeah, about thirty five."

"No. Thirty-one."

"Yeah," Howard said grinning; then he nodded and walked toward the steps.

Outside, Howard looked up at the sun off in the west as he was unlocking his car door. The sun here looked dirty for some reason, not like the sun he saw at the beach in Saugatuck. Looking over the top of the car at the broken glass and paper littering the street, he shook his head. He winced when he saw the broken television set stuffed in a cardboard box with other trash—the box label marked "FACIAL TISSUE."

A sinking feeling came over him with the realization, suddenly, that this was his life. This was how he went through the days, scratching for money in the street. Just getting by.

He thought of Marian, as he stood looking, thinking of her at the dining room table having dinner, neatly dressed, the grass out front neatly trimmed—no trash at the curb.

For the first time the realization of his position in life, compared to the life Marian had, hit him. Up until now, he had only been thinking of the boy-girl relationship they had. Now, he was hit with the question of where that relationship was going—how they would live.

"Wow," he said, slowly sitting down in his car. He felt as if someone punched him in the stomach. This is what he could offer Marian, he thought, living out here for a lifetime, a life of scuffling in the street.

He shook his head, then hit the steering wheel with the flat of his hand.

"It ain't going to work," he said, moving his head from side to side forcefully. "She isn't going to leave her comfortable life with daddy's money—to live with a reporter with a rocky future."

Putting the key in the car ignition, he said slowly, "I've got to talk to her." Then turning the key, he said in a loud voice, "Oh, God—I can lose her."

~~~

The morning following Howard's second registration and full payment for fall classes at the university, a Sunday, he stood up at the side of his bed in his parent's house. Reaching for the clock on the dresser, to press the light bar to see the time, he was hit with a jolt that knocked him back down on the bed.

"What the hell—was that?" he said out loud, looking up at the dresser, then getting up on his feet, holding the edge above the drawers.

He did not know if it was lightning, or electric shock, that knocked him down. He had heard the bones crack in his spine when he was hit.

His right thigh "burned" at the place he was struck.

He sat back down on the bed to rub his thigh, that slowly seemed to be going numb, now, at the spot of the jolt.

"Wonder if it was lightning—of some kind," he said, softly, moving his leg out.

He stood up slow, and looking out the window, saw it was a clear day. There was no storm of any kind, no clouds that could give him a hint of what happened, what gave him the jolt.

He looked down at the rug, "maybe it was static electricity from down here," he said quietly, dragging his foot across the carpeting. "Or maybe," he said picking up the clock, looking at the cord for fraying, "the clock had something to do with it. Could have been something—like that."

When he set the clock down on the dresser, he tapped the light bar and the face lighted. It was ten minutes to eight.

He shrugged and sat on the bed.

"I don't know what it was," he said quietly, "but I'm not going to tell—say anything about it—to anybody." He grinned, and said, "they'd just laugh anyway", and began to take off his pajamas.

Later Sunday evening, Howard and Marian went to the Harbor Bar, a former boathouse, built on a dock out over the Detroit River, the water flowing under the floor. The wooden shack was built up plush now, a padded bar overlooking the river with wide windows and a row of tables. Marian wanted to sit at the bar, so they did, facing the windows.

"I took classes the nights of Monday, Wednesday and Friday," Howard said to her. "Most of the City Council meetings are Tuesday nights," he said to tell her his schedule as a point of information. "And sometimes there are Planning Commission meetings with newsworthy items—all at night, babe. I'm going to be busy—nights."

"How much do they pay you? she said, rattling the ice cubes in the tall glass of rum and coke.

Howard turned red with embarrassment, and looking away from her, watched a guy in a white shirt and tie climb on the stool next to him.

Turning back to Marian, he said in a low voice to her face, "It's only part-time work, babe. They give me ninety bucks a week."

"When you take out the taxes—and all that," she said, while poking at the lime slice floating in her glass with the straw, "there isn't much left."

"Well, babe," Howard said leaning toward her, "it's better than nothing." He had noticed the guy in the white shirt listening to them talking, so he spoke in a low tone. "Look at it this way—it's a step up on the ladder toward a big-city newspaper—and the big money."

When Marian looked at him, he could feel her disappointment.

"We won't—have much time," she said slowly, poking the straw to make the ice cubes jump in her empty glass, "to be together—do things?"

"Don't worry, it'll work out, babe."

"I'm thinking of getting a job, too," she said looking out the window at the Detroit Edison freighter passing by on the river. "I hear J. L. Hudson's is hiring in the sports department—sales people."

"Cripe, babe, skiing isn't *that* expensive," Howard said, raising his glass to the bartender, signaling for a refill, "that you have to get a . . . job."

"I want to go to Vermont," she said looking at him. "Stowe, Vermont. I want to ski their Mount Snow—and it's not cheap."

When the bartender came and stood in front of Howard, he said to her, "Want another drink, babe?"

She nodded and Howard said to the bartender, "Make it two please," and when he spoke he felt a span opening between himself and Marian.

"Two Cuba Libres," the bartender said, and when he dumped the ice cubes out of the glasses into a metal sink below the bar, making a crash sound, Howard jumped.

The skiing, and the ski trip now, upset Howard; she was getting independent of him, he felt.

To show her he could plan too, that he was moving ahead with his life, Howard said, "I'm wrestling with the idea of buying a better car—maybe, even, a new one."

"You certainly need one," Marian said, smiling.

Howard sat silent for a moment; then the bartender returned, and spread out fresh napkins in front of he and Marian, and placed their drinks on the papers.

Howard felt Marian had put him down, but what made it worse, she was able to talk from a high position—the position of money.

"Well," he said, "it's easier to finance—get a loan—on a new car," and picked up his rum and coke.

"Oh, Howard," she said in a whisper, "I wish you could come to Vermont."

He liked her for saying that, it made him feel included again.

"Maybe next season, babe," he said looking at her, holding his drink out in front of him. "I'm caught up in the newspaper business right now—my first job and all that."

"Doesn't it count," she said lifting her glass, "that you wrote for a college paper—all those stories?"

"That was a journalism class requirement," Howard said, and shifted his weight on the stool; it was then he noticed the white shirt guy next to him was listening to their conversation.

When Howard looked at him, the guy picked up his drink, in an attempt to act disinterested, and took a sip.

"There was no payment—involved," Marian said before looking forward out the window, and sipping on the straw in her rum and coke. "They didn't give you—anything?"

"Yeah," Howard said looking at her, "call it training."

Lowering her glass, she said, "Honey, I'll think about you when I'm racing down the snowy slopes—skiing my heart out—and I'll wish you were there."

"Who are you going with," he asked, "to this Mount Stowe in Snow, Vermont?"

"It's Mount *Snow* in *Stowe*—Vermont, honey," she said smiling. "And I'm going with the Grosse Pointe Ski Club, to answer your question. The whole group makes the—pilgrimage on the bus we hire."

He had to smile at her directness—loosened a little by the rum and coke. He liked to hear her talk in that independent manner. He remembered the first time he heard it—when they had only been going together for a few weeks. John Kennedy was being sworn-in as President on television while they were watching at the Campus Bar.

He said the ceremony drove shivers down his spine. And she said, "How come? You know he's a Democrat."

"Why are you smiling?" she said now, rattling her ice cubes in the glass. "You look like the Cheshire Cat. What I said wasn't *that* funny."

"I know," he said slowly, looking at her face to see the rum effect on her demeanor, "But to me, it was."

"Sometimes, honey," she said looking at him with her head tilted to one side, "it's hard to understand you—you know that?"

"Not to change the subject, babe, but did you register for classes—at the university?" he asked and took a quick drink of rum and coke, while still looking at her.

"Yep," she said nodding. "I'm only taking two this semester."

"Daytime classes?"

"Uh-huh, I'm going to get a job—for the afternoons. Why? Is there something I should know?"

"I have to know your schedule," Howard said setting his glass down on the bar, "that's all. So we can work out our lives—to spend some time together. That's all."

He put his hand on her arm and squeezed it gently.

"Can I have another one of these?" she asked, but did not look at him, holding up her empty glass.

"Sure," he said, and held up his glass for the bartender to see the refill signal. "You know babe, I feel bad—about u being separated so much—this fall."

"You know," she said, turning awkwardly toward Howard, him seeing the rum getting her drunk, "Daddy thinks—we see too much of one another."

Howard broke into a wide grin; for some reason, no matter what she said, it did not hurt.

"Well," he said, "it's not every guy at the university that can meet a girl with a father in the Gestapo."

"He's just protecting his daughter."

"From what, babe?"

The bartender came and went through the ritual with the napkins and the fresh drinks.

For a moment, Howard looked at the river outside, the sunlight fading, but he could not forget how the McArthur Bridge to Belle Isle showed white in the sun against the blue river, when he was driving Marian home to Grosse Pointe down Jefferson Avenue. And he felt a fondness for the Chrysler arch over Jefferson Avenue at the auto plant, when they passed under it at Conners, the clock in the center of the arch that stopped working. It all belonged to the magic of being with her. They could be in Paris or Rome when they walked through the Detroit Art Museum, it did not matter, they were together, that was thrill enough, making each day sweet.

"He sort of said," she said reaching for her drink on the bar in front of her, "that you drink too much, and it's rubbing off on me."

"He said that too, babe?"

"Uh-huh. I guess, honey, you're not exactly on his hit parade," she said and took a sip from her glass.

"Yeah, it shows, babe. Whenever I come over to your house—he's about as subtle as a sledge hammer."

"He's a father, honey. He's just being—protective."

"What is he protecting, babe?"

"Ah-h, I guess," she said looking out the window for an instant, where a large Chris-Craft Constellation cruised by slowly, going up the river, "he's protecting my future."

"Oh man," Howard said, and inadvertently turned toward the guy in the white shirt, who now sat rolling up his sleeves, while listening to them talk. Howard was sure of it now; the guy was an eavesdropper, but he turned back to Marian and said slowly, "You can't blame him, I guess. Every father would like his daughter to marry a dentist."

Oh, Howard, that's funny," she said grinning.

He smiled back at her and felt a sudden foreboding; she seemed about to tell him something. He looked at her face, looking for a clue.

"Well, babe, he's got a big investment in you—that plush school you want to go in New York . . ."

"He thinks," she said setting her glass slowly down on the bar napkin in front of her, "I should—go out with other people."

Howard felt the top of his ears burn, then his cheeks.

He looked at her face, thinking back to the first week they were together on campus in the fall sunshine, walking hand in hand, stopping in front of the Boesen Rare Books and Fine Prints shop with its sophisticated decor of black window borders and gold lettering. She, her long blonde—streaked hair, wooly crew sweater and pleated skirt, her marvelous long legs with the rounded calves showing, looking every inch—expensive. He felt so fortunate, and took a selfish pride for being with her. All this was in jeopardy now.

"When," Howard said, his voice weak, "did he say that?"

"About—a month ago," she said watching him set his drink down. "Does that answer your question?"

There was movement next to him, and Howard turned to see the guy in the white shirt standing up, reaching for his bar bill. He watched the white shirt go to the cashier counter to pay his tab, over near the doorway.

When Howard turned back to look at Marian, he said in a flat tone, "all the times you and I—traveled—you said it was all right, going out of town together. I mean, you said your folks 'trusted' you—and all that."

"They do trust me," she said and reached for her glass. "Otherwise they wouldn't of let me go—would they?"

Howard reached for his glass, then hesitating said, "Then—why are you telling me about this—now?"

He sat looking into the glass.

"You—asked me," she said, taking a drink, not looking at him. When she picked up her glass she said, "Whooo, I'm getting dizzy . . . ."

"Maybe we should go, babe."

Outside, walking down the gangplank from the bar, that was part of the nautical theme of the building, Marian stumbled and leaned over the rope railing.

Howard caught her by the arm, pulling her upright.

"Ease—y, babe," he said, "take it slow."

"Too much rum and coke," she whispered.

"Yeah," he said putting his arm around her shoulders as they walked, "that stuff can known you for a loop."

"You're good to me, Howard," she said as they started the steps on the riverbank that led up to the parking lot. "I like when you're good to me, How-ward. I like you—but I don't *love* you. You now that?" She waved her free hand as they stopped on the top step overlooking the parking lot.

Howard stood stunned for a moment, "C'mon, babe, take it easy—you had a lot to drink."

"Did I ever say I loved you?" she said, pulling up her sweater back on her shoulders, that had slid down, the sweater she always wore in air conditioned buildings. "I want an answer," she said in a loud voice.

"No, you haven't said you loved me," Howard said to the side of her head, just above the ear, "and I haven't said I love you either."

"See what I mean? she said in a loud voice.

Howard looked around the parking lot to see if anyone was listening, feeling embarrassed.

"I always—ah—thought, babe, that it was *understood* about us. That we didn't have to—admit—use words . . ."

"That's no answer," she said pulling the sweater up with both hands.

Over in the corner of the lot, next to a pick-up truck, Howard saw a light-blue Ford with the interior light on, the white shirt guy leaning, his head lowered, as if reading something down on the seat.

"You're right, babe," he said leading Marian down the row of parked cars, "I should be more—demonstrative."

"You can't just—leave me hanging—in space, she said watching him open the car door for her.

"I've been inconsiderate, he said as she sat down in the car. "I can see that now. Yes," he said quietly.

Walking around the car to the driver's side, Howard glanced over and saw the white shirt guy still there, looking down.

"Maybe he's just some salesman," he muttered, "writing a report that's got to be in by morning."

As Howard was sliding in behind the steering wheel in the car, Marian asked, "Can I have a cigarette? I need a cigarette."

"I'll make it up to you, babe," he said shaking the pack.

"Don't be silly, Howard" she said taking a cigarette.

Lighting hers, then his cigarette with the car lighter, he sat looking at her. She made him defensive.

"Even your father knows we're crazy for one another," he said. "That's why he wants to break us—apart."

"And you," she said blowing out smoke, "are helping him—you and your night classes and day job—with studying in between. He just wants me to go with some guys from Grosse Pointe—once in awhile."

"It won't be long, babe. Just this semester. I'm pretty close to graduating." Holding the cigarette, wetting his lower lip with his tongue, he added slowly, "Maybe we can work something out with the skiing. Take a trip together."

"Yeah," she said, "skiing and fucking—man, that ought to do it."

"Take it easy, babe."

"No I won't 'take it easy, babe,'" she said blowing smoke at him. "I've taken it *too* easy, in fact. There's got to be more, Howard—a fucking—commitment. Not just a lot of—movement. Okay?"

Howard knew no matter what he said now, that it was not going to make a difference.

When he reached over and put his hand on her thigh, she touched the back of his wrist with the hot end of her cigarette.

"Hey," he shouted.

His first impulse was to swing, a backhand at her face, but he caught himself, and sat rubbing the burn.

"Hey, what?" she said.

"Don't be so—German."

"You're German too, so what."

He sat thinking that if he swung, he might have broken her nose, or something. She was just like him; they were two people who reacted and did things on impulse—things they did not worry about. He liked her too much; that stopped his swing.

"You didn't have to do that," he said.

"I want to go home," she said pushing her cigarette out the window. "Take me home, Howard. I feel terrible."

When they turned and drove up the driveway at her house, Howard did not see any lights on.

"Your folks aren't home, yet," Howard said turning the car lights off, leaving them sitting in total darkness. "You said they would be home before dinnertime."

"I lied," she said. "They're up at the summer house."

"You—didn't have dinner, then?"

"No dinner," she said.

"That's why the rum and coke hit you so hard," he said softly. "You were drinking on an empty stomach."

"I wasn't hungry," she said opening the car door, "I got a lot of stuff on my mind."

"You should eat something, babe," Howard said and opened the car door on his side. "Scrambled eggs; if you can't make them—I'll give you a hand."

"No you won't help me," she said. "Don't come in, Howard. You're not invited—to come in the house."

He watched as she stepped out of the car and slammed the door, the dome light coming on for a moment.

"Are you *that* upset?" Howard said, opening his car door again, standing. "What's the matter?"

"If you come in I'll—call the police," she said, taking two steps back. "Is that enough—*upset*?"

"Take it easy," he said slowly, sitting down in his car, looking at her in the dark. "I've—never—seen—this part of her before," he said quietly to himself. "Man, the hostil—ity. Man."

"I'm going in the house," she said and turned to step up on the low front porch.

Standing out of the car again, Howard said, "I'll call you tomorrow."

She was unlocking the front door, but turned to say, "I may go up to the summer house," in a loud voice. "I'm not sure."

When she closed the front door, the heavy cover over the mail slot made a loud *clang*.

"Okay, okay," he said, starting the car, "have it your way, babe. The way you *always* have it."

Driving down to the corner, he stopped at the sign.

"She gave me the bums-rush," he said putting his hand on his forehead, "because—because somebody is coming—somebody is coming later. Oh, man."

He turned slowly onto the cross street, between the large houses then went around the block. He parked three houses away from where Marian lived. It was dark here, the street light at the corner. He turned off the car lights.

"I won't stay too long," he said, quietly, feeling his throat go dry, not able to say anything more.

He had the odd sensation he was sinking right down into the seat.

He was sliding his hand on the top of the dashboard in the dark, searching for the pack of cigarettes, when he saw the headlights of a car turn from the cross street.

When the car turned up at Marian's driveway, and Howard sat up holding the steering wheel, trying to stop blinking.

It was a light blue Ford.

Howard watched as the guy in the white shirt walked up and rang the front door bell. The door opened and the guy went inside.

Howard lit a cigarette.

"Everything," Howard said, "we said at the bar tonight—was for this guy—to hear. Can you imagine that? For this bastard."

When he stopped at the cross street again, Howard wretched. He had dry heaves and held onto the steering wheel hard.

Chapter 10

Monday, Howard went to work at the Suburban Press newspaper office. At lunch time, he phoned Marian's house, but there was no answer.

He thought she probably went up to the summer house, like she said she might, and he went back to typing stories.

The other reporter, Missus Lorraine Warren, sat typing at her desk at the back of the narrow newsroom. She was shapely in a way that it could not stay that way for long. Her husband was a business manager for the *Detroit News*, and they rented a house in Grosse Pointe and had a daughter in high school there.

The managing editor of the paper was a woman, also. Karen Trombly was out covering a luncheon, herself, that was held in support of a Negro woman running for Detroit City Council.

Missus Trombly favored human rights, and women's rights, even more, so she was covering the story herself. She told all this to Howard when she was interviewing him for his job as a reporter.

The owner of this string of newspapers, Howard found out, had a son at Princeton, and Howard figured that was why he paid such stingy wages. Calvin Beamer, the boss, needed every cent he could get hold of.

When the door of the newsroom opened slowly, Howard looked up from his typewriter.

"Can I talk to a reporter?" the guy in the doorway asked. He wore a blue work jacket and cap, and over his left pocket was a tag with "MARTY".

From his desk, Howard could see the man's hands and fingernails were stained.

"What can I do for you?" Howard asked, leaning back.

Lorraine stopped typing, looking to see if the man was a threat.

"I own a gas station—up on Conners Avenue. Well, I keep getting robbed. I've had nine break-ins in a row."

Howard nodded and asked, "Have you reported all this to the police?"

"Yeah, four, five times," the man said, tipping his cap back on his head, then glancing at Lorraine, 'but it don't do no good. I still get broke into—and they take tools, tires, and sometimes, new batteries."

"If the police can't help," Howard said, "how can I help?"

"One night I sat in my station in the dark—waiting," Marty said quietly. "About one o'clock the back window slides up and I turns on the lights."

"You got the crooks?" Howard asked, surprised.

"They was cops—in uniform. One in the window, the other out in the alley."

"Wow," Howard said, and he heard Lorraine blow air through her teeth and go back typing.

"I went to the shift Sergeant at the police station and told him," Marty said slowly. "He said he'd check it out—see what was going on."

"Did he look into it?" Howard said, writing on his note pad.

"Yeah, he called me on the phone two days later. He said they were investigating a robbery, they'd found the window open, and climbed through to check."

Lorraine blew air through her teeth again, making a *sh-u-u* sound.

"Okay," Howard said after writing Marty's name and address on his pad, "I'll look into it."

"Thanks," Marty said, and turned and stepped to the door. "Hope you can do *something,*" he said opening the door, "before they put me out of business; the insurance dropped me because of all the robberies."

When he was gone, Howard said to Lorraine, "He's got trouble all right—with the cops, yet."

"Forget it," Lorraine said lighting up a cigarette. "He can't prove anything. It's his word against theirs."

Later, near five o'clock, Howard called Marian before leaving the office. Ardis, her sis, answered.

"No, she's not here," Ardis said. She's got classes down at the university."

There were no day classes, this late. Howard knew Ardis was lying for her sister. There was a smile in her voice; she was not good at lying.

"Okay," Howard said calmly, "I'll call again, later." He sat for a moment looking at the phone, thinking Marian had changed so fast, he could hardly believe it.

That Thursday, he phoned her again, and she told him she was going up to the summer house that weekend, it was the Mother's birthday.

Howard was unsure if she was stalling him again, but said, "I'm going to celebrate my first paycheck at that lobster place downtown, tomorrow. Would you like to join me?"

"Sure," Marian said. "Sounds good."

"Okay, babe, I'll pick you up after work. About six," Howard said, a little surprised, but pleased. "See you then."

The Lobster House was a restaurant in an old residence near the Fisher Building in Detroit. It was a landmark type of place with loyal customers. And executives from GM, and some well-known entertainment names frequented the establishment.

There was a lobster tank with live lobsters near the door where you came in, each with a number tag. You picked a crustacean and gave the number to the waiter that showed you to a table in the crowded dining room. The tables were only a few feet apart.

Marian sat smiling, sipping white wine from an oversized goblet, listening to Howard.

"So my editor says, next week when President Kennedy comes to the city airport," Howard said quietly, "I want you to ask him, "'is there any relief for the laid-off skilled tradesmen here on the east side—from the auto industry?'"

"Are you nervous?"

"Yeah, for Pete's sake," Howard said holding his goblet in front of his face, "I'll be talking to the *President*. I keep saying—practicing—what I'm supposed to say—I don't want to forget—you know, I'll be excited."

"That's pretty good, Howard," she said. "You're just getting started in the newspaper business—and here you are—interviewing the President."

"Yeah," Howard said, then taking a quick sip of wine, "they've even assigned their part-time photographer to be there—you know—when I shake hands with Kennedy and ask him the question."

"No wonder," Marian said, "you're all excited, honey."

"The governor will be there, too," Howard said, looking at her face across the small table, wanting to kiss her suddenly, "and all the big-wigs from the unions."

"I'm happy for you, honey," she said reaching back to adjust the swirl of her hair at the back of her head. "Things are—going good for you."

He sat looking at her, thinking she was the only person he ever really cared about. He could not help himself; she just did that to him.

A waitress came to the table next to them, and slid it against the table over in the corner booth.

"Holy Mackerel," Howard whispered to Marian, "everybody in the country is looking for him. The government, CBS, the newspapers—He stopped every truck in America. Well, his union did. Jeez."

"Is that him?" Marian whispered back. "Are you sure?"

"Yeah, it's him, babe. Everybody wants him to let the trucks roll again—everybody's looking for him. The whole country is at a standstill."

"It' can't be," she said quietly. "What's he doing here?"

"Having lobster," Howard whispered back.

The waitress reached over Howard's shoulder and set a large platter with a cooked lobster in front of him. After she tied a bib around his neck, she reached over to serve another platter to Marian, then tied on her bib.

"What's this stuff?" Howard asked the waitress, pointing at the crust covering the underbelly of the lobster.

"We just started doing that," the waitress said quietly. "It adds flavor; it's a baked almond paste."

"Can I get one without the paste? Howard asked. "I just want a lobster. No paste."

"I'm afraid they *all* come that way," the waitress said setting a bowl of melted butter on the table between the platters.

When she went away, Howard shrugged, then leaned forward over his lobster and whispered to Marian, "You think—I should phone the *Detroit News*—tell them Jimmy's here?"

"Why?" Marian said, straightening her bib.

"Well, because—I'm a newspaper man," Howard said as he began scraping off the paste on his lobster with his fork. "I'm supposed to be fearless in seeking out news—along with accuracy—and good spelling."

"No, honey," Marian said, bending her lobster's claw to break it off, making a grimacing face. "Let someone else do it," she whispered. "You might cause trouble."

He felt a relief she was not judging his newspaper ethics or his integrity. She was letting him off the hook in the face of the situation that could turn ugly—even violent.

"I suppose you're right," he said, thinking she must have taken a course in avoiding problems at Grosse Pointe High.

As he cracked the lobster open with the pliers-like devise, he cut his thumb on the shell's jagged edge. The blood seeped out, and not wanting to stain the linen napkin, he pressed the cut against the cold of the water glass.

"Howard," Marian said when she saw the blood in the water, "what happened to your thumb?"

"I cut it on the piece of the shell," he said, raising the thumb to look at the wound.

"That looks awful," Marian said, making a sour face. "I'll ask the waitress for a band-aid—or something."

"No, no, babe," he said quickly. "It's all right."

"Are you sure, Howard? It looks," she said pointing with her fork, "pretty bad."

"Naw, it's okay, now. Honest."

He held up the thumb, and when the blood came out again, he pressed it against the water glass.

Her concern over the thumb made him feel good, but what he really wanted was to find out what was going on with the new guy in the white shirt she was dating. Ever since he picked her up at the home, Howard had been trying to devise a casual way to ease into the subject. He did not want to show he was affected, yet he was eager to learn about his competitor.

A man wearing eyeglasses, and holding his hat in both hands, came through the kitchen door, went over to Jimmy and whispered in his ear.

Howard watched as the tables covered with bread, salad bowls and water glasses, were pulled out, and Jimmy stood up, then moved quickly to the kitchen door, and go out.

Howard looked at Marian, then grinned.

She raised her eyebrows as if to say that someone knew where Hoffa was, or see, you did not have to get involved.

When he nodded he understood, she reached over, smiling, and patted his hand. The hand with the good thumb.

For dessert, the waitress brought orange sherbet in tall parfait glasses.

Howard could not hold back any longer, so he asked while picking up a long dessert spoon, "How are you and your new friend getting along?"

"Freddy?" she said. "You know, we're just getting acquainted. He likes to watch Jack Parr—on late television."

"Freddy—do I know him? Is he a student?"

"He was—a student down in Coral Gables, but dropped out the second year. His uncle is Daddy's business partner."

"I didn't know Daddy had a business partner," Howard said, and put a spoonful of sherbet in his mouth.

"Yeah," Marian said untying her bib and setting it on the table. "Well, it's like this, Daddy is a retailer and once a year, he and Karl Aschenfelter pool their funds, then Karl goes up to Canada—North Bay—to the fur auction. Karl buys a ton of furs and ships them to Europe. When the furs are sold in Paris, Belgium, Germany, and down in Rome, they split the profits."

"This Karl is a furrier?" Howard said, looking at his cut thumb for a second, turning it to see if the bleeding slowed, then pressing back on the water glass.

"No," Marian said after swallowing her sherbet, that she took only small portions of on the tip of her spoon. "Karl has a tool and die business, out in Warren, somewhere. And, Freddy—Frederich—is his nephew."

"How did Daddy meet Aschenfelter?" Howard asked, wiping a bit of sherbet from the side of his mouth, the napkin in the hand with the good thumb. "Some German social club?"

"Lochmoor," Marian said, scraping at the sherbet mound in her dish slowly. "They're golf partners; they *were* until Daddy had the heart attack—you sound like you're—interrogating me, Howard. Stop."

"Sorry, babe," Howard said, looking at his dessert spoon of sherbet, "I'm *concerned*—about you. Who you go with, that's all, babe."

"Howard, honey," Marian said leaning forward, "I have to do this—my father wants me to go out with other—men. That's all. You are the only one I care about. Truly."

"I don't like all these guys," Howard said, leaning forward over the table, "coming at you—taking a bite of the sandwich. My sandwich, babe."

She smiled at the sandwich analogy, and said, "But you still have the sandwich, honey."

He looked at her for a moment, and though of saying, 'who would want a sandwich with a bite taken out', but instead asked, "Where does Fred work? What does he do?"

Howard felt his newspaper instincts come into play.

"He's a car salesman out in Birmingham," she said setting her spoon carefully on the saucer under the parfait dish. "He sells—used—cars—those plush German ones."

"He makes big money, then?" Howard said dropping his spoon in the empty parfait dish, making a *clang*. "That's what Daddy—why Daddy—fixed you up with this Fred."

"I guess so," Marian said. "he's kind of a playboy. We're going to a Piston's game on our next date."

"Why does he drive," Howard asked slowly, "a light blue Ford—if he's flush with money?"

"How do you now, what kind of car he drives, Howard?"

"I went around the block," he said, "the night after the Harbor Bar. I had to, babe, I was going crazy."

"That's not—healthy, Howard. I mean, it's not like you. It almost borders on—sick."

"Yeah," he said, leaning back in his chair. "it was a bad taste—in my mouth, too."

"But—I forgive you," Marian said. "I realize that me going out with other guys—has you climbing the walls. But—I have to do it—Daddy is pushing me."

"That why I—went around the block, babe. that's when I saw the light blue Ford."

"The car is from his uncles' tool shop, a business car," she said, sliding her parfait glass and saucer to one side. "You know what he told me; there's an apartment upstairs in the shop with a bed, sink, table—even a shower. His uncle Karl stays there sometimes. And there's a small window, that he can look down on the whole shop—see what's going on."

When the waitress came, they ordered coffee.

"Fred says he has a Porsche—it's in the body shop—the side was hit in an accident. I don't think it's a new Porsche."

Howard said, "Thanks for telling me all this, babe," just as the waitress returned and set coffee cups and saucers in front of each of them. "It sort of makes—it easier to swallow—all this."

"I know," she said. "I know—you're suffering, honey. But—what can I do? I just have to go along with it, too. My father wants me to—meet other guys." She said lifting her coffee cup. I have to do what he wants."

"It sounds," Howard said lifting his cup, looking at her, "so—medieval, or something."

She was wearing a navy blue suit with a cream-colored shirt—the color of coffee—and Howard wished he could drink her—keep her away from all these other guys.

"I know," she said holding the cup in both hands, "but there is nothing I can do."

"Was this Fred at the Harbor Bar?" Howard asked setting his cup down slowly onto the saucer. He did not like to ask.

Marian nodded, lowering her eyes.

"He was playing golf with someone—at the Country Club. A customer—who wanted one of his cars and didn't want to wait." she wiped her mouth with the end of the napkin. "He wasn't supposed to come until late, but he came over when he was done—and he saw us get in the car and go to the Harbor Bar. He followed us—he told me later that night, he waited for you to go to the men's room—or something—but when you didn't—he got up and left. He wanted to talk to me—tell me he had to go to New York for awhile. A week maybe, or more."

"He's really creepy," Howard said slowly. "He might be a crook—maybe mixed up in some kind of shady stuff." Looking at his cut thumb that had stopped bleeding, "It could be—dangerous, babe. I wish you could—stay away from him. You know?"

"Oh, Howard, don't be so silly—and dramatic."

He shrugged.

"I'm worried about you and this Fred," he said.

The waitress came and refilled their cups, and slid the bill on the corner of the table. She did not speak before she walked away.

"There's a boy in my history class," Marian said calmly, "who asked me to go to a hockey game at the Olympia. Maybe you think he's a hood, too," she added, smiling.

"Maybe I know him," Howard said lifting his coffee cup. "What's his name?"

"Hartwell," she said softly, almost inaudible. "Kevin."

"Marwil?" Howard said looking over his cup. "He has the same name as the campus bookstore? Is he related?"

"No, How-ard," she said, "his name is Hart-well. Kevin Hartwell."

Howard was drinking his coffee, thinking she was amazing because she could appear reticent and unaffected at the same time while talking about his guy.

"No," Howard said slowly to her, "I guess I don't know him—after all."

This program of Marian's father was putting a strain on their relationship. Her telling him about other guys she was dating, was grinding Howard, who did not want to hear about these guys. It was the same for Marian; she did not like the questions about the people she went out with.

Maybe that was why Daddy started this campaign of having Marian dating other men. Howard thought to himself. Eventually, it would cause enough conflict—become so abrasive—they would separate.

When they each lighted cigarettes and sat talking, Marian said her history class friend was an "engineer at Burroughs Adding Machine Company" and Howard nodded.

He knew a company would not hire anyone without a degree and let them do engineering, but he just nodded.

"Rhode Island," Marian said, after Howard asked where the engineer was from. "His father is a stock broker," she said, and Howard nodded, while putting out his cigarette.

When Marian said in an offhand manner, "Yeah, Kevin and you are neighbors. He lives at the Patterson Hotel—just up the block from your old apartment," Howard flinched.

"Oh, yeah," he said, knowing the hotel has been vacant for two years, condemned like the other buildings on his apartment block, slated for demolition. It was part of the university's expansion program.

The only thing living in the Patterson building was the dumpy bar on the ground floor, that was allowed to keep open until the liquor license ran out.

Her talking about the apartment brought back the memory of the time he and Marian had fried eggs for lunch. They had only known one another a few days then, and he had no spatula to flip the eggs, and the next day, when he opened the mailbox out by the front door, a spatula fell out.

He stood smiling at the spatula out there in the doorway, he remembered, thinking how caring she could be.

There was another time at the apartment he could never forget, a time that he felt so attracted to her, it scared him. He could not get through a day without her. He had to be *with* her, but when his Ford broke down, and had to be taken to the garage, he could not drive her home to Grosse Pointe and she had to ride the bus.

Howard walked her to the bus stop up on Woodward Avenue. They had just made love on the couch in the apartment and he could not keep his hands off of her. He kissed her and pulled out her baggy sweater to look down at her boobs knowing she never wore a bra.

The bus stop was on the sidewalk out in front of the Patterson Hotel on Woodward Avenue.

When Marian climbed on the bus, Howard felt deflated and alone, and thought of having a drink at the ground floor bar behind him. The CAMEL sign lighted in the grimy window, the cigarette part gone, was to show the bar was still open for business despite the building being vacant.

Howard did not go in the bar, he remembered, it was a place for derelicts.

This guy in Marian's history class did not do his homework very well in checking on the status of the Patterson Hotel. Howard's newspaper instincts were up and running and he wanted to protect Marian, or at least warn her that the guy was a fraud. But, he did nothing.

"I want to go to the little girls' room," she said pushing back her chair from the table.

"I'll meet you at the door—next to the cashier," he said, "when you're ready."

Howard was mad after paying a quarter of his earning for the lobsters, and when he said, "I don't like their almond paste," to Marian, as they walked across the parking lot to the car, he was really saying this was his last visit.

"It was smart not to ask the waitress," Marian said, "about Hoffa being there. She would be on the spot to say yes or no."

"Yeah," Howard said, "that happens a lot in the news business. You step on a lot of toes."

Back at Marian's house, sitting in the car in the driveway, Howard kissed her and when he slid his hand under her shirt, she leaned away.

"I've—got to go," she said quietly, "Ardis is home."

"It's early, babe," Howard said, looking to the rear of the house, where he could see all the lights on in the kitchen. "We can go someplace . . ."

"No, honey, I've got to help Ardis—she's making coconut cake for mother's birthday tomorrow." she opened the car door and the dome light came on, then she closed it enough to put out the light. "Daddy and mother are up at the summer house—we're going up in the morning—about six, in time for breakfast."

"Oh, I see, babe," Howard said, as a cold feeling of being an outsider—an intruder, came over him. Every time she talked about her family, he had the same cold feeling.

"I promise, honey," she said putting her hand on his face, "we'll make up—for the time—we're—separated."

"You're going to drive me crazy, babe."

"I know," she said, "I know how you feel. I can't even sleep at night—I'm so mixed up."

"Well, maybe you could get rid of this—Fred guy. Things—would settle down—a bit—if you did, babe."

"it's not that easy, honey. Daddy likes—the background Fred has, and all that, and he's pressing me to . . ."

"Jeez, babe, now what?"

She moved to put both hands on his face, and holding it, said, "Honey, I have to tell—you."

"Okay," Howard said feeling her warm hands.

"Fred—wants," she said quietly, "to buy an engagement ring for me. He wants us to become engaged."

"Wha-at, babe? You only met this guy a month ago."

"More like seven weeks," she said sitting back, her elbow bumping the car door, the dome light flickering, "I was as dumbfounded as you are, honey."

"What—what did you tell—answer, babe, when he said that?"

"I said I wasn't sure—I needed more time to think about it." She sat up straight, looking forward through the windshield at the lights in the kitchen. "I'm just being honest about the whole thing. I mean, it's a big decision—a big move—and I have to be sure."

Howard though now, that all a woman wants is a ring and marriage. If a proposal is dangling in front of her, she cannot resist.

"Je—eez," he said, looking away from her, out the window at the dark on his side of the car, "I can—hardly breathe."

When he reached over to hold her, she said, "No. No, Howard, I've got to go—inside—now. things are all—different," she said pushing his hands down. "Oh, I'm so mixed up—I'm getting dizzy."

When the dome light came on, she added, "Don't get out of the car—please."

In the light, Howard saw she was crying.

"I'll call you Monday," he said quietly, leaning out the window.

"Yes," she said, not looking back.

He turned on the car lights, catching her in the glare as she walked up the driveway near the house. The view of her rump, the tailored suit, the blonde-streaked hair back in a swirl. "Oh, man," Howard whispered, "how can *anybody* not want that? Oh, man."

Starting the car, and back down the drive, he felt as if a hand were inside his stomach, pulling his insides down.

Somehow the Toddle House restaurant, where he turned onto Jefferson Avenue, looked different. Before, the tiny building set back on the long lawn, was a landmark that meant he was almost to Marian's house; it made him feel good.

Now it was just a house with tiny square windows and a blue sloping roof, like a drawing in a child's book of fairy tales. But the charm was gone.

On the overpass of the Expressway, half way home to his parents house, he turned abruptly, and drove down the ramp, into the flow of speeding traffic, headed to downtown Detroit.

"I can't sleep," he said quietly, "my stomach is on fire. I need a drink—to put out the fire. Hell, a lot of drinks."

Walking into the Campus Bar later that evening, Howard saw Tim Etherly sitting on a stool reading the sports page.

"You reading about the Lions?" Howard said sitting down next to him.

"Naw, I got a bet on the Red Wings, they're playing the Blackhawks."

"How much?"

"Fifty." Then he turned to look at Howard. "Hey, that reminds me—you still owe me for those opera tickets."

"Right," Howard said, reaching for his wallet. He took out a ten and gave it to Etherly.

When the bartender came, Howard ordered a beer and one for Tim also.

"You must live in this place," Howard said.

"It's sort of my office," Tim said. "Jeez, you look rough, man. You have a fight?"

"I just got word from Marian—she might get engaged to some creep."

"And he has money," Etherly said. "The creep's *always* have the money to get married."

When the bartender came with the two beers and set them on the bar, Howard said, "Give me a shot of Kessler."

"We don't have Kessler now," the skinny bartender said. "We changed to Old Thompson. It's just as good—and it's a dime cheaper."

"Okay, Old Thompson."

"Don't try and drown your troubles, Howie—it don't work. They'll still be there in the morning—tomorrow."

"You're probably right, Tim, but I got to have something. I feel like I've been kicked in the gut."

Howard lifted the shot glass, and drank the whiskey slowly, leaning his head back.

"I know booze don't help," Tim said quietly, "because when Sylvia cut me loose—I drank like a fish."

"I have to survive," Howard said, picking up his draft beer, "what the hell else can I do to get numb?"

"There's only one cure, Howie, "and that's to find *another* girl—that way you bury the sting—you survive," Tim said, finishing his beer, then reached for the one Howard bought.

"But," Howard said, "I can't forget Marian—she's one of a kind. How can another girl compete—take Marian's place? It wouldn't work for me."

"C'mon, Howie, people are breaking up every day—and there's all kinds of girls—in circulation. You can't stop living—because of a break up."

"Damn," Howard said, "I miss her so much—I feel sick."

"Oh-h," Etherly said looking at his watch, "I've got to go. I've got to pick up my girl for dinner tonight."

Howard watched as Etherly drank most of the beer quickly, and set the glass on the bar, figuring the guy just wanted to be away from his sad story.

Howard sat looking in the mirror behind the bar, and saw when Etherly slid off the stool, he was standing directly behind.

"My girl works for a law firm—they've got a big case and they put in long hours," Etherly said. "I'm not running out on you."

Howard saw Etherly talking to him, using the mirror, looking at him.

"I know, I know," Howard said to the mirror, grinning. "Hey, good luck with the Red Wings bet."

"Forget the hard booze, Howie. Stick with the beer if you're going to get smashed. And remember—start looking for a new girl—it's the only way out."

Howard nodded, watching Etherly in the mirror go out the door.

"'Dinner tonight', my foot," Howard said, and drank the rest of the beer in his glass.

He sat the glass down, and ran his hand through his hair, looking in the mirror over to the booth that he and Marian used most of the time when they came here.

"Damn," he said, "I feel—half-dead—without her. How am I going to—survive," he said, "if she gets married?"

He slapped the bar with his hand flat.

The bartender, came from the end of the bar, where the overhead television set was on the Jack Paar Show.

"Another Old Thompson?" he asked, thinking the slap a call.

"Yeah," Howard said.

Chapter 11

Saturday morning, Howard was home trying to read his Geology textbook, but every time he thought about the university, he felt down. when he remembered the places on campus Marian and he spent time in, he was overwhelmed by the loss of her now.

Outside, he could see the tree in the backyard was bare, and the leaves, because it had been raining off and on, were wet on the ground.

It was almost eleven o'clock when he left his room and went downstairs, giving up on trying to study.

"What's on the menu, for dinner tonight, Mom?"

"Pork chops," she said looking up at him from the table, peeling apples. "Father got apples from that boss who has a farm up in Romeo."

"Every year we get a bushel," Howard said, "like clockwork. Hey, where is Dad?"

"Downstairs in the den—George Pierrot's program is on. Father knows all those travel films by heart."

Howard smiled, recalling how his father always talks about taking a driving trip to Alaska.

His mother had gained weight in recent years, and her hair was gray, but her mind as still sharp.

"You will be here for dinner, son?"

"Yes," he said, sensing what she was driving at.

"You're not going with that Grosse Pointe girl—anymore?"

"We—sort of—broke up," Mom."

"That's too bad. She was very nice."

He stopped home to get his camera one evening last summer, Marian in the car. He brought her in the house, downstairs in the recreation room, where his parents were watching television, and introduced her.

He remembered he was shocked at the contrast; Marian so sleek, and his parents in their middle-class dowdiness.

Surprisingly that day, his father was wearing a green cotton work shirt and pants, and looked like a custodian. Howard remembered introducing his parents, feeling embarrassed; they looked like a frumpy working-class couple on the couch, looking up, in the pine-paneled recreation room.

His father's job was supervisor for the tools and shipping department with an international bridge construction company. Howard had never seen his father dressed like that before, and he felt let down. Here was his father dressed like a laborer, when he was in charge of a six-man crew that shipped tools to work sites around the country, bought new tools, even replacement machinery. There was a constant parade of tool salesmen in his office, resulting in gifts of every kind, especially at Christmas: booze, fruit baskets, even cigars.

His father never got his hands dirty at work, and here he was dressed like a worker on the day Marian visits.

Now, Howard stood watching his mother peeling apples in the kitchen. He took a slice from the bowl on the table and popped it into his mouth.

"Yeah," he said to his mother, rolling the piece of apple around in his mouth, "she was nice—a real winner."

"Maybe it's for the better, son, that you broke off with her," his mother said, not looking up, continuing to peel. "A girl like that—you couldn't keep her in handkerchiefs. You wouldn't be happy with a Grosse Pointe girl. There's too big a difference."

Howard stood silent, looking at the old sweater his mother was wearing, both elbows worn through.

He swallowed the apple slice, nodding.

"Where's my know-it-all little sister?" he asked. "What's Kathy doing today?"

"Her AYH group is on a bus tour," his mother said as she quartered an apple, "to someplace that makes maple syrup. They won't be back until evening."

"Good," Howard said grinning, "as in Good Riddance."

"Behave," his mother said looking up sharply. "You'll miss her—she might take a trip with those Youth Hostels to Europe this summer."

"Maybe," Howard said. "I was just teasing." He took another section of apple. "Think I'll go downstairs and see where father is 'travelling' today."

"I'll start lunch as soon as I get these apples cooking," his mother said looking up. "Don't go out until you have something to eat."

"Yes, mother," Howard said smiling, opening the door to the basement.

Downstairs, Howard found his father leaning back in a lounge chair, his legs up, and empty Stroh's beer bottle sitting on the side table.

"What's on Pierrot today?" Howard asked.

"That photographer guy that goes all over Arizona—and sleeps in the back of his truck. He calls the pickup truck, 'Gus'."

Howard dropped onto the couch and said, "That's one way to cut travel expenses. Sleep in the back of your pickup."

"Hey," his father said, pointing at him, "I checked the oil in your clunker—and I had to add two quarts. You keep that up and you'll be walking. That engine will burn out the bearings, if you don't add oil."

"Thanks," Howard said.

"There were four parking tickets stuffed in the glove box," his father said picking up a stubby cigar out of the ash tray on the side table.

"Yeah," Howard said, watching his father lighting the cigar, flinching at the intrusion of privacy at the glove box, "the cops, every once in a while, ticketed the cars parked on the street in front of the apartment. Those tickets are a couple of months old."

"One of the colored guys in my crew," his father said blowing cigar smoke, dropping the burnt match in the ash tray, "has a wife that works in the Traffic Fines office downtown. I'll see what I can do."

"Great," Howard said, smiling.

"You shouldn't let those tickets pile up like hat, son. They put out a warrant out for you."

"I forgot about them, Dad. They're from a couple of months ago . . ."

"You look like you were drawn through a knot-hole kid. You hung-over?"

"Naw," Howard said and hesitated, "Marian—we broke up—sort of—we're not together—anymore."

"If you had a tiff," his father said flicking the ash from his short cigar, "that's normal. You'll patch it up. You'll be back together—you'll see—things like that happen."

"Naw," Howard said crossing his legs, "we *really* broke up, Dad. She's got some other guy."

"A man don't let some other guy take his girl away—not if he's a man," his father said glancing at the television set for a moment.

Howard's father had served in the Pacific with the Seabees during World War II. He liked to tell stories about how fighting with the Japs went on in the islands while his outfit was building airstrips. Sometimes at the end of the runway, the fighting would go on.

Other stories, he told to Howard, were about Jap snipers taking pot-shots at the men who operated the bulldozers and graders as they were working, building the airfields.

"Yeah," Howard said, "but I'm up against money here; really big money is involved. I don't have—much money."

"Who's fault is that, Howard?"

"I'm working," Howard said, "uncrossing his legs, then leaning forward, his elbows on his knees, "but I'm just making peanuts."

"Get a better job, son," his father said through the cigar smoke. "Beat the bushes—find what you need."

"But I'm still a student at the university," Howard said leaning back on the couch. "I can't work full—time and take classes, too."

"You'll work it out," his father said looking at the television. "Don't get down in the dumps—every time you hit a bump in the road, kid. That's for pizz-willies. A man just keeps looking for better opportunities—until he finds one."

"I've got to get my degree," Howard said thinking. "That comes first, I guess."

"Just get out there and do something, son. You'll feel better about yourself, you'll see. Moping around the house don't get you anywhere. And things change; you never know what's coming your day—from day to day."

Howard smiled.

"I guess you're right, Dad."

"Of course I am," his Father said looking over at him, "there's no other answer. Just keep looking. And if the girl don't like you for what you are—get *another* girl Get a girl that agrees with what you think. That way there's less trouble—for the long run."

"Hey, you guys," Howard's mother shouted down the stairwell from the kitchen, "I made tuna salad—and tomato soup—when you're ready for lunch."

"We're coming, mother," his Father shouted back.

When his father stood up from the lounge chair, he said to Howard, "You know—you should get rid of that bucket of bolts—get a good car. When you work, you got to have reliable transportation. That thing you're driving is on its last legs."

"Cars are expensive, dad," Howard said getting to his feet. "I don't make a lot of loot."

"You go over to Ver Hoven Chevrolet," his father said, pulling down his sweat shirt, that slid up when he got to his feet, "and ask for Ray Alexander, the sales manager. I sent a lot of people from work over to him. Tell him he owes me a favor."

Howard smiled, "Okay, I'll tell him that."

His father picked up the beer bottle and went to the door of the laundry room, where he had an old refrigerator from the kitchen, and next to it a shower stall, a sink and a toilet. This room, built next to the laundry tubs, was all closed in with pine panel boards. He cleaned up here after work.

"That girl," his father said, holding the pine door open, "the one with the money. Just remember this, kid, a lot of guys got killed in the war—I lost a lot of friends—and they never got the chance to make the mistakes—like we all do."

When his father went through the door and closed it, Howard started up the stairs, unsure of what he meant.

~ ~ ~

The afternoon of the second day he bought his new Chevrolet, Howard phone Marian from work.

"I've got a new set of wheels, babe," he said over the phone, sitting at his desk, grinning. "It's a Chevy convertible, Super Sport, gold with a white top. I'll come over—take you for a ride down Lakeshore."

"You bought a *new* car?" she said. "That's terrific. Not that you needed one."

"Yeah," he said, grinning, "it's mine and the finance companies. I got three years of debt."

"Good for you, Howard."

"Can I pick you up around six?"

"Well," she said, and there was a pause, "I've got to tell you—I'm engaged. Fred gave me a ring."

Howard closed his eyes, as if hit in the face, "but—we're just going for a ride—in my new . . ."

"Fred asked me," Marian said slowly, "not to see you—anymore," and her voice cracked.

"Jeez," Howard said in disbelief, "just like that? He's sure in a hurry—isn't he?"

"Yes, Howard," she said softly. "Ple-ease understand."

He could tell she was crying.

"Okay. Okay, babe," he said leaning back in his office chair, "I understand. Maybe later, or sometime, we can go for a ride," he said softly, "I understand."

"I'm sorry, Howard," she said in a high voice, "I'm going to miss you—we had so much fun—doing things."

He tried to speak, but his throat was too tight.

"I—understand," was all he could manage to say.

"Howard—I have to go now," she said, and he heard her sob.

"Okay," he said, and he heard the phone click on the other end.

He sat looking at the telephone on his desk.

"That Fred was sure in a hurry," he said. "Damn." He sat there feeling as if he had been told Marian had been killed in a auto crash. "She's gone. Damn."

Chapter 12

Howard kept looking at the girl sitting next to him on his first night of class for The Growth of American Democracy Since 1865. He knew her from some place, but he could not remember where.

When the class ended, the bell ringing, he leaned toward her and said, "I've met you before, but I can't place—where."

She smiled. Her lips were full, like the actress Leslie Caron.

"I think it was in the student center," she said slowly, as if it was an item buried deep, she was recalling, "and you were sitting with Marian Harbaugh at a table in the cafeteria."

"Oh, okay, I remember," Howard said as they both stood up from the student chairs. "It was St. Patrick's Day and we were talking about drinking green beer—when you walked up and talked to Marian. That was it."

The girl smiled, looking up at him, as they walked in the hall.

Howard noticed she was shorter than Marian, as they walked, her body slimmer. She wore a Calico blue shirt that was blousy, and he could not see the outline of her boobs, nor the rest of her.

When she had walked away from the table in the cafeteria, Howard recalled asking Marian, "Who was that?" Marian said, "'A girl I know from Grosse Pointe High,'" and Howard had a mental picture of them talking on the grass in front of the school tower and spire on Fisher Road.

He remembered, too, they spoke so quietly, that he did not hear what they were saying, above all the noise in the cafeteria.

"So you're a Grosse Pointer, too?" Howard said.

"Not exactly," she said as they walked in the hall slowly, "since my parent's divorce, I've been living in Indian Village—with my mother—and her new husband."

"You and George Pierrot," Howard said offhand.

"Pierrot lives two streets over," she said and looked up smiling. They own the lot next door to their house, and his wife keeps a giant garden—it's all fenced—they have parties in the summer out there in the garden."

"I'm Howard Keck," he said smiling, "before you—tell me too much."

"I'm Julie Picard—and my step-father is Dunbar."

"So you're the Picard in Grosse Pointe," he said looking down at her, "and Dunbar in Indian Village?"

"I suppose you could say that," she said, as they came to the edge of wide steps leading down to the doors.

"I suppose you're engaged?" Howard said, half kidding. "*Everybody* you talk to these days, is engaged."

"No. Not quite."

"Marian is engaged," he said as they started down the steps, "so I'm back to being—a freebooter—so to speak."

"Yes," Julie said looking down at the steps as she moved down, "I heard about it."

"The Grosse Pointe newspaper?"

"No. At church," she said. "We go to the same church over on Jefferson Avenue."

"Small world department," he said.

"You could say that," she said. "I guess."

They walked out into the dark outside, and Howard asked, "Where are you parked? In the lot across the street?"

He was beginning to enjoy asking her questions. The answers she gave, were different, not what he expected, and he was smiling, playing a new game.

"Uh-huh," she said, closing her duffle-coat, looping the wood toggles into the loops with her free hand, holding a notebook in the other.

"I'm over yonder," Howard said, pointing across the lot, lighted with tall overhead lamps. "Out on the back street over there in the dark. Where it doesn't cost *anything*."

Julie nodded and said, "I see," as she stepped up on the cement curb at the edge of the lot.

"Where's your car?" Howard asked.

"There," she said pointing with her notebook at a red MG.

Howard saw it was a vintage model, built just after the war; narrow tires and a cotton convertible top.

"Cripes," he said, looking in the windshield, "the steering is even on the right side. This thing must of come directly from the English countryside."

"My step-father," Julie said slowly, was in England for two years—working over there. He brought it back when he came home."

Howard watched as she opened the small door with an ising-glass window, sat down, and moved her legs together, up into the car.

Even though she wore dark blue slacks, Howard saw her leg movement as graceful, almost enticing, and he was aware, she was aware of it.

"You don't have any problem shifting the gears? he said.

"I'm left-handed," she said, grinning.

"You were made for each other," he said grinning.

"You could say that," she said, and started the small engine that gave out a tinny whine.

"Bye," Howard said holding up his hand.

She looked up, smiled, and nodded.

Watching her drive off in a cloud of gray smoke, he said to himself, "Who-wa, I think I'm going to enjoy this history class."

He turned, walking toward the end of the parking lot, where there was a street, over in the dark.

~~~

On the third week of classes, a Friday night, Howard and Julie sat drinking coffee in the cafeteria, when he asked, "You like gypsy music? Yesterday a friend I met in the bar from the Music School, told me about a bar in River Rouge—with authentic Gypsies. They play violins," he said grinning, "roaming around to the tables. And, sometimes, they even spit on the floor."

"Sounds," Julie said smiling, showing perfect, even, teeth holding her coffee cup, "revoltingly authentic—not to mention—unsanitary."

They both laughed.

"I hear it's better to go on a weekday," Howard said setting his cup in the saucer, slowly, "because the place gets really jammed on weekends. When it gets too crowded, you can't enjoy the music."

"Sounds—intriguing," Julie said. "Something that should not be missed."

"We can go, if you want," Howard said, the first expecting a polite refusal, looking at her smiling, those full lips, "that is if you had a Tetanus shot recently."

She laughed, and said, quote I can't—stay too late."

"No. No," Howard said, noticing her nipples showing through her white shirt when she sat up straight, "I have to look fresh-faced at work tomorrow—and wholesome. I got an early interview."

She laughed, and when they stood up, pulling on their coats, Howard looked at the nipples again, that the wide leather belt, and down at the tweed skirt, wondering what she looked like without skirt.

"Maybe we should go in one car," she said, as they were walking to the door of the cafeteria. "So I don't get lost."

"Right," Howard said following her out the door, feeling himself getting excited, "I'll show you my newly financed Chevy."

They walked out in the dark to where his car was parked on a side street.

"Like that new-car smell," she said as they drove down Woodward Avenue toward the Detroit River.

"Yeah," Howard said while turning onto Jefferson Avenue, heading down river, "I'm trying to keep that smell—as long as possible. I don't even smoke in the car."

He grinned at her, then realized he was driving in the opposite direction from Grosse Pointe, and shook his head; with Marian he was always headed the other way.

In River Rouge, across from the Dancing Magyar Cafe, Howard counted only seven cars in the small parking lot. He parked at the far end of the lot, near the base of a metal frame structure, a tower, that's ported heavy wires from the Edison electric plant down the street.

"Uh-h," Julie said when they were walking to the front door to the café, "what a *smell* that is. Phe-ew."

"Yeah," Howard said smiling, "that's from Zug Island, just down the street. They make tar."

"So this is Del Ray," Julie said, pulling a strip of oversized leather purse, "where the Hungarian population lives."

"Yep," Howard said, and reached to pull open the weathered front door; when he did they heard the first of the music, violins playing wildly.

Only three of the tables were occupied by couples, who all seem to be seated close to the bar. Cigarette smoke hung in a light-blue cloud in the room.

Howard picked a table against the wall, just right of the door. When he pulled out a chair for Julie, she slid out of the quote and dropped over the back of the chair, and sat down.

"This is really—that—to the point of being unbelievable," she said to Howard.

He tried not to look at her breasts, and said, "you ain't seen nothing yet."

Three violin players were following the lead player, a short man in a tan suit, who plays violin sideways, moving the bow straight up and down. The group was playing at a table, were a woman in an orange dress, sat listening to the music violin not more than 2 feet from her ear. Her escort, a thin man, pushed money in the breast pocket of the tan suit.

After the waiter brought their Vodka and orange juice drinks, Julie leaned to separate the person the floor next to her like. When she did, her white shirt fell open, and Howard saw her breasts.

"I'll call them to our table," Howard said Julie, knowing now, she was leading him on.

"Where do Gypsies come from?" She asked, after taking a drink from the glass, which he now held their her face.

"I read somewhere they might be from Egypt," Howard said back. "That's where the word "Gypsies" comes in, meaning Egypt. But," he said leaning toward her, taking a sip of his Vodka and orange juice, "some historians say they migrated to Europe—from India. I'm not sure."

"They're terrific," Julie said. "In that music—so compelling—and the guy in a tan suit—unbelievable."

"My friend tells me the tan suit is a king," Howard said, smiling. "He's the Gypsy King for the Detroit area."

"I believe it," Julie said. "He looks—noble."

When Howard ordered refill drinks, he asked the waiter to send the musicians to play at their table.

When the lead Gypsy came over and began to play, Julie leaned back in her chair, smiling, as if absorbing the music.

Howard said grinning, looking at her full lips pursed, as she listened to the mournful music next to her ear.

Howard had urged to hold her, and the Gypsy King seemingly sensing their feelings, made the music wail even more.

Julie crossed her legs, slowly, Howard saw, as if someone had put a hand between them.

Howard took a drink from his glass, but he could not stop watching Julie.

One the background violin players, wiped his face with a handkerchief, then spit on the floor, before resuming the play.

More people were coming in then sitting at the tables, almost all were occupied now.

Howard leaned over and touched Julie's arm, then said, "it's getting late. We can go—when you're ready."

"Not yet," Julie said. "I've never seen anything like this—just a while longer. All this is—so—basic."

Howard smiled, nodded, then took a sip of his drink, wondering how long you have to wait. He wanted her.

It was just after 1131 they left the café, and walking in the parking lot, Julie said, "oh, that music—it goes right *through* me."

"Yeah," Howard said, "it's worth a trip down here to hear it."

When he was unlocking the car door, Julie leaned against his shoulder. He pulled the car door open, then leaned to kiss her, and she put her arms around his neck. He sat down holding her, kissing her hard, feeling her handbag slipping off her shoulder onto the floor of the car.

He leaned back, pulling open her blouse, then sliding back and the seat, her on top of him, her nipples hard, he kissed her breasts.

She reached back and pulled the car door shut.

Neither spoke,—pushed up his shirt, then land him, her face burning, kissing.

Howard turned, feeling the steering wheel against the side of his head, while removing his pants, when she pulled up her skirt, and said, "No, stay there. I'll do it—stay there."

She was almost setting up, pumping with her hips, her breasts rising and falling with her body motions above him.

A bolt hit Howard, beginning at the top of his head and going down the spine. He felt himself go numb from the shock. He could not get an erection. Something had made him numb.

"What the hell," Julie whispered. "Get it up."

"I can't," Howard said. "Damn, what happened?"

"Try," she said. "C'mon, man. Do it."

"I can't," he said after a few moments.

"Shit," Julie said.

"That never," Howard said, swallowing hard, "happened before."

"That's what they all say," Julie said closing her blouse, lifting her legs off Howard, sitting on the corner of the seat as he pulled up his pants.

"Maybe, I drank too much," he said thoughtfully.

When he looked at Julie, he sensed it was as embarrassing for her, as it was for him, so he turned on the radio when he started the car. They rode in silence.

Back at the campus parking lot, she slipped her handbag strap up on her shoulder, and said "I really have to get going home. It's late."

"Right," Howard said and leaned across the seat and kissed her.

She pulled away from him, and said quietly, "thanks for showing me that Gypsy place. I enjoyed it. Really."

She opened the car door and stepped out, Howard looking at her when the interior lights came on, trying to see her face, looking for forgiveness.

"See you in class Monday night," she said before closing the car door.

"You bet," Howard said in a loud voice.

In the headlights, he watched as she climbed into the low, red, MG., Started it, and drove toward the exit.

Howard sat for a moment, thinking, and asked the question to himself, "maybe it was a shock from the high-voltage cable tower?" He shook his head, "Naw, because it happened at home to—when I climbed out of bed."

He thought for another moment, then said, "could someone be—deliberately—trying to keep me from making love the girls? But why? And who?"

He sat for moment more, then said, "I need a drink. I'll go to the Campus Bar."

He drove slowly out of the parking lot.

Julie decided to drive the Expressway down to Van Dyke Avenue, a thoroughfare that ended in Indian Village.

Taking the down ramp from campus on the Expressway, she failed to see the heavy gas tanker truck, pulling a trailer "pup" behind, lumbering along at an even speed on the inside slow lane.

Driving the MG from the right-hand side, her view was blocked by the grass bank that sloped down to the Expressway to her left.

The gas truck hooked her car front with its high bumper, dragging it into the concrete wall, crushing it into a wedge.

Julie died instantly, her head and chest crushed.

The truck driver worked the brakes to stop, worrying the shooting sparks might ignite a fire, slowing the heavy vehicle in stages

Howard stopped at the Campus Bar. It was nearly empty, only an elderly couple, neighborhood regular customers, he recognized from when he lived nearby. They were friends with the old, night bartender.

After a second draft beer, Howard decided to head for home. He did not like sitting alone, listening to the senior citizen conversation about prescription drugs.

On the Expressway, Howard saw the accident as he drove, following the other cars around the line of police flares burning, but he did not see Julie's MG pinned against the wall on the opposite side of the truck.

An ambulance siren sounded behind him, and when Howard looked in the rearview mirror, he saw the orange flashing lights, when the traffic in front of his car moved, he drove ahead, following.

~~~

Sipping coffee from a paper cup the next morning, Howard walked slowly to his desk in the newspaper office. He began leafing through the pile of notes from the switchboard operator; people who wanted return calls.

Sitting back in his chair, he saw the folded *Detroit Free Press* sitting on his IN box. It was folded so the headline showed: GROSSE POINTE WOMAN KILLED IN TRUCK CRASH.

Missus Warren, knowing Howard covered the Grosse Pointe's for his news beat, must have put the *Free Press* in the box so he would be certain to see it. She must have put it there before she went out this morning.

Howard read: Ms. Julie Picard, 22, a Grosse Pointe Farms native, was killed when her sports car was struck by a gas tanker truck as she descended the Woodward ramp to the Expressway at 11:56 PM last night.

Howard dropped the cup, splashing coffee on the floor.

"Son of a bitch," Howard said slowly. "It can't be—son of a bitch. No."

He continued reading, coming to the line, "police were uncertain if alcohol played as a factor in the fatal crash, and stated an autopsy on the body later this week will make that determination."

Howard leaned back in his chair, covering his face with his hand.

"Poor Julie," he said quietly. "What a loss—that beautiful eagerness gone. It's not fair. Damn." He picked up the paper cup and threw it into the wastebasket. "Her firm body," he whispered, "what a loss—is hard to understand. Gone."

As he thought about the tragedy, he slowly began to realize his part, his involvement, his being with Julie at the Gypsy bar hours before the crash.

How would his being out with her look to people, he wondered. Then he felt a pang of fear, thinking how the police investigators would react. He was involved and he might be accused of something—a complicity in her death. He could be facing criminal charges.

Howard's first reaction was to run, Canada maybe. But he could be traced there, he realized, besides, it would look like he was guilty if he ran—disappeared.

The best plan was to stay, he decided. But he could not decide what to do next. He thought of going to the police, tell them about being with Julie hours before the crash. But then, and awareness to stay put and do nothing until the events unfolded, came to him.

Missus Warren walked into the newsroom, saying, "we see the story about the girl killed in the crash?"

"Yeah," Howard said watching her past, picking up the newspaper from his desk. "I was just thinking what I can write for our paper—about her."

"The usual," she said, slapping her notebook on her desk, then pulling off a raincoat, her full breasts out, rising, she worked her arms free. "What the family says, what her boyfriend says, and was she engaged to be married, that kind of thing."

Hanging her coat on a wall rack, she said, "and be sure to get a recent photo of her."

"Right," Howard said, lifting the newspaper to look at the headline again.

"You look pale," Missus Warren said, standing in front of Howard's desk; he had not seen her approach, and he flinched. "You all right? You look—sickly—your face is white."

"Naw," he said, setting the newspaper down on his desk, "I've got *money* problems." Shaking his head, trying to sound concerned, acting; after saying the first thing that came into his mind, not wanting to reveal his real cause for concern.

"Don't we *all* have money problems," she said smiling.

"I've only been here about a month," Howard said quietly. "I don't—know—how to ask the boss for—more money."

Missus Warren shook her head.

"You're in the wrong place, Howard," she said. "you're working on a weekly newspaper—and they don't pay much. You've got to go to a daily, a big newspaper, and land a full-time job. that's where the money is better."

"Yeah," he said, becoming absorbed in his diversion, that he had thrown out, that was becoming real. "I guess I knew that all the time."

"Lorraine," he said, "I've got to try—anyhow. I'm going to ask for more money."

He surprised himself by saying it.

"You're wasting your time, Howard."

"I know. I know," he said looking up at her, trying to avoid looking at her breasts in the loose sweater. "But I've got to do *something*. I'm working, and I'm not much better off than I was before."

"Welcome to the club," Missus Warren said, while walking back to her desk. "Everybody working here," she said sitting down, looking at him, "is under paid, kiddo."

"Yeah, yeah," Howard said.

"Have you talked with Karen Trombly? She carries a lot of weight," Missus Warren said. "Maybe the boss will listen to his lady managing editor, if she puts in a plug for you."

Before Howard could answer, Missus Warren's phone rang, and she picked it up and began talking.

Later that morning, when the newspaper owner, Calvin Beamer, came into the office and was settled at his desk, Howard walked in and asked him for a raise.

He refused.

"I'm giving notice," Howard said, feeling his face flush red. "In two weeks—I'm leaving."

He astounded himself; his reaction. He did not know where the force of the decision came from.

~~~

Investigating police talked with students in Howard and Julie Picard's history class. A girl, whose boyfriend was a member of the Grosse Pointe Sports Car Club, and who Julie, was eager, after talking it over with her boyfriend, that although she was not in the same history class, and was taking a different class, told police detectives she had seen Howard and Julie together in the cafeteria a few hours before her death in the crash.

Contacting Howard at home, the police asked him to make a statement at the Conners Avenue Precinct station near his home.

He entered the station the next day, crossing the bare floor, remembering that on his 16th birthday he came in here to get his first drivers license.

The Sgt. at the desk sent Howard to the Traffic Bureau office, where he met another sergeant named Doyle.

"Yeah," Howard said across the scarred old table, "it was after a night class we had together at Wayne State," watching the Sgt. writing. "I'd heard the Gypsy Band was playing down at the bar in River Rouge. I told Julie, and we went to see them play."

"What did you have to drink?" Doyle asked without looking up from his note writing.

"Both me and Julie had vodka and orange juice."

"How many vodkas?"

"Two," Howard said, folding his hands and watching the writing. "We only stayed a little more than an hour. I mean, we didn't make a night out of it."

"She got in her car, and drove from the bar?"

"No," Howard said quietly. "I drove. Her car was back at the campus parking lot. We left the bar, I drove her back to her car."

"She drove from the campus lot to the Expressway?"

"Right," Howard said nodding. "That was the last I saw of her, when she drove away."

"About what time was that?"

"Eleven-thirty," Howard said. "Around that time."

"Did she appear okay?"

"Yeah," Howard said quietly again, "she didn't act like a person who had too much to drink, or anything like that. I'm not sure, but I don't think she even finished her second Screwdriver. She was more interested in the Gypsy music—listening to it—then she was in drinking."

"All right," Sgt. Doyle said when he stopped his writing, then pushed back his heavy chair. "I'll have this type then you can sign it—and will be finished."

"Okay," Howard said, leaning back in the heavy oak chair.

Three weeks later, the autopsy on Julie's body revealed a low amount of alcohol, but it was determined by the Wayne County Coroner, that alcohol was not a cause of her fatal car crash.

The twenty-three year old gas truck driver was issued a ticket, accused of negligent homicide, and a court date was set by the Traffic Bureau for hearing in Circuit Court.

Howard did not know about the court date. He had been thinking of leaving Detroit—going to Florida.

~~~

Howard's father drove his car into Bernie's Friendly Marathon gas station for fill up, the same day his son went to make a statement to the police.

Carl Keck always came the Bernie's for gas; he and Bernie had served together in the Seabees during the war.

"How's the world treating you, Carl?" Bernie asked from his standup desk near the gas station door.

"Can't complain," Carl said. "Look at you, on your feet at the desk. Don't that bit of shrapnel in the hip give you hell?"

"Ah, sometimes. You know?"

"Why don't you go to the VA hospital and have them take it out?"

"My wife keeps asking me the same thing, Carl. When too busy right now, you know?" Bernie said wiping his hands in an oily rag. "Hey, I got something important to tell you."

"Shoot." Carl said.

"Wait a second. I'll tell the kid to pump your gas and we'll talk," Bernie said and pointed to the side room where he stored new tires. "Step in there."

In the tire room, Carl leaned against the workbench.

"What's this all about?" He asked Bernie when he came through the doorway.

"It's about your boy—Howard," Bernie said in a low voice, wiping his hands again.

"What about Howard?"

"That accident were the Grosse Pointe girl got killed—some people think—he was sort of the cause of the whole thing."

"Naw," Carl said standing up straight, "he was cleared by the cops, about the drinking and all that."

"Well," Bernie said lifting his, then setting it back of his head, "let me tell you what I heard at the VFW post. Okay?"

"Okay, shoot."

"This girl who was killed has got some guy who thinks Howard drinks too much. He was supposed to learn about your kid from some guys in Grosse Pointe who know about Howard. They checked him out when he was going with some other fancy Grosse Pointe girl."

"Dammit," Carl said rubbing the side of his face, "who is this 'guy'?"

"I heard he owns a big tool and die shop in Warren, someplace. He does a lot of military work—hush-hush stuff, making parts for the government. He hires a lot of former GIs, some who were Military Police, and they got friends who wound up getting jobs as cops. He knows a lot of cops."

"Did you hear all this, Bernie?"

"At the Euchre table," he said, "there was a game and the guys were talking."

"So why does this guy think Howard had something to do with that girls dying in the crash?"

The telephone out on the standup desk rang with the loud *ding-ding*.

"Just a second," Bernie said, "I got to answer the call. I'll be right back."

"Okay," Carl said and shrugged. "Okay."

Wimberley came back, he said, "the cops know that the father of that dead girl was a metallurgist. They got the report from some detective agency. The father worked in South America for a while, and they went to England for some reason—I guess to work there. The wife had suspicions, I guess, and hired a detective. A photograph of the father, walking, holding hands in London with a young ballerina—well, the mother divorced him."

"What has all that to do with Howard, Bernie?"

"That girl that was killed in the crash—" Bernie said patiently.

"Julie," Carl said.

"Okay, Julie," Bernie said trying to clean the oil off his index fingernail with the rag, "was from Grosse Pointe, and some guy Grosse Pointe had your kid checked out—and it came out he was heavy boozer."

"'Checked out'," Carl repeated.

"Investigated, Carl," Bernie said quietly, tucking the wipe rag into his back pocket, leaving part hanging out. "Some girl's—father I think it was—had his friends check out Howie's bad habits."

"Okay," Carl said, "I see—and this nosey guy—who lives in Grosse Pointe, too—he got wind of Howie's habits—and now he's spouting off that my son had part in the crash."

"Right," Bernie said, leaning against the tires, his arm extended. "The way I hear it, the guy is saying Howie had the girl drink too much at that bar, the night of the crash—he influenced her to drink too much. He was the fault she was killed."

"That's wrong," Carl said. "The cops *know* they didn't drink much that night."

"Right," Bernie said, "the reason I'm telling you all of this is—because—the tool and die guy has a lot of connections—with the cops. He's fixing—I hear—to get Howie in some kind of scrape with the law—so he gets arrested."

"Damn," Carl said, taking off his cap, running his hand over his white hair, "this is serious. You know what kind of scrape their cooking up?"

"Not yet, pal," Bernie said. "But don't say nothing about what I've spilled, Carl. They can hurt my business—tell my customers to go someplace else, if they find out what I've told you. Okay?"

"Okay, Bernie. And thanks for telling me."

"Sort of reminds me of the South Pacific—and that squabble," Bernie said. "All over again. I got a run. The gas kid put your fill up on the bill for the end of the month. He says your oil is about a pint low."

"Thanks again, Bernie."

Chapter 13

"Your father is very much upset you quit your job at the newspaper, Howard."

"Mom, it paid peanuts. I'll get another one—I just have to look around."

"I've never seen your father so upset," his mother said, leaning forward from her chair in the living room. She spoke soft, near whisper. "Not since your sister had that appendix-attack—and we rushed her to the hospital."

"I'm—sorry, mom," Howard said from where he sat on the couch opposite her, "but I want to go away—take a trip for a while. Maybe go to Florida. So—much—at happened lately. I need to take a break."

She leaned back in her stuffed chair, heavily. Howard knew he was interrupting her afternoon nap, that she always took, before beginning to cook supper and do the dishes later.

"It looks like you're running away, son," she said softly. "It looks like you're a *fuga-tive*," she said, mispronouncing the word.

"I know, mom. I know and I'm sorry it *looks* like that, but it's nothing like that—at all. Things are coming at me from every side right now. I'm just going to take a breather—for a while."

"And what about your classes, Howard? What are you going to do about college?"

"If I drop them by the end of the third week," he said rubbing the back of his neck, "I get a full refund. I'll use the money to finance my trip."

"Your father thinks you can't hold a job," his mother said, her head tilted to one side for emphasis. "He's disappointed you don't have a steady job—so you can settle down with a nice girl—like everybody else."

"Jee-ze," Howard said leaning forward, elbows on his knees, "he's never said anything like that to me."

"You're a big disappointment to him, son."

"I'm sorry he feels bad, honest, mom. But, right now, I've got to get away from things here. That's all."

"You said something like that too, Howard, when you rented the apartment down at the college—and moved out of the house."

"That was different, mother."

"It's *always* 'different' with you, lately, son."

"Ah," Howard said, wringing his hands, elbows still on his knees, "mom, I got a big favor to ask of you."

"What is it, Howard?"

"My car payments," he said slow. "I—have to ask you to make a few—while I'm on the road. Maybe a month or two. That's all. When I get a job—down there in Florida, I can start making them again—and I can pay you back for the ones you paid."

"How much are they?" She asked, looking out the front window into the bright of the afternoon sun, squinting.

"A little over forty bucks a month," Howard said, and pulled the payment book out of his shirt pocket, riffling the edges of the stubs for each payment.

"Give it to me," she said reaching for it.

"Otherwise, I'll lose my new car," he said handing over the pay book. "It'll give me time—while I look for a job."

"Don't tell your father," his mother whispered and slipped the pay book's into her thick recipe folder on the side table next to her chair. "But—I can only do it for a while."

"Oh, yeah, mom," Howard said, leaning back on the sofa, relieved. "It's just for a couple months—at most," he whispered.

"Go," his mother said, "I want to nap a bit."

Howard stood up grinning, then leaning down, kissed her cheek. "You're a pal," he said while straightening up.

"Remember," his mother said, tilting her head back, eyes closed, "it's only for a few payments."

"Right," he said, turning for the door to the kitchen, "thanks."

Two days after he had dropped his classes at the University, Howard was sitting at the dinner table, when his father came up from the basement laundry room.

After work, Howard's father always "washed up", which meant he had been nipping from the "magic bottle" before dinner. The bottle itself, was a Four Roses decanter, given to his father at Christmas years ago by a sales representative from a construction materials company.

Howard's mother called it the "magic bottle" after finding out every time the whiskey was low in the decanter, the next day it was *always* up. She would check the whiskey level when doing laundry, or cleaning up the rec room, and looked for the bottle on the workbench, next to the old cigar boxes filled with nuts and bolts. She knew Carl would buy a pint of whiskey and pour it into the decanter, and she wondered if he drank Four Roses because her first name was Rose.

"Hi dad," Howard said from his chair next to the stove. "Everything okay at work?"

"Ah-h," his father said, pulling out his chair, sitting down slowly, "they're talking in the yard—about going on strike again. They want more money."

"Will that affect you, Carl?" Howard's mother asked, stopping from mixing flour in the frying pan, making gravy.

"Naw, don't worry, mother, my job is classified up with the supervisory staff. You don't have to worry."

Howard noticed his father's face was flush-red, and he figured that was from drinking the Four Roses too quick.

"Strikes never do any good," Howard's mother said, carrying a platter of Swiss steaks to the table and setting it down. "And it's hard on the families."

"Where's Kathy?" Carl asked looking up at his wife. "Isn't she going to have dinner?"

"It's Wednesday, father. She's over at Jenny's for dinner. The mother drives them to dancing class."

"Oh, yeah, dancing class," Carl said quietly well spooning mashed potatoes onto his plate. "Why doesn't she take up bookkeeping—or something practical? Dancing class."

"Now—father—don't start," the mother sitting down in her chair near the stove.

When Howard lifted the steak from the platter, he said, "I'm heading for Florida—tomorrow, dad. I should be down in Miami in a couple days—it's only about fifteen-hundred miles."

"Be careful on the road, Howard," his mother said, spooning peas and carrots on her plate. "And when you get tired driving—stop and take a rest."

"Sure, mom," Howard said and put the stake on this fork into his mouth.

"You got your mind made up?" Howard's father said in an even tone of disapproval. "That's what you want to do—go to Miami?"

Howard nodded. "Yeah, I've got a few leads for a job down there," he said line. "And with the Michigan winter coming now—it would be like a vacation."

"Vacation from what?" His father asked, spooning peas and carrots from the bowl. "Why can't you look for a job around Detroit—we can help you here—if you get in a jam."

Howard shook his head.

"I'll be all right," he said, cutting the steak on his plate. "If things—don't work out—I can always come back here—and look for work. Besides, I sort of just want to go—someplace. Florida is as good as any for a trip."

His mother looked at him and said, "are you going to Miami because you broke up with that Grosse Pointe girl? Does that have anything to do with you going Florida?"

"Naw," Howard said, swallowing twice, "it's just that I don't have to see her—every day—and have the freedom—is about all Marian has to do with it."

"Well, you're old enough to make your own decisions," his father said in a weary tone. "If you need help, let us know."

"Thanks, dad."

Howard could not help feeling his father seemed relieved somehow, that he was going away. It was an odd feeling Howard had, when his father did not react the way Howard thought he would about Florida. It was as if Howard had solved some problem for his father—who was grateful.

"I hope you find your way, son," his mother said, "down there in Florida."

"You never know, mother."

"I hope that's what you're looking for, son," his mother said reaching for the bowl of mashed potatoes.

"It's not dangerous—or anything, mom," Howard said, cutting his Swiss steak and pieces, slowly. "Like I was going back in the Army—something like that."

"Were all done with that," his father said quietly, looking across the table at him, as if saying the Army was hard for mother to accept.

"I'll write—as soon as I get situated down there with a permanent place to live," Howard said, nodding.

"Phone us if you get in a jam," his father pointed his fork at him.

"I sure will," Howard said, nodding.

At six the next morning, Howard climbed out of bed and went downstairs to the laundry room to use his father shower. He flipped his pajamas into the laundry basket.

Excited about starting for Florida, he pulled on a pair of clean Chino pants, then realized he forgot to bring down the belt from his room. When he saw an old belt of his father's hanging on the back of the pine door, he took it off the peg, and seeing the crack going across leather to the fourth hole, grinned, because it had broke for his father.

He slid the belt into loops, despite seeing more cracks, and grinned again, when the end stuck out a foot too long. He tucked the extra length into loops at the side of the pants.

He planned to change the belt after he had cereal and some coffee upstairs.

~~~

Driving self, Howard noticed the trees were still green, they turned off the car heater. He grinned when he thought of everything turning brown in the October chill up at home.

On the afternoon of the second day of driving he was in the city limits of Miami, and began looking for a cheap hotel.

He found the Palm Tree Hotel in a rundown part of the city, but it was within walking distance to Flagler Avenue, so he decided to stay here. You could walk around town, learning Miami, and keep his car parked.

The hotel room rates were low, and the first morning he came down the lobby to drop his key at the manager's desk, he saw four women.

As he walked to the desk, Howard heard one woman say to the one sitting next to her, "he says he's a football player from the college, this guy last night, and all he did was piddle-piddle. Finally, I says, 'If you ain't gonna do anything, your time is up. We're done.'"

Howard looked at the woman, smiling; she wore black framed glasses and a black wig. She was talking to a woman who had a full-rounded body, like in a masterpiece painting.

Still smiling, Howard dropped off the key at the desk to the manager, a short man, who looked like a New York cab driver. And he talked like one in a raspy voice.

The kid who worked at the parking lot next door to the hotel, came through the front door as Howard was going out.   •

Overtime, Howard heard him asking, Gloria, the full-bodied woman, who had an eight-year-old daughter, for a free session upstairs for parking her car all day free. She looked at him, shaking her head, her legs pulled up, under her, on the lobby couch.

Howard liked walking, and usually went to Seventh Street in downtown Miami, stopping in a different bar each day. He saw Cuban stores along the street, and heard the rapid speaking Cubans on the sidewalk. They were everywhere.

He found the Winners Circle Bar near the US—1 The Hwy, that ran south to Key West, and back up north along the Atlantic sure, and started stopping at the bar regularly. The bar patrons were tourists, horse players, and local business owners.

It was on the television set at the Winner's Circle he saw the Russian ship loaded with missiles for Havana, as it turned and headed home. He had seen all the American Army trucks in the streets of Miami, but the next day, they were gone. He knew it was an alert of some kind, but the crisis had passed. Some of the soldiers had come to the bar for a beer in the evening, but in a day or so, they did not come any more.

It was a week later, Howard walking in the morning down 17th Street from the hotel, passing a church, he saw the crowd out front. Most of the men wore khaki pants and shirts, and were with their families, all speaking Cuban.

On television at the Winner's Circle he saw the news report that the prisoners from the Bay of Pigs invasion had been released from Cuban jails. President Kennedy had worked a deal with Castro's government for the release, trading medical supplies for the release.

The next morning, as Howard walked past the church, he saw a podium on a stage built directly across the street from the church, and a barrel-chested man speaking. The cloud clapped politely as the man spoken Cuban.

Howard thought it was probably some city official welcoming the released prisoners, and continued walking toward the bar.

Then, the following week, Howard saw on television, Pres. Kennedy himself, speaking to the same group of ex-prisoners at the Stadium where the Orange Bowl is played. The heavy-set man was standing at the president side during the ceremony. Howard figured him a CIA man.

Howard began to feel he was missing all these news events as a reporter. He should be reporting, not watching the news on television, and he began making the rounds of the papers for a job. He began at the top, *The Miami Herald*, and worked his way down to the last prominent newspapers. No one was hiring.

Sitting in a juice bar, reading down the list painted on the wall of what juice was good for what part of the human anatomy, like cranberry for the kidneys, and coconut and pineapple for the stomach Howard thought of Marian. Suddenly it hit.

He thought he would send her a postcard, then shook his head. It was hard on him, thinking of her up north. But he could not shake the image of her. He had let her go.

"The distance," he said the tall glass of piña colada, "instead of helping, is making it worse. I keep wondering what she's doing now, up north, there in Grosse Pointe. Damn."

When he lifted the glass, he saw the juice machine on the back cover of the juice stand. It was a stainless steel appliances size of a gallon jug, that looked like a miniature washing machine. It used centrifugal force to extract the juice of fruit and vegetables.

He remembered seeing the same machine at Marian's house, sitting on the counter in the kitchen. Her father, she said, used it for making juice from grapefruits. He drank a lot of grapefruit juice after his heart attack.

Setting the half empty glass of piña colada down, he said quietly, "this stuff isn't working. I need something stronger. Damn."

Instead of Kessler whiskey, the Winner's Circle Bar used Bellows as the bar whiskey, and he sat drinking shots with this beer.

He began sleeping later each day, he quit job hunting, and to feel better, he went back to the bar for more shots and beer. They usually made a night of it.

One afternoon, sitting on the edge of the creaking bed in the small room, waking up, he opened his wallet, checking his cash, and found he only had nine dollars left.

Thanksgiving Day was next week, he owed his parents a letter, so he would write, and figured he would ask for one hundred bucks on loan at the same time.

After writing a letter, he went outside the hotel looking for a mailbox, and passing the parking lot next to the hotel, saw his Chevy sitting in the sun. He felt guilty about neglecting the car, knowing it should be run, keeping the oil up in the engine and all that.

He climbed in the car, the seats blistering hot from the sun through the windshield, and drove, looking for a mailbox.

He mailed the letter, and for some reason, maybe enjoying being on the move again, drove over the causeway to Miami Beach, then north along the role of plush hotels, the *Eden Roc*, *Kennilworth*, and continued driving, passing the houseboats where the TV series "*Surfside Six*" was filmed.

In the town of Hallendale, he knew from the map he studied before coming to Florida, that Fort Lauderdale was just up the road. The Fort Lauderdale of the college kids spring break, the mecca in the sun for fun. The Fort Lauderdale of the movie, "Where The Boys Are," was made.

In the city of Fort Lauderdale, he drove along the beach, grinning, and turned on Las Olas Boulevard, looking at sites, and at the same time, looking for a place to turn around for the trip back to Miami.

That was when he spotted the long, white, three-story building with the giant letters: *Fort Lauderdale Press*.

"Damn," he said out loud, "if I wasn't so scruffy-looking, I'd go in and ask for a job."

He had not shaved in two days, and the Polo shirt he wore, had stains on the front.

Then, reasoning went away, and he was confronted by the face, he was here, and he should try for a job. He needed a job.

Parking in the newspaper lot, he walked into the lobby, and half-heartedly filled out an application for a reporting job at the employment office.

Two days later, returning from a walk downtown, stepping into the lobby of his hotel, the manager said from his desk, "There's a phone call for you."

"Me?" Howard said, groggy from drinking.

"Yeah. Fort Lauderdale Press called. They left the number for you to call back," the manager said, holding a yellow piece of paper out at Howard.

"Yikes," Howard said reaching for the note, "I might have a job."

"Good for you, pal," the manager said, turning away when the switchboard buzzed with a call.

Chapter 14

The letter from Marian was over four weeks old when Howard opened it.

Sitting in his apartment in Lauderdale-By-The-Sea, he read her letter first from the pack of mail his mother sent in a large envelope.

Howard, Dec. 3, Friday

I have broken off my engagement to Fred.

My parents are frantic. Meet me on the second floor cafe at J. L. Hudson's. Please.

We can talk.

Love, Marian

"Wow, he said out loud, excited at her words, that were a shock of exhilaration. He was going to see her again. At the same time, he had the feeling you get when you have won something.

"Oh, babe," he said, looking at her handwriting, "I wish I had been there. I'd give my right arm to have been there."

He thought of writing her a quick response letter, but on second thought, he hesitated, rationalizing that her parents might see the letter first, and read it, maybe destroy it.

A phone call to her house would be just as chancy; the parents would simply say she was not home.

"I've got to do *something*," he said shaking the letter, making the paper flutter. "I've got to reach her somehow."

Sitting back in the chair, looking up at the ceiling, he said, "I don't want to lose her—*again*. I can't flub this chance. Damn. I've—got—to call her. Now."

Scooping the change off the top of the dresser, he pulled on a rayon sport shirt decorated with loud yellow pineapples, and lurched out the door.

Across the street from his apartment, there was a motel with a switch board and pay telephones. When he entered the phone booth, he sat for a moment to catch his breath, then slowly dialed Marian's home number in Grosse Pointe.

There was no answer. He looked at his watch, listening for someone to pick up the receiver.

"It's six-thirty," he said quietly, "they should be having dinner," he said, continuing to look at the watch. "You think someone would be home—the end of the day. Dammit, why doesn't someone in that family answer the phone?"

After three more rings, Howard hung up the phone, and sat looking at it. "Maybe something happened," he said, "and they all went out somewhere. Well, whatever the reason, they're not home." he said standing up, opening the booth folding door.

Walking back across the street, Howard saw the small light-green Chevy, parked two buildings away from his apartment.

Last night, when he came home late from the Cottontail Club, Howard was sure he saw the head of someone sitting in that Chevy. When he turned the parking lot in front of his ground-floor room, and the headlights caught the car, there was no one.

Now, he saw a head again.

"It's someone all right," he said stepping up on the low porch in front of his door, "and it's obvious he's watching me come and go. But, why?"

Inside, closed the door, he said, quietly, while thinking, flipping a light switch on, "if I can get the car license number—I can ask someone that shares department to check the registration for a name and address."

Everyday, Howard's job as police beat reporter, had in making the rounds of the Sheriff department, city police, and the Florida Highway Patrol. Also the Everglades Port Authority office.

He was just starting to make friends in all the offices, friends he could rely to give him details, when a police story broke.

Sitting down in the stuffed chair in the front room of his apartment, he saw the Manila envelope on the low table in front of him, where he had dropped it. Upending it, looking through the pack of mail his mother sent him, a folded note fell out.

"Son,

Father has been asking where all the food money goes, so I have to stop making your car payments for you. I will send up the pay book in a separate envelope today.

Mother."

Howard smiled at having to ask his mother to be deceitful, and her doing it. She was a helping hand, and he appreciated it; more so, because she did it against her sense of what was right.

That night, Howard could not sleep, thinking of Marian. At work the next morning, he telephoned twice from his desk at the *Press* newsroom, but got no answer. He wanted to get in touch with her desperately, now that she was free again.

"Maybe the family all went up to the summer house," he said looking at the phone on his desk. "But why be *incommunicado* silence?"

He took a sheet of yellow copy paper and rolled it into his typewriter.

"I'll write her," he said, looking at the blank paper for a moment, "to cover why I haven't answered her note—until I can get her on the phone."

"Marian, Jan., 5

Just got your note re: break-up and then calling GP house, but get no answer. Great to hear you are "free" again and am desperate to talk. Miss you fierce, babe.

My home address: 1805 N. Ocean Blvd.,

Lauderdale-by-the-Sea, Florida or *Press* office phone 544-6060, ext. 439, work hours. Write or call. Longing, Howard."

After he typed her address on the large envelope with the *Press* logo printed on the corner, he folded the letter slowly, shaking his head.

"Wish I could climb in the envelope—be there when she opens it," he said.

Downstairs at the newspaper business office desk, he set the envelope in the tray to be stamped with outgoing mail for the day. The secretary had a postage meter for stamping the volume of newspaper letter sent. Back in his news desk, reading the morning edition for new stories that need more information, sipping coffee from a paper cup, he was interrupted by the assistant news editor stepping up to the desk.

"Keck, go see McGuire in his office," the editor said and turned.

"Right now?"

"Yeah. He's got an assignment for you."

"I'm going."

Howard picked up two pencils in a sheet of yellow copy paper, that the glass-enclosed office, knocked on the door.

"You cover Port Everglades, Keck, so this is your story. You got a Port Pass?" McGuire asked looking up, sitting at his desk.

"Yes," Howard said noticing McGuire's thinning blond hair on top of his narrow face.

"Our photographer took these pics," McGuire said and slid several large photos out of an envelope and spread them on his desk. "These two boats—ships—in the harbor—old World War I sub-chasers," he said pointing, "we think are being used for raids on Cuba."

"Wow," Howard said turning one photo, looking at the grey painted ship in the picture. "Huh, it looks like it's made out of wood."

"They *are* wood," McGuire said turning back the photo, "and this canvas cover back here," he said pointing with a thin finger, "we think is a machine gun mount. Then, over here in the deck, these two outboard motor boats, we think are used for close in raids, or maybe landing commandos."

"Small boats have twin outboards," Howard said, looking close the picture, "they look like twin fifty-horse motors," he said twisting his neck to look.

"Right," McGuire said stacking the photographs, sliding them back in the envelope. Then he took out a small white envelope, and slid on a single picture, "and our photographer took this pic also, a Chrysler Imperial—dark blue—parked near the boat dock. It's probably the boat Captain's car. We checked the license with Tallahassee motor vehicle registration for the address. It's on the back of the photo. Check it out."

Howard looked at the blue car, then turn the photo over.

"It's a Coral Gables address," he said, looking back at the photo, then at McGuire, thinking Coral Gables is a long way from Lauderdale.

"Right," McGuire said holding the white envelope of Howard. "I want you to drop whatever stories you're working on—and go down to Miami, and start checking. This could be a big story if we catch these guys raiding Cuba. Official Washington says no raids from American soil. If they're doing it, it's against the law. You understand? Kennedy will have a political stink on his hands."

Howard looked at McGuire, thinking what he heard from the office rumor mill, about McGuire being the top student in his journalism class up at Gainesville.

Another thing, Howard felt, was if the Cubans wanted to raid Castro's Cuba, why not let them. Leave them alone. But it came to him slowly, that for some reason, the newspaper wanted to give Kennedy a headache.

"Okay," Howard said to McGuire, "I'll get started right away."

"Whatever stories you got working in the pipeline for the police beat," McGuire said watching Howard collecting all the photos from his desk, "turn them over to Burrel to work on."

"Okay," Howard said waving the envelope in one hand, "and I was to cover the Navy League meeting tonight at the Pier Sixty-Six restaurant."

"Give that to Burrel, too."

Driving down the A-1A Highway toward Miami, Howard said out loud, "these jerks on this paper seem more interested in fighting President Kennedy than they do Castro. Let the Cubans fight communism down there. Leave them alone, for Pete's sake."

Lighting a cigarette with the car later, Howard said, "maybe they are Republicans—and they want to scuttle President Kennedy and his Democrats?"

"And that super-editor McGuire," Howard said as he drove past the Gulfstream Racetrack, "should know better, after all he was top man in his class up there in the home of the Gators—and their Gator-aid."

Howard had to smile, thinking of Gator-aid, the drink invented by a doctor. at the University of Florida. The mixture replaced vitamins and minerals the football player sweated out during practice in the hot sun. No one passed out anymore with Gator-aid.

"Maybe," Howard said using two fingers, throwing away his cigarette butt, "I could flub the story—tell them I couldn't find anything out." He thought a minute, "But if someone else starts tracking this boat story—they would know I lied. I better not."

All of a sudden, he said, "What the hell am I doing down here in Florida? Yeah," he shouted, gripping the steering wheel with both hands, "how was I supposed to know she would break up with that Fred character—the interloper?"

He smiled.

"I like it she's free—again," he said smiling. "Oh yeah," he shouted, "I like it. It makes me feel good."

He thought of quitting this newspaper, driving back up to Michigan. He would see Marian again, be with her again.

"Wow," he said, moving his head from side to side. "Wow."

Ahead, the City Limits sign for Miami appeared at the side of the road and he reached across the seat to the glove box to get the street map out. Driving, he found Coral Gables, then the street where the Captain's house would be located, and set the open map on the seat.

"I know Marian," he said grinning, driving. "I know how she thinks—how she reacts. And that's my secret weapon. She isn't the type to *kow-tow* to anybody; if you push, she's going to react, fight you. If things don't go the way she wants, you got a fight on your hands."

Grinning, looking for the street of the Captain's house, "She won't take orders from some guy," he said. "She'll go with some guy, for awhile, but if she isn't boss, it's all over. That's what happened—this engagement," he said, grinning. "I know—I know this," he said showing his teeth, "because we're both the same."

Reaching for his notebook, he found the house address, and began checking house numbers.

"I better hold on to this job," he said, "you know, at least until I find out—for sure—what's going on with Marian up there in Michigan."

He found the house with the address.

"I'll try phoning again tonight," he said parking at the curb in front of the house. "Maybe I'll make contact."

Stepping out of the car, he looked up, "Man, that sun is hot," he said walking toward the yellow stucco house with a small carport on the side.

All the windows were glass jealousies, all tilted shut.

Ringing the doorbell, he heard an echo inside.

"This place is empty," he said, beginning to check the windows for a place to look inside. At the back of the house, he could see into the kitchen.

"Huh," he said, cupping his hands around his eyes to block the sunlight, "I don't see any chairs or table even."

"Hello, there," a voice came from behind him. "Can I help you?"

"Yes," Howard said calmly, deliberate, "I'm looking for Mister Riva," as he turned around.

"I live over there," a bearded man in shorts and sandals said to Howard, pointing, "and I've never seen Mister Riva—or anybody—at this house."

Howard looked at the stringy beard the guy was pulling at near his mouth, and said, "I have this address for Riva," taking out a small notebook from his shirt pocket, "but this place—seems—unoccupied. That's strange."

"Are you from the police?" the man said, bending to scratch his bony knee.

"No, I'm a reporter from the Fort Lauderdale Press. I'm doing a story—I'm supposed to talk to Riva."

"Hey," the thin guy said, breaking into a wide smile, "I'm a writer, too. I freelance pieces of magazines, mostly."

"No kidding?" Howard said, feeling easier about being caught snooping. "Well, I'd appreciate any help—to find Mister Riva."

"Like I said before," the thin guy said, moving his head from side to side, "I've never seen *anybody* at this house."

"Are you sure?" Howard said looking at his notebook.

"Yeah," the thin man said, tugging at his bear slowly, "Some guys come every month-end—they wear suits and sunglasses—like cops. They look the place over, then go away. Some kid cuts the grass. That's about all I've seen going on—nobody living here."

"Okay," Howard said, nodding, sweating in the sun; putting the notebook back in his shirt pocket slowly.

"Hey," the thin man said looking over at his house, "you got time for a cold beer?—That sun's hot."

"Cold beer sounds good," Howard said, grinning.

Walking across the grass toward the house, the man held out his thin hand, "I'm Paul Redmond. What kind of story you working on for your paper?"

"I'm Howard Keck—I'm working on a story about—insurance—a big-money claim—for a suspicious fire," he said lying clumsily.

"Well," Redmond said, pulling open the glass patio door to the kitchen, "those guys who check the house every month—could be Feds."

"You mean the house is a dummy address," Howard said, taking the Budweiser can, handed him by Redmond holding open the refrigerator door, feeling the cold. "An accommodation address."

"Yeah," Redmond said popping the beer can top. "It could be part of the cover-story for somebody—doing government work, maybe."

Somebody began typing—somewhere in the house. Howard heard it before, he thought, but it had stopped for a while.

"That's my wife typing," Redmond said, before taking a drink of beer. "She's working on her Miami crime novel. C'mon."

Howard followed Redmond down the hall to a back bedroom.

When he pushed open the door, Redmond said, "Sylvia—this is Howard Keck—reporter for the Lauderdale Press," and waved his can at the two people introduced.

The woman in long black hair, stood up at her desk below the wall of shelves crammed with books. Her breasts showing through her t-shirt, she said, "Hello," looking at Howard looking at her breasts, "always nice to meet a fellow scribbler."

Instead of shaking hands, she smudged out the cigarette left burning in the ash tray.

"Didn't mean to intrude," Howard said, "while you're working," looking at her face, making eye contact.

"No bother," she said folding her arms under her breasts. "It happens all the time," she added sarcastically.

"We'll go out on the patio," Redmond said to her, "leave you alone to work."

"It's going slow today," Sylvia said sitting back down at her desk. "I *needed* a break—I haven't done much typing today."

"What are you writing?" Howard asked and took a sip of beer.

"A crime novel," she said. "It's my *genre*—I was a crime beat—police beat reporter for the Herald," she had not turned around as she spoke from the desk.

"I hear crime books sell the biggest," Howard said.

"Hope so," she said, looking at the page in the typewriter, rubbing her fingertips together.

"C'mon, Howard, we'll leave the new Agatha Christie to do her work." Redmond said, pointing with his beer can to the door.

There was more than professional jealousy here, Howard felt walking in the hallway; the marriage had died.

Outside on the patio, when Howard sat down in a canvas chair opposite Redmond, he heard the typing start.

"She's close to finishing her book," Redmond said quietly. "She's working like mad to finish it."

"It's a real grind," Howard said, "writing a whole book."

"You don't know the half of it," Redmond said looking into the glare of the sun outside patio. "I—was thinking about the house next door," he said, not looking at Howard, "and I have to ask—does that story you're working on for your paper—ah, does it involve Cuba?"

"I'm not sure," Howard said, taking a quick sip of beer, unsure what to say.

"Well," Redmond said turning to Howard, "if it has anything to do with Cuban exiles—and toppling the Castro regime—I might be able to help you."

"I see," Howard said, nodding, not wanting to tip his hand, "but I'm just, just beginning to—"

"That house over there," Redmond said, lifting his chin as if pointing with it, "has got to be a front for someone using the address."

The typing stopped for a moment, then began with a rapid burst of energy, suddenly.

"Yeah," Howard said holding his empty beer can, lifting it, draining the last morsel into his mouth, "yeah, it could be something like that."

"Your newspaper story," Redmond said quietly, "isn't about Cuban exiles—and the raids on Cuba, is it?"

At first, Howard thought of getting up and saying he had to get back the office. Then he reconsidered, thinking Redmond was on the level, and might have some information.

"You mean," Howard said, "since the Bay of Pigs—other raids have been going on?"

"All the time," Redmond said, and lifted his beer can to train what was left.

"But the federal government," Howard said slowly, "has outlawed raids in Cuba—especially from American soil. It's a law—official—foreign-policy."

Redmond leaned back in his chair, arms behind his head, his wife's rapid typing going on behind him.

"Most of the Cubans here in Miami—Little Havana—are giving money to groups—to make the raids over there."

"How—can you be so sure?" Howard asked.

"I have contacts," Redmond said lowering his arms, "with some of the groups who make the raids—I've even gone on some of the raids."

Howard looked at him for a moment, then said, "you're not just saying that?"

"I even *write* about it," Redmond said, pulling at the beard from his chin with two fingers. "South Florida is a hotbed of anti-Castro activity—land, sea and air."

"And the newspapers," Howard said, scratching his head behind his ear with a single finger, "don't know anything about all this? That's hard to believe."

"If they do," Redmond said slowly, "they're keeping quiet about it."

"Okay, give me your phone number," Howard said standing up, hearing another burst of rapid typing in the other room. "I'll check with my editors to see if they want to get the newspaper involved in this Cuba-raider thing. If I get the green light, I'll contact you."

Howard winced looking for somewhere to set the empty beer can, when Redmond said, as he stood up, "It's a big story—like I said—involving most of South Florida. You'll see."

Howard pulled out a small notebook from his shirt and held it and a pencil to Redmond, juggling the beer can in his hand.

"Write your phone number," he said to Redmond, "and I'll call you in a day or so. That's all I can promise."

"Fair enough," Redmond said, taking the pad, writing.

When Howard bent to set the empty can of the low table near the window, he saw magazine with Redmond's name emblazoned on the front cover. The feature article, titled, "The Barefoot Mailman" was over Redmond's name.

"Is that your article?" Howard asked.

"That was my last sale—two months ago," Redmond said handing the notebook back to Howard. "It's an article about a legendary mailman back when Florida was subtropical. Back at the turn-of-the-century. Florida was all swamp."

Howard looked at the big-time men's magazine, putting the notebook and pencil in his shirt pocket. He began to understand; that must be the reason Redmond's wife was angry—the two months since the last paycheck.

"Well," Howard said the Redmond, who pulled open the house front door, holding it open, "thanks for the beer and the—information."

"You bet," Redmond said, tugging at the side of his beard.

Inside his car was like an oven, the sun white-hot overhead, and to cut down the glare, Howard fumbled for his sunglasses through his sport coat on the seat. It was when he put on the glasses, looking in the car rearview mirror, he noticed the gray Ford parked down the street. Two men were sitting in the car.

Driving past Collins Avenue in Miami traffic, Howard did not see the car following anymore; he shrugged looking in the mirror.

"Wonder who they were?" He said out loud. "Cops maybe—who knows. Spooks, even. After all, this is Little Havana."

Chapter 15

Driving in Fort Lauderdale, Howard turned off the car radio, and said "let's take a look at these two spook-boats—see what they look like, first hand."

Turning off the A-1A Highway toward Port Everglades, he smiled, saying, "besides—it's too early to go back to the office. It's not quitting time yet."

At the port, he looked for the buildings he'd seen in the background of the boat photographs, to locate where they were docked.

When he came to the spot he recognized, he stopped the car, looking, and said, "where—are the boats? They're not here. Huh, they're gone."

He picked up the envelope from the car seat, and slid out the large photo, checking the buildings in the background.

"Yep," he said, "they should be right here. Ha."

In the newspaper parking lot, getting out of the car, Howard grinned, saying "what will be *Wunder Kind*—editor say, when he finds out his spook Navy has disappeared?"

On the steps up to the newsroom, he said, "maybe the paper will drop the boat story. We will scrap the whole shooting match. That would be hard to take—I'd be off the hook. I don't want to do the story anyhow—whose side is his newspaper on anyhow?"

After typing a three-page note, Howard rolled it into the platen on McGuire's typewriter, so he would see it first thing tomorrow morning. The note had all the details of what Howard found at the house in Coral Gables.

With the switchboard shut down for the day, Howard could not use the telephone at the newspaper. He would have to call Marian from the pay phone at the motel across from his apartment.

Stopping at the Lighthouse Restaurant for dinner, he ordered the shrimp and corn on the cob, yet Howard could barely eat half of the senior citizen platter. He was so excited about talking to Marian, he had the remainder of the meal put in a doggie bag.

In Lauderdale-by-the-Sea, he saw the grey car again, up the road from his apartment building. A man, a young guy, was sitting, holding up the newspapers of reading it.

"There's that bastard, still snooping," Howard said, parking his car. "Someday, I'm going to get the cops to asking for identification. But not today, I'm too busy."

In his apartment, Howard hung his sport coat in the closet, and took off her shirt and tie.

Pulling a dark blue polo shirt over his head, he said "time to try calling Marian—maybe I'll get lucky."

Sliding the coins from the ashtray on the dresser, where he'd been dropping them now, for his telephone fund, he went quickly to the door.

Crossing the street to the motel telephone, again he looked at the small head in the grey car.

"One of these days," he said, trying not to look in the direction of the car, "I'll make sure, buddy boy, you get what's coming to you."

"Hello?" Marian's voice came like music on the phone.

"It's Howard, babe," he said, smiling.

"Oh, honey," she said quietly, as if in relief, "it's so *good*—to hear you—again."

"I didn't get your note—for a month."

"It doesn't matter, honey. Oh, Howard, you can't imagine how glad I am you phoned—"

"I've tried calling you, babe—ever since I read your Hudson's note."

"We've been up at the summer house—all of us," she said softly. "Daddy had a second heart attack. We rushed him to the hospital in Lapeer, and they transferred him to Sparrow Hospital in Lansing—for a heart by-pass."

"Wow, babe, you've sure had a double dose of trouble—"

"It's mother, now," Marian said in a reverent voice, "she's not taking all the excitement—too well. Ardis and I came home to get some clothes and things to take back up. Honey, you're so lucky you caught me at home—"

"I'm lucky to—*know* you, babe."

"Oh-h, you're so sweet. That's *charming*," she whispered. "I wish things were different—so we could be together—now.

"Just talking to you, babe, gets me *all* excited." Howard choked. "I feel like jumping in my car and driving—back up to Michigan—right now."

"No no, honey. Things are hectic here—don't come up. We don't want to lose mother—she won't leave Daddy's side—I mean, we have to stay with her until Daddy's better. You—understand—don't you?"

"Is that Fred guy around?" Howard asked. "Is he holding your hand?"

"No, honey," she said, "Fred is not around at all. He wanted to pick up the pieces of our engagement—start over—he even began crying, but I told him no."

"You saw him, babe?"

"No. We talked—on the phone, honey."

"I've got to come up to Michigan, babe—I don't want to lose you—again. I couldn't take it."

"Howard, please don't come back—just yet, honey. It'll be a few weeks—I'm sure—before Daddy is okay. I'm so upset with him so sick—and now, mother, too. I got so much on my mind. Oh, so much has happened lately—since you went down to Florida. I don't need any more—I can barely handle what I've got now. Please. Stay in Florida a bit longer."

"My heart is pumping like mad, babe, just talking to you again," Howard said in an even tone. "*I* might need a by-pass—if I don't see you."

"Don't kid about something so serious, Howard. Please."

"Marian, I'm not kidding—you don't know how excited I am just to hear you—again. My heart is thumping like it's going to jump right out of my chest. Really."

"I'm sorry, Howard. The way things have worked out."

"Do you think, babe, your break with that Fred—had anything to do with your dad's heart attack?"

"Oh, God, Howard, I can't even *think* about that."

"Okay, okay, babe. I'll stay in Florida—like you ask."

"Just—wait a while, honey. A week, or two."

"Okay, babe. Can I phone you up at the summer house?"

After Marian gave Howard the phone number, she said, as if realizing all of a sudden, "do you think—all that has happened lately—is because of me?"

"Naw, it's nothing like that, babe. You just did—what you *had* to do. and sometimes, things, they take a turn for the worse. You're not to blame, babe. It's just life—things keep happening. Sometimes things turn against us. That's all. We don't have any control."

"I still feel—sort of—guilty, honey."

"That's normal, babe. But you can't blame yourself for *everything* that happens in people's lives. You're only *one* of the players."

"I'm not sure what to think, Howard. I've been so upset, I can hardly eat or sleep lately. Everything in my life is in turmoil—it seems. Everything is upside down."

"Have a rum and Coke," Howard said. "That's what I always do."

"Oh, you-u—charmer—you," she said with a smile in her voice. "You *always* know what to say."

"I mean it," Howard said quickly.

"I've got to run, honey. Ardis is calling me from upstairs."

"Okay, babe. I'll phone you in a day or so."

"How-ward, I miss you—so."

"In my case, babe, that's putting it mildly—I feel like I'm a volcano."

"Don't—Howard."

"Okay—then I'll just say good-bye for now."

"Bye, honey."

Hanging up the telephone in the booth, dropping the coins in the slots for the call, it came to Howard that he and Marian never said words like 'I love you'. But what they had between them, what they did for one another, was even stronger than the words. They did not need words.

When she bought the spatula for his apartment, when he bought a pair of expensive opera glasses at J. L. Hudson's for her twentieth birthday, then she spent months knitting a heavy wool cable sweater, an intricate, complicated pattern, for his birthday, and when one day it was raining, he was putting on his light raincoat in her kitchen at home, and she reached around him from behind, pinning his arms, holding him, resting her head against his neck, how they felt about one another came in a burst of pure emotion.

He sat smiling in the telephone booth, thinking, the memory of things like that, was a photograph on the mind that would last a lifetime. He could call up those memories, and he would get the same sensation; pleasure.

~~~

The next morning, Howard, a cup of Seven-Eleven coffee in his hand, was reaching for a copy of the morning edition from the stack on the copy editor's desk.

"Keck," he heard; looking up he saw McGuire in the doorway of his office. "Come in here a minute."

"You get my note?" Howard said following McGuire into the office.

"Yes," McGuire said sitting down at his cluttered desk. "Close the door."

Howard, standing, sipping coffee, pushed the door with his foot.

"Our boats are both down in Key West."

"I'll be darn," Howard said, nodding, grinning.

"Get down there—and talk to some of the crew—anybody—who will talk."

"You want me to go to Key West?" Howard asked, over the top of the cup he was sipping coffee from.

"Yes. Today. This is a very important story," McGuire said looking up. "Our—owner and boss—thinks it has—international—implications. He wants us to give the story top priority. And we always do what the publisher wants, right?"

"Okay," Howard said thoughtfully. "And what about my expenses?"

"Keep a list o your expenditures: motels, gasoline, food, and the paper will reimburse you."

"My note about all the Cuban clandestine stuff—"

"Yes," McGuire said picking up Howard's typed notes, "we've been hearing rumors about these raids for some time—and these anti-Castro groups—for some time."

"Oh, I see," Howard said, tilting his coffee cup to look inside for a second.

"You're doing okay," McGuire said holding up the note papers, "keep on it."

"Right," Howard said.

At his apartment in Lauderdale-By-The-Sea, Howard changed clothes, hanging up his sport jacket, putting on his Chino pants with his father's tattered belt, and a dark blue t-shirt. He took off his socks before he slid on the worn deck shoes.

The hot sun overhead, Howard passed Miami and started driving down the Keys, thinking the sun was intense like it was last summer on Marian's raft. No long shadows, he recalled.

"It's odd to think that down here," he said driving Highway US-1 as the road sign "Key Largo" appeared.

For an instant, he saw Marian in his imagination. She wore her light-blue shirt and fitted Bermuda shorts, and she stood on the porch of her summer house.

"Man," he said out loud, "I need a drink. I must be tired—or something."

He drove into the parking lot of a building the color and shape of a concrete bunker. A sign said this was the location for the filming of the movie, "Key Largo", with Edward G. Robinson and Humphrey Bogart.

"Ah, anything to get those tourist dollars," he said.

When he stepped out of his car, Howard felt his pants sliding down.

"What the hell?" he said pulling the Chinos up, standing close to the car. It was then he saw the crack in the belt leather at the buckle catch, the crack having pulled open from his movements.

"I got to get a new belt in Key West," he said pushing the foot-long excess of belt into the loops along his side, after re-buckling the belt. "I can use my expense account."

Walking up to the front of the building, showing a poster of Clair Trevor, the female lead in the "Largo" movie, Howard felt the *tingle* in his right thigh again. Two days now, the spot where he was shocked that Sunday morning getting out of bed, has been doing a slow burn.

"It's like somebody telling me—they got their hooks in me—or something," he said, walking into the lobby where a good part of the movie was filmed. "Maybe it's Marian's Daddy zapping me—somehow. Naw, he's sick. Well, maybe it's one of his henchmen—and he's using one of those dog-training electric shock gadgets."

Taking a seat at the bar in the rear of the building, where a picture window looked out over a large pond, it reminded Howard of the Harbor Bar in Detroit. He ordered a rum and Coke the way he and Marian did, when they were there.

Thinking of Marian and the Harbor Bar again, he wanted to head for Michigan—instead of Key West, but the only word that came out, was, "Damn."

Sipping his drink when it came, the more he thought about Daddy, the more Howard felt he was the one responsible for the taking Marian away. He forced her to date "other guys".

"Yeah," Howard said quietly, "he must of went to Central Casting and got that Fredrick character, who fit all the requirements for a suitable husband for Marian; the best that money can buy."

After taking a long drink, he felt calmer and a little cooler.

"You can't fault the old bastard, I guess," he said slowly, looking out at the pond for a moment. "He wanted her to marry somebody—dependable. Someone who will keep her in a Grosse Pointe comfortable life."

Howard sat thinking, inadvertently rattling the ice cubes in his glass, "and that leaves out the scribbler—me—who wanders all over the place. But—it didn't work—the thing backfired on Daddy. His daughter dropped that Fredrick bastard on his head. She broke-up with him—engagement and all."

The bartender appeared, thinking Howard had signaled for a refill when rattling the ice cubes. Howard gave him the glass without speaking.

Howard turned to look down the bar. At the far end, two young men sat with a model race boat sitting on the bar in front of them. One, a fat man with glasses, was tinkering with something with wires to the boat, which looked like it was made of red plastic.

The second man, who wore glasses also, sat, arms folded, leaning on the bar, watching intently what the fat man was doing. Both of them looked college age, dressed in t-shirts and shorts.

Just as the bartender came back with a fresh drink, and set it in front of Howard, the lobby doors opened and a man and woman came in quickly. They sat down two stools away from the boat, looking at it. They did not look like tourists.

The woman's face, Howard saw, was hard, as if she had seen a lot of bad things happen; the man had a fleshy face and wore his hair combed back like a Latin playboy. Howard shook his head as he picked up his rum and Coke.

"Let's try it," the fat man down the bar said. "I think we got it fixed."

The other man lifted the boat model off the bar. They both went out the twin doors that opened out onto the sand around the pond outside.

Two tourists, short, heavy people, came in the bar, and not only did the man and woman look alike in size, they both wore t-shirts with GARDEN STATE on the front. Howard smiled.

The man ordered banana daiquiri's for them, then said, "Let's go out there, Muriel. They got a radio-controlled boat like Ralph's."

Howard finished his drink, put a dollar on the bar and stood up. "Time to go—enough of this," he said quietly.

When he stopped at the small gas station and store building on Tavernier Key to use the bathroom, Howard felt obligated to buy something. He bought a pint of Bacardi Rum from the small store. He reached in the car and slid the flat bottle in the paper bag under the driver's seat.

The humidity was rising with the hot sun, and walking around the car, he rolled every window down, saying to himself, "the next car I buy is going to have air conditioning, for sure."

The plastic back window of the convertible was on a zipper, so he had to kneel on the back seat to pull the zipper tag around: that was when he found the cut in the fabric just behind the seat. Pushing open the cloth, he saw the spare tire gone.

"Damn," he said looking in the vacant trunk, "that was a brand new tire and rim." Shaking his head, he tried to think who would have taken the tire, and immediately thought of the parking lot kid, who always pestered Gloria at the motel. "Wouldn't put it past him," Howard said slow, dropping open the window. "I hope my insurance covers the tires."

Driving the long Seven-Mile-Bridge, wind gushing through the car and out the back window, he shouted out loud, "On the left, the Atlantic Ocean, and over here on the right, we have the Gulf of Mexico—hell, it all looks like the same water to me."

On the island of Key West, he turned off highway US-1 onto Duval Street, driving for the docks on the other side of the island.

He had been here before, two months prior to being drafted into the Army. A friend from high school was delivering a new Cadillac to Miami, driving it down for a friend of his dad, and Howard rode along. They took the old Cadillac back up to Detroit. Howard rode along because the trip was "free". They drove down to Key West, the hundred-fifty miles, a "sneak" trip, before turning the car in.

Driving Duval Street, Howard remembered the writer Hemingway's house on the left. And further down, on the right, Sloppy Joe's Bar. Both places looked pretty much the same.

On Green Street where it met the harbor, Howard spotted the two raider boats he was looking for. They were docked side-by-side at the dock. He parked his car at the curb.

It was supper time, and Howard could smell onions frying, as he walked slowly toward the boats.

The closest boat had the name "Prospero" painted on the stern, the other was named "Caliban".

As Howard walked closer, a man appeared on the stern just across from him.

"What flag is that?" Howard shouted from the dock.

"Honduras," the man shouted back.

"You the Captain—of the ship?"

"No," the man said, laughing, then lighted the stump of a cigar in his mouth.

"Where is the Captain?" Howard asked stepping to the edge of the dock near the stern rope.

The man shrugged, then rested both hands on the railing.

"When he comes—we go out," he said.

"Are you from Honduras?" Howard asked.

"No," the man said, smiling widely. "Columbian."

"What is the Captain's name?"

"Martinez," taking the cigar out of his mouth and looking at it for a moment.

"What—does this boat do?" Howard asked, spreading his hands wide.

"Scientificos," the man answered, then began puffing on the cigar. "For the fish—you know."

"Does this boat ever go to Cuba?"

"If the water is—unruly. Sometimes."

"Is this ship an old sub-chaser? It looks like that kind of boat," Howard asked, his hands on his hips.

"Are you a police man?" the man asked leaning forward on the rail with boat hands. "You talk like the police."

"No, I'm a reporter," Howard said, shading his eyes from the sun in the west, getting lower in front of him. "I work for a newspaper in Fort Lauderdale."

"I thought you were police—you ask the questions like the police."

"Yes," Howard said smiling, "I know that—but we even ask questions of the police, they don't like it either." Pointing, he said, "Can I ask what's under the canvas—up front there?"

"Scientifico," the man said calmly.

"I see," Howard said, then paused before he asked, "Can I step on board—look around a minute?"

"Nobody on board," the man said gripping the rail tight. "Much scientificos on board. Equipments cost much money. Nobody comes on board."

Howard knew the answer before he asked the question, but asked anyway.

"When with the Captain—Martinez—come again?"

The man shrugged, then took the cigar stub from his mouth and flicked off the ash.

"Okay," Howard said, shading his eyes from the sun, "thanks for talking to me."

The man nodded, again holding the rail.

"Nada," he said quietly.

Walking to his car, Howard said, "Yeah, 'nada'—nothing. I drove down here for 'nada'. I'll call McGuire tomorrow morning and tell him I haven't found out anything new."

Chapter 16

Knowing he should be out looking for a motel, Howard sat in Sloppy Joe's Bar slowly drinking a rum and Coke. He was sitting where the bar curved, making a loop, so that he sat facing a young Negro, dressed in a maroon shirt that looked like silk, who kept buying vodka and orange juice for an old Negro man in a long overcoat buttoned up to the neck.

Howard wondered if the old man was the father of the young Negro, or maybe the old man had suffered some great calamity, or had some fatal disease like cancer, and the young man was trying to make up for it by buying him drinks. The old man tried leaving twice, but the young man stopped him each time, taking hold of his arm.

Everyone at the bar was watching the two, pretending at the same time, not to be looking at them. Howard caught the other bar customers sneaking a look at times.

Most of the customers were tourists, jamming the bar under a red white parachute that hung overhead from the ceiling, trapping a giant cloud of blue cigarette smoke. they would all be able to say they had been to famous Sloppy Joe's in Key West. When Howard looked up at the parachute, from time to time, he kept wondering what the parachute motif had to do with Sloppy Joe and Key West.

After ordering a third rum and Coke, Howard, looking for the men's room, stood up, and caught the young Negro watching him a moment.

On the wall near the lavatory door, Howard saw the large photo of Ernest Hemingway, and read the notation under it, that said the author had frequented Sloppy Joe's Bar, while writing his novel, *"To Have and Have Not"* in the 1930's.

When Howard stepped back, turning to the bathroom door, again, he caught the young Negro looking in his direction.

When Howard was standing, using the urinal, again he found the belt end hanging down and with his free hand, pushed it back into the loops at his side.

Coming back out of the bar, Howard was sliding up on the stool, when he saw coming in the side-street door, the man and the hard-faced woman from Key Largo. He was sure it was them; the man had combed-back hair.

They were passing behind Howard to take seats down the bar, and Howard turned and said to them, "Didn't I see you people up in Key Largo this afternoon?"

"No," the man answered, putting his hands up to hold his sport jacket lapels, "we just got off our boat."

As the man stepped away, the woman asked, "are you in the Navy?"

Howard, feeling the effect of drinking a fourth of the pint of rum in the car, while he scribbled his notes after talking with the crewman on the boat, and with the two drinks he had downed here at the bar, he was feeling light-headed.

"Naw-w," he said grinning wide, turning around on the stool to face her, "I was in the Army."

"You weren't in the Army," she said, as if mocking.

"Yeah, I was," he said. "Here, I'll prove it," and he reached back for his wallet.

After he handed her his worn Certificate of Service, he sat wondering why he just did that.

She stood looking at the card, as if memorizing what was on it; name, rank, serial number, and dates of service.

Watching her face, Howard knew she had to be some kind of law enforcement. She had duped him into identifying himself.

"I believe you now," she said, and handed the card back. "I've got to go," she said, and walked down the bar and sat on the stool next to the sport jacket man.

As Howard sat sliding the card back into the plastic folder, his wallet wide-open, he saw the edges of a five-dollar bill and two singles showing. But he knew he had eighty dollars in twenties, hidden under the "secret flap", and put the wallet in his back pocket, feeling he had tricked the world.

A girl bartender, who had served Howard his first drink, and who had large gray eyes that Howard had teased her about, was filling a plastic bucket with ice cubes near him.

"Storm warnings," she said to Howard, who was looking again at her eyes. "Storm warnings," she said again and moved away.

The young Negro in the maroon shirt, who had been away, came back to his stool and lifted his drink.

Howard was beginning to tire. It was after eleven; he had a long day, the drive down the Keys catching up with him, fatigue setting in.

He finished his drink, and when he set the glass on the bar, and stood up from the stool, the girl barkeeper came down the bar and quietly said, "Go out the side door, and—keep going."

Howard was too drunk to look at her, but did walk out the side door of the bar. He walked down the sidewalk next to the wall of the bar, along the string of cars parked at the curb.

When he found his Chevy, Howard stood, putting the key in the door lock, but dropped the ring of keys. Then he could not see where they fell, and began looking under the side of the car.

"Hey, you," someone shouted from the corner up at Duval Street, and was coming down the side street toward Howard.

"You talking—to me?" Howard said, kneeling, patting the pavement with his hand under the car, searching for the ring of keys.

It was dark here on the side street, but as the man came closer, Howard could see the Negro had big shoulders, like a weight lifter, or a fullback. He was not young; forty, maybe.

"Gimme your money," the man said as he came up to Howard.

Howard stood up, wishing he was inside the car, safe.

"I'm broke," Howard said, "I drank up all I had."

"Gimme your money," the Negro said again, and Howard heard a *clunk* against his car fender. Howard saw the metal of the 'brass knuckles' in the darkness as the fullback slid them on his hand.

"I drank up all I had," Howard said, dragging his foot under the car for the keys. "I don't have—" he began to say, but stopped when the young Negro from the bar came up.

"You got trouble, Bobby?" he said to the fullback.

"Says he's tapped out. Broke."

"Let me look at your wallet," the maroon shirt said.

"Drop dead," Howard said.

When the maroon shirted man reached for the wallet in his back pocket, Howard pushed him away, hard.

The fullback swung hitting Howard above the left eye. For a second, everything went blank for Howard, and falling, he grabbed forward, his fingers catching the maroon shirt, tearing down the pocket making a narrow rip.

"That's a seventy-dollar shirt—you bastard," the young Negro shouted. He pulled the pocket of Howard's t-shirt, and half of the shirt ripped away from the shoulder.

Howard grabbed the throat of the Negro man; he could not see, the blood running down his face from the cut made by the brass knuckles. Then, gaining his balance, Howard threw all his weight to the left in a thrust, and both he and the young Negro man fell to the ground.

Howard sat up, squeezing the Negro's throat, when he felt a sharp blow, again over the left eye, but this time saw a bright flash of light.

"Stop. Stop it," a thin voice shouted; a woman. "Don't hit him again." When Howard looked up, using his right eye, closing the left, he saw a blackjack in the hand of the fullback guy.

Then he saw the two men with the woman in the street, and in the background, heard a siren, but could not tell if it was the police or an ambulance. He felt relief.

When the two men pulled Howard off the young Negro; the fullback was gone.

When Howard sat up on the curb, holding his ripped t-shirt against the bleeding eye, for some reason he thought of the brass knuckles and blackjack—and recalled they were both new, as if just out of the package. It was as if someone had just provided these weapons for these thieves.

"What did you hit him with?" Howard heard someone ask the maroon shirt.

"With my fist," the young Negro said.

Howard, looking with his good eye, saw a man in a dark brown suit, standing above him; the crowd behind, the ambulance backing up with flashing lights.

"Are you in the Navy?" the suit man asked.

"No," Howard said, "I was in the infantry," and as he said it, realized he was talking to some sort of plainclothes cop.

"Let me see some identification," the suit man said, and Howard reached and pulled out his wallet, still sitting on the curb, handing it to the man.

"Okay, man," the medic said looking at Howard's head wound. "You'll be okay now. We'll fix you up."

Howard felt him press a wad of gauze on the cut.

"Is it bad?" Howard asked.

"C'mon, man, get in the back of the ambulance," the medic, a fat man, said. "We'll take you to a doctor."

Howard, laying in the back of the speeding ambulance, siren wailing, "Where are we going? What hospital?"

"Stock Island," the medic said.

"Never heard of it," Howard said.

At the hospital, the doctor was stitching the wound closed, Howard laying on the gurney under bright lights, when the nurse said, "he just reeks of alcohol." Then to the doctor, "can you smell it?"

"Rum," Howard said, feeling the doctor pulling the stitch tight. He lay, keeping his eyes closed.

A man came and said to the doctor, "the guy who hit him says he did it because he was walking around in the bar—with his dildo hanging out. I got to get this guy's side of the story—for the police report."

"Go ahead," the doctor said, "he's conscious. Drunk, but conscious."

"I don't want to make a police report," Howard said, keeping his eye shut. "Forget it."

There was a pause.

The doctor said slowly, "write the same thing the other man said—and give it to the police."

When Howard sat up after the doctor was done, a nurse came and pressed his wallet into his hand. He checked and found his eighty dollars under the hidden flap.

Behind him, Howard heard the nurse say to the doctor, "he's a reporter—from Fort Lauderdale."

The police report man came back, carrying a press camera. "Lay down," he said, "I got to take a picture. Take your pants down."

"Are you kidding?" Howard said.

"Just lay back and pull your pants down—your shorts too," and when Howard lowered his pants, the man pulled down the shorts.

"No way," the man said as the flashbulb went off. "He don't have no foot-long schlong."

Another man came, and said, "take a shot of that belt hanging down." Then to Howard, "Hold that belt out for a picture."

Howard held the foot of the belt out, and the second man said, "turn it over, so the light side shows. that's it—snap a picture of that."

When the photographer was done, and Howard was pulling up his pants, the doctor came back.

"You're all right," he said, "but you'll have a king-size headache in the morning. Don't do anything strenuous for a few days. I'll give you a prescription—for the headache."

Howard took a taxi back to his car, and when he found the ring of keys under the rear tire, climbed into the back seat. Taking a t-shirt from his athletic bag, he pulled it on, then lay over on the seat and went to sleep.

The bright sun woke him the next morning. It was just after seven he saw looking at his watch, then sitting up, arms resting on the front car seats, looking in the rear-view mirror, he looked at the eye.

"Wow, what a shiner," he said touching the blackness under the left eye. Touching the stitched cut, it was tender, but it did not hurt.

"Man," he said sticking out his tongue to the mirror, to look at it, "have I got a hangover. I need a drink."

He remembered the pint of rum under the seat, and he climbed out of the car, and sitting in the driver's seat, reached under for the bottle. After a long drink, he took a short one, and put the pint back under the seat.

"I need a coffee," he said getting out of the car, locking it. "Maybe some eggs, too."

Walking Green Street near the harbor, he saw both of the raider boats missing.

"They're gone," he said checking around the harbor to see if they had just been moved. "Yeah, both of them—they sneaked away in the night. McGuire is going to flip, when I tell him."

Standing with his hands in his pockets, looking across at the rows of shrimp boats tied up at the docks, he said, "Well, I got about an hour before McGuire will be at his desk—"

When he turned around and started walking up Green Street, he saw the sign, ÉLECTRIC KITCHEN", in the front yard of a wooden house painted a dusty blue.

"Don't know what that name means," he said, "but, maybe I can get some breakfast there."

Opening the picket fence gate, he crossed the yard, and when he opened the door, he found people sitting at tables around the house's former living room. He sat down at the table near the door.

A heavy woman came out of the kitchen with a coffee pot and two cups.

"Morning," she said looking at his black eye, "you look like you could use a coffee."

"Yeah," Howard said grinning up at her, "I was looking for those science boats over in the harbor—but they disappeared."

"They're an odd bunch," she said pouring coffee. "They come and go at all hours of the day and night. There's something funny about that outfit."

"Yesterday," Howard said, "they were here—in the evening—"

"They're a bunch of foreigners, I think," the woman said holding the coffee pot out at a distance, "and I don't know what they do—but I got a sneaking feeling it ain't good. You, know?"

Howard lifted his coffee cup.

"Well, I can't wait around until they show up," he said.

"That's quite a shiner you got, sonny," she said grinning.

"Yeah," Howard said quietly, "her husband came home."

"Some people never learn," she said catching that he did not want to talk about it. "What would you like for breakfast?"

"Ham and eggs," Howard said and sipped coffee.

"I'll give you some grits, too," the woman said stepping away, pouring coffee for the other customers at the tables.

After breakfast, Howard telephone McGuire, and asked, "You want me to stick around and see if the boats return?"

"No-o," McGuire shot back, "We'll just wait—see where they show up. Come back to Lauderdale and write up what you got so far—and maybe we'll have to take a different tack."

"Right," Howard said. "I'll head back to Lauderdale today." He did not mention the robbery and fight.

After filling the car gas tank, Howard was driving out of the station, and saw standing in the driveway, a thin, bald man, a suitcase at his feet, holding a white shirt on a hanger. He stood, holding out his thumb for a ride.

Howard stopped the car next to him.

"I'm going as far as Lauderdale," Howard said through the open window. "How far you going?"

"Miami," the man said looking in the window.

"You got a driver's license," Howard asked. "Can you drive a car?"

"Yes," the thin man said, looking at Howard's black eye.

"Put your stuff on the back seat, and take the wheel," Howard said. "You do the driving."

"Okay," the thin man said, opening the car door.

Howard slid over to the passenger seat in front, and reached for the rum pint in the bag under the seat. He put it under where he was sitting.

"I'm going up to Miami to get married," the skinny man said, adjusting the seat forward to fit his small frame.

Nodding, Howard did not believe him. Lately, he had a hard time believing *anything* people said.

"What kind of work you do?" Howard asked him.

"I'm a cook—I'm working at the La Concha hotel."

If a man was working, he could afford a bus ticket up to Miami, Howard thought. if he did not have much money, how could he get married and support a wife?

"I was crewing on a forty-foot sloop," Howard said, "and the boom swung—hit me in the noggin. I saw stars for a while."

"Your eye is all black," the tin man said looking forward, driving. "You look like you were in a fight."

Howard was going to say to the man he looked like an undertaker, but said, "I've got some rum—you want a snort?"

"No. I'm driving."

The man was beginning to perspire, Howard saw.

"I've got a ring for the wedding," the thin man said, and reaching in his shirt pocket, took it out, and held it up.

"Oh yea," Howard said, before sipping rum, rolling his eyes.

It was a cheap ring, the kind people buy to wear when they are not married: this man had a story so pat, that it was not believable.

After another drink of rum, Howard said, "I'm pretty tired. I'm going to sleep a little."

He slid the pint under his seat, folded his arms, and closed his eyes.

Later, the sun lower, the thin man said, "Miami is just ahead," loud enough to wake Howard.

"Already," Howard said sitting up, touching his cut eye slowly.

"I'll get out at Sixteenth Street."

"Right," Howard said looking, trying to figure what part of Miami he was in.

When the thin man stopped the car at the curb near a busy street corner, he said, "Thanks for the ride." Howard watched as the man took his suitcase from the back seat.

"Good luck, pal," Howard said, after the thin man slammed the car door, as Howard was sliding over behind the steering wheel. "You're going to need it."

After readjusting the car front seat, and driving off, he added, "You're not even a good liar." Then grinning, he said, "he didn't believe me, either."

Tilting his head to look in the rear-view mirror, Howard said, "I can't go into the office at the newspaper—looking like this. I'm going to ask McGuire for a couple of days off."

"If that skinny creep knows I was in a fight—so will the whole office. Damn," Howard said, taking another quick look at the cut eye in the mirror.

Chapter 17

At the *Fort Lauderdale Press* news room, Howard sat typing notes for his editor, McGuire, wearing sunglasses. The other editorial staff were gone for the day, only the printers were down in the press room running the morning edition.

When Howard finished typing details he had found in Key West about the two raider boats, he went into McGuire's office, rolled the two pages into McGuire's typewriter, then wrote a note in pencil, saying he was taking two days medical leave.

Tired from not getting enough sleep last night in Key West, he drank the last of the rum from the pint bottle as he was driving to his apartment.

"I'm going to need more rum," he said touching the stitches above his eye. "Tomorrow this cut will feel like it's on fire. I better get a fifth of rum."

Ahead, he saw in the dark, the lighted liquor store, the size of a supermarket, banner signs in the window announcing sales, and said, "Ah, they don't call it 'Fort *Liquor*dale for nothing".

He turned off highway US-1 into the parking lot beside the building wall, and climbed out of his car.

At the corner of the building, he stepped up to the front door, but had to stop abruptly. Someone was coming out.

"Ah, the *Fort Lauderdale Press*," Redmond said grinning. "Man, what happened to your eye? You look like you got hit with a baseball bat."

"Right," Howard said grinning, looking down at the bearded man, holding a six-pack of Lone Star beer.

The sign on the door behind him said the beer was on sale this week for ninety-nine cents.

"You can fill me in later about the eye," Redmond said, shifting the six-pack to his free hand, pulling Howard away from the door. "There's something on tonight—a fly over—Cuba. Interested?"

"Does it have to be tonight?" Howard asked. "I'm just getting back from Key West—"

"Yeah, your newspaper ran a picture of the two CIA boats this morning," Redmond said quietly. "The story said the boats had been docking at Port Everglades—making raids on Cuba." Looking in both directions off in the dark, he said, "There's a leaflet flight tonight—I can fix it for you to go. But, it's tonight—you understand?"

"Jeez," Howard said looking at the door, "I didn't get to read today's paper—"

"Before the Feds clamp down on South Florida, man, they are going to hustle a flight tonight. I can help you meet the pilot—involved."

"Okay, okay," Howard said grinning. Redmond was excited, pulling at the side of his beard, looking up at Howard, waiting for an answer. "I got to clean up—"

"You got till eleven," Redmond said. "Meet me at my house down in Coral Gables."

"What are you doing up here in Lauderdale?"

"I came to my sister's house in Lighthouse Point," Redmond. "I had to borrow some money—my wife took all the cash in the house—she had to run to New York and meet with her publisher—some problem with her book."

"Okay," Howard said, "I'll come to your house at eleven. I got some stuff to do, now," he said reaching for the door. "I hope—this flight—is worth the trouble."

"You won't be disappointed, man," Redmond said, and added before he stepped around the building corner, "Eleven."

Howard turning into the parking lot at his apartment, looked down the street for the watcher; but the small Chevy was not there.

"Someday I'm going to go over and yank him out of his car—pound him until he tells me who he's working for," Howard said parking, reaching for the bottle of Bacardi Rum.

After taking a shower, Howard had a rum and Coke, then went across the street and phoned Marian from the motel.

No one answered the phone at either number.

Sitting in the apartment, sipping another drink, he said, sitting back in the chair, "Ah, to hell with Redmond and his Cubans. I'm just going to sit here and get smashed." He sat quiet for a moment. "Dammit, why can't I get in touch with Marian? That hurts—more than the eye does. It's something ominous, her not answering. I can *feel* it in my bones. I know her father is sick, and all that, but that's only part of it. Okay, she's with Daddy. But that's not *all* of it. There's something else that's happened."

He drank what was left in the glass, and wiping his mouth said, "Maybe I should head up to Michigan—drop everything here—and just go."

Looking at the ceiling for a moment, he said, "If I sit here drinking rum, I'm going to go crazy, if I keep this up."

Setting the empty glass up on the desk next to his typewriter, he said quietly, "I got to stop thinking about her—reserve thinking—until I hear from her. Okay, I guess I'll go find Redmond and his Cuban friends—just to keep from going bonkers."

~ ~ ~

They were driving in Redmond's jeep that had one headlight.

"You're kind of corko," Redmond said, driving in the dark, looking forward. "I saw it when you came into the house. Well, I hope you don't fall out of the plane."

"Yeah," Howard said, "I called my girl at home—no answer. So I took an analgesic—rum and Coke—Cuba Libre."

"That's my wife's drink, too."

"Hey, what would happen—if we had to—well, crash-land in Cuba?"

"They'd lock us up and throw away the key. Uncle Sam couldn't help us in Cuba. You'd be eating fish heads and rice the rest of your life."

"Sounds like a strong argument," Howard said picking at the stitches, "to stay right here in Miami."

"Yeah, it does," Redmond said, turning a corner.

Howard could see the lights of the main part of the Miami airport off in the distance.

Redmond turned again, the Jeep's single head light caught the sign ahead: GOLD COAST CHARTER FLIGHTS.

A night light was on in the office, but Howard saw no one inside. Redmond parked, and turned off the Jeep light.

"There's the plane," Redmond said, "over on the right. It's a Beechcraft—not exactly the newest model—but reliable."

"Twin engines," Howard said quietly.

Another car approached in the dark, and Howard saw it was a Thunderbird, as he climbed out of the Jeep.

"Thought it might be cops," Redmond said.

"Took the words right out of my mouth," Howard said.

A man dressed in a tan jumpsuit came up to the Jeep, carrying two suitcases. A girl with black hair followed him.

"This is Raoul," Redmond said to Howard.

"Hi," Howard said looking at the girl; she was thin, and had full lips like Julie Picard.

"The plane is being watched," Raoul said quietly, "so try to act like tourists—flying to the Bahamas. I'll go in the office—file the flight plan."

"Where do we go?" Redmond asked.

"Go to the plane," Raoul said, handing Howard and Redmond each a suitcase. "There's an interior light switch on the left, just inside the door. I'll only be a minute."

Walking to the plane, Howard said, "Is his daughter coming with us?"

"That's his girl," Redmond said, "she's from Montserrat." Redmond added grinning, "She don't fly."

When the lights were put on in the plane, Howard saw eight seats, four on each side, each with a window. Bundles of papers were stacked on the seats and in the aisle way.

"Is there a bippy?" Howard asked.

"That door behind you," Redmond said sliding a bundle of paper off a seat to the floor, making room to sit.

When Raoul came into the plane, closing the door, he said, "You have to fasten the seat belt—until we get off the ground."

He went front of the cockpit.

"I hope we don't have any surprises on this trip," Howard said across the aisle to Redmond.

194

"Relax, man," Redmond said, "he flies to all these islands; he takes rich people out there every day. Buckle up, man."

"There is a lot of ocean out there," Howard said, touching his stitches, now beginning to itch; then buckled the seat belt.

When the engine started, the whole plane shook.

Looking out the windows plane taxied, Howard saw the rows of lights of the runway. The engines revved, then began the roar, and Howard was pushed back in the seat, the lights flashing by his windows plane sped down the runway, and he felt it lift off.

This sky was complete darkness, the only lights were those twinkling far below in Miami. Ahead, it was dark; Howard knew they were out over the ocean.

Suddenly, the plane lurched, dipping the right wing, turned, then leveled off again.

"We're headed south now," Redmond shouted above the engine noise. "You can drop the seat belt."

The only lights Howard could see now were in a string, and he shouted to Redmond "that must be the Keys down there."

Redmond nodded, then shouted, "now we go down close to the water," Redmond shouted across the aisle.

"How come?" Howard shouted back.

"Radar," Redmond shouted. "We confuse it."

"I hope Raoul don't hiccup," Howard shouted. "We'd go right in the drink."

"Yeah," Redmond shouted, grinning, "we're only two-hundred feet off the water."

Howard said, "Wow," to himself.

Redmond saw Howard's face sink, and shouted, "Don't think about it." Then Redmond pointed at the window, shouting, "That's Key West down there—we're ninety miles from Havana now."

"Hey," Howard shouted, "the lights on the wings just went out." He no more than spoke, when all the cabin lights went out. "Now what?" Howard shouted in the dark cabin.

"We don't want them to see us coming," Redmond shouted in the dark. "We're sneaky."

Looking out the window, Howard saw only the white streak of the phosphorescence—the light made by the waves.

He sat in the dark listening to the din of the engines running evenly, feeling the plane vibrating gently.

He was going to say something about Key West, but he forgot what it was. Instead, he shouted to Redmond, "Hope this plane—is well maintained."

"Don't worry," Redmond shouted back in the dark, "Raoul knows his stuff."

"How much does he get—for this trip?" Howard shouted.

"Twenty-five hundred," Redmond shouted. "He needs it—he's got four kids."

"What about Montserrat?"

"He's divorced."

"Hey, you two," Raoul called back from the cockpit. "Come up front. I want to talk to you."

Following Redmond, Howard climbed over the bundles of leaflets in the aisle way, moving toward the green lights of the dials on the instrument panel.

"Sit there, Howard," Redmond said. "The co-pilot seat."

When Howard sat down, he could see the orange flame of the engine exhaust just outside his window.

Looking forward, he saw a glow in the shape of a dome on the horizon.

"Is that Cuba?" he asked. "Up ahead there?"

"Havana," Raoul said. "We'll be over it in a few minutes."

"Wow," Howard said, "this is really something."

"Better than a rum and Coke," Redmond said slowly; he was standing between the two seats, hunched, looking through the windshield, holding to the back of the seats. "You give me the call," he said to Raoul, "when to pop the door—like last time."

"Yes," Raoul said, tapping a gauge on the dashboard with a finger, "and I want you two to be careful back there when the door is open."

"Right," Howard said.

"You bet," Redmond said nodding,

"Just to be sure," Raoul said to Redmond, "I want Howard to stay behind you—at all time. Away from the door."

"Understood," Redmond said.

"Right," Howard said on top of Redmond's 'understood'.

"And", Raoul said, "if you guy's write about this trip, don't use any specific names." he was looking forward, the lights getting brighter, spreading wider on the horizon.

"Right," Howard said.

"Okay," Raoul said, "get back by the door. I'll yell when to start tossing leaflets out. And be alert—until the door is closed again."

"You bet," Howard said, excited, climbing out of the seat to follow Redmond back over the bundles of leaflets. "I've got to tap a kidney," he said to Redmond when they were back by the door.

"Go quick, man," Redmond said. "You'll miss the whole show," he said calmly. "Press the panel light in the john—it's like a flashlight. But close the door first—so there's no light in the cabin."

When Howard was coming back out of the lavatory in the dark, he heard Raoul shout, "Okay, open the door—and start the leaflets."

"Right," Redmond shouted back, and turned the handle to unlock the door. When he had it partially open, he forced a cushion into the bottom, then hooked a bungee-cord on the handle and stretched it to hook the other end on the wall fire extinguisher.

When Howard heard the rushing wind and the full noise of the engine, he covered his ears.

Redmond began stuffing leaflets out the narrow opening, taking handfuls at a time.

Howard began sliding stacks of leaflets to where Redmond was working. They both moved rapidly.

The cabin was lighted now, from the lights below; they were directly over Havana.

Finally, Howard shouted, "There's only three bundles left to go," as he handed what he held to Redmond.

Redmond shouted back, "Too bad we don't have a bomb. that's the president's palace right below—where Castro lives."

Howard took a quick look, but could only see leaflets fluttering from his window in the light below.

"Next time," Howard shouted, and stepped up the aisle to get the last of the leaflets.

"We're done with the paper," Redmond shouted to Raoul after the last of the leaflets were out.

"Lock the door," Raoul shouted. "Good work. Relax."

Howard watched Redmond unhook the bungee, pull the cushion inside, drop it, and lock the door by pulling the safety arm down.

"Wow," Howard said grinning, sitting down on the arm of a seat, "my heart is going a mile a minute."

"Told you," Redmond said, "it would pump you up."

The cabin lights came on.

Howard saw a crumpled leaflet on the floor and picked it up.

"What does this say?" Howard asked Redmond. "I can't read Spanish—Cuban."

"It tells the people of Cuba," Redmond said putting the bungee cord in the overhead cabinet, "to resist Castro—that help is on the way. Stuff like that."

"Psychological warfare," Howard said.

"Yeah," Redmond said.

"Think I'll save this one for a souvenir."

"Put it in your pocket," Redmond said moving up the aisle. "Let's go up front."

Folding the leaflet and putting it in his pocket, while entering the cockpit up front, Howard saw only dark again out the windshield.

"We're going to set down on Grand Cayman," Raoul said looking at a unfolded map on a clipboard, "just long enough for fuel. You guys can have breakfast. Then we buzz to Jamaica—Kingston. From there we go to Great Niangua in the Bahamas."

"From the Bahamas," Redmond said to Howard, pointing at the map, "we hop back to Miami. Some trip, huh?"

"Yeah," Howard said, "I didn't even miss the sleep."

"Who needs sleep, man?" Redmond said. "We had the old adrenalin pumping."

"I might pick up a passenger, or two, in Kingston," Raoul said adjusting the knob on a gauge. Then looking out the side window, added, "We're coming up on Cayman. You guys go back to your seats and buckle up."

"Right," Redmond said, hitting Howard's arm. When they were in their seats, Redmond shouted, "I could sure use some coffee."

Howard looked at him from across the aisle, "I want to write a postcard," he shouted back above the noise, "and tell my girl I'm down here in Cayman—explain where I am—if she's been calling the newspaper."

Redmond nodded.

At Bridgetown, while Cayman officials were inspecting the airplane, and it was being refueled, Howard and Redmond went to the airport cafeteria.

Howard bought a post card with the photo of palm trees and a sandy beach and wrote:

"Marian,

No answer when I called GP and summer house. Will not be in news office until Monday on work hours. Am in SCUBA center of universe, Grand Cayman island.

Miss you fierce. Rum and Coke forever.

Howard"

When Howard finished writing, Redmond said, "You should get married to that girl."

Howard sat grinning, watching Redmond scoop his scrambled eggs onto a piece of toast, then pour catsup on the eggs, before setting the other toast on top.

"I'm sort of worried about her," Howard said, looking across the table as Redmond lifted the sandwich to his mouth, "I phoned her before we left—and got no answer."

Catsup dripped off the bottom of the sandwich, when Redmond bit into it.

"Maybe—," he said pausing to swallow, "is there another guy around?"

"Nothing to worry about," Howard said taking a forkful of eggs from his plate. "There was—but that's over," he said biting off the corner of his toast.

"Yeah, sure," Redmond said, "and you're not worried. Why else would you be writing that card, man?" Redmond said and bit into the sandwich.

199

"Okay," Howard said taking more eggs on his fork, "I'm worried. You're right."

Raoul came in the cafeteria door, and walked over to the table. He was eating a Milky Way candy bar.

"Ten minutes to take off," he said chewing, "and I've got medical passengers. That's the reason for the rush."

"That was a quick re-fueling," Redmond said looking at the corner of the sandwich left in his hand.

"I only took a hundred gallons," Raoul said. "The fuel is too expensive here—I'll wait to fill—up in Kingston."

"We're coming," Redmond said, "as soon as we pay the cashier."

Raoul turned, taking a bite out of the candy bar, as he walked back to the door.

"I got to get a stamp for my post card," Howard said.

"The cashier's desk has stamps," Redmond said, chewing.

The passengers were an elder Negro man and woman, the woman with a gauze bandage taped over her right eye. The couple sat up front, the seats behind the pilot.

After take-off, Howard leaned back in his seat while taking off the seat belt, turned his face away from the light of the window, and let the drone of the engine put him to sleep.

He was tired of worrying about Marian.

"Seat belt, man," Redmond said, shaking Howard's shoulder from across the aisle. "We're landing."

"Wow," Howard said fastening the seat belt, "I really conked out there for a minute."

"Your adrenalin is wearing off, man," Redmond said.

Raoul helped the elderly couple off the plane, and stood watching them walk to the small terminal door.

"She needs eyes surgery," he said to Redmond. "They came to see a specialist here in Kingston."

Howard looked across to the international terminal and saw the giant BOAC and PAN AM airplanes. He was here in front of the terminal marked CHARTER FLIGHTS CONCOURSE.

"Maybe I can sample some Jamaican rum," Howard said, automatically touching his eye cut. "I'm beginning to crumble."

"We'll find a bar," Redmond said, grinning.

"Don't be too long, Raoul said. "As soon as I get fuelled, I want to go."

"Right," Redmond said looking at Howard.

When they were walking toward the concourse, Howard said, "Wish there was some way to call my girl." Looking at his watch, "It's almost eleven. She'd be up now, it's morning at her house."

"In a few hours we'll be in Miami, man," Redmond said reaching to pull open the concourse door when they approached. "Why pay the price for an international phone call?"

"I suppose you're right," Howard said going through the door. He felt a strong wave of foreboding now.

Inside, they found the small bar with only five stools.

Howard sat drinking, feeling a sense of loss; the way you feel after losing your wallet.

"Whew," he said to Redmond, "Guess I'm getting drowsy, and the rum is just making it worse."

"You can sleep all the way back to Miami, man," Redmond said rattling the ice cubes in his glass. "Great Inagua is just a pit-stop for the hop across the Gulfstream."

"Then our night-adventure is over," Howard said, while touching his cut eye, feeling the dull ache it had turned into, and looked over at Redmond.

"Yep," Redmond said grinning, "back to the daily grind."

Chapter 18

Monday morning, getting ready for work, Howard shaved, then dabbed talcum powder on the dark under his left eye.

He had slept most of the day Sunday, telephoning Marian's houses at two hour intervals, but after five attempts, gave up when there was no answer.

At his newspaper desk, he shifted to the notes for phone messages, "nothing—there's no calls from Michigan at all," he said quietly. "Damn—something is *really* wrong."

While making the rounds of the Fort Lauderdale police station, and the Broward County Sheriff's Detective Bureau, he could not shake the sinking feeling that he had lost Marian.

It was after 10 o'clock in the morning, when he finished phoning into the newsroom, two stories about robberies, and the fatal crash report from the Florida Highway Patrol, from the press office in the county building, then headed back to the newspaper office.

"Man," he said to himself, "I feel like a zombie," as he rolled two sheets of paper, with the carbon between, in his typewriter. "Heh, "he said grinning, "and I probably look like one."

He typed, "Night Flight" for the slug line on top of the page first notes about the leaflet drop over Havana. He was writing these notes to give to McGuire for the ongoing investigation about the raids against Castro's Cuba.

When the assistant city editor came up to his desk, Howard looked up, leaning back from typing.

"McGuire wants you in his office after lunch," the assistant editor said flatly.

"Okay," Howard said, lighting the fresh cigarette off the burning stub of the one in his ash tray, then going back to typing.

It was twenty minutes after noon when he finished typing and looked up, separating the carbon copies from the original pages, and caught McGuire looking at him from the glassed-in office.

"Probably wants an account of what I've been doing the last few days," Howard said to himself, tapping the copy papers to make them even. "Wait till he reads this leaflet-drop yarn—it'll curl his socks."

As Howard walked through the door into the office, McGuire said, "Close the door."

Howard, reaching for the door and pushing it shut, caught McGuire moving a white envelope on his desk, then resting his elbow on top of it.

"I've got a whale of the story," Howard said sitting down in the chair in front of the desk, holding up the typed pages.

"It's about a leaflet drop from the anti-Castro bunch—from a plane that buzzed Havana—Saturday night. That's where I've been—"

"That's quite a mouse you got over that eye, "McGuire said.

"Oh, yeah," Howard said, touching the stitches. "It looks much worse than it is—"

"Keck, this is a family-owned newspaper," McGuire said slowly, as if searching for words, "and we serve the news to the families of Fort Lauderdale—our subscribers."

"Okay," Howard said, trying not to grin, thinking McGuire was kidding, "but this Cuba raid thing you assigned me—"

McGuire interrupted Howard, saying, "Lauderdale PD got a report from Key West PD about a fight you had down there—over a—moral—issue."

"Yeah," Howard said grinning, "the two of them wanted my money—that's about as *moral* it can get."

"Well," McGuire said, "Chief Lister says you've been around Lauderdale—drinking excessively."

"Yeah," Howard said grinning, "and sometimes it's off-duty cops I'm drinking with."

"This drinking," McGuire said moving the white envelope under his elbow, "can affect your work here—"

"How's that?" Howard said, holding up the flight notes. "Here's an account of a leaflet drop over Havana—a first-hand account from Saturday night. I flew with—"

"I should have known," McGuire said slowly, "you were living in that sleazy hotel—in a run-down part of Miami—when we called you for an interview for this job.

"We should have put two-and-two together," he said, glancing out to the newsroom beyond the glass.

"What about the hotel in Miami?" Howard asked.

"It's a residence for—derelicts," McGuire said in an even tone. "Drunks—and drug users."

"What cheap hotel isn't?" Howard asked.

"Like I said, Keck, this is a family newspaper. What happened down in Key West goes against the grain. You're indecent exposure of your privates in Sloppy Joe's Bar—and you're not being married—is all against our policy.

"I'm going to have to let you go."

"I didn't *expose* anything in Sloppy Joes—indecent or—otherwise."

"The police say different in their report."

"They got it wrong."

"Nevertheless, Keck, today you're no longer an employee at this newspaper," McGuire said looking down at the white envelope. "Do you need money?"

Howard stood up, "Hey," he said waving the notes, "I don't believe this. You're misinterpreting that police report—."

"Let's not drag this out," McGuire said opening his desk drawer, and after sliding the envelope in, closed it slowly. "Mister Doyle wants you to leave the newspaper—he doesn't want the paper's reputation—sullied."

"Doyle," Howard said rolling the copy paper sheets into a cone, "can go to hell—and take his newspaper with him.

"Tell him that—you messenger-boy."

Howard pulled open the door, and walking to his desk, tore up the notes of the leaflet flight and slammed them in his wastebasket.

From his desk he took his calendar, rolodex, notebooks, pencils, and his ashtray, and dropped them all into the waste basket.

He walked out of the building without speaking to any of the reporters, partly out of embarrassment, partly because of anger.

Crossing the parking lot, he said out loud, "That bastard—he even stiffed me out of two-week's severance pay." Opening his car door, he said, "Yeah, that sort of sums up McGuire all right."

~~~

Grinning, Howard was thinking, while driving on highway I-75 north toward Georgia, about the look on his apartment manager's face when he told him about leaving, going home because of a medical emergency.

"He didn't know whether to believe me or not," Howard said out loud, shaking his head, grinning. "Well, I'm paid up for eleven days yet—until the end of the month."

Howard had thrown the old belt away, pulling it out of his Chino's, when packing his clothes. He broke it at the crack, and dropped the pieces in the trash basket.

"Dad's belt," he said, grinning, "fixed it—fixed things—so I'd be returning home. Strange," he said shaking his head. "Strange."

He was exhilarated about going home, glad for the chance to see Marian again, be with her.

Instead of going to a bar, moping about being fired, having fellow reporters buying drinks and trying to console him, he felt glad to be fired, as if a weight had been lifted off of him. Actually it was; the decision to leave the newspaper was made for him—and he was out the door, and, now, on the road home.

It was getting dark when he stopped for gas in Orlando. He stood pumping gas into his car, thinking of Marian; how he had seen other women with blond streaked hair, swept up at the back, and how it gave him a jolt—as if it were her.

He shook his head, thinking how was he to know she broke the engagement to that Bozo, down here in Florida.

"Wow," he said shaking his head, "it's hard to believe I'm going back—to pick up where I left off with Marian."

Driving again, he eased down the ramp to the expressway, into the line of headlights, then picked up speed.

Thinking of returning to Marian made Howard think of the girl he met in the bar two-weeks ago. And what she said.

He did not believe her when she said she had left her husband. He did not believe her when she said she had just had a baby.

But when they were making love on the narrow bed in his apartment, the hair between her legs was a stubble—as if it had been shaved off at the hospital and was growing back—after she delivered a baby.

When their love making became so active—her on top, straddling him, and his head slipped over the side of the bed, he remembered her saying, "Oh, be careful—don't hurt your neck," and, he remembered smiling, just before he ejected, feeling everything going up into her.

"Hope I didn't start something in there—" he said quietly, driving, "that was quite a load."

He felt guilty, he remembered, and went back to the same bar two days later. The woman was with a man at the bar, and after a while he heard her tell the bartender, the man was her husband, and that they had made up, and decided not to divorce.

Looking forward, intent on driving fast, both hands gripping the steering wheel, Howard said out loud, "People get caught up by events—that's all. They make a move—like the girl from the bar—and Marian and me, too—and they think they know how things will be; then, bingo, the situation changes, and you find out—that events did not turn out the way you figured they would."

Lighting a cigarette, he said to himself, "Amazing—it makes you wonder—how come life is so—changeable.

"How the hell are you supposed to know," he said waving his right hand, "if a decision you make—is right?"

"Ugh," he said making a sour face, "I've got to stop smoking so much," and flung the cigarette out the window.

"Marian got engaged to that—interloper—and I wandered down here to Florida to get away from all that. Then—boom—I find out she's not engaged and all of a sudden, I find myself in the *wrong* place. Unbelievable."

After gassing up the car just before Atlanta, Howard was driving through the city, he saw a hitchhiker, standing on the down ramp under the streetlamp.

He looked at the thin young man in tight pants and a light green sweater, standing with one hip high, his thumb up.

"No doubt where he wants to go," Howard said.

Then his thigh, the right one hit by that Sunday morning shock, felt warm, as if it were a hand that was trying to stimulate him.

"Shit," he said, "I must be crackers, or someone is messing with me," he said rubbing the spot on his thigh.

Once, he recalled, he walked past a parked car that had a burglar alarm system, and it went "*beep-beep*", the alarm activated.

"Maybe it's some electronic device," he said driving in the city traffic that was filtering down onto the Expressway, "that somebody can control."

He thought of the night he was with Julie Picard and failed to get an erection after feeling a "shock". It can be used to stimulate, or the other way, to make you fail to get stimulated, he was aware now.

"Maybe," he said out loud, "it can be used as some sort of tracking device too—give off a signal that can be followed by somebody."

He shook his head, "But who would want—to track me?"

Ahead, on another down ramp, Howard saw two young girls in short skirts standing under the street light, their thumbs up.

"Hey," he said looking and grinning, "they won't have to wait long for a ride. Yikes." After he passed them, he added, smiling wide, "Hope they don't cause a traffic-jam—or maybe a pile-up—with those legs."

Then Howard's face dropped. He thought for moment, and said, "it's too—easy," he said out loud. "It's some sort of set—up—that effeminate kid—than the two dollies. Someone wants someone to stop—take the bait."

He drove in silence for a while.

"Me?" he said quietly. "Would someone want me to stop?"

He thought a moment, "I wonder if all of this has anything to do with that couple in Sloppy Joe's—the woman with hard face?"

Then he added slowly, "and I wonder if there's any link with that couple and those two guys who tried to rob me—that ended in that brass knuckle fight?"

He shook his head from side to side, slow, thinking, "damn, could it be—someone is really out to do a job on me? I mean, trying to scuttle me; get me in trouble with the law?""

Out of the lights from the city, he drove the highway dark on both sides, thinking, "it seems that there is not part of my life, that hasn't been left alone. It's like someone is pulling the strings in my life."

Each right-thinking, who would benefit from him hitting the wall.

"That's a hard question," he said reaching in his shirt pocket for cigarette.

"Yeah," he said lighting a cigarette with the car lighter, "if I find the *who*—that—might explain all these crazy events taking place in my life—lately. Yeah."

"You know," Howard said putting his right hand on the back of his neck, stretching his shoulders muscles out, "if I tell anybody about this electric stuff—they'd probably think I was crackers. Better keep to myself—at least until I find out—more."

Lighting a cigarette with the car lighter, he said quietly, "they seem so well organized—they seem to be *everywhere* I go. It must be a network," he said thoughtfully, reaching to put the lighter back in the hole. "Yeah, one hell of a network."

It was growing colder now, and when Howard stopped to gas up in Tennessee, he dug his jacket out of his duffel bag in the trunk. It was the third week of November.

Standing with the car door open, pulling on the jacket, he said out loud, "Everything changes, but Marian and me, that will *never* change. You can take that to the bank."

~ ~ ~

"There's some meatloaf left over from dinner," Howard's mother said. "I'll make you a sandwich—if you're hungry."

"Sounds good," Howard said from where he sat at the kitchen table.

The black under his eye was mostly gone, and he had told his mother about the fight in Key West. All of this now was part of his reentry back into the life of the family; he would have to give an account of his trip to Florida.

"Father and Bernie are bowling," his mother said, and pulled open the refrigerator. "He usually comes back about ten."

Howard saw beer bottles in the refrigerator.

"Can I have a beer with my sandwich?"

His mother reached to set a bottle of Pabst on the table in front of Howard, then carried the meatloaf platter to the sink, and carefully began to unwrap it. She took a knife from the drawer and began sliced the meatloaf.

"What are you going to do now, son?"

Howard knew that question was at the top of the list; it was part of the price for being part of the family. He reached from where he was sitting to the drawer where the bottle opener was always kept.

He was about to answer his mother, prying off the cap of beer, then taking a swallow.

"Oh, you're here," came his sister's voice from the kitchen doorway. "Mom said at dinner you called them and were on your way up—from Florida. Howdy, brother."

"Hi," he said and took another drink of beer. "Doing your homework?"

"Uh-huh," she said. "Geography." She watched as Howard took a long drink of beer. "You don't look sunburned or anything. You're *supposed* to have a tan—when you've been to Florida."

"Kathy," Howard's mother said in her firm tone, you get back to your homework, young lady—or you can't watch *I Love Lucy* tonight."

The telephone rang, and Howard, smiling, watched his mother, turn and reach out to answer the wall phone.

"Oh, she said listening. "Just a minute, Marge."

After his mother punched the hold on the phone, she slid the plate of meatloaf on the table in front of Howard, then took the mustard and relish jars from the fridge, and set them on the table, and said, "I'll be on the phone in the front room." She went out waving her hands.

"It's probably Mrs. Bonkowski," Kathy said the Howard, smiling. "They'll talk for an hour."

Looking to see if her mother was gone, his sister whispered to him saying, "a letter came for you this morning—returned from Florida. I saw it. Mom's got it."

"You don't miss much, do you?" Howard said to her, then biting into the sandwich he just made.

He was thinking about the note he sent to Marian from the newspaper office.

Cupping her hands around her mouth, like a megaphone, Kathy said, "the writing on the front said, 'married and moved out of state'."

Howard set the sandwich down on the plate quickly. His throat grew so tight he could barely breathe; he put a hand to his chest, as if shot.

"Your face is all white," Kathy whispered, "Are you sick—maybe the sandwich?"

At first Howard could not speak; he shook his head, holding a hand up in front of his face, the palm out, as if to deflect a blow.

"Are—are you," he said in a weak voice, "sure, Kathy? You're not just saying this?" he added while rubbing his chest.

"No—honest," Kathy said leaning on the table, both hands down. "Mom's got the letter—I gave it to her after I got the mail."

Her tone was serious now, not kidding Howard.

"Damn," Howard said quietly, folding his hands on the table in front of him. Then in a distracted voice said, "Damn," again.

"Don't tell mom I told you," Kathy said looking intently at Howard. "She'd get mad at me for telling."

When Howard felt his stomach heave, he tried taking a deep breath to ease the tightness. But he could not draw in the air.

"You better go," he said to Kathy slowly. "Go and do your homework," he said taking shallow gulps of air.

"Okay," she said. "Wow, Howard. You look like you've seen a ghost."

"I'm just worn out from all the driving," Howard said. "It's catching up with me—not getting sleep."

"I wouldn't of said anything about the letter," Kathy said, rubbing her left elbow, looking at it, distracted, as she spoke. "But I thought—you'd want to know."

Howard nodded, then waved her away.

"Be sure not to tell that I told you."

"I won't."

Kathy turned, and quickly went through the doorway, almost bumping into her mother coming in.

"Howard," his mother said, "you only took a bite out of the sandwich. You don't like the meatloaf?"

"It's great, mom. I'm tired, that's all—those fifteen-hundred miles I drove from Miami—are catching up with me. I didn't realize—I was so tired."

"Well, son, your room is ready," his mother said and began covering the meatloaf with plastic wrap. "I turned down your bed."

"Thanks, mom," he said getting up from the table, both hands spread to steady himself.

"Oh, did you save my mail?" he asked calmly pushing in the chair under the table.

"Yes," his mother said, opening the refrigerator, sliding in the meatloaf platter, "and there was one you sent that Grosse Pointe girl returned. I'll get all that came."

Howard stood staring at the handwriting on the envelope: *Married. Moved out of state,* thinking it must have been Marian's mother, or maybe, Ardis; it was a woman's handwriting.

"Ah, damn," he said walking into his bedroom, sitting down on the edge of the bed, holding up the letter. "Ah-h, what the hell—happened? I can't believe it."

He heard his father's voice out in the kitchen, and after silence, then the words, "Huh, he came home to die," in a mocking tone, after Howard's mother must have told him their son had returned.

Howard stood up, folding the letter, and walked into the kitchen, "No," he said from the doorway, "I just didn't want to miss Thanksgiving turkey dinner."

"Well," his father said grinning, "if it ain't the big shot back from Florida. So you made it home?"

"Yep," Howard said, aware now his father had been drinking at the bowling alley, his voice louder than usual. I drove straight through—only stopped for gas. Now I'm feeling like a truck hit me."

"Go get some rest, son," his mother said calmly. "You and your father can visit—later."

"Okay," Howard said waving his letter hands, "tomorrow dad, I'll fill you in—on what it's like down in Florida."

"Go," his mother said.

"Night, everybody," he said.

"Don't let the bedbugs bite," his sister shouted from the front room where she was studying.

When he was back in his bedroom, Howard hear his father say, "It's starting to snow—it's only November." Then after a pause, added, "he's got quite a mouse over his left eye."

"Tomorrow," his mother said, "we can hear all about it."

Laying in bed, Howard asked himself about Marian, her decision to get married in such a hurry, but, when he turned on his side, fatigue took him to sleep quickly.

~~~

Two days later, Howard woke up after eleven in the morning, and heard his mother crying. He had been out drinking last night with friends at the university.

"Mom?" he shouted. "You all right?"

"Terrible," she said from the kitchen, her small television set talking in the background. "Somebody shot President Kennedy," she said crying, "down in Texas."

"Wha-at?" Howard said, getting up out of bed, going to the kitchen door. "How bad is he hurt?"

"He's dead." His mother sobbed, and said, "They killed that nice, young man, down there."

"Oh, man," Howard said, putting his hands on each side of the doorframe, head down, "it can't be true."

"It's on all the stations," his mother said softly. "Come see—for yourself."

Howard stepped back into the bedroom and pulled on a pair of pants after shedding his pajamas. Barefoot, he moved back to the kitchen and sat at the table. Walter Cronkite was speaking in the stentorian voice on the small black and white screen, adding to the gravity of the news.

"Who—who did it?" Howard asked staring at the screen.

"They don't know yet," his mother said over at the sink, wiping her hands in a towel with a yellow flower pattern. "Who could do such a thing," she said quietly. "The President of the United States?"

"Hope it wasn't a Russian," Howard said, listening to the set for details. "We'll be at war tomorrow."

"Your father will have a fit," Howard's mother said looking at the screen. "He thought the world of Kennedy—being in the Navy like him in the big war."

"Yeah," Howard said, watching the television segment showing the presidential car moving and the actual shooting sequence.

"Oh, poor Mrs. Kennedy," his mother said watching.

"Damn," Howard said, "a sniper shot him. Where the hell were the security people?"

"I can't watch it anymore," his mother said. "I've seen what the bullets did too many times. It makes me sick."

"It's hard to believe," Howard said shaking his head, "that something like that could happen—to our President."

"East some breakfast," his mother said. "I made coffee—and if you want eggs, I'll scramble some," she added, looking out the kitchen window.

"Just some cereal," Howard said looking over at her. "Where's dad?"

"The dentist," his mother said opening a cabinet overhead, taking out a box of Cheerios. "He took a sick day at work—one of his fillings came out," she said filling a bowl with the cereal. After pouring milk from a carton, she set the bowl in front of Howard, "I hope he doesn't get too upset—father's heart isn't too strong—and the shock about Kennedy."

"Dad will be all right, mom," Howard said watching her return the milk carton to the refrigerator. "He'll have a few beers," he said taking a large spoon from a drawer, reaching from his chair, then leaning back, "and he'll be all right. Don't worry."

"You were out late last night," his mother said flatly. "I hope you're not going to make a habit of—gallivanting all night, mister."

"Naw," Howard said taking a spoonful of cereal, "I was talking with friends last night—about my idea of taking classes—getting my degree—before going back to newspaper work."

"I heard that before," his mother said coolly. "You moved home—you decided—and were going to work and go to school."

"I'll get through quicker," Howard said after swallowing a mouthful of cereal, "if I carry a full-load of classes at the university. And—Marian is not around—it shouldn't take too long. After I graduate, I can concentrate on getting a big-time job on a big-time newspaper."

"I held up giving you that letter," his mother said quietly. "I was waiting for the right time—to give it to you—not when you came home—came in the door—but after a while. I knew it would shock you."

"Yeah," Howard said nodding, "you're right—it was a shock all right. Her getting married so quick," he said slowly, "and then reading about it on the front of an envelope—for *everybody* to read."

He hesitated, then took a spoonful of cereal.

"Maybe you're better off, son. She was nice, but she was used to having things you couldn't begin to afford. You are better off—in the long run—because I don't think you and her could have stayed together very long."

"I don't know," Howard said stopping his eating for a moment, "how I feel. Finding out her getting married—hit me like a ton of bricks. It hasn't sunk in yet—I mean, I don't know if I believe it, or not."

"I can see how you feel, son. It's like President Kennedy here, being shot," his mother said pointing at the television set, "It's so shocking—it's hard to believe it's true."

"Yeah," Howard said and took a spoonful of cereal, "it seems that everything—is unreal—all of a sudden."

"What are they doing?" Howard's mother asked, looking at the television screen. "Oh-h, that's Jackie Kennedy. Look."

"They're swearing in the new president," Howard said looking. "Johnson was the vice-president before."

"Oh, lord," Howard's mother said, putting her hand to the side of her face, "Jackie has blood on her suit. Look, there," she said pointing. "That—poor—woman."

"Yes, I see it," Howard said. "I've seen enough," he said standing u from the table. "I don't want to see any more."

~ ~ ~

The day of the Kennedy funeral, Howard was sitting in the campus bar, watching the procession on television. He heard the drums beating a military dirge, and saw the president's casket riding on a gun carriage. People lining the streets in Washington were crying.

Etherly came in the bar, dressed in his khaki pants and shirt, work dress for the university ground maintenance crew.

"Everybody on campus," he said sitting down on the stool next to Howard, "is watching the funeral on TV—all the offices—the student center—even the cafeteria."

"Man," Howard said, "the whole *world* is watching." After he took a drink of draft beer from the tall glass, he said, "It wouldn't be too hard to figure what the world thinks about American today. I mean—the world probably thinks we're still living in the Wild West days. You know—buffalo Bill and Billy the Kid—shoot-'em-up's."

"Boy," Etherly said, "are you in a good mood," watching the bartender draw the draft he ordered from the tap. "But, I guess I can't blame you Howie,—I heard about Marian getting married." He watched as the bartender slid the glass over in front of him. "I know how you feel—when Veronica and I broke up—hell, I didn't see any sense of even living any more. I know—first hand, man,—what you feel."

Howard, grinning, said, "I never got to think that way—the part about 'life not worth living'."

"Wait until it sinks in," Etherly said and took a long drink of beer.

"I guess," Howard said looking at Etherly, "I'm still in the—confused—stage. I mean, I'm still trying to find out why—it happened. Why she got married."

"Money, sport," Etherly said. "You got snookered by money. He has it—you don't. It's simple—I know. The same thing happened to me and Veronica."

Howard sat shaking his head back and forth, slowly.

"Okay," Howard said, "maybe you're right about the money part, but I got a hunch—there's more involved—something else."

"C'mon, Howie, use your head—what else could it be?"

"Maybe it was that I was snookered from the start," Howard said, looking in the mirror behind the bar, studying Etherly's reaction. "Maybe somebody was doing a job on me, you know—working behind the scenes to make me crash."

"You and the whole world," Etherly said waving his hands, "are *always* looking for a conspiracy. It's *always* a conspiracy that brings you down—makes you fail. Well—I guess that's one way to explain why you flopped. Some dark force was responsible for your failure."

Howard, realizing he would get no understanding from Etherly, said quietly, "I was just thinking out loud."

"Let it go," Etherly said. "Here, let me buy you a beer and we'll both drink to the girls we lost."

"Okay," Howard said sliding his empty beer glass on the bar for the refill, "I guess you're right about the—reality of it."

Looking up at the television screen, he saw the honor guard at Kennedy's gravesite firing a twenty-one gun salute.

It made him think that Marian may be gone away—but she's not gone, as in death. She was gone, but it was not a final-gone. Her being away was not final—there was hope it seemed to Howard, of being with her again. He could feel it all the way down to his shoes. He knew Marian, he was sure. Her being gone would crack—someplace.

"Here's to the girl's we knew," Etherly said holding up his beer glass, talking to Howard's reflection in the mirror behind the bar.

"To our girls," Howard said and took a drink, nodded.

He did not want to alienate Etherly; he was a good source for facts. He was the one who told Howard about vets being eligible for twenty-four credit hours for their military service. The university gave credits for physical training and the other classes taken in the military. It was a boost for Howard, who needed only twelve credits more after the military credits, and he would have the one hundred and twenty needed for his degree.

This boost is what prompted Howard to complete his requirements for the degree, now. It was a bright spot.

Howard had found a direction to move.

Chapter 19

Howard stamped the snow off his shoes and started up the steps to the office of his Journalism advisor, Doctor White, when Melanie Marsack came out the professor's door.

"Hey, Howard," she said pulling on her plaid overcoat, "how you doing? Are you working on a newspaper?"

"Naw, I'm finishing school," he said grinning. "this March will end my last term—then I can start making the rounds—for a job."

Unzipping his jacket, pulling out the scarf, felling sheepish about not working, he looked down at his wet shoes.

"Well," Melanie said, flipping her hair out, caught under the coat collar when she pulled it on, "I've landed a crackerjack public relations job with a hospital in Wyandotte. What do you think about that?"

"Wow, Melanie. Good for you," Howard said, grinning.

"An-nd," she said in a boasting tone, "I got a new apartment there in Wyandotte—with a balcony and a view of the Detroit River."

Howard nodded; talking to her always reminded him of talking to his little sister.

"That's great," he said smiling.

"Me and my roommate," she said pressing the front of her coat, "are giving a house warming party, Saturday. I'm inviting you. Will you come?"

"We'll have to see," Howard said looking down at his shoes again, "what the weather is like. If there's a big snow—I mean I can't promise."

"Bring your girlfriend," Melanie said smiling. "Who—are you going with—now?"

"To tell the truth," he said still looking at his wet shoes, "I'm sort of—in between—romances, right now."

He could tell she knew about Marian getting married.

"I told you she would break your heart," Melanie said touching his arm. "I know a girl who was one of the guests at the—big wedding—out in Grosse Pointe."

"Yeah, Melanie, you're a regular—Cassandra."

"No I'm not," she said shifting her shoulders inside her coat to make them comfortable, "because Cassandra predicted tragic events—not lovelorn advice. It's a wonder you ever passed that class we had in Shakespeare."

"Well, Melanie, you know what I mean—you look into the future—and make predictions. How's that?"

Melanie was pulling on a glove she took from her coat pocket, "You know she married a guy, some people said, was a cop of some sort—and other people said he was a hood. I guess you can take your pick, Howard."

He blinked, then said, "I haven't heard anything."

"I've heard they're living in New York City," Melanie said smoothing the fingers of her glove. "They're renting someplace—and I hear they do a lot of skiing."

Howard's throat tightened; he could only shake his head up and down.

"I've got to run, Howard," she said pulling up her coat collar with both hands. "Be sure to come to my party, Saturday. Okay?"

"We'll see, Melanie."

"That will have to do for an answer, I guess," she said, and started down the stairs. she stopped, and turned to look up, and said, "Howard—be careful."

He grinned, looking down at her and nodding.

"You too—Melanie," he said, wondering to himself, why she had said that.

Outside Dr. White's office, two girls were sitting on the chairs in the hall, waiting to see the professor. They were both from Howard's Journalism class.

"Hi," Howard said, sitting down on the only chair left, next to a girl name Iris, who worked with him on the college newspaper as copy editor. "Waiting long?"

"Ten minutes," Iris said. "Doctor White's talking with Dave Hammond from the Dearborn newspaper."

Howard was about to say something else, but the office door opened. When Hammond came out, everybody began talking; they all knew Hammond was a working newsman, struggling to fill the requirements for a degree.

"Still at it?" Hammond said to Howard, referring to the working for his degree.

"I'll be done this March."

"Lucky you."

"Yeah."

"Well, I got to run," Hammond said walking toward the stairs.

Both the girls had gone into the office, the door was closing.

Howard was getting warm, and when sliding off his quilted jacket, what Melanie said about Marian marrying a cop, struck home. He must be a New York cop, Howard reasoned, because they're living there—but what the hell as he doing in Detroit?

Stuffing his scarf into one pocket of the jacket, Howard grinned, "No wonder he said he lived in the dumpy hotel—he doesn't know anything about Detroit. He just picked the name because it was near campus.

Then it entered his mind, the guy Marian was married to, might be a federal cop. Howard sat holding the jacket over his knees, thinking the guy might be from the Bureau. That would make the story he told Marian—about being an 'engineer' at the Burrough's Adding Machine Company all baloney too.

Howard sat thinking, this Fred character, was in an awful hurry to get back to New York City, after getting married, just as the office door next to him swung open.

Doctor White sat behind his desk, his hat with its short brim, pushed back on his head, looking like a race-track tout.

"Since it's only a two-hour credit," he said to Howard, "I usually ask students who take this class—to research and write—a ten page, or so, piece—on the history of some publication here at the university."

"Okay," Howard said from the chair in front of the desk, jacket folded on his knees. "Is there *any* publication in particular you want?—"

"What comes to mind," Doctor White said leaning back in his desk chair, "is the yearbook."

Howard raised his eyebrows, then grinned.

"Okay," he said, "I'll write a piece on the history of the yearbook at Wayne State University," and almost added the remark, even though it sounds like a joke.

Here was Doctor White, the author—or editor—of the book, "*By-line: Ernest Hemingway,*" that was over ten weeks on the best seller list, Howard sat thinking, handing out a crummy yearbook assignment.

"You don't have to bother coming in to my office," Doctor White said, "until you have finished the piece—history. Just bring in the typed script to my office. I'll grade it, and submit it for the credits at the end of the term."

"This class," Howard said, "is my last one. It gives me enough credit to get my Bachelor's Degree."

"Good," Doctor White said, sliding the folder with Howard's grades, and notes on his journalism classes, into a side drawer of his desk. "Then you can start working—as a professional. Your degree will open a lot of doors—for employment."

"Thank you," Howard said as he stood up.

"The university library," Doctor White said looking up, has a collection of yearbooks going back to the nineteen-twenties. Make friends with the librarians—they can help a lot with your research."

"Right," Howard said. "Well, I guess I have my work cut out for me for the next ten weeks," he added while walking to the door. "That's for sure."

～～～

Howard was at home, sitting at the kitchen table. His father came up the steps from the basement after 'washing-up'; which included drinking three fingers of Four Roses whiskey.

"Father," Howard's mother said turning to look at him from the stove, "we have your favorite today—pepper steak—with rice."

"Hi Dad," Howard said grinning, "I registered for my final class at the university today." After a pause, he asked, "How was work today?"

"Good. Good," his father said, pulling his chair out from the table. "Mother, where's the little one?" he asked sitting down.

"Over at Martha's," Howard's mother said from the stove, while spooning pepper steak into a bowl, "they're making fudge; and Martha's mother is making spaghetti dinner for them, she said on the phone."

"Fudge for whom?" Howard asked.

"The girls want to sell it—at school," Howard's mother said, setting the bowl of pepper steak on the table, then a bowl of rice. When she opened the refrigerator and took out a large bowl of salad, she said, "They want to make money to buy new uniforms for the marching band."

"Kathy isn't in the band," Howard said taking a scoop of rice.

"No," his mother said sitting down at the table, "but Martha plays the clarinet in the band—and needs help."

"We had a lot of excitement," Howard's father said, "at the shop today." Using tongs, he was filling his salad bowl. "The cops were out in the back alley. I want to watch the news at six o'clock on television—they should have the story."

"What kind of story?" Howard asked as he ladled pepper-steak over the rice on his plate.

"They found some guy this morning," his father said picking up his fork, "laying behind the dumpster—at the tool and die shop—across the alley from our building. His head was bashed-in."

"Was he dead?" Howard asked.

"I don't think so," Howard's father said, and held a forkful of salad for a moment, while he added, "but he was one of those guys who wears a motorcycle jacket—and has a lot of tattoos."

"How did he get there?" Howard's mother asked as she scooped rice onto her plate. "Did someone leave him—or what?"

"That's just it," Howard's father said, stabbing his salad for another forkful, "because the cops were saying there's been two—three break-in's lately at companies in the neighborhood. And that tool and die shop across the alleyway—I hear—makes some kind of tank parts for the army. Hush-hush stuff."

"Then," Howard said, intrigued, "It's possible one *put* him out of action—on purpose?"

"Yeah," Howard's father said pouring more Thousand Island dressing over his salad, "because there's talk that the tool and die shop has some guys from the sauerkraut army working there—skill tradesman."

"Germans?" Howard asked.

"Yeah," Howard's father said screwing the cap back on the salad dressing bottle, "they're World War Two, SS guys, I hear. Former—SS troopers."

"You think," Howard said looking across the table at his father, "these SS troopers wacked the guy in the motorcycle jacket—for snooping around?"

"Oh-h," Howard's mother said, "I forgot the dinner rolls I put in the oven—to warm up."

She pushed back her chair, and stood up.

"Well," Howard's father said looking at him, thinking, "the cops did find a large screwdriver in the alley = that must of belonged to the motorcycle jacket guy. Somebody—the cops were speculating—hit him in the back of the head with something like a lead pipe—because he's in the hospital in a coma, they said."

Howard's mother set a basket filled with dark brown dinner rolls on the table.

"The rolls are a little well-done," she said sitting back down in her chair, "but they're still good."

"Someone might have been laying," Howard said slowly, "for the guy in the motorcycle jacket—you know? I mean, somebody might have been—waiting."

"They make parts for the new German *Werwulf* tank over there in that tool and die shop." Howard's father said taking a forkful of rice and pepper steak, "so I hear. And they have a lot of precision instruments—tools—over in that shop, somebody told me, that are worth a lot of money."

"Howard, hand me the butter dish," Howard's mother said.

"Sure," he said to her, and handed it over. Then to his father, he said, "You think they'll have more answers about the motorcycle guy on the six o'clock news?"

"We'll see," his father said, then reached over to take a dark dinner roll from the basket.

"They're a little over-done," Howard's mother said.

"I like them crispy," his father said, smiling.

Howard's mother smiled back at him.

"Mother, maybe Kathy could not miss dinner with us," Howard's father said breaking the roll with his fingers. "I miss her at dinner—it's the only time I get to talk to her."

"I know," Howard's mother said, "but she's at that stage where she's making a lot of friends." After reaching to put the butter dish in front of Howard's father, she added, "But, I'll have a talk with her—ask her to plan her activities—around—the dinner hour."

"Good," Howard's father said reaching with his knife for a pad of butter.

"What about me, dad?" Howard said. "You miss me too?"

His father grinned, buttering his roll.

"You're the *first one* at the dinner table," his father said looking at him, "and you *never* miss a day."

"I'll take that as a compliment," Howard said looking at his mother, shaking her head back and forth, smiling.

After an apple dessert, Howard's father was having coffee when he turned to look at the kitchen clock.

"C'mon," he said to Howard, "it's time for the news on television." Getting up from the table, putting a hand on Howard's mother's shoulder, he said slowly, "Wonderful dinner, mother. You would win first prize—anywhere."

She reached up and patted his hand on her shoulder.

In the living room, Howard saw the snow covered dumpster on television, a reporter pointing to the spot the man in the motorcycle jacket was found.

The reporter said police speculated the man might have been injured in a fight that was gang-related.

Then, a thin man in a tailored overcoat appeared next to the television reporter, and after being identified as the tool shop owner, he went on to say something about burglaries in the buildings nearby in recent weeks. But, he told the interviewing reporter, he had no knowledge as to what happened to the man in the motorcycle jacket.

Howard noticed the owner's overcoat had epaulets on the shoulders, that it was the sort of tan wool overcoat British officers wear over their uniforms.

Then the name, Horst Aschenfelter, flashed on the bottom of the television screen, identifying the tool shop owner.

"Mackrel," Howard said, loud, almost shouting.

"What-at?" Howard's father said from his chair, startled by the outburst. "You—know him?"

"Sort of," Howard said. "He's a partner—business partner of my girl friend's father. And he's one of the group that owns the marina—in Saint Clair Shores. I came across him when I was doing a story—a grand opening party."

"Take it easy, Howard," his father said firmly. "You keep jumping like that—you'll get a heart attack." Then after a pause, he added, "Or give *me* one."

What Howard did not tell his father, was that at the grand opening celebration, Aschenfelter sent a steady stream of cognac to Howard's table at the Yardarm Tavern. Howard drank too much, there overlooking the marina docks, as the party wore on, and the cognac in the snifter glasses continued to come over to the press table.

On the way home, Howard was stopped by police, arrested and taken to the police lock-up in St. Clair Shores. The shift sergeant, in going through Howard's wallet, found the State Police press card, issued to identify all reporters, and the note typed on the back by the police chief.

It read: "Give all assistance possible to this reporter. Chief, Edward Groesbeck, St. Clair Shores"

When Howard first came on the weekly newspaper beat, and was going around introducing himself, Chief Grosbeck, Howard recalled, took the card after looking at it, typed and signed the note. He did it on his own, Howard remembered, without being asked.

"Are you a reporter?" the police desk Sergeant asked Howard.

"Yes," he remembered saying. "I work for the Grosse Pointe Press—for the Calvin Beamer newspapers."

"You can go," the Sergeant said, and tore the report made by the arresting officer in half. "Go get some coffee."

When the excitement passed, Howard remembered, walking back to where his car was parked, he thought of the steady stream of cognac that kept coming his way at the party. It came from Aschenfelter, and it seemed he was *deliberately* setting up Howard to get arrested: but why—Howard kept asking himself. He decided then, he would have to dig into the background of this Aschenfelter.

All he knew, was that Marian mentioned the name once, when she said the guy was a part-time partner in her father's fur business.

"Sorry, dad," Howard said over to his father in the living room chair, "I just got excited—about the news story."

~~~

Howard was tired of reading old copies of the yearbook. Leaning back in the heavy oak chair in the university library, he rubbed his eyes, using the heels of his hands. He had read through most of the yearbooks of the nineteen-thirties, and was about to begin the nineteen-forties, when the name of the university then, was simply Wayne College. the school was named after Mad Anthony Wayne, Howard found out by reading, the hero of the battle of Fallen Timbers down in Ohio, during the War of 1812. He also found out, Wayne County where Detroit is located, was named in honor of the general, after the war, too.

Notes Howard had written, seemed to conclude that there were fewer students enrolled in the early days of the school, but beyond that, the yearbooks were much the same. It was not much to show for the two weeks he had been reading. Howard felt, as he stretched.

Still sitting, Howard pushed against the oak table, sliding his chair back. Then he stood up, and walked slow to the end of the long room, heading for the drinking fountain out in the hallway.

"Keck," someone said. "Hey, Howard," someone called from the hall.

Howard looked out and saw Hal Parsons from his Journalism class, carrying a stack of microfilm rolls in his hands.

"How you doing, Hal?" Howard said quietly, stepping out into the hall.

"I thought you were in Florida," Parsons said grinning.

"Naw," Howard said. "I missed Michigan, so I came back," he said and shrugged. Then added, "I'm working to finish—get my degree. I just have one class to go, and I'm done."

"I read in the Journalism Newsletter about you being in Fort Lauderdale—on a daily paper."

"The police beat," Howard said, and leaned over to drink from the spout on the water fountain. "It got to be sort of boring," Howard added, when he straightened up, wiping his mouth. "The same thing—over and over—only the names change."

"Well," Parsons said, his head to one side, "I'm working at the *News*—downtown."

"No kidding?" Howard said. "Good for you. That's impressive. I bet Doctor White—is—proud of you."

"Yeah," Parsons said thoughtfully, "I'm a dad again—a girl this time. I—can't fool around. I mean—I got to make a decent living."

"I should say so," Howard said, feeling himself running out of things to say.

"What happened with you," Parsons asked slowly, "and that Grosse Pointe girl you were going with?"

"She—got married," Howard said leaning to take another drink from the water fountain, feeling Hal already knew the answer to the question; he was the guy who advised Howard, he remembered, to marry a middle-class girl, and leave the girls with money alone.

"That figures," Hal said, moving the rolls of microfilm in his hands to a more comfortable position.

"I'm finishing my last class for graduation," Howard said to change the subject. "Doctor White has me researching the growth—of yearbook publication—at the university."

"Sounds exciting," Hal said grinning.

"Okay, I deserve that—it's a clunker of a subject—you're right, Hal. But—it's the last assignment for my degree. So cornball, or not, I don't have no choice."

Howard was waiting for Hal to say he understood.

Instead, he said, "Have you heard about the *Detroit News* opening up a Suburban Bureau?" as he shifted the stack of microfilm from one hand to the other.

"No—I've been busy with all this stuff for my—degree," Howard said, trying not to act too interested.

"They're planning to insert a page of local news for each of the suburbs," Hal said watching for Howard's reaction closely. "They figure it will—increase circulation."

"You mean they're doing—new hiring?" Howard asked.

"Yeah, I've already been over there," Hal said as if he was proud of himself, "and I applied to cover downriver for them. I've covered the downriver beat for the weekly I worked for—almost two years."

"Maybe," Howard said quietly, "they'd hire me to cover the Grosse Pointes—where I worked on that weekly?"

"Tell them you already got your degree," Hal said. "You're close, anyhow. And maybe because you covered the Pointes for that weekly—they'd consider you over somebody who hasn't. It's worth a try."

"Okay," Howard said, looking at Hal's face, avoiding a study of the acne scars, "and thanks for cluing me in about the job openings." Then Howard, attempting to act friendly, added, "You got time for a beer?"

"Not today," Hal said. "I got to finish this research," he said holding up the micro-film. "It's about an education department scandal."

"I bet it's about," Howard said grinning, "some sap of a school superintendant—misappropriating funds—spending school money—for entertainment?"

"Yeah," Hal said hefting the micro-film, "the same old baloney—but this superintendant *sliced* it different." Then he said in a brotherly tone, "Be sure you get over to the *News*—and fill out an application."

"Don't worry," Howard said, "I'll go today."

"Lucky I ran into you," Hal said before he turned away.

~ ~ ~

Howard's sister, Kathy, said, "You got paint drops on your face," from where she stood in the doorway.

"When you paint the ceiling," Howard said, looking down from the ladder, "you get drops. Okay, smartie."

During the past two weeks he had painted the living room, the dining room, and was now on the first of three bedrooms. He felt he owed the family something for letting him live home while he finished work on his degree.

"Mom sent me," Kathy said. "She says the *Detroit News* is on the phone. They want to talk to you."

"Why didn't you say so," Howard said, setting the brush on the edge of the can of paint, then stepping backward down the ladder onto the floor covered with newspaper.

"I just did," Kathy said grinning. "Dad says you're doing a good job—I heard him tell mom."

"Look out, I don't want to get paint on you," Howard said, wiping his hand with a rag, stepping over to the doorway.

"Don't get paint on the rug," Kathy said backing up. "Mom will kill you if you do."

"Okay, boss."

Two weeks ago Howard had gone to the personnel office at the *Detroit News* and wrote the job application. His heart was jumping hard now.

In the kitchen, his mother handed Howard the telephone saying, "His name is Gibbons—he says he's an editor at the *News*.

"Thanks, mom," Howard said and cleared his throat.

~ ~ ~

"What did Gibbons say, besides you start at the beginning of the pay week?" Hal asked Howard, then took a sip of beer.

"Not much, really," Howard said grinning, feeling content about getting the reporting job. "He seemed sort of pre-occupied with the dates on my application—checking for gaps in employment, I guess. He kept flipping the sheet over—checking one side, then other."

It was just after eleven, and they were sitting at the Anchor Bar, the place most reporters from the *News* and the *Free Press* gathered, a few of which were drifting in for an early lunch.

"I told him," Hal said, "I knew your work from way back in our journalism class. But he seemed more interested in the fact you knew your way around Grosse Pointe. I think that's what got you hired."

Howard picked at the paint on his fingernail, "Yeah, Gibbons says I'm responsible for the five Grosse Pointe cities, Harper Woods and Saint Clair Shores—my old stomping grounds—for his Suburban Bureau. I fell right into it."

"Did he tell you about your expense account?" Hal asked, showing a twinge of pride for Howard getting hired.

"Yeah, yeah," Howard said setting his beer glass down, and I had my photo taken for the press card identification thing, too. Ta-da. Now I've graduated from suburban weekly to suburban daily." After a pause, he added, "You're a big help, Hal. I owe you."

Despite all Helps help, Howard always felt suspicious of him; he was too solicitous, too eager to involve himself in Howard's problems, too ready to offer advice. Howard never gave any indication of how he felt. He kept silent.

~ ~ ~

The story Howard was writing about the history of the yearbook at the University had grown to four pages.

He sat in an oak table in the library writing; he began with a description of the thin first yearbook, describing its contents, a 1928 edition.

Then the thought crossed his mind: how can I work to Grosse Pointe again without thinking of Marian. Everything in the place reminds me of her. Damn. It will be hard.

The librarian came up to the table, carrying another stack of yearbooks for him to leaf through.

"We would like a copy of the report," she whispered, "for files—when you complete your work."

Howard looked up at her, a portly shape, classes over a soft face, and smiled, as she set the books on the table.

"Certainly," he whispered back. "You've been a great help. I'll be sure to give you a copy."

She smiled, touching the string of amber beads around her neck, then walked away.

After Howard wrote two more pages of his yearbook story, and began a third, he felt tired, and began rubbing the back of his left shoulder. He looked up at the clock on the wall, above the bookshelves; it was just before three.

Rush-hour traffic began about four clock, so Howard decided to head for home to beat the crowd. It was Friday, people would be leaving for work in a hurry to get home start the weekend.

Walking to his car in the campus parking lot, he passed a restaurant with a newspaper stand out front.

He knew the home edition would be on sale, and stopped to read the headline:

"CO-ED SLAIN IN ST. CLAIR SHORES".

He stooped to read the story—this was on his beat beginning Monday. Eager, he read the first line of the story.

"The pajama clad body of Melanie Marsack, 22 was found laying in the living room of the apartment at—"

Howard almost dropped his yearbook note papers, catching them by raising his knee.

"Naw-w," he said sliding the note papers on his leg, so he could hold them again. "That can't be—Melanie—from my classes. It *can't* be-."

Reading quickly, bending forward, he skimmed the story for the details.

"Police said she was struck with a heavy object, possibly a table lamp with a square base, one corner puncturing her skull."

"Not Melanie," Howard said reading, hunched over, "it must be some kind—of mistake."

229

The article, Howard read, went on to say, "police estimated time of death at approximately 3 AM for the part-time student at Wayne state University, who works for the public relations office of—"

Two girls came out the restaurant door, and one stood for a moment looking at Howard stooping to read the newspaper. One other girl came out the door, he realized she had been waiting for her, not scrutinizing him, as they all walked away, talking.

When Howard went back to reading the article, he came to the line, "Continued on page 5."

It was then he set the yearbook notes on his shoes, to keep them off the ground, and dropped three dimes on the mailbox of the newspaper rack.

He opened the newspaper to page 5 and read: "the building custodian told police the victim had only moved into the apartment about 10 days ago."

"What the hell was Melanie doing living and St. Clair shores?" Howard said looking at the newspaper. "She told me she had an apartment down in Wyandotte—downriver—below Detroit, there, balcony and all."

Shaking his head, he said, "this is unbelievable—Aw-w, it can't be true. it can't."

Reading again, the article stated, "The custodian told police, a middle-aged man frequently visited the victims apartment. This man, the custodian added, wore a coat with military style epaulets on the shoulders."

Howard close newspaper, then folded it in half, "Epaulets!" He said. "What the hell's going on—with 'epaulets'?"

He was walking again toward his car, "Could it be that tool and die shop owner?" He said. "He had epaulets on his coat—I saw him on television when the motorcycle jacket guy was found bashed in the head."

Unlocking his car door, "But, how the hell would he know Melanie? And what's the connection with her and epaulets and her living in St. Clair Shores?"

Driving his car down the ramp, out of the parking lot, he said, "The first thing I got to find out—is if this epaulets guy—is the same guy involved in both these bashings. Yeah."

The next day, Sunday, Howard was back at the library writing his yearbook history: he had twelve pages.

When he paused, taking a break from writing, leaning back in the oak chair, stretching, he thought about going to work tomorrow morning, and smiled.

Then he thought of Melanie and St. Clair Shores, and the feeling that it probably would not be wise to mention, when making the rounds of departments, to tell the Shores detectives he knew Melanie from his journalism class.

He might come under suspicion, if he told police he knew her. They might even lock him up.

He left the apprehension past, and went back to writing the draft of the yearbook story. He was ready now, about World War II, where officer training for the services was being offered at Wayne University, some of the candidates sleeping on cots in the gymnasium, which had been converted to a billet.

Slowly the thought came into Howard's mind, tomorrow he would have to play it by ear, regarding Melanie's murder. If he had to, he would tell he was a classmate of hers—but only if there was no other way.

He did not feel like writing anymore on the yearbook draft. He snapped off the green shaded lamp, stacked his yearbook story pages.

Pulling on his coat, Howard said, "Poor Melanie. I wonder what she got involved in—that—got her killed."

Walking to the library hallway, he thought it was a lousy way to begin a new job—writing about a murder—of a classmate of all things. They did not cover that in any of the journalism classes he took.

He shook his head; but still he felt excited about starting on the new job, he had to admit that.

"Maybe that's what they call—professional," Howard said walking to the top of the stairs.

Chapter 20

At home, Howard stamped the snow off his shoes, and walking in the back door into the kitchen, saw a letter lying on the table.

Bending to see who it was addressed to, he saw his name, dropping his pack of yearbook notes on the table, he picked it up.

"It's Marian's writing," he said quietly, feeling a jolt in his chest. "What could she be writing me about?" He said reaching for a table knife to open the envelope.

"Howard," his mother called from the living room, the television set on loud, "dinner will be late—about an hour. Father and Bernie went to the VA hospital to see a friend—who took a turn for the worse. And there's a letter for you—it came yesterday, but no one checked the mailbox. I found it today."

"Okay, mom. Thanks," Howard shouted back, opening out the folded letter.

Howard read quickly, the round, full letters of Marian's handwriting, he knew since their days at the University.

"Dear Howard, 9, January

I left Frederic and I'm staying with Nancy

(the airline stewardess) at her apartment.

Phone number at bottom of page. I can't stand being told by Frederic how to do everything. And I mean *everything*.

Believe me, I was about to go crazy listening to that every day. Daddy likes Fred, flipped when I phoned home me to tell I left him. Daddy says I should go back to Fred. In- deed, it was Daddy who pressured me to marry him in the first place.

I should have not given in, but Fred cried, and Daddy said he was a good catch. Fooey!

I will go back home to Detroit after a while, when my family settles down a little.

P.S. I sent this note to your house in Detroit because I do not know your Florida address. The news in Lauder- dale said you left, when I called there.

Nancy's phone number is—4458-6841."

Howard waited until just after seven o'clock, then called Marian in New York; he sat at the kitchen table that had been cleared and the family moved to the front room and watch television.

"Oh, Howard," Marian said speaking close to the phone mouthpiece, "It's always been you—you know that, honey."

"I ache so bad," he said, "when I think of you, babe. I nearly went crazy—when you married that creep. It felt like I was in a vice, or something—I could barely breathe."

He paused when he heard her crying.

"I know, honey," she said and choked. "I'm sorry I hurt you so bad." Then she said in a high, strained voice, "But I knew right away—right after I was married—it wasn't going to work."

"I thought of shooting that bastard," Howard said, "for butting in our lives—what we had together."

"Frederic carries a gun," she said, offhand.

Howard almost did not hear, he was shaking at hearing her voice again.

"What?" Howard said, his head down.

"Fred carries a lot of money," Marian said, "for his car business—and he carries a small gun."

"Yeah," Howard said slowly, "that phony-baloney—. If he isn't a hood—he's something close to it."

"I think they have been following you, Howard. I've heard Frederic talking, sometimes, maybe with his boss on the phone. I think they even were following you in Florida."

"That would explain a lot of things, babe. Some things happened down in Florida—well, I'll just say it looked like I walked into a trap—a set up."

"I heard Fred talking once," Marian said slowly, "and he mentioned your father's name, so I listened while he talked on the phone; something about electricity at night used on your father—to give him a heart attack. But, they said it didn't work. He got out of bed the next day."

"The bastards," Howard said flushing red in the face.

"Honey," Marian said, "I think they tried to get rid of you—but you went down to Florida. You got away from them"

"May they rot in hell," Howard said gritting his teeth.

"It's *all* because of me, Howard. I can just feel it. Please be careful, honey. I couldn't stand it if something happened to you. I'd just die."

"I'll keep my eyes open, babe. And I mean *all* the time. I promise," Howard said and took in a deep breath: he felt excited, angry, and a little frightened, all at the same time. "I'm—so-o glad to hear we'll be together again," he said and felt a slight sense of calm. "When are you coming back to Detroit?"

"When the dust settles, I guess," Marian said in an exasperated tone. "When Daddy calms down; then I'll go home. He didn't like me leaving Frederic at all, but mother and Ardis will get him to simmer down. Maybe in a week—or two."

"I hope this Fred character doesn't find you there in New York, babe," Howard said running his hand over the side of his face.

"No, I'm way ahead of you, honey. He doesn't know about Nancy—where she lives and all that. I don't go out. There's food and wine here," she said thinking, "and she doesn't go on a flight for two days yet. So, I'm okay."

"Good," Howard said sitting up straight. "And I got a bit of good cheer—I got a reporting job on the *Detroit News*, their new Suburban Bureau—heh, covering the Grosse Pointes, yet."

"Oh-h, that's terrific, Howard. Wow, good for you, honey. I'm so-o glad to hear—yeah, that is a bit of good cheer."

"I begin tomorrow," Howard said, and laughed. "Things are beginning to move *our* way." After a pause, he added, "So—the sooner you get home—the better, babe. Oh, man, I want to hold you, babe."

"Me too, honey, she said in a low voice. "I feel the same way—I miss you terribly." Then in a distracted toned, she said, "I've been so stupid to listen to other people. I can't wait to be with you, honey, and this time for good."

"Phone me, babe, as soon as you arrive home. Please. I'm a bundle of nerves, babe."

"Yes. Yes," she said softly. "That makes two of use with *nerves*, honey. I was so stupid to marry—the way I did."

"That stuff is over," Howard said to reassure her. "Don't think about the past. think about the future—how the two of us—will be together."

"You make me," she whispered, "feel good—*all over.*"

"Hearing your voice again," Howard said whispering back, "makes me feel like I've just come alive again. I want to hold you so much—I'm going to—explode."

There was a pause.

Howard heard Marian speaking to someone away from the telephone.

"I've got to go, honey. Nancy wants to use the phone the check her flight schedule."

"Okay, babe," Howard said exhaling hard. "Do what you have to—I'll be waiting for your call—when you're coming home."

"Good night, honey," she said softly.

"'Night, babe."

Howard hung up the phone slowly, thinking.

"That creep, Fred, was sure in a hurry to get married," he said quietly. "But, why?"

Sitting back in the kitchen chair, he put his hands behind his head, interlocking the fingers and said quietly "who would benefit the most?" Shaking his head, getting up the kitchen table, he said, "that's what I've got to find out, and I think I should start with that character that owns the tool and die shop."

Walking into the living room, where his father, mother, and sister were watching television, the "*I Love Lucy*" show, he said, "Marian's getting a divorce—she's coming home."

~ ~ ~

Monday, his first day on his new reporting job for the *Detroit News*, Howard made the rounds introducing himself at the City Halls. First the five Grosse Pointe cities, and after a stop in Harper Woods, he found himself sitting in the car in the parking lot of the police station in St. Clair Shores.

Snow flakes were falling on the windshield, as he sat looking at the two-story cube of cinder blocks, after taking the key out of the car ignition.

"Do I tell them I knew Melanie from my journalism class?" he said quietly, his breath steaming in the cold. "Naw, I'll just do my job routine—and if they find out she and I were classmates—I'll play dumb. I'll say something—something like—I didn't think it had anything to do—with the investigation."

The desk Sergeant with a name tag, Hiller, looked Howard stamping the snow off his shoes, standing in front of the desk in the lobby.

"I'm Howard Keck, a new reporter for the *News*. I've come to check the blotter—and who you have in the lock-up."

"You have a Press Card?" the Sergeant asked in a routine tone. "Some identification."

"Oh, yeah," Howard said pulling out his wallet. Then, while the Sergeant was looking at the card and photo, he asked, "Where is the Detective Bureau?"

"Up those steps," the Sergeant said handing back the press card. "But I think they're all out right now."

"Okay," Howard said putting the card back in his wallet, "I'll check with them next time."

The Sergeant slid the complaint log on the counter for Howard to read through. It was a clip-board with large rings, the information on printed forms filled out by the officers, who answered calls and wrote a report of what they found.

"We don't have anybody in the lock-up," the Sergeant said flatly.

"Okay, then," Howard said as he finished leafing through the complaints, sliding the board back to the Sergeant. "I guess that will do it for today. Thanks, Serge."

The Sergeant was nodding, when the telephone rang and he picked up the receiver.

Howard, standing and zipping up his jacket, looking through the plate glass door at the falling snow in the parking lot, suddenly, saw the man from the television newscast outside.

Howard was sure it was Aschenfelter, who owned the tool and die shop where the motorcycle jacket guy was clubbed. Watching the thin man, as he locked the door of his dark blue Mercedes, Howard saw the officer coat with the epaulets on the shoulders; now he was sure it was Aschenfelter.

Holding his note tablet over his head, as if to block the falling snow, Howard covered the lower part of his face with the other hand, and outside the door, walked quickly toward his car, at an angle, away from where the Mercedes was parked.

Catching a glimpse of Aschenfelter's face, who turned to walk toward the Police Station door, Howard noticed it had the features of a skull, the cheek skin sunken.

"Wonder what that creep is doing here?" Howard said to himself as he climbed into his car. After he started the engine and turned on the windshield wipers to clear off the snow, he said, "Maybe he's checking on the investigation about Melanie's murder. He seems to be around when all the rough-stuff is going on. I wonder what he's into—besides that tool shop? Where can I find out?"

Driving out of the parking lot, Howard said, "Hey, maybe the archives at the *News* have some clippings on this guy. Yeah—I'll check it out."

Moving slow with the traffic on the snowy street, he thought of the last thing Melanie said to him, that last time he saw her outside Doctor White's office; "Be careful—Howard."

Back at his desk at the *Detroit News* press room, Howard typed a feature story about a new carillon being installed behind the Water Pump Station in Grosse Pointe Farms. After filling out a slip to assign a photographer to take a picture of the new bell tower, he dropped the story and photo request on the Suburban Editor's desk, on his way out the door, heading for the library at the university.

Sitting at the oak table in the library again, he sat writing about the Depression Era affect on the yearbook, and the college's lower enrollment rate. He wrote out five pages to cover the subject of the economic downturn, bringing his yearbook history draft to a total of thirty-one.

Stacking the new pages with the others in his folder, Howard whispered to himself, "maybe six or seven more pages—and I can start typing—get this report ready to turn in to Doctor White's office. Ya-hoo."

He would finally have his degree, he thought, but felt it was just getting rid—eliminating an obstacle, rather than feeling a sense of accomplishment—what he was supposed to feel.

He grinned, lifting his jacket off the back of the heavy chair, then snapping off the reading light on the table, thinking of how his father and mother would feel proud of him for earning the degree. But to him, it was an anti-climax now, he already had a job on a big newspaper.

~~~

His mother was dropping spaghetti noodles into a pot of boiling water, when Howard walked into the kitchen.

"Ah-h, spaghetti," he said, "you can't beat it for dinner—make a lot of it, mom."

237

"Father is going to stop at the Italian bakery," she said without looking at him, "on his way home from work—and get a loaf of sesame seed."

"Super," Howard said, setting his yearbook notes on the edge of the kitchen table, and pulling open the refrigerator door. "The snow is really coming down out there, now."

"How was your first day at work?" his mother asked, stirring the cooking noodles with a large wood spoon.

"Ah-h, no problems—it went smooth," he said lifting a carton of orange juice out of the refrigerator, bumping the door closed with an elbow. "I knew most of the people—from when I worked on that weekly newspaper, so I was really just saying hello all over again."

"There's some news from the Caldwells next door," his mother said in an even tone, which she used when she disliked something. "Betty and Ray sold their house—they're going to move."

"Yikes," Howard said pouring orange juice into a small glass, "that's kind of a shock—I mean it's so sudden," he said while putting the orange juice carton back in the refrigerator.

"Well, his mother said while stirring, "Ray just retired last year from Sears, and Betty said they want to get a smaller place—a condo out in Sterling Heights."

"It's odd though," Howard said and set the empty juice glass on the sink. "You think she would have mentioned something about it. They were more than just neighbors—you and Betty were good friends."

"I know," his mother said, trying not to show her disappointment, "but I guess, you can never know about people—what they will do. I thought she was a friend."

"I wonder," Howard said, "who will move in next door, what we'll get for neighbors," while picking up his note folder from the table. "Boy, will dad be surprised."

"Howard," his mother said, pouring the noodles and hot water into a colander in the sink to drain, "let me tell father. I'll wait—until after dinner."

"Okay, mom," Howard said walking to the kitchen doorway. "I won't say anything. I'm—going to be doing some typing—after dinner—for my class work."

"A young couple is moving in next door," his mother said lifting the colander, setting it in the pot she had poured the hot water from, making a cloud of steam rise from the sink, "and they have a little girl about three."

Howard shrugged, making a bored face, and said, "I wonder where they came from—in such a hurry."

His mother was upset about the sudden move, but Howard could not suppress the feeling of suspicion. He felt as if something was going on behind the scenes; someone was pulling the strings. He could feel it on the back of his neck.

"I'll call you when dinner is ready," his mother said with her back to Howard. "So don't turn that radio on too loud with that classical music—you won't hear me again."

"Right, mom," Howard said grinning about the classical music.

From the hallway, Howard saw the front door swing open out in the living room. His sister, Kathy, came in carrying her books in her arms, leaned against the door to close it.

Her loden Duffle coat was covered with snow on the shoulders.

"You look like a snow man," Howard said, grinning.

"I had to *walk* home," she said setting her books on a small table near the door. "The school busses can't get on the road with all this snow."

"Don't get my living room rugs wet," Howard's mother shouted from the kitchen. "Kathy—come out here to the kitchen."

Kathy made a face, but moved quickly with her books to the kitchen.

"You should use the back door," Howard said after her, grinning.

When no retort came, Howard shook his head, and went to his bedroom. He snapped on the desk light, and dropped his yearbook notes on the desk, next to his typewriter. Then he turned the class music station on the radio. when reading through his notes, he found he had the Depression Era segment of the history, instead of *before* World War II, had it after the war segment. He made a note to change the chronology when typing that page.

Rolling two sheets of paper with a carbon between, into the platen of his upright typewriter, he sat for a moment engrossed in thought, the Holberg Suite playing on the radio, then began typing the history of the yearbook, his last assignment at the university.

He had been typing for twenty minutes, when Kathy appeared in the bedroom doorway.

"The mailman brought this letter with a bunch of other stuff," she said holding the letter out to Howard. "I saved him a trip up to the porch—when I came home."

Howard looked up at her, "Thanks," he said, watching her drop it on her desk.

"It's a girl's handwriting," she said, "and it's from New York."

Howard felt his heart jump looking at the small envelope, before he picked it up, and using a pencil, tore open the top.

"Dearest Howard,

Just a note to say I'll be arriving in Detroit at 7 P.M. on Tuesday, Jan. 12, flight 220 from New York.

Please pick me up.

Love Marian.

P.S. Nancy asked I quit running up the phone bill, ergo this note."

Howard sat looking at the note, savoring the message, re-reading it slow, feeling his heart pounding hard.

"Man," he whispered, "I feel like I'm just coming back to life—that I got my life back. I didn't realize how much I missed her. Man."

He sat staring at her writing on the note because it was part of her; the radio station playing, "The Lark Ascending."

"Howard," his mother called from the kitchen, "get ready for dinner."

"Okay, mom," he shouted, blinking, coming back to reality, smiling.

He folded the note slowly, and slipping it back into the envelope, tenderly, he said, "She'll be here tomorrow night. I'll be with her tomorrow night—man, that's all that counts now."

He remembered how before he could not bring himself to think about her and be realistic about marrying her, or buying a house, or furnishing it, not even where they would live, not any of those things.

When he went with her before, he remembered he was only concerned in sharing a good time with her, going places, doing things that were interesting—boy and girl things that were exciting.

Being with her now, he knew would be different; he knew he would have to take the responsibility of being with her.

Standing up at his desk, he said, "Well, at least I have a job now. A steady income will make a difference—a big difference," he said snapping off the desk lamp.

At dinner, Howard's father told everyone he had seen a young couple in the front room next door when he came from work, and Howard's mother told him the house was sold.

Howard thought his father would react a lot stronger, be upset, more than what he was, and it struck Howard, that was unusual for his father. He knew his father and Ray next door had been friends for years. Something was wrong, Howard felt; his father was acting out of character.

After dinner, Howard's father went downstairs to watch the George Pierrot travel show on television.

Howard went back to his bedroom and sat down at the desk, glancing through the yearbook notes. He was too excited about Marian's homecoming to type anymore. He decided to go downstairs and watch the evening news with his father.

Downstairs, Howard dropped on the couch in the recreation room. He faced the side of his father, stretched out on a leather lounge chair, legs raised.

"What's this guy?" Howard asked; the news had come on television.

"That's the head of the J Edgar Hoover's bureau in Detroit," his father said. "They caught some guy snooping around the Tank Arsenal plant."

"He sure dresses like a dude," Howard said, "and he looks like that actor—Zimbalist. That suit he's wearing must cost a bundle."

"He's probably got a government clothing allowance," Howard's father said waving a hand. "Edgar wants his boys to look spiffy."

"Cripe," Howard said, "take a look at his hands—he's even got a manicure—look at those fingernails. He's a spiffy one, all right, maybe—*too* spiffy."

Howard's father rolled onto his side in the lounge chair, his face him.

"I—had to go to the nurses office at work today," he said to Howard in a low voice. "Don't tell your mother—she's upset enough—about Betty moving away."

"Okay, I won't say anything," Howard said nodding, but looking as father was concerned. "How come you had to go to the nurse?"

"I just got dizzy," his father said quietly, while throwing up his hands. "I damn near fell over—I went forward—and dropped to one knee."

"Wow," Howard said, leaning forward, elbows on his knees, to better hear his father, "that could be serious."

"The nurse said I should go to see a doctor right away," he said speaking low, "and that I should get an EKG test."

"You better do what the nurse says, dad. You can't go fooling around—when it's the heart."

241

"I'm not so sure," his father said, "it is the heart."

"That why you got to go to a doctor, dad, so you can find out—'for sure'—what it really is."

"I can't tell mother," his father said rolling back to lay flat in the chair again, "she'll get upset—and worried—and she doesn't need that on top of losing her pal Betty."

"No, dad," Howard said raising both hands, pointing both index fingers, "just go up and tell mom. She *has* to know. She has a right to know—Betty be damned."

His father sat silent, thinking a moment.

"I guess—I'll go to a doctor," he said sitting up in the lounge chair. "I'll go tell mother first."

Howard stood up from the couch, studying his father's face, and for the first time he noticed the dark circles under his eyes.

"I had some good news today," Howard said to break the somber atmosphere. "I got a letter from Marian saying she's flying home tomorrow night."

"That Grosse Pointe girl again," Howard's father said pulling up his pants by the belt. "Why do you want to get mixed up with her again? She's way out of your class."

Howard, grinning, watched his father walk toward the stairway, turned to look back, "you should go to a doctor too."

"Who's going to a doctor?" Howard's mother said from the top of the stairway.

"Nothing serious," Howard said grinning, following his father upstairs to the kitchen. "Father thinks Marian is too good for me."

In the kitchen, Howard's mother and sister were washing the supper dishes; the tiny black-and-white television set was on the news, the volume low.

When his father and mother walked out to the living room, his father telling her about his heart scare, his sister Kathy walked behind them, listening.

Howard stopped to look at the television picture, when he saw the man with the epaulets appear on the screen. He was talking with a reporter with a microphone, but the volume was too low for him to hear.

The epaulets man was standing, his hand holding open the door of the dark Mercedes.

"What the hell is he up to now?" Howard said, reaching to turn up the volume, unable to find the correct one for the row of small knobs. "He pops up everywhere."

In the picture on the television set switched to the Detroit Bureau office, showing the man in the expensive suit sitting at a desk, the nameplate: WALDRON. Howard was turning all the knobs, when the volume rose, "and the investigation is continuing," Waldron said.

"Investigation of what?" Howard said throwing his hands up in a futile gesture. "Why does the guy with the epaulets keep showing up? Who the hell is he?"

Howard heard his mother say out in the living room, "I'll call Doctor Steinburg's office, tell them you're coming—while you change clothes."

~~~

At the airport terminal, the first thing Howard noticed was Marian's legs, the round calves, full down to the ankle as she walked toward him with a suitcase.

"Oh, man," he said rising from the chair in the lobby, watching her walk in a pleated skirt, "she's even more beautiful than I remember."

"How-ward," she said, smiling when she saw him. "I'm so glad you showed up—I was worried."

He kissed her softly, after watching her set the suitcase down.

"Wild horses couldn't keep me away, babe," he said looking closely at her face. "this is like a dream—us back together. I think I'm in heaven."

"I wish Daddy felt the same—about me coming back to Detroit," she said watching Howard pick up her suitcase. "He wants me," she said, as they walked, shifting her overcoat to her arm away from Howard, "to stay in New York—and stay with Frederic—work through our—"

Shaking his head, Howard said, "I'm glad you didn't take his advice again," while trying not to look at the way she moved, walking next to him: he was getting excited. "He's the one who touted you to marry that creep—in the first place."

"I know how you feel, honey," she said looking at the side of his face, "but look at me, what I have to live with. Daddy claims I disgraced the family—in his eyes—and now I have to go live in his house again."

"Naw, babe, you don't have to go back home," Howard said when they stopped in front of the revolving door. He stood watching her pulling on her winter coat. "We can get a place—together."

"Not just yet, honey—ple-ease," Marian said and stepped into the revolving door.

"Oh, man," Howard said quietly to himself, before stepping into the door section behind Marian, "this family thing won't go away. I think—it's going to be a long drawn-out session. I can see it coming."

243

At the car in the parking lot, Howard slid the suitcase on the backseat, and when he climbed behind the steering wheel, kissed Marian. She put her arms around his neck, but when he slid her skirt up, she said quietly, "Not now, honey," and pushing down her skirt, added, "I'm just too upset. I have a lot to handle."

"Talk about 'harder,'" Howard said. Then he whispered, "Damn, damn—I prematurely ejaculated. "Aw-w," he said, "I came in my pants—I'm wet, look." He lifted the front of his pants up.

"Oh-h, honey," Marian said, putting her hand to the side of his face, "please try and understand—I've got to go through the come home scene—and it's going to be—very emotional."

Howard nodded, and sat straight, looking down, below the steering wheel, where his wet pants spot showed dark in the light from the overhead parking lot lamps.

The car windows were beginning to fog-up from his heavy breathing.

"I haven't been making love much in the past months," he said to Marian. "Only a couple of times down in Florida. I'm like a bomb—and seeing you again, babe—I can't help—exploding."

"Honey," Marian said, "I'll make it up to you—when all of this is over. We'll have the rest of our lives together," she said, her hand squeezing his forearm. "I'll make you happy. I promise."

Nodding, Howard started the car.

"See you still have the new Chevy," Marian said to change the subject.

They were both silent, driving past the piles of snow on the boulevard past the airport terminal, that led out to the Expressway back to Detroit.

"I suppose you've been making love like a rabbit with that creep," Howard said. Turning to take a quick look at Marian, he asked, "Hey, you're not pregnant—are you?""

"No, honey," she said, "I *made sure* I didn't get pregnant. You should know better—than to ask."

"Good," Howard said driving, looking forward, "I mean, I'm glad that creep—didn't give us—that kind of trouble."

"When he started telling me what to do all the time," Marian said in a distracted tone, looking outside as they drove past snow pile-up along the roadway, "it got to be too much."

"Yeah," Howard said, "that would get to you after awhile—I can see that."

"He even told me what to *wear* one day," she said, a hardness in her voice.

Howard took a quick look at her, as they passed under the overhead street lamps, and saw her jaw set.

"I don't blame you, babe," Howard said and dropped his hand on her thigh and squeezed it. "I'm—glad—"

"*You're* glad," she said, meaning she found relief by leaving Frederic.

"Uh-huh," Howard said. "*I'm* glad—that you've come home, babe."

She smiled, looking at him, slipping her hand on his.

~ ~ ~

"Ah, I haven't been here for awhile," Howard said turning into the driveway at Marian's Grosse Pointe home. "It hasn't changed much—just the piles of snow—they won't last."

"I wish you were right, Howard. Thanks for trying to cheer me up."

Ardis pulled open the front door, after Marian rang the door bell.

"You're not welcome here," Marian's father shouted from the living room.

"Is he talking to me, or you?" Howard quipped.

"Come, come in," Ardis said holding the door open. Hugging Marian, she said quickly, "It's good to see you again."

Her mother, coming from the living room, said to Marian, "Oh, dear, are you all right?" After Marian kissed her cheek, the mother straightened, her hand to the side of her face.

When Marian began pulling off her overcoat, Howard started to take his off also; everyone in the vestibule was watching one another closely.

Then Howard remembered the wet on the front of his pants, and said, "I'll get the suitcase," and slipped the coat back to cover the wet spot.

"My daughter is a married woman," Marian's father shouted when he heard Howard's voice. "You have no business here—you are against the law of man—and God."

Marian put her hand on Howard's shoulder, "Don't take him seriously. He'll calm down. Go get the suitcase—please."

"In a way," Howard said grinning, "he's right."

"Oh, Daddy," Ardis shouted toward the living room, "he's just a friend from college—helping her out."

"He should not be here," the father shouted back, "and neither should she. She should be with her husband—her *lawful* husband."

"Go get the suitcase," Marian whispered to Howard.

"Oh, Daddy," Ardis said, excited, "come and say hello."

Howard heard her as he was closing the door, going for the luggage.

"Whew," he said outside, the snow on the driveway crunching as he walked, "that's like a buzz-saw in there."

Pulling the suitcase off the back car seat, slamming the door, he stood for a moment in the dark and cold. Looking at the row of large houses up the street, all lighted, he suddenly felt intimidated—everything seemed *larger* for some reason.

"Whew," he said unable to find a reason for the feeling.

Back inside the house, Howard found the family all out in the kitchen, the father wearing a robe over pajamas.

Marian stepped over to Howard when he appeared in the kitchen doorway.

"I'm going to run," he said in a low voice, setting the suitcase down.

"Oh, stay for some coffee," Marian said quietly. "It's early yet—"

"Don't put me on the spot, babe," Howard said, his hand over his mouth, "ah, like the one on the front of my pants—if you get my drift."

"Oh, yeah," Marian said grinning and putting her hand on his shoulder.

"Is this *all* your luggage you have?" he said bumping the suitcase with his foot.

"I put it in storage," she said. "It's in a warehouse in New York—I just have to send for it."

When they were walking to the front door, he stopped and wrote his news office phone number on a piece of paper from the small note pad he always carried.

"Thanks for coming to meet me at the airport, honey," Marian said looking at the note paper. "Tomorrow I have to see a lawyer—I'll be busy."

"I'm glad you're back here, babe. You don't know how glad—despite your father's outbursts."

"Me, too," she whispered, just before he kissed her.

Chapter 21

At his desk in the newsroom the next day, Howard typed a feature story about "Bubbling" a boat for the winter; it was a new process he learned about at the marina in St. Clair Shores. the bubbles kept the ice from forming around the hull, that would be crushed by the ice, ordinarily.

After he finished the story, and was writing a request for a photographer to take pictures at the marina, a tall girl came in and sat at the next desk.

She wore a black patch over her right eye.

"I'm Suzy Whitaker," she said, after shedding her coat while seated, pushing it over the back of the chair, then unzipping her briefcase on the desk. "I cover Warren and Centerline."

Howard smiled, nodding, trying not to look at the eye patch.

"I'm Howard Keck—I cover the Grosse Pointes, Harper Woods and St. Clair Shores."

"My eye is infected," she said in a matter of fact tone, reaching to touch the patch lightly. "My doctor gave me this thing to cover the medication—then my mother thought it looked too—plain—so she sewed sequins on it."

Howard, working not to smile, nodded, gathering up the pages of the "Bubbling" story scatted on his desk, then tapping the stack edges to make them even.

"I used to work on a weekly out in the Pointes," he said, just to be talking. "That's how I landed this job. I get my degree from Wayne State at the end of this term. I'm just finishing the last class. But the formal graduation won't come until June—when the dean has a ceremony."

"I graduated from Michigan State," she said smiling, pulling open a side drawer. "I worked on a weekly out in Warren—for almost a year. I've been here for almost a week now—they hired me too, because I know my way around Warren."

"The only big event happening out in the Shores," Howard said in a bored fashion, "is the murder of a co-ed—that the cop-shop is investigating."

"Uh-huh," Suzy said. "I heard that girl was supposed to marry some guy from Warren—two days—before she was killed. He's an engineer from Germany. They were going to get married in one of the Wedding Chapels out there in St. Clair Shores."

"Well," Howard said, holding back that he knew Melanie Marsak from journalism class, before she was killed, sat silent for a moment, then said thoughtfully, "I haven't had much chance to read-up on the detail stuff."

"Her getting killed that way," Suzy said, taking two notebooks and a leather bound telephone list out of her briefcase, putting them in the drawer, "really upset the German community in Warren."

He sat watching as Suzy took a dog-eared, paperback Thesaurus, and dropped it in the flat desk drawer just above her legs, "Yeah," she said, "it's kind of an open secret—they work at the Warren Tank Arsenal. They're designers and engineers from Germany helping the government. Most of them brought their families—and they have a German neighborhood—a German community."

"And the girl that was murdered," Howard said leaning back in his desk chair, "was supposed to marry one of these Germans. Boy—that story is loaded with all *kinds* of possible leads."

"Maybe," Suzy said, "someone didn't want them to get married."

"Yeah," Howard said, folding his hands behind his head, now, while leaning back, "if a foreigner marries an American, they can stay here—indefinitely—they don't have to return to their country."

"That might have something to do with it," Suzy said sliding her briefcase to the side of her desk top.

"Maybe," Howard said slowly sitting upright, "I will check out the background of this engineer guy from Germany."

"That whole neighborhood of Germans—is protected. but good luck," Suzy said. "They're being here—is sort of hush-hush," she said just as her phone rang. "I mean it's not publicized," she added and picked up the telephone.

Howard stood up, then walked over to the suburban editor's desk to drop off the "Bubbling" story and the photo request.

When he glanced back at Suzy, she was hunched over, talking into the phone quietly, smiling.

"I wonder," Howard said watching Suzy talking, "what Melanie got into with this German hush-hush stuff—and if any of it—was the reason—she was hit with a lamp."

Al Carmody, the editor was away, and Howard looking for a clear place to set his story, looked at the clutter of photos on the desk. One figure in a picture caught his eye.

"Damn," he said slowly looking closer, "if it isn't him in the military coat." Picking up the photo he saw the coat on a thin man, standing in a group, that was watching a wall being knocked down by a bulldozer.

The cutline under the photo read: "Making way for the new Warren Industrial Park, business leaders watch as the first of the abandoned buildings at Campbell and Mound Roads is demolished. Soon, a new industrial park will occupy the site, bringing new industry, jobs, and an increased tax-base for the city.

From left, the businessmen are:

Howard counted to the third name, Robert Aschenfelter.

"Now we're getting somewhere," Howard said looking at the name again. "I have to find out what this guy's connection—why he keeps showing up at crime scenes."

Walking out to the hallway of the newspaper building, Howard saw the cafeteria down at the end and started for it to get coffee.

Near the cafeteria entrance, a small sign extended out from the wall: LIBRARY.

"I should see what information the newspaper has on this Aschenfelter," Howard said reaching for the doorknob on the frosted glass door. "Just for the heck of it."

Going through the file, Howard found only clippings of awards given Aschenfelter by retail merchants and city officials for his community service.

"Naw," Howard said closing the folder. He was sitting in the outer room of the newspaper library, that reminded him of an old style dentist's waiting room. "Nothing here—that could help me."

He stood up, and was crossing to the counter to return the folder, when the door opened and Suzy Whitaker came in carrying a paper cup of coffee.

"Doing some research, huh," she said, lifting the lid on the coffee cup, taking a sip. She turned her head sideways and read the name on the tab. "Aschenfelter," she said as if reading, "what you want to know about that guy? I sort of know—rather—know *of* him. Maybe—I can help you."

"I see him all over," Howard said. "On television—out at the Shores police station—and he seems to show up where crime takes place, for one reason or another."

"Well, I don't know about the crimes," Suzy said, "but he's sort of the un-official—mayor—ombudsman for that German community we talked about. He helps with the legal stuff, and the taxes; problems they have with the utility companies, that sort of thing. They keep him busy."

"Okay," Howard said, "that would explain some of why I see him around so much."

"He has a daughter at college in Colorado," Suzy said, before taking a long drink of coffee, after blowing on it, "and his wife plays Bridge all the time."

"That sounds like he has a lot of free time," Howard said looking at the name on the folder, then shaking it.

"Ah, you want dirt," Suzy said, grinning. "He has a girlfriend—some German woman, who's supposed to be an aristocrat from someplace near Dresden. Her family raised horses, before the Russians took over. She has a son."

"Where did you pick up that information?" Howard asked.

"When I was going to classes at Oakland, I had an apartment in Rochester," Suzy said. "Eva Schroder lived in the complex building across the parking lot. Rumors were flying about the Mercedes showing up in the parking lot—sometimes all night."

"Aschenfelter," Howard said, "that rings a bell." He had flinched when he heard the name, but Suzy did not notice. His first name isn't Frederic, is it?"

"I'm not sure," Suzy said, "but I hear he's sort of a playboy—and got kicked out of college in Miami."

"How did Aschenfelter know Missus Aschenfelter?" Howard asked.

Her husband and Ash were army buddies—Aschenfelter was an engineer at the Tank Plant—until he passed away—with Leukemia," Suzy said holding the cup in the palm of her hand now. "He helped Ash get work for his tool shop—everybody in town knows that."

Howard nodded, biting his upper lip, thinking.

"Oh, Miss," the woman behind the library counter said, "no coffee please." She pointed at a sign on the wall, that said: NO FOOD OR BEVERAGES ALLOWED IN LIBRARY.

"We were just going," Howard said sliding the folder on the counter back to the librarian.

"I have to check out a name," Suzy said, and drank the remaining coffee before dropping the cup in the wastebasket. "My girlfriend met a guy—who owns a golf shop; she wants to know if he's married." she said smiling at Howard.

Howard walked to the door and stopped. "What happened to the—playboy?" Howard turned and asked Suzy.

"Ash got him a job in Birmingham, selling foreign cars, I heard. He must be doing pretty good—I hear he married a girl from Grosse Pointe."

Howard wince.

"Ah-h," Suzy said smiling, "the plot thickens."

"Naw," Howard said feeling his face flush, "she was in one of my classes—at Wayne State."

"Uh-huh," Suzy said, grinning, "Go on—"

~ ~ ~

"Hey, Bob-o, this is Howard calling from his desk at his new job on *The Detroit News*. Suburban Bureau, specifically.

There was a pause on the phone, then Bob Foskett said, "Good for you, man," slowly as he comprehended. "I always had you figured to make it big-time in that newspaper racket."

"Yeah," Howard said, "expense account included."

"Hey, Howard, how are you and that sweetie, Marian, getting along?"

"Aw, she married some hustler-bozo with money," Howard said closing his eyes. "they were living there in New York, but now she's back here in Detroit—filing for divorce."

"Jee-ze, what a mess, man," Bob said in a flat tone, that did not offer sympathy. "How did she get away from you—in the first place?"

"I guess her father didn't think I had much potential," Howard said. "he sort of 'found' a husband for her—with money. But, I'll fill you in on the details later—right now—I got to ask you for a favor."

"Okay," Bob said, "I'll do what I can—if it's legal."

"You know someone who can do—investigating?" Howard said slowly.

There was a silence, then Bob said, "I use a snoop to check out clients—see if their finances are shaky. This guy is an ex-cop—he uses his connections here in New York."

"You really snoop on clients?" Howard asked grinning.

"Yeah," Bob said defensively, "some of them. I don't want to do a lot of design brain-work—and not get paid for my efforts, man."

"I don't blame you," Howard said, picking up a pencil off his desk, tapping the eraser on the telephone base. "I'm checking this guy's surrogate father at this end, but the guy I'm after spends a lot of time in New York City on some kind of foreign car business. He carries a lot of cash, and he carries a PPK."

"Like James Bond," Bob said.

"What?" Howard asked.

"Bond carries a PPK."

"Yeah,—Okay, man," Howard said. "In a nutshell, it's a plain old investigation of this yahoo—and it might turn into a news story on this end."

"No," Bob said, "You want this guy who married Marian investigated because you thinking he's a crook—out here stealing what he can in New York."

"Right," Howard said, "since you put it that way, Bob. I only have to add that the *News* will cover all expenses—and if they don't I'll put it on my expense account."

"Well," Bob said, "that's good to hear—I was just going to ask about the cost—being covered. You must of read my mind, man."

After giving the name and address of Marian's husband, Howard, to break-up the seriousness of the conversation, said, "You been working hard on your boat—this winter?"

"Yeah, some," Bob said, then added, "man, I've found a forty-two footer. I want to buy it, but Deborah wants to re-model the kitchen at the house in Sag Harbor. So—the matter is—under arbitration—so to speak."

"Ah-h," Howard said, "life is full of problems."

"When you get married—someday, I hope—you'll find out, buddy-boy."

"Yeah—", Howard said, hearing another phone ringing in Bob's office before he could speak further, then hearing Bob talking on the other line.

"I've got to go to work," Bob said. "Duty calls—and I'm the only one in the office right now—."

"One more thing," Howard said after giving Bob the phone number at his news desk, "If you find out when he's heading for Detroit—buying an airline ticket—could you let me know—pronto?"

"You're worried about the PPK—aren't you?" Bob said.

~~~

Opening the front door, Marian came out into the night cold, holding the door almost closed against her back.

"Honey," she said softly, the cold air making her breath steam, "it's not a good time to come in—Daddy's having a fit. Ever since dinner—he keeps saying me and Frederic should go to a marriage counselor."

She put her hand against the side of Howard's face, "He wants—he insists—we patch-up the marriage."

"Jee-ze," Howard whispered, setting his hands on her shoulders, "he's *always* 'insisting on something."

"Well, honey, I went to the lawyer today—" she said before Howard kissed her, pulling her against himself. "No honey, not out here," she whispered stepping back. "Not on the front porch."

"I'm going—crazy, babe," Howard said slowly, watching her leaning against the door. "I want you so much."

"I know—I know," she said and put her hand on his lips. "This trouble will be over soon," she whispered, "and we'll be together, honey. But right, now, we just have to—"

"No-o, babe," Howard said, putting his hands back on her hips, "we should make our move—right now. Get away from all this—get a place together—and let the rest of the world twist in the wind."

"That wouldn't be practical," she said putting her hand on his arms holding her, "the legal thing would be changed—and Daddy would disown me—not to mention the scandal that it would cause."

"I have a decent job," Howard said watching Marian's face, his breath turning to steam in the cold, "so you won't have to worry about money any more—"

"I know, honey," she said looking him in the face, "but I have my family to think of—what it will do to them if I run off." Squeezing his arms, she said slowly, "let's get the divorce done first—just now. That's the most important thing—issue."

"Can you get out tonight? Howard asked, in a tone that surrendered to her practical thinking. "Can you get away for a while?"

"No, honey. Fred is coming to Detroit tomorrow—to sign legal papers—we meet the lawyer at his office downtown in the Penobscot Building. So, I have to stay here—until that's over."

"Our news office is just down the street from the Penobscot; I can pound a typewriter until you're done with the lawyer. Will you call me, babe? We can get together."

"Yes," Marian said, pushing back to open the door.

"Marian," her father's voice came from the living room, "you are still married."

"Coming, Daddy."

"Your husband is coming here," her father said in a slow rhythm, "tomorrow."

"Yes, Daddy."

Howard stepped forward and kissed her, pulling at her heavy wool sweater as she backed into the house.

"Tell him to go back to watching his wrestling on television," he said.

"See you tomorrow," she said quietly. "I miss you—*all* of you, honey," she whispered, before she closed the door slowly.

Turning off the porch, Howard shook with being cold, and looked up at the stars. It was a clear night, but cold.

"That old bastard," Howard said, stepping off the porch, "just because he's got money—he's *always* right."

~ ~ ~

The next morning, after reading the headline: "Tool Shop Owner Arrest in Co-Ed Murder," Howard drove to the St. Clair Shores police station to do a follow-up story.

"They got the bastard," he said walking past the piled snow in the police parking lot. "I'd like to know how—for more than one reason."

"Yeah," the young detective said, "this Aschenfelter came in to make a statement about how he knew the deceased. He's a partner in a marina project that wants to build a high-rise apartment and hotel building on the waterfront. They plan to have shops, bars, restaurants, theatres—all along a waterfront boardwalk—a giant boater's Mecca."

"How did the deceased fit into all this?" Howard asked wanting to know about Melanie.

He was sitting at the detective's desk, writing in a tablet he held on his knee. He glanced for a moment at the name: Detective Troy Klebba on the upright plastic name plate.

"The investors needed someone to handle the public relations for the marina project," the detective said all-knowing, as if he single-handed, solved the case. "They advertised for candidates—his Melanie Marsak showed up—she was the one selected for the job."

"I see," Howard said, "and she moved in at her apartment to be near the project?"

"Yeah," Klebba said, "we got all that information from this Aschenfelter guy when he came in to make a statement a few days ago."

Howard nodded, and began writing in his notebook. He remember seeing the gaunt Aschenfelter in the snowy parking lot a few days ago.

"But," Howard said, "what led to his arrest?"

"Okay," the all-knowing Klebba said, leaning back in his desk chair, "this Aschenfelter pays this Melanie a midnight visit. He parks his company car, a light-blue Ford, out front of her apartment building—but he parks it in a restricted zone near the doorway."

"How did you know it was Aschenfelter's company car?" Howard asked while writing.

"A snow removal guy with a plow on his truck was clearing the parking lot that night. He was miffed the car was near the door, so he writes the license plate number down to give to the building maintenance guy—to ask the tenant to move the car. He goes around the building to the other side to plow—when he comes back, the car is gone—about twenty minutes later."

"What time was this?" Howard asked not looking up from writing in his notebook.

"About twenty minutes to one in the morning," Klebba said. "The coroner's report estimates time of death between twelve and one."

"Is that all you have on Aschenfelter?" Howard asked.

"No," Klebba said leaning forward, his elbows on the desk, "an elderly couple in the next apartment was up—the old man has kidney problems—heard shouting in the apartment. A man and woman arguing—that stopped—abruptly—about one, they said."

"Ah-h," Howard said, "so you arrested Aschenfelter?"

"No, the sheriff's department went to Aschenfelter's tool shop later that morning with a warrant," Klebba said in an all-knowing tone, "he's got an apartment—living quarters—upstairs fixed up in the tool shop. They arrested him. And they found a stain on the shoulder of his fancy overcoat—that he'd tried to wash off—"

"Blood stain?" Howard asked.

"I'm not sure, Klebba said. "they took it to the lab for analysis. We're waiting for the report."

"Wow," Howard said, "that would clinch the case."

"We're pretty sure it's a blood stain," Klebba said.

The telephone on the desk rang, and Klebba picked up the phone, and sat listening for a moment.

Howard closed his notebook, then stood up, and said, "Thanks."

Klebba, nodded, then picking up a pencil began to write.

Going down the stairs to the police station lobby, Howard said quietly to himself, "that coat with the epaulets—will be the downfall of that creep Aschenfelter yet." Then, thinking of Melanie, he said, "that creep went to the wrong girl for sex favors. Poor Melanie."

Chapter 22

It was almost four that afternoon, when Howard finished his rounds of the City Halls on his beat, and started up the stairs to his desk at the *News*.

Entering the Suburban Bureau on the second floor, pulling off his overcoat, Suzy Whitaker said, "from where she sat at her desk, "You got a phone message." As Howard passed her, she added, "it kept ringing—every ten minutes—so I answered it. I thought it might be important."

She lightly touched the skin under her eye patch, then rubbed it. Howard could smell her perfume.

"Thanks," he said laying his coat across the vacant chair next to his, before sitting down and slapping the notebook with the Detective Klebba details on the desk.

The note written on a square yellow pad read: "Fred coming for dinner tonight at father's invite. I'm grounded. Marian."

Howard's neck burned at the back; he felt as if he had just missed a train, or plane, and was standing, watching it move away.

To keep from lowering his forehead down on the desk, he reached back, and put his hand on the spot where it burned.

"Howard," Suzy said, "you okay?" She stood up from her desk, and walked over to Howard, smoothing the skirt of her dark blue suit. "It must have been important—your face is as white as a sheet."

"I'm just—tired," he said looking up at her. "I don't get enough sleep—it's catching up with me."

"It isn't because this Fred—moved in on your girl, is it?" Suzy said quietly, putting both hands on his desk, leaning forward.

"That's part of it," he said catching a view of her breasts in a black see-through bra, that showed because she wore no blouse. "He's her husband—who she's divorcing."

"Uh-huh," Suzy said grinning, standing upright, folding her arms under her breasts, "it's all coming clear now—it looks like father wants to keep you out of her life—he wants you to move on, kiddo."

"It ain't like high school," Howard said leaning back in the desk chair, "there isn't any 'moving on'."

"When I went to Andover," she said, "*all* the kids said that—but—they all moved on—eventually."

"Where's Andover?" Howard asked, to side-track her, trying to cover up feeling sheepish about spilling how he felt about Marian.

"Out in the hills—Birmingham," she said absently, running her hands to smooth her skirt over her rump. "I'm sorry to be nosey—but I came over when you went pale—I thought you were going to pass out."

"I'm just worn out," Howard said to her back as she walked to her desk.

Another reporter came in and sat at the desk opposite Howard's. This reporters' name was Cobb, but Howard did not know his first name; he missed it when Cobb introduced himself. Cobb, after rolling in paper and a carbon sheet, began typing rapidly as if unaware Howard and Suzy were in the room.

Howard watched as Suzy smoother the back of her skirt before sitting down, and saw the roundness of her thighs, when the skirt pulled tight, as she sat down.

She is what is labeled as full-figured, Howard thought. Soft, in all the right places.

Howard's phone rang, and he almost jumped. It was the Recreation Director from Grosse Pointe Park, who he talked with over forty minutes last week about the plans to enlarge the city's swimming pool. The Director was calling to say the City Council had approved the plan; Howard could write the story for the newspaper.

It was just after six when Howard finished writing the pool story. He was filling out a slip for a photographer assignment request, and did not see Suzy walk over.

"Since your girlfriend and her husband are having dinner together, "she said, pulling on her overcoat, the outline of her breasts showing, "what are you planning for supper—a bowl of chili?"

"I haven' given it much thought," Howard said looking up, sliding a paper clip on the five pages of the pool story and the photo request.

Glancing at the wall clock, "Yikes, I didn't know it was this late."

He picked up the phone, dialing home.

"Mom? Yeah," he said quietly. "I'm working late tonight, so don't hold any dinner for me. Okay?"

Suzy stood grinning, listening, flipping the cover of Howard's dictionary up and letting it fall.

"No, I'll get something to here downtown," Howard said turning sideways. "Okay, bye."

"You live home, huh, tiger?" Suzy said, not in the tone of a question, but more like a statement of disclosure.

"I didn't have a job until this month," Howard said. "I had to live someplace," he said rubbing the side of his face. "I couldn't be too fussy."

"Well," Suzy said and shrugged, "my steady boyfriend is down in Miami—tonight."

"What's he doing down there?" Howard asked grinning, leaning back in his desk chair.

"He flies an airplane for a small air service," she said, rubbing her face below the eye patch, lightly. "He won't be back until *tomorrow*—night."

"Well," Howard said leaning forward, "I guess it's a bowl of chili for the both of us, then."

"I can do better than that," Suzy said buttoning her overcoat. "We'll go to Sherman's they have the best prime rib—in the country."

"I'm on a chili budget," Howard said standing up, reaching for his coat on the chair. "I made a car payment this week."

"I can loan you a few bucks," Suzy said turning toward the doorway.

Walking behind her, pulling on his raincoat, Howard could smell her perfume; he could only say half-heartedly, "I don't like to—"

"It's just a loan, Howard," Suzy said, turning her head to one side, as they walked toward the stairway, adjusting the black eye patch. "You have to pay it back."

From the moment Howard and Suzy entered Sherman's Prime Restaurant, he could see every eye in the room go to the black eye patch. He felt like a celebrity, escorting Suzy.

A thin waitress, dressed like an airline hostess came over and said to Suzy, "there is about a twenty minute wait, dear." Howard watched the waitress discreetly studying the eye patch; she was a middle-aged woman, her movement quick no nonsense, but he saw her bonding with Suzy, no matter what the cause for the eye patch was.

"Okay," Suzy said, holding her briefcase in one hand, slipping her coat off her free arm.

"You are number forty-seven," the waitress said handing a plastic chip to Howard with the number on it. "You can wait at the bar—I'll call you."

Howard nodded, and after setting his and Suzy's briefcases on the bench near the bar, hung the coats on a stand.

He had to work to keep from smiling; he knew the men in suits, mostly were lawyers, were all curious about why Suzy wore the eye patch.

Sitting down at the barstools at the far end of the bar, Suzy crossed her full legs, and Howard could hear the nylon against nylon zipping sound. it excited him, but he looked away.

"They make a terrific martini here," she said, fishing for a cigarette in her crumpled pack.

"I need *something* strong," Howard said, "after the day I had today."

"I know what you need," Suzy said just as the bartender came over. "Two Martini Specials," she said, and picking up the plastic tag Howard set on the bar, "for table forty-seven."

Looking at the tag, the bartender nodded, then moved away.

"You must come here a lot," Howard said to her, looking at the long painting behind the bar, showing a fox hunt, covering the entire length of the wall.

"Over at the Press Club," Suzy said, "down the street," blowing smoke, "all they talk is shop. to get away from those people, I come here. I found this place a couple of days ago."

Howard took out his pack of cigarettes, looking at Suzy's legs, where their knees were touching. He wondered if she was enjoying it too. She did not show any sign.

"Who is this Wonder Woman—whose husband is coming for dinner?" she asked, blowing smoke away from Howard, and watching the bartender set the Martinis in front of them.

"A Grosse Pointe chick," he said lifting the toothpick with the olive out of the drink, and seating it. "I met her at a class at Wayne State."

"You better be careful, Howard," Suzy said without looking at him. "The G P protection society could step on you. The wealthy are very—protective—especially of their daughters."

"I don't blame them," Howard said.

Melanie, Howard remembered, said the same thing, in the same words, almost, about "being careful." Poor Melanie.

"Well," Suzy said holding the tall-stem glass, "here's to the good life." She took a long drink of the Martini.

"Right," Howard said before drinking, trying to keep his eyes off Suzy's legs as she uncrossed them.

The space under her skirt emitted a faint odor of her perfume.

Howard felt warm, an erection beginning; he set the empty Martini glass down, slowly.

"Hey," Suzy said smiling," you made short work of that Martini, tiger." she put her hand on his arm. "Relax, Howard."

"A table is open," the waitress said suddenly from behind them. "Follow me, please."

As Suzy leaned to sit down at the table, Howard caught another glimpse of her breasts, when her suit jacket lifted open, forward.

He knew now that the effect she was having on him was all being staged. He grinned.

"Everybody," he said, quietly, "at the bar—is looking at us." He thought a moment, then added, "must be that we got a table—there are some who were there before us."

"Maybe it's just the eye patch," Suzy said lifting up the menu. "they're wondering, maybe—if we're celebrities."

Howard ate the rib-eye and most of the "cottage" fries, while watching Suzy eat only some of the steak, and pick at the Cole slaw. He held back on making a comment about her appetite; he could sense she was preoccupied.

A light snow was falling when they stepped out the restaurant door, Howard holding it open for Suzy.

"You weren't too hungry," he said to her. "That rib was among the best, I've ever had."

"I feel more like drinking—than eating," she said pulling her coat up around her neck. "You're very perceptive," she said smiling, taking his arm, holding it against herself as they walked.

Howard could feel her soft breast against the back of his arm; they were crossing the street, walking to the newspaper parking lot.

Her Lincoln Town Car was dusted with snow at the rear of the lot, Suzy pointing to it, before digging her keys out of her large purse.

Howard kissed the back of her neck as she was unlocking the car door; neither of them spoke.

She sat down behind the steering wheel for an instant, then reached for Howard's arm while sliding over to make room on the seat for him. He sat down, pulling the door closed. He leaned across the seat to kiss her, and when he put his hand on her breast, she moved his hand.

"Wha-at?"

"We're out of high school," she said.

When Howard slid her skirt up, she helped remove the panty-hose, and the scent of her perfume filled the car.

Her thighs shone white as Howard moved, half-kneeling, half-lying on top of her, while she slid down on the seat.

"Uh-hm," she moaned when he entered her, pulling at him, pulling him hard against herself.

Feeling all of for softness and moisture, Howard put all his pent-up emotion into his love-making.

"Whe-ew," was the only sound he made, his face now wet against hers, the rest of him thrusting.

"Keep—kee—ep," she whispered, "Hold—hold—How—ard, hold."

When Howard lost control, and he could no longer hold, and after feeling himself release, he lay against her while breathing heavy.

She was breathing hard in his ear, and after kissing the side of his face, she began straightening her clothing.

"Will you be all right?" Howard asked.

"I wear a diaphragm," she said putting the pantyhose in her handbag. "If that's what you want no—my boyfriend had a doctor fit one—when we started—early on."

"Hope he don't hear about us," Howard said watching her close her coat around herself.

"He won't," she said putting her hand against the side of his face. "What about your Grosse Pointe girl?"

"What do you mean?"

"Does this change anything?"

"I'm—not sure, Suzy."

He was quiet for a moment, feeling trapped.

He liked doing it with her, but now he wanted to go—be away. He never felt that way with Marian. With her he wanted to be with her *all* the time. He could not explain it, or give a reason, it was just the way he felt about Marian.

"My boyfriend goes to Miami," Suzy said quietly, "and sometimes Dallas and Tucson—he's gone two, three days at a time. We could—get together—when he is away. If you want," she said pulling her coat around herself.

Howard nodded. He wanted her, but how could he say he wanted Marian more, and not refuse her offer.

"We'll see what we can work out," Howard said slowly, thinking, sitting up and putting both hands on the steering wheel. to change the subject, he said, "Your windows are all covered with snow."

"Good," Suzy said pulling her coat collar against her face, "it makes for more—privacy."

Howard smiled, but did not say anything when he turned to look at her, watching her slide the eye patch around to make it feel comfortable.

~~~

The next morning, Howard was at his newspaper desk when the phone rang.

"Honey," Marian said in a cheerful voice, "I'm going up to the summer house—until the divorce is final. Will you come up?"

"Great," Howard said smiling, leaning back in his desk chair, "that's good news, but," he said looking up at the wall clock showing nine-thirty," I can't get away until four or five—I've got two interviews scheduled." He inhaled, "You know I'll come up."

"Everything is frozen up there," she said, "but Daddy leaves the heat on in the house. I'm taking some clothes and Daddy's Olds—I'm going up this morning."

"Okay," Howard said, "I'll come up as soon as I can get away, babe."

"Fred and Daddy were working on me all through dinner last night—trying to make me change my mind about getting the divorce. It was just too—much."

263

She began to cry.

"Take it easy, babe," he said sitting up erect at the desk, "things will be okay—you'll get your freedom. It's always like this in the beginning," he said trying to reassure her, feeling upset over her crying.

"I—know," she said, sniffling. "I realize that."

"It's bumpy now," he said softly, "but it will turn smooth—you'll see, babe."

She was going against everything she knew, Howard realized. her comfortable life in Grosse Pointe, friends, school, and even her family, she was pushing aside. It was almost too much to ask—of anyone. And it was all because of how they felt about one another.

"Okay," she said in a high voice, that was caused by Marian wiping her nose, "come up as soon as you can—I'll have the fireplace going, honey."

"Terrific, babe. As soon as I can, I'm on the way."

"I miss you so much," she said in an even tone. "I—made a mistake with Frederic. It was stupid to marry him."

"You had a lot of pressure, babe—from all sides—they pushed you into a picture-book marriage. But real life has a lot of bumps in the road."

"Oh, hurry, come up," she said. "I've got to have you with me—I've got to have you to talk to." There was a pause, then she said, "I'm going to go now. I'm calling from Howard Johnson's by Lockmoor Golf course. See you in a while. Goodbye."

"Bye, babe," Howard said and set the phone on the cradle slowly. The dry in his throat made swallowing hard.

Suzy Whitaker came into the newsroom carrying a briefcase and a handful of large photographs.

"Hi," she said dropping the case and photos on the desk as if they were heavy. "It's really cold out there."

"Howdy," Howard said, watching as she slid off a brown tweed coat; she wore a brown suit with an orange scarf. "You're chipper this morning."

"You bet," she said touching lightly at the eye patch strap where it was close to her ear. "You got time for coffee?"

"I've got to run," Howard said thinking, "I've got a court session to cover." Then looking at her round thighs, felt himself getting excited, added, "Maybe a little later on."

"Right," she said, "I understand," and as she was walking to the door, smoothed her skirt with her hands over her thighs.

The telephone rang.

"A collect call from New York city," the operator said. "Do you accept the charges?"

"Yes," Howard said, surprised.

"Hey, man, this is Bob," he said. "I've got news."

"Bob," Howard said leaning back in his chair, "good for you—good to hear from you so soon."

"Howie, we checked-out this Fred guy—you asked about. The ex-cop was too busy, so I hired a junkie I know who has connections like you wouldn't believe—and I gave him two hundred."

"Okay, Bob, I'll Western Union you the money," Howard said leaning forward on his desk. "What did you find out?"

"Okay, he carries a gun—like the one Bond does," Bob said in a tone that there was a lot more to come.

"A PPK," Howard said.

"Yeah, and the reason he does is—he's walking around with about forty grand in his pocket," Bob said, and Howard could tell he was smiling. "He needs it for his business."

"What kind of business does he do, Bob?"

"He's in the car importing business—and this will knock you for a loop, Howie—"

"C'mon man, spill it Bob."

"Here it is," Bob said sounding proud of his work. "It seems that when Sergeants up and go overseas on the Military Transport ships, Uncle Sam will ship the family car, along with all the other household stuff—furniture, dishes, and all that."

"How does this fit in with this Fred guy's business?" Howard asked while writing notes at his desk.

"Now when the ships come back to the States," Bob said slowly, "it ain't always with the family Chevrolet. Your Fred has the Sergeant buy a sport car overseas just before returning stateside—mainly coupes, the kind with those gull-wing doors."

"Everybody wants those gull-wing cars," Howard said.

"Right," Bob said getting excited, "when those coupes hit the dock in the U.S., the price triples, man. But our businessman Fred only gives the Sergeant four—five hundred bucks—cash—and drives off to Detroit—with the title in his hand."

"I see," Howard said writing quickly. "Someone must give cash to buy another car to the Sergeants in Europe."

"Right," Bob said.

"People must be lining up in the plush suburbs to buy those cars," Howard said. "And this Fred has no import tax, sales tax, none of that—and Uncle Sam picks up the transportation cost. This Fred is making out like a bandit."

"Yeah," Bob said, "he make a bundle on every car, man. He must have a waiting list of customers as long as your arm. He doesn't lack for takers—that's for sure."

"Wow," Howard said, "this thing is pretty big—even Uncle Sam is involved. I mean—it's overwhelming."

"Ah-h, this Fred guy is playing with fire," Bob said. "He'll get caught."

"Could you get a picture of one of these cars on the dock?" Howard asked. "You must have a camera."

"I got a Polaroid," Bob said, "that I use at work to take photos at construction sites—"

"Good," Howard said, "try to get me a picture of this Fred taking delivery of a car—if you can."

"I'll try, man," Bob said thoughtfully, "when the next ship comes from Europe." Then after a pause, he added, "The only thing I got left in my notes is that he drinks Southern Comfort on the rocks—and that he gets swacked often in a bar called "Dakota" up near his apartment."

"You've done a damn good job of investigating this guy, Bob. You'd make a good reporter," Howard said grinning.

"You know, Howie, I kind of like this snooping around stuff—it gets your blood racing—like when you're sailing fast in a boat."

Howard, grinning, said, "Don't be seen by this guy. Be careful, Bob."

"I know, I know," Bob said, "when a guy carries a gun—there's always a chance he'll *use* it."

"How's your boat?" Howard asked to change the subject.

"I got it stored inside," Bob said. "I'm installing a weather radio—and a ship-to-shore phone, this winter."

"Hey," Howard said grinning, "You're really going—technical, Bobbo."

"Yeah," he said, "but it's all for safety sake."

"Well," Howard said, "I've got to go back to the grind here—so I've got to run for now—but when you get a photo, let me know. Okay?"

"You bet," Bob said.

~ ~ ~

Payday for Howard was two days away; he did not like it, but he went to the bank and withdrew forty dollars of the fifty-seven he had left in the account.

Across the street from the bank he saw a liquor store with a telephone on the wall near the front door. After he phoned home, telling his mother he would not be home for supper, he went into the liquor store and bought a fifth of Bacardi Gold Rum.

He had been driving north for just over an hour, when he turned off the Expressway at the Five Lakes Road exit. He drove the narrow path made by the snowplows, along the high piles of snow, looking for the HARBAUGH house sign.

"They got a lot more snow, then we did down in Detroit," he said driving slowly, looking for the road up to Marian at the summer house. "Yeah—and I hope it's enough snow to keep Fred from showing up."

He spotted the HARBAUGH sign, and turned up the road that went up the hill, all the way back to the house hidden in the bare trees.

When he saw the large house ahead, lighted, smoke billowing out of the wide stone chimney, he smiled.

"Man," he said, "it's like coming home." He shook his head and said, "Marian and myself—back together."

He beeped the horn twice, as he came nearer the house, then parked his Chevy in front of the two closed garage doors.

Marian came out on the porch, waving. She wore tight ski pants and a baggy wool sweater; then she stood with her arms folded against the cold.

"Hey," Howard shouted, walking in the snow to the steps, "this is like a scene in the movies." He waved the bag with the rum bottle, "All we need is the music."

"Okay," Marian said back, "how about 'Moonlight In Vermont'." She was smiling, watching him come, "What's in the bag? There's all kinds of food in the freezer—Ah, you didn't bring—?"

"No," he said coming up the steps, "it's nothing solid." He kissed her, leaning over her folded arms. "I brought some rum, babe. The stuff they call 'demon rum'—by those who don't use it."

"Thanks for coming, honey," she said smiling, pushing open the door behind her, lighting the porch with the lights from inside. "It's freezing out here."

"Wild horses couldn't keep me from coming," he said following her in to the kitchen watching her bottom move in the ski pants. He set the bottle in the bag on the kitchen table, and put his arms around her, "You don't know how much I've thought about you."

She stepped back, away from him, "What about when you took Julie to see those Gypsies? Were you thinking about me that night?"

She moved to stand with one hand on the sink, her hip cocked to one side, a combination provocative and confrontational stance.

"What was I supposed to do, babe?" Howard asked unwrapping the seal on top of the rum bottle. "I mean, you were out playing house with that creep Fred."

"Touché," she said, grinning and turning to take two glasses from the cabinet. "You know, honey," she said shaking her head, "I love talking to you—I never know what's going to come out. You're more than just—entertaining. You're more like—startling—I guess that's the word."

"It wouldn't be 'startling'," Howard asked pouring rum into the two glasses, "if I ask if you have any cokes in the refrigerator?"

She pulled open the fridge door, "We got orange juice," she said smiling. "Will that do?"

"Okay," he said, "We'll pretend we're at Gulfstream Race Track drinking Florida daiquiris."

"It's all that's here," she said handing him the carton of juice."

Howard took hold of her wrist above the carton.

"You don't know what I went through in Florida—after you married that creep," he said. "I had to keep telling myself you were gone—and keep trying to tell myself that I would have to get over the idea of having to live without you—I nearly went nuts with you gone, babe."

Marian let the carton drop to the floor and splash, and pressed both of her hands on Howard's chest.

"I know," she whispered. "I know—because I felt it too. I'm—sorry I listened to Daddy."

He could not resist her closeness, and slid his hands up under the sweater, cupping her breasts. When she did not resist, he felt a pause, that he took as a sign for him to go on; a waiting, an encouragement to go on.

"Oh, babe," he whispered to the side of her face, his against hers, just above the ear, "you are the only one—I ever wanted."

When he slid down the ski pants, they both moved down on their knees on the rug.

"I would think of you," she said slowly in a tone that was almost a plea, "all the time—I couldn't let go of you—I couldn't forget what we had together."

"For me, babe," he said using his hand on her, "there will never be—any—one—else."

"There," she whispered, "Ah-h—there—yes—yes."

They moved together, each giving all there was, that one person can give to another. A total giving.

After, when they lay spent, both breathing heavy, Howard wiped the wetness from her forehead.

"It's so-o right," he said slowly. "It's so right our being together—when we're apart, I want you even more. I can't help it—the feeling is so—strong."

"I feel it too," she said. "We just *have* to have each other—there is no other way. I don't care what happens—as long as we can be together—like this, honey."

"Right," Howard said lifting himself up on one elbow, "no more separations."

He leaned over and kissed her.

"Thank you," she said, "for being Howard."

When they sat up, pulling on their clothes, Howard smiling at her, she smiling at him, each knowing they felt a contentment few people ever witness.

"Hey," Howard said, kneeling again, helping her get to her feet, Maybe I can have that drink now."

"I wish we had Coke," Marian said smiling, standing up, holding Howard's arm as he got to his feet. "We'll have it—and we'll have it the rest of our lives, honey."

"And limes," Howard said picking up the orange juice carton from the floor, "and tall glasses—with ice cubes that rattle."

"We can have everything we want," she said, "because we're together now—forever." She picked up the two glasses off the table, and held them for Howard to pour what was left of the orange juice. "There were—mistakes in the past—"

"Babe," Howard said quietly, "that's all in the past." He poured juice in both glasses and set the carton in the sink. "Don't look back—look at what we have—what we're going to do."

Smiling, they *clinked* glasses.

"To us," Marian said, "who are really just one."

"Right," Howard said and slowly took a drink; he felt Marian was turning morbid, as if she sensed doom.

Wiping her lip, she said, "Honey, let's go down to the lake where we swam last summer. It'll take us back to the good time—and wipe away all the *unpleasantness* since—as if it never took place."

"It's cold out there, babe," Howard said before he swallowed what was in his glass. "But if it makes *you* happy—it makes *me* happy."

"I'll get my coat," she said grinning, and handed Howard her glass. "I don't need rum," she said walking over to the wall rack for her ski jacket. "You're all the stimulation I'll ever need, honey."

Howard drank her rum, set the glass on the sink, and reached for his raincoat on the chair, grinning, following her to the door.

"Hope the lake doesn't melt," he said going down the porch steps, slowly, in the darkness. "We're both burning like hot embers."

"Uh-huh," Marian said taking his arm, walking the snowy slope down to the lake, "and forest fires—we've got to be careful not to start the woods ablaze."

The raft they had sat on last summer, was pulled up on the shore, covered with snow. Howard kicked one barrel as they walked past and it made a hollow sound.

"Remember how we had to swim to the far side of the raft," he said as they walked out on the icy lake, "when I wanted to kiss you?"

"All the eyes up in the house were on us down here," Marian said leading Howard by the arm. "We were about here—when we kissed last summer," she said pointing, stamping one foot at the spot.

"Okay," he said wrapping his arms around her, kissing her. "No, babe, we're right back where we were last summer—with all the stuff in between—gone. Okay?"

"Daddy said you drank too much," she said evenly, looking down at the ice. "He said you were—unsuitable—to be a husband—that you would be—unreliable."

"So he touted you on to Frederic," Howard said putting his arm around her shoulders.

She nodded, continuing to look down at the spot on the ice.

"He said Fred had a high—income," she said slow, "and I would be able to live—pretty much—the way I lived before—at home in Grosse Pointe."

"What were your feelings, babe? I mean after all the practical stuff your father poured out—what did you feel about this Fred guy?"

"I never loved him at all; not even close to what we have," Marian said moving her foot in an arc on the ice. "He was just—convenient—and Daddy was so—insistent." Daddy said Fred's mother was from a German family of nobility—but after a while I was sure I didn't want to have a child with him. I want you Howard, your child. So I knew I had to run away."

"Why didn't you run away—before—you married him?"

She nodded.

"That's too—hard," Marian said. "too—dramatic."

"So you married him?"

"He was so—forceful," she said. "From the beginning, I didn't like it. I thought he would change as time went on. But it didn't—it got even worse."

Howard was rubbing the back of her neck to relax her.

"Very few people find real love—in their lifetime—it's very rare," he said, wondering where that thought came from, looking up at the stars, then looking down at the ice.

"He made all the decisions," Marian said. "I found out what I felt and had to say—didn't seem to mean anything."

Howard pulled her against his chest and kissed her forehead to console her.

"We're back together now," he said. "We can pick up where we left off—and I have an income now."

"It's getting colder," Marian said in a voice that seemed to come from a distance. She was looking up at Howard, when she said, "Oh, look at all those stars up there."

"Let's go back in the house," Howard said concerned. He had a sudden wave—a premonition—he was losing her.

They walked in the snow, without speaking, up the slope to the house, holding hands.

When they neared the top, they saw the car headlights down in the trees, coming up the road from the county highway.

"We got company," Howard said. He stopped walking. "Does your ex how where this place is?"

"I'm not sure," Marian said, her voice hard. "But someone could have told him," she added, releasing his hand.

"I know Ardis wouldn't," Howard said watching the lights getting closer. "Your mom—neither."

"Daddy," she said, pulling her jacket zipper up at the neck, "he might of even drawn a map."

They could hear the car tires *crunching* in the snow as it came closer.

"Could it be the Sheriff," Howard said, "checking on the house all lighted up—or something?

He felt Marian moved closer, pressing his arm.

"I don't think it's the Sheriff," she said. "I don't recognize the car—either."

"Marian," a shout came from the car as it came closer. "You are still married to me."

"It's Fred," she said, "and he's drunk. I'm going inside and call the Sheriff."

She ran up the steps, Howard following.

A shot rang out, and the glass in the door Marian left open, shattered as Howard passed going inside.

"That crazy bastard," Howard shouted, ducking.

Marian punched the bottom button on the phone on the kitchen wall.

"There's a man shooting here," she said. "Yes," she said, "the Harbaugh House off Five Lakes Road—hurry—send the Sheriff."

Two more quick shots rang out.

"Uh-h," Marian said, "it hurts," and dropping the phone, put her hand on the back of her neck, below the right ear.

When Howard saw the blood, he reached for the dangling phone. "A woman has been shot," he shouted in the receiver. "Send an ambulance—quick."

He released the receiver, letting it dangle, and quickly took a kitchen towel from the rack, and wadding it, pressed it against where the blood was running down Marian's neck.

"Can you move over to the chair, babe?" he asked, holding her by the shoulders, guiding her to the kitchen chair.

"It hurts—terrible," she said sitting down. "Oh—oh, look at all this blood."

There was the sound of a siren in the distance.

"You'll be all right, babe," Howard said pressing the blood soaked towel on her wound. "they're coming—help is coming."

Then, car headlights flashed outside the window, and faded quickly, as Fred, wildly turned his car around.

"That bastard is going to make a run for it," Howard said, watching the lights move away.

"He's not coming in the house?" Marian asked weakly.

"No, babe. No—he's going."

"Oh-h—it hurts—burns," she said, lowering her head onto her arm resting on the table. "All this blood—I'm getting—dizzy."

Howard put his hand on her shoulder, as if to feel the way she was sinking. He was scared now.

"Hang on, babe," he said quietly. "Hang on."

A second siren sounded in the distance.

"The am-bulance," she said in a weak voice. "Where—?"

Headlights flashed in the window.

"They're here, babe," Howard said. "They'll fix you up—the ambulance is here—you're going to be okay."

When he took the towel off the wound on her neck, the blood surged from the bullet hole; he only wanted to look at it, to see if the flow was subsiding. It was not, and he winched as he pressed the soaked towel back.

"I feel—like I'm going to—faint," Marian said.

"You're going to be okay, babe," Howard said quietly, and took hold of her hand, and he felt her coldness.

<p style="text-align:center">~~~</p>

"I think he was shooting at me," Howard said to the detective in a gray suit, sitting across the kitchen table, writing, "and he hit Marian—talking on the phone."

"But you said before, her husband shouted, 'you are still married to me,' and then he fired. Now that sounds like he was shooting at *her*."

"Yeah," Howard said, leaning back in the chair, looking out at the snow outside the Harbaugh house kitchen window. The sun was up, glaring on the whiteness, but offering in no warmth. "But—I *feel* he was shooting at me."

"Well," the detective said touching his sagging jowl with pudgy fingers, "it's murder one, if the shooting is pre-meditated, that this Fred can be charged with. If you get into this other thing, about him shooting at you and hitting her—it would be manslaughter—or maybe only an attempted murder."

Howard nodded, not liking all this talk about murder; he wanted to get away to the hospital, see Marian. How she was doing.

"I guess," Howard said, "I was just *speculating,*" suddenly realizing the seriousness of what he told the detective.

"This Fred guy shot his wife," the detective said, "and that's your statement." He slid the papers across the table and offered a pen, "sign at the bottom."

"Her father, Daddy Harbaugh shot her," Howard said signing the paper. "The furrier, Harbaugh—did it."

"Come again?" the detective said.

"Her father shot her," Howard said sliding the papers back. "he shot her—by meddling in her life—forcing her—coercing her—to marry that creep. He might as well have pulled the trigger on her—after that."

"Oh," the detective said, "I see what you mean." He tapped the ends of the statement pages against the table to make them even. Well, a father has to—guide—his daughter in life. That's part of his responsibility—as a father."

Howard nodded, looking across the room at the wall phone. The police had hung it up. He could not look at the bloody floor.

"You're at the *Detroit News;* you work for the *News*. Right?" the detective asked standing up from the table.

Howard nodded.

"We know where to contact you," he said, "if we need more information."

Howard nodded.

"—And the court date," the detective said pulling on his overcoat. "We'll be in touch."

Howard nodded.

Chapter 23

Marian died just before eight that morning, and Howard telephone the Harbaugh family in Grosse Pointe from the hospital in Lapeer.

"The doctors said it was a brain hemorrhage," he told Ardis, who answered the phone.

"Daddy and mother," she said crying, "are really broken-up—about the call from the hospital last night. Daddy can't speak—" she said before she began to cry so hard she could not talk.

"Sorry," Howard said, "that all this—I had to tell you—". When she did not talk, he added, "I have to go now. The police caught Fred—I have to go now. Goodbye, Ardis," he said before slowly hanging up; an act of reverence.

~ ~ ~

At home in Detroit the next morning, Howard slept until ten minutes before twelve.

When he walked into the kitchen, his mother said, "Your father is upset—very upset—about you being involved in that shooting—of that Grosse Pointe girl."

"Yes, mom," he said pouring cold coffee from the pot into a saucepan to warm it, "I understand—I can see he would be. I'm sorry, mom."

Howard set the saucepan on the stove and lighted the burner under it.

"I'm worried about him," she said from where she was peeling potatoes at the sink. "He's turned—so sickly lately. something is wrong with him—and this shooting episode—has taken him down—even more."

276

"I noticed he looks—tired," Howard said pouring hot coffee into a cup. "He seems—exhausted.

He walked over and sat at the table.

"It seems odd," she said not looking at Howard, "that all of a sudden, he turned to get so sickly. he was always pretty healthy. I can't understand what is taking him down like this—all of a sudden. And the doctor can't pinpoint it either—he's no help."

Howard sat at the table holding the cup in both hands, looking at his mother.

"Maybe he has some disease," he said, "that we don't know about yet."

"He gets up in the night now four—five times now."

Howard noticed his father's problems began soon after the new neighbors moved in next door. He decided not to say anything to his mother; he did not want to scare her.

He recalled his mother told him that the neighbor's wife said her husband was an "electrical engineer" one day when they were talking over the fence.

That rang alarm bells for Howard, and for some reason he felt the "engineer" was a plant; someone sent to cause him and the family harm.

But he knew it was one thing to *know* about the threat, but he had to be able to *prove* what he knew.

If the damage was being done "electrically"—surreptitiously—by this evil neighbor, it would be hard to prove. Any damage, a heart-attack, or kidney trouble, would appear normal in people as part of the aging process. to say otherwise, Howard knew, he would appear mentally unstable if he made such accusations against the neighbor.

But Howard sensed—something—was going on.

Last night he woke up suddenly—and he found his bedroom lighted—indirectly—from some unseen source. And nights before he saw a red flash and *knew* it was a Laser beam. It could be a Laser guide for a thermal-imagining device, where the body-heat can be tracked in darkness.

Someone was tracking him, Howard was sure.

One Saturday, Howard remembered seeing the "electrical engineer" going to his car in the driveway. He remembered he was a slight, blond guy with short hair, glasses. He did not look menacing, but quite the contrary. But that same day, Howard sensed the "electrical engineer" had something to do with Marian. It was a feeling that came from nowhere, just a premonition, he recalled thinking about it now. But for some reason he could not explain, and even though she was gone now, it continued to stay with him.

Thinking about it, again, the Laser could be a locater, but the white-light stuff might be fiber-optics. In that case, the transmitted light of the fiber optics, can allow electricity to travel on it, like it does in a copper wire. The electricity can be used to damage a person physically if the fiber-optic light is on him over time.

Howard had to find a way to prove this tech stuff is nothing more than a new way to hurt people. But he had to come up with a way also of not appearing like a crackpot.

Another thought crossed Howard's mind; all this sophisticated electrical equipment is very expensive. Whoever is footing the bill, must be wealthy. Cost, no concern.

Howard did not mention any of these thoughts to his mother, he sat silent at the table now, while she scrambled eggs at the stove.

"Make your toast," his mother said evenly, "your eggs are done."

He reached from where he sat and pushed down the handle on the toaster where he had dropped two slices of bread before.

He sensed his mother was suffering—silently—much more than just what his father was going through.

He did not know about the "tricks" played on her—electrically. The light bulbs suddenly burning out in a bright flash, when she turned on a light. The refrigerator motor suddenly going on the second she opened its door, the electric clock on the stove, when she was cooking, jumping to "oven mode" and going off with a dry ringing, and the oven thermostat "burning out" suddenly, so that she had to call a repair man.

Also, she did not mention the water pipe breaking downstairs, soaking the winter clothes hanging underneath on a rack, the belt suddenly breaking in the washer, then the clothes dryer, so she had to call a repairman. Then, there was the furnace, which spewed cold air when it was supposed to be giving heat, and the air conditioning that ran at high-speed, the motor revving so high is nearly jumped off the mounts, providing little, or no cool air in the hot summer.

Her television, when she was alone, flickered, jumped, and when she turned up the volume, the sound went down lower.

She was afraid to tell any of the family about how dizzy she got when looking out her kitchen window when the sun was bright. She fell to the floor, once, but did not tell the family.

Nor did she mention the intense light, that burned almost, when she sat in her living room chair on sunny afternoons to take a nap, the drapes partially closed over the front window. Nor how her legs "burned" during the day, and her feet "ached" to the bone at night in bed.

She was afraid to mention any of these things, along with how the neighbor's dog was let out when she worked on her flower bed near the fence; the dog barking from the other side of the fence, mere inches from her face. Or how suddenly she grew fatigued, as if a heavy weight was put on her shoulders, when the sun was high overhead. She opened a lawn chair in the shade inside the garage to sit and rest.

She felt afraid to mention it; thinking it all due to her advanced age, so she kept quiet.

"Is that Grosse Pointe girl's funeral today?" she asked Howard while sliding the scrambled eggs on his plate.

"No, Mom," Howard said picking up a fork, "it's tomorrow, just about noon." He began eating, then added, "I'm going to the office in a while; I have a story to write. But I'll be back at dinner."

"Your sister is going to a Sock-Hop at school," she said setting the frying pan on the stove. "We'll start dinner when father gets home."

"Okay," Howard said lifting a forkful of eggs. "Today is payday at work," he said hesitating, "so I have to get there—if I have to crawl."

"It's all so sad," his mother said picking up the frying pan, shaking her head, moving to the sink.

"You mean about Marian?"

"Everything," his mother said, her back to him, running water into the pan at the sink. "It seems—everything has turned so sad in our lives—all of a sudden."

"Yeah," Howard said looking down at his plate, unable to look up, "I never realized it. I see—what you mean, mom."

~ ~ ~

At the *News* office, Norman Poe, the Suburban Editor, said, "You know Keck a reporter is supposed to *report* the friggin' news—*not* be part of it," when Howard stopped in front of his desk.

Howard nodded at the editor's referring to Marian's shooting at the summer house.

"I know," Howard said, taking the admonishing word, but, more intent on reaching for his paycheck Poe held out to him. "I've run on to a whopper of a story—I'm going to type it now. It's big—it involves cars and the military."

"This envelope came for you," he said. "It's from New York—I had to sign for the damn thing."

Howard took the large manila envelope, saying, "It's a photo. Part of the whopper-story I have. Thanks."

"New York city is not exactly on the suburban beat, Keck."

"I know," Howard said quietly, "but you'll see the connection—very soon. How it ties-in with our suburbs. I'm going to write it now—how a local businessman has a racket importing stuff from New York."

"Okay, Keck, but this better be good."

"It is, boss. You'll see," Howard said before turning to go to his desk.

Howard typed steadily on the story that ran nine pages, finishing just before eleven that morning.

After he separated the carbon papers from the original sheets, he took the photo of two men standing on a dock next to a gull-wing coupe, the doors up. The red interior of the shiny black car showing behind the two men, one in an army uniform, shaking hands, both grinning. The other man, Aschenfelter.

"That will be the end of that scam," Howard said as he dropped the pages and photos on the center of the editor's desk, so he would see it when he returned.

"Fred's hash was settled with the shooting," he said going back to his desk for his rain coast. "Now we got that tool and die creep, too. When the army tracks back and finds that Dutchman is the money for buying those cars—he'll be a guest in the Federal pen.

Pulling on his rain coat, and going out the newsroom door, Howard straightened the black tie he put on for Marian's funeral.

"Aschenfelter is so greedy," he said going down the steps, "that working for Fred at the dock, got him caught."

~~~

At the cemetery for Marian's funeral, Howard kept control of his feelings, while watching the Harbaugh family, hanging back in the Grosse Pointe crowd.

But when Ardis put her hand on the casket as it passed, then pressed her forehead on it, the tightness in Howard's chest, that he had blunted by swallowing to keep from rising up in his throat, came out in an "Ah-h."

He felt the rush, the overwhelming sense of loss; the woman that was so exciting to be with, Marian, was gone—forever. It came to him in a wave—that he would never see her again.

Howard turned away from the crowd, holding his chest, and walked slowly to his parked car. He had to step around where the snow was melting in the sunshine.

He stopped for a moment in front of a large tree with bare branches.

"Too much," he whispered.

~ ~ ~

Walking in the hallway at the *News* cafeteria, Parsons stopped Howard.

"Hey," his Wayne State University journalism classmate said cheerfully, "where the heck you been? I haven't seen you for almost a week?"

"Court mostly," Howard said watching the coffee swirl in the paper cup he rotated. "First the murder trial, now a Federal case about cars—that I'm not supposed to talk about."

"Your name," Parsons said smiling, "is in the program for the June graduation ceremony—you're joining the alumni. Liberal Arts—Baccalaureate. You going to the ceremony in a cap and gown—to get your degree from the dean?"

"Why?" Howard said shaking his head.

THE END

7 May, 2011

St. Clair Shores, MI